LORI

Charlene Wexler

Books by Charlene Wexler

LAUGHTER AND TEARS SERIES
Book 1: Lori

COMING SOON!

LAUGHTER AND TEARS SERIES
Book 2: Murder Across the Ocean
Book 3: Milk and Oranges
Book 4: Elephants in the Room

FAREWELL TO SOUTH SHORE SERIES
Book 1: The Coming of Age of a Former 1950s Girl
Book 2: We Will Not Go Back

NOVELS
Murder on Skid Row

LORI

Charlene Wexler

SPEAKING VOLUMES, LLC
NAPLES, FLORIDA
2023

Lori

ISBN 978-1-64540-897-0

In honor of my three Granddaughters,
Lily, Bella, and Sage.

Acknowledgments

I would like to thank my editors, Bill Bike and Erica Mueller who corrected my mistakes. I want to thank my family and friends who pulled me through the death of my son, and encouraged to write about it.

Prologue

2001

"Girl, that is one snappy outfit. Do you all work for Madame Cheng?"

Startled, Lori turned around to see a thin young girl dressed in a skimpy beaded halter-top, short black leather skirt, stiletto heels, and wearing tons of makeup.

"No!" Lori whispered, dragging Adele up the steps and into the main room of the Chicago Avenue police station.

"What was that about, Lori?" Adele asked, looking over her shoulder as she was pulled by the arm by her friend. "Oh, my God, did you see how that woman was dressed?"

"She thinks we look like hookers..." Lori replied numbly, still trying to wrap her brain around the night's events.

"You're kidding," Adele said. She looked from Lori to the young, scantily clad prostitute milling around the police station.

Lori stopped pulling her friend and stopped walking. "Why not?" she said as she looked down at her dress, then at her friend. Both women were lavishly dressed in sequined evening gowns with plunging décolletage, three-inch heeled sandals, and adorned in their finest jewelry. It was two in the morning and they were in a police station. "I guess she took an educated guess," Lori replied, smiling wryly. "I only hope Madame Cheng runs a classy outfit, if I looked like I belonged to *her*." Lori tried to make light of their situation, considering.

"I think we just look out of place," Adele answered. The women made their way towards the desk where Adele's husband, Jim, stood in his black tailored designer tux among the prostitutes, derelicts, and unhappy perpetrators of some minor misdemeanor. Adele noted gratefully how handsome Jim looked in formal dress.

Right, Adele, Lori thought to herself. *Just out of place, like two older middle-aged couples dressed to the hilt would normally hang around here at this hour. Stop it, Lori*, the voice in her head screamed. *Just be thankful they are with you. What if you were alone in this wretched place?* Lori looked about, taking in the dingy, small concrete and brick building bustling with policemen and people from the world of night prowlers.

“Jim,” Lori asked, “Where’s my husband?”

“I don‘t know,” he answered, smiling weakly at Lori.

"When the policeman threw Jerry in the paddy wagon, he did say, ‘I’m taking him to the Chicago Avenue Station,’ didn’t he?” Lori asked, trying to keep her voice from shaking. She held fast to Adele’s hand.

“Yes, he’s here, but where, they don’t know yet,” Jim explained, shrugging.

The three well-dressed adults looked around, watching the early morning mini dramas unfolding before them. Some folks were arguing over a traffic accident, one young man had obviously been brought in on charges of drunkenness, and the prostitutes had been brought in for simply having chosen the wrong profession.

Dropping Adele’s hand, Lori slumped against the desk’s counter top, thinking, *How could this evening end here? I was so happy, laughing and dancing with family and friends. How wonderful the evening had been until...*

“There’s Jerry,” Adele announced calmly, pointing with her index finger.

Yanked back to the present, Lori looked up to where Adele was motioning. Horrified, she watched as two policemen tried fingerprinting her husband, Jerry, while he jumped around, holding his hands up in two fists.

That did it. Not realizing he was behind a plate glass barrier and couldn't hear her, Lori shook her third finger at him and ran towards him screaming, "How could you do this to us? AGAIN!"

A tall, heavyset policeman grabbed her and pulled her away from the window. "Lady, he can't hear you, and you aren't allowed back here."

Lori resisted and headed back towards the glass barrier. Staring through the clear glass at a room that was now empty, she turned to the policeman and said, "He's gone! What have you done with my husband?"

"He's in a jail cell," the officer answered as he again grabbed hold of her.

Lori proceeded to pound the officer with her fists as she said, "Let go of me. A jail cell? You can't put Jerry in a jail cell!"

Adele approached from behind and pulled her away. "Lori, quiet down before you're arrested too."

The officer had put his thick arms out in front of his chest to deflect the woman's attack. He was tired and bored with the same old scenario, well accustomed after twelve years on the force to the craziness of upset wives, of upset crazy people in general. "Get her to calm down, would you, Ma'am?" He shot a quick dirty look at his attacker and then moved away down the hall.

Adele quickly maneuvered Lori into the women's restroom, where she calmed down and finally let the tension, which had taken hostage every part of her body, release into a flood of tears.

Holding Lori in her arms, Adele tried to ease the situation. "Lori, don't be so hard on yourself," Adele soothed. "He was just celebrating his son's wedding." She released her embrace to reach into her tiny sequined purse and handed Lori a tissue.

Lori wiped the tears from her eyes with the tissue and answered, "Adele, he started drinking again, and he embarrassed the hell out of me at the wedding, and then he provoked that policeman!"

Adele looked at her friend and thought, *How can I make it less painful? She has been through so much, and it really looked like things were going well until tonight.*

She handed Lori more tissue. Lori was a wreck. Her hair, once dark but now mostly graying into a lovely silver, earlier done up so pretty for her son's wedding, was now askew, with errant tendrils sticking every which way. Her eyes were red from crying, and blotches appeared on her pale face and chest, her lipstick gone.

"Lori," Adele admonished, "your cheeks are black from mascara. Wipe them."

Lori never really wore mascara, and now she knew why. Very few days went by without her finding something to cry about. Her son's wedding should have been a joyful day.

She moved toward the row of porcelain sinks, turned on one of the faucets, and began rinsing her face off with cool water. She could not stop crying, even if she wanted to. She looked up to see her bedraggled reflection and began crying anew.

"Think about it, Lori," Adele said. "Jerry was really well behaved at the wedding, toasting everyone with Shirley Temples until the last half-hour, when stupid Sy handed him a glass of Johnnie Walker Scotch and insisted they toast the newlyweds." Adele kept her hands on Lori's shoulders as Lori continued the tasks of rinsing her face and trying to get under control.

"Anyway," Adele continued, "most people were gone by then. That poor young policeman couldn't control his horse. You have to admit, Jerry was funny when he told him to take his horse back to the country club." Adele attempted to stifle a giggle. "I never knew police horses were kept at the South Shore Country Club. Did you, Lori?" She was trying her best at making light of the situation.

Lori turned off the water and moved toward the paper hand towel dispenser to wipe at her face. Taking the stiff brown paper to her face, Lori spoke. "Come on, Adele. When the cop said, 'Get out of the street,' all Jerry had to do was move. Not my husband. No, he had to hit the horse and mouth back to the cop." She wiped at her eyes once more and leaned back against the sinks.

"Lori, just one drunken episode in four years is a pretty good record," Adele said.

Lori's compassionate, naïve friend had no idea what Jerry's drunken episode could lead to. Shaking her head, she looked past her friend and focused on the dirty, gray, chipped concrete wall across the restroom and answered, "Look where being drunk and funny landed us. The real problem is this drinking episode could ruin everything. He can relapse with just one damn drink. No more denying it. My husband Jerry is an alcoholic."

Lori turned and busied herself before the mirror, trying to reassemble strands of her hair into some semblance of order and propriety. Then she burst into a fit of laughter and said, "Adele, you're right, it was funny watching that policeman trying to maneuver his horse, and Jerry's remark was clever—that is, if it came from a stranger."

Adele relaxed her shoulders and smiled.

The restroom door slammed open. Two scantily dressed girls moved in. One lit a cigarette and said to her companion, "I ain't seen that f.... since I was brought in here."

Lori and Adele quickly exited. Jim was waiting for them.

"I knew you'd be in there," he said softly. "I contacted a lawyer friend of mine," Jim explained. "He's working on getting Jerry out, but it could take hours. Let's move to a less congested area, maybe the vending machine room, where we can sit down and get some coffee." He smiled without being patronizing and then looked down at his black dress shoes as he made his way to the vending machine room.

Lori smiled a weak smile, grateful for having Jim to turn to during tough times. Jim was so efficient and tactful. Lori silently thanked God the kids were already off on their honeymoon. Oh, God, how would she ever face her daughter-in-law Anne's parents? They probably wondered what kind of a family their daughter had married into.

She remembered another time Jerry had sent her to a police station. It was when he had totaled their car. He had survived his collision with a tree because of his inebriated state. That was when she was young and naïve, when she believed in her husband, when she denied that he was an alcoholic causing the problem, not an innocent victim.

The stench of alcohol, cigarettes, and sweat filled the room. As long as the well-dressed threesome managed to avoid the two inebriated bodies on the floor, Jim's guess was right; it was less crowded in the snack room but still seedy. Adele and Lori sat down on the straight-backed chairs near the wall while Jim tried to figure out how to get just plain black coffee from the new type of vending machine offering ten different concoctions of presumably warm beverages.

Lori looked at her two faithful friends, musing about how much she truly missed them. Several years ago, Jerry and she had moved from Chicago to Arizona. They simply had fallen in love with the state after Jerry had spent months there in a rehabilitation facility for alcoholism. Their son's wedding had brought them back to Chicago for the weekend.

Adele and Jim were their closest friends. The four of them had a history going back many, many years. Adele, Jim, and Lori were friends from high school. Jerry and Jim met in college. Jim fixed Lori up with Jerry, and they had been a foursome ever since. Jim, a tall quiet intellectual, and Jerry, a short, loud, funny tumult maker, meshed in an Abbott and Costello sort of way.

From their first day together at Northfield High School in the posh north suburbs of Chicago, Adele and Lori bonded. They were both from similar backgrounds and were romantics who loved Johnny Mathis, cashmere sweaters, dancing, and, of course, boys. Lori was more of a tomboy than Adele, who held herself like a princess, dressing in all the classic fashions. Living in an affluent northern suburb of Chicago made life relatively easy. They shared clothes and secrets.

Lori watched Adele get up to refill their coffee cups. Almost forty years later, her hair was still black and shiny, she still wore a size eight, and she still believed in people. Lori wondered how Adele did it. Most women, when they reached their late fifties, became fat, especially in the middle. Lori's hair was well beyond graying, her dress size was twelve, and she was just emerging from another bout of depression. She kicked off her shoes, removed all her jewelry, and sat back in the chair. Looking around the room at the other occupants who were eyeing them with curiosity, Lori thought, *Yes, even affluent middle-class people get arrested.*

It was four in the morning by the time they left the police station. The usual hour ride to Adele's house in the northern suburb only took forty-five minutes. Lori had never seen the Edens Expressway so deserted, but she usually wasn't out at this time of day. Jim was exhausted and went right upstairs to bed. Jerry was fine. He had two hours of sleep while in the jail cell and another forty-five minutes of sleep in the car. Adele and Lori were totally stressed but wide-awake.

Adele busied herself by making coffee and taking out pastries, while Lori took the opportunity to yell at Jerry: "How could you do this to me!"

Jerry, at the onset of Lori's verbal attack, managed to escape up the steps to one of the bedrooms and bolted the door. Adele, the eternal peacemaker, shuffled Lori into the kitchen.

"Calm down, Lori," Adele said. "He'll go back to Arizona tomorrow. He'll be guilty and apologetic and go back to not drinking."

Lori took another drink of coffee, and put the cup down. She leaned forward in her chair, looked into Adele's eyes, and cried, "Can you believe the hell I've gone through with this man for the last thirty years? If he starts drinking again, I swear, Adele, I'm gone." Lori ran her hands through her now deconstructed hairdo and continued. "Oh, Adele, I should have run as fast as I could after meeting Jerry's crazy family. I was so damn young and naïve."

Chapter One

1970

Lori was wiggling around and staring out the window like a cat ready to bolt.

"What's wrong with you?" Jerry asked. "We're just going to my family's house for a Friday night Sabbath dinner. They won't bite you. They're eager to meet you."

"Jerry, I'm not used to driving through bad neighborhoods, okay?" Lori said as they made their way through the section of Chicago that held the Cabrini-Green housing development. Lori looked warily out the window and said, "I'm checking windows for flying bullets. Why didn't you stay near the lake on the outer drive where its safe?"

"Hey, Lori," Jerry replied, "you're twenty-four. Maybe it's time for you to venture out of Northfield."

He drove on through the dirty streets filled with groups of black teenagers mulling around dilapidated buildings, thinking, *I should have taken a different route knowing she was with me.* Then the thought came to him, *Maybe Mom was right. Maybe Lori is too much of a Jewish princess for me.* The thought of what his mother said left him as he turned and look at her. He melted, quietly noting how cute she looked with her long curly black hair, enormous green eyes, and those beautiful legs showing through her short skirt.

Lori relaxed some as they drove out of the low-income housing project, turned east on North Avenue, and then right on a street called Orchard.

When they approached Jerry's house, Lori noticed that contrary to most buildings on the block, Jerry's house had a very large vacant lot next to it. This was unusual in an area that was congested with houses, apartment buildings, and stores.

Thinking of the recent riots that took place in their city, she asked Jerry, “Was the house next to yours burned down after Dr. King was shot?”

“Lori, that was two years ago, and this part of the West Side was not where the riots were,” Jerry responded. “Close, but not here. And anyway, I highly doubt any riots are going to break out tonight.” He tried to be reassuring and maneuvered the conversation to a less sensitive subject, adding, “There were never any buildings on this lot as long as I can remember.” Jerry maneuvered his car into a parking space on the street and stepped out of the car, opened the door on Lori’s side, and helped her get out, saying, “We’re here.”

Nervous about meeting the family as well as having driven through the seedier parts of Chicago she had only heard about and never actually seen first-hand, Lori grabbed onto Jerry’s arm as they got out of the car and walked up five wide stone steps to the entrance of an old one-story bungalow. The two white stone lion heads that stood on either side of the building reminded her of the Art Institute. The door, heavy and wooden, held within its frame a beautiful stained-glass pane with pictures of blue birds and red flowers. On the right side of the door was a small mezuzah. They entered an open door and quickly passed through an average-size front room with plastic covered furniture. The interior of the house was much smaller than Lori thought it would be.

She asked Jerry, “How did your family manage with only two bedrooms and four kids?”

Jerry gave her a funny look. *What a strange question*, he thought.

“When my sister Eileen was living here, she used the den, and my brothers and I slept in the second bedroom,” Jerry explained.

He walked Lori into his bedroom. The room looked like the young men had never moved on. There was one bunk bed, one twin bed, and two dressers. The walls were still covered with sports team posters, especially banners sporting the logo of the Chicago Cubs baseball team. There were toy trucks and a basketball on the floor, and a red lava lamp sat on the dresser.

Lori opened her mouth, ready to say something, but before it came out, Jerry said, "Yes, as the youngest, I slept on the top bunk."

She smiled but didn't say what she was really thinking. *It must have been very crowded. My single bedroom with the princess bed was twice this size.*

"Where do you sleep now?" she asked.

With a broad grin, Jerry answered, "On all three beds."

Lori smiled as they moved on through the other rooms of the house. She glanced at the numerous family photos on the walls of the hallway, then rested her eyes on the ones of the boys. It was easy to find Jerry. He always had a devilish grin, or he was in a funny pose. *That's my guy*, Lori thought as she reached for his hand. *Life with him would be fun.* She noted an absence of photos of Eileen, but before the thought fully formed, Jerry had moved her into the dining room. She noticed that even though the family's furniture was at least forty years old, it was in perfect shape. The green and pink patterned sofa was still covered with plastic and looked like nobody sat on it. Every counter and tabletop had a knickknack resting on an embroidered doily. Radiators warmed the house, and open windows, adorned with lace curtains, cooled it.

The family had watched their neighborhood go from being a poor Jewish area to a predominately poor black one, and now in 1970, it was on an upswing to becoming a middle-class area.

To Lori, their whole way of life seemed to be out of another century, the old country.

She and Jerry passed through the dining room into a large red and yellow tiled fifties kitchen containing a Roper gas stove, a metal sink, a patterned linoleum floor, a chrome and vinyl kitchen set, and a counter covered with plants and knickknacks.

As they entered the kitchen, they encountered Shelly, Jerry's mother, who was busy with a dish of food.

"And make sure the wine's on the table!" Shelly ordered. "Carol! Carol, honey, take this from me, will you? I have to check the oven." It was immediately obvious that Jerry's mother—standing only five feet tall, weighing barely one hundred pounds, sporting a head of gray hair, and endowed with a formidably booming voice—was definitely the boss.

"Jerry, you're late!" Jerry's mother screeched, slamming down the platter of food onto her Formica kitchen counter. "Where is Carol?" she mumbled to herself. "The sun is down, it's time for the candles." She waved her hand impatiently at her son and moved to the stove, not once looking up to greet him or Lori. "Go, seat your girl next to Carol."

Lori joined the family in the dining room around the table as Shelly, in her floral-patterned, loose fitting house dress and traditional lace head covering, quickly followed them into the dining room, lit the Sabbath candles, and recited the prayer. Following Shelly, Jerry's father, Jack, held up his glass of wine and recited the *Brachah* over the wine: *Baruch atah Adonai eloheinu melech ha olam borei brie hagoffin.* All at the table held up their own glass of wine. At the end of the prayer, in unison they said "amen" and then took a drink of wine from their glasses. The sweet Mogen David wine brought back to Lori memories of her youth.

Lori looked around the table at the family she planned to join. The Brill brothers' physical features were as different as their parents. Jerry and Steve were short and stocky, similar to Shelly's build. They had hazel eyes and thick black curly hair. Joel, with straight sandy brown hair and green piercing eyes, was tall, thin, and wiry like his dad. Darrell and Danny, Steve and Carol's twelve-year-old twins, were adorable with their matching dimples. There were some missing family members. Lori knew Jerry had a sister, but she couldn't get him to talk about her, and she knew Joel was married, but his wife was also absent.

Dressed in a casual tan sweater and brown pants to match her brownish-red hair, Carol was about Lori's height and build, only much heavier. As the friendliest of all the family, she hugged Lori with open arms and said, "Great to meet you! Jerry's told us quite a bit about you!" She turned and winked at Jerry. "All good, of course. Come and help with the serving so we can talk and get to know each other."

Lori smiled shyly as she and Carol joined Shelly in the kitchen. Shelly handed them soup bowls. She never looked at the two young women in the face. She didn't talk, not even a friendly hello; she just loudly issued orders like a short-order cook.

"This bowl goes to Steve," Shelly ordered. "He likes extra matzo balls. And this one here goes to Joel. He likes an egg in his soup."

The doorbell rang. Carol leaned in to Lori and winked. "Go answer the door. You're dressed too nice to be serving soup."

Lori was relieved. She would hate to spill soup on her new blue knit skirt. *A wash-n-wear polyester pantsuit would have been more appropriate*, she said to herself as she smoothed down her short skirt with her hands and moved to the front of the house and answered the door. Two women dressed in shabby and faded cotton house dresses similar to Shelly's rushed pass her, shouting salutations to an unseen Shelly.

Shelly yelled out, "Rachel, Emma, you're in time for dinner. Pull up a chair!"

Both women joined Shelly in the kitchen and quickly took over the serving. Lori went back into the dining room and sat down next to Jerry. She tried to say something to him but quickly gave up. It seemed like everyone at the table was talking in loud, fast voices. They seemed so at home. She looked around her. Wasn't this what she longed for? A large, busy, happy family, something she never had. She would try her best to fit in.

Rachel, one of the women similarly dressed as Shelly, walked into the dining room, put down a plate of brisket on the table, picked up a bowl of broccoli, and with a big grin, yelled back to Shelly, "I knew you would have broccoli! It was on sale at Phil's Grocery."

Jerry's brother Joel joined in the conversation by yelling into the kitchen, "Nineteen cents a pound at Jewel. Mom, did you beat that?"

Soon, everyone but Jerry's dad seemed to be shouting something at each other.

As Carol picked up Lori's soup bowl, she leaned down towards her and said, "Get used to it. This family strives on bargains and arguments."

"Carol, who are those two women?" Lori asked of the two new members of the dinner party. "Are they family?" she asked softly.

Carol laughed. "That's another thing you'll have to get used to. Shelly's house is a cosmopolitan rendezvous."

"A *what*?" Lori asked.

"An open house, with people from everywhere coming and going," Carol explained.

Lori nodded and then reached over for some food. With each taste of the traditional Jewish Sabbath dishes of well-done brisket, garlic roast chicken, and perfect moist and crispy potato kugel, she found herself lingering between bites as memories of her youth when her grandmother, her father's mother, lived with them and cooked like this. So engrossed was Lori in her memories that she failed to respond to the excitement around her until Jerry poked her, saying, "They're at it again."

She looked up to see a serious scuffle between Jerry's two brothers, with Joel punching Steve in the arm and screaming, "You're cheating me out of money!"

Like a bat out of hell, Shelly came running out of the kitchen with a rolling pin.

"Enough!" she yelled. "Joel, take out the garbage. Steve, help Carol in the kitchen!"

The boys quieted down and obeyed without saying another word. Lori noticed that throughout the excitement, their father sat in front of the TV in his green vinyl lounger, ignoring everyone. In fact, the only thing the man said all night was the blessing over the wine. Speaking of wine, Lori wondered what had happened to the expensive bottle she had brought as a house gift.

Carol and Rachel brought out tea and strudel, and everyone sat back down, dismissing the fight like it never happened. After dessert, the table quickly cleared of its occupants. The men moved to the living room, but instead of sitting on the furniture, all three brothers plopped down on the floor in front of the television, next to the twins, who were watching a football game.

Carol sat down next to Lori and asked for her phone number, saying, "We should get together now that you will be part of the family." Carol was the only one to acknowledge that Lori and Jerry were planning to get engaged soon. Steve had said, "Hi," and the twins had waved when Jerry introduced her as, "This is Lori," and his parents barely acknowledged her presence.

She didn't talk to Joel until she and Jerry ended up walking out of the house with him, and he took her arm and maneuvered her towards a bright red Corvette parked in front of the house.

Grinning, he asked, "Why would you go out with my baby brother when you can travel in style with me?"

"Aren't you married, Joel?" Lori said, sweetly.

He smiled and got into the car. She moved back to where Jerry was waiting for her and got into his five-year-old Chevy Nova.

She turned to Jerry with a million questions about his family. "Jerry, Steve said he was a financial planner. What does Joel do?"

"It depends on the day," Jerry responded. "By the way, the Corvette belongs to his friend. He wrecked up his car again."

"Where was Joel's wife?" Lori asked.

"Caryn usually doesn't make it to anything," Jerry responded. "She's always sick."

"What about your sister?" Lori asked.

"She lives in California," Jerry said, warning, "Don't ever mention her name around my parents!"

"Why?" Lori asked.

Jerry dismissed the question as he drove on and found himself dodging many of Lori's inquiries about his family. When they pulled up in front of Lori's house, Jerry pulled her to him, gave Lori a big kiss, and said, "Honey, you ask too many questions."

Lori was surprised to see the lights on in her house. Walking in, she found her father waiting for her.

"Why are you still up, Dad?" Lori asked.

"I wanted to find out about your evening," he responded.

"Dad, you won't believe what it was like. It's like I'm marrying Woody Allen or something. What a crazy family!"

"He's from a more traditional Jewish family, Lori. It's going to be different than our Reform Jewish family in many ways."

Lori rolled her eyes. "Plastic on the furniture, old ladies in house dresses. The house hasn't been redecorated probably since Jerry's folks were first married, but they all seemed so comfortable with each other.

Lori laughed at her recollection of the chaotic family get-together. "I can hardly wait to talk to Adele and tell her all about it." She bent to kiss her dad on the cheek, saw a piece of luggage near the chair where he sat, and asked, "Why do you have a packed suitcase?"

"Honey, I'm leaving on business early in the morning," he explained.

"I thought you were slowing down."

"This trip can't be helped."

"Where's Mom?"

"Sleeping, with a migraine."

"Dad, make sure you will be here for my wedding," Lori half-seriously admonished. "No surprise extended trips away from home!"

As Lori headed up the stairs she thought, *At least Jerry has a large family, not a mom who is always sick, and a dad who is always gone.*

Chapter Two

Lori and Jerry were married on August 20, 1971, at the Sheraton-Blackstone Hotel, located on Michigan Avenue in downtown Chicago. Being an only child, Lori had no siblings to stand up at the wedding. Her best friend, Adele, was her maid of honor, and her two future sisters-in-law, Carol and Caryn, were in the bridal party with Jerry's brothers and his two friends, Jim and Sy. The room—gold and white, with its terra cotta walls, painted ceiling, massive crystal chandeliers, and surrounding balconies—was decorated in various shades of pink, one of the lighter shades matching the color of the bridesmaid's dresses. Her parents had gone all out, spending over ten dollars a dinner per guest, plus the cost of the extras like an open bar, the band, flowers, and a wedding consultant.

Two hundred people were seated with their bodies turned towards the back of the room in anticipation of the bride coming down the aisle. Lori—with a pearl tiara sitting atop her beehive hairdo and dressed in long, satin, pearl-inlaid, ivory-colored wedding gown—waited for her turn to walk down the pink flowered aisle to her groom. She smiled as the band started to play her song, *Sunrise, Sunset*, from the play and movie *Fiddler on the Roof.* Soon, Beth the vocalist would start to sing, and Lori would start to walk.

She looked around for Suzi, the wedding consultant, but Suzi had disappeared. Lori became nervous. When Suzi finally appeared through the closed door, Lori asked, "What's wrong? Did Jerry change his mind?"

In an effort to calm Lori down, Suzi took her hand and smiled at her.

"No problem, just a late guest who walked down part of the bridal aisle instead of walking down the corridor," Suzi explained. "All is well now, and we'll start the music again."

Soon, Lori was floating down the aisle to *ahs* and *ohs* delivered by loving friends and family. Standing under the rose flowered *chuppa* waiting for Jerry to break the wine glass, Lori quickly forgot about the delay. It wasn't until a strange-looking woman approached her in the receiving line that she got a clue to who caused the problem. The woman—tall, slim, and dressed in a long black dress, black leather gloves up to her elbows, black pointed leather boots, white, silver, and black makeup, and long thick black hair reaching down to her *tuchas*—smiled at Lori, and in a loud voice she blurted out, "You have just married into a very dysfunctional family."

Before Lori could respond, Shelly had grabbed the woman by the hair, and the woman in black awkwardly bent down to clench her fists in Shelly's face. Jerry's brothers, Steve and Joel, disentangled the two brawling women and manually escorted the woman in black out of the room, while Suzi the wedding consultant desperately tried to restore order, repeating, over and over, "Everything is fine. Please make your way into the room for dinner."

Jerry looked at Lori a moment before saying "That…was Eileen." His brows knit tightly upon the bridge of his nose, and he scowled slightly at his new bride and shook his head, adding, "You invited her, after I told you not too."

Lori looked up at him sheepishly and then back at his brothers, who frowned in disapproval. "I…I thought I could bring your family together," she stammered.

The wedding consultant took hold of both of them. "Mr. and Mrs. Brill, it is time for your entrance.

Chapter Three

Lori stood by the window of her Lincoln Park high-rise apartment, looking down fifteen floors to Chicago's magnificent clear blue Lake Michigan. Jerry, her husband of four months, came up behind her and gently kissed her neck.

Her face aglow, she looked up at him and smiled. "Good morning," she murmured sweetly. Turning back to the window, she said, "What a beautiful view."

He slipped his hand down her skimpy nightgown, poked his head over her shoulder, and hummed, "Oh, yes."

She turned around and removed his hand from inside her nightgown. "Honey," she said, "we better get dressed and go to work if we want to keep paying the rent on this place."

Jerry smiled, embraced his wife, and said, "My mother almost died when she heard we were paying $170 a month for a one-bedroom apartment in Lincoln Park."

"Did you tell her it was a brand new high-rise that included parking?" Lori asked.

Parking was hard to find in the area, so the indoor lot in the building was important to Lori. Lincoln Park was a changing neighborhood, with a conglomeration of ma and pa type stores like Goodman's Rexall Drugstore, Angelo's Grocery Store, and Ricky's Deli next to too many taverns.

Slowly, new places like Michele's gourmet French restaurant were taking over. To the south and north of the area, near the lake, lived the town's wealthy families, and to the west, Chicago's bums and prostitutes.

Besides gifts from her parents, Lori and Jerry picked up interesting items from the many re-sale and furniture stores along Clark Street. Lori was especially fond of the oak antique roll-top desk with its many cubby holes and bright brass knobs. She immediately took possession of it, placing it right near her side of the bed. She grabbed the car keys from atop it and threw them into her purse.

Lori beat Jerry in the race to the shower. Dressed and waiting for him, sitting at the high bar separating the kitchen and living room, Lori lit her cigarette. She took a deep drag, sipped her coffee, and checked the clock, noting it was 7:45 a.m. She was due at her teaching job at 8:30 a.m. She and Jerry liked to leave together, but it was getting harder and harder. Jerry soon proved to be the late one in the family. He had no exact working hours since he was a salesman for a medical supply company.

She yelled into the bedroom, "I have to get out of here in fifteen minutes."

He came out of the bedroom half-dressed and said, "You better go, honey. By the way, since you have the car, will you pick up a birthday cake for my dad for tonight's dinner?"

Lori's eyebrows narrowed, and her lips pursed. She walked over to him, hands on hips, and said, "We have a party to go to tonight in Northfield."

He looked at her, exasperated, and said, "Why would you accept a date to a party on a Friday night? You know we are expected at my mother's every Friday for family Sabbath dinner."

"Fine," she said as she grabbed her coat and books. Swearing to herself on the way out, she knew she was stuck there this Friday, because of the birthday, but she'd be damned if she had to go there every Friday night. Something had to be done about that!

That evening, Lori walked into the Brill house and graciously handed Shelly a luscious chocolate raspberry whipped cream birthday cake from Chef Allen Pastries.

Shelly reached up and took the box, inspecting it as she delivered Lori a look of scorn. “You bought a cake from that fancy rip-off place?” Shelly looked hard at Lori and squinted. Her voice rose to an unpleasant volume. “Are you crazy?”

Looking in Carol’s direction, she roughly handed the boxed cake to her other daughter-in-law and picked up a plate with a homemade white cake topped by a pink plastic *Happy Birthday* sign. Pointing to it, she announced for all to hear, “*This* is a birthday cake for our family from someone who *knows* how to save money!”

All at the table sat in sudden quiet.

Turning beet red with embarrassment and anger, Lori grabbed Jerry’s arm and said, “Let’s *go*.”

“Why?” Jerry asked, clueless. “What’s the matter with you?”

Lori turned around and ran out of the house. If she had taken her coat and the car keys, she would have been gone before Carol came out after her, dragging Jerry along with her.

Carol talked first, saying. “Lori, you have to learn to ignore Shelly’s remarks. Everyone else does. Shelly is like the old Yiddish saying, ‘What’s on the mind is on the tongue.’”

Lori turned to Jerry, her jaw firmly set in anger and disgrace. “I will *not* go back in there,” she asserted. “Give me the keys.”

“Honey, please,” Jerry pleaded. “It’s my dad’s birthday.”

Lori stared at him. She soon realized he wasn’t coming with her. He just stood there, hands in his back pockets, eyes off in the distance, scanning the area for an escape route like a cat ready to spring.

She held out her hands and demanded, “The *keys*.”

Jerry handed Lori the keys and watched as his wife got into their car and took off.

He turned to Carol and said, "I don't know what to do with her. She hates my family."

"Jerry, she comes from a different neighborhood and background, and you know your mother is a tough one to deal with," Carol countered.

He smiled a devilish grin at that one, shook his head, and asked, "What should I do?"

"Wish your dad a happy birthday, and go home to your wife," Carol explained. "Steve will give you a ride."

Jerry followed only part of Carol's advice; he went back in, but he did not leave right away. Jerry stayed and noshed on some of his mom's brisket and strudel, then kissed his dad and made it home an hour after Lori. When he entered the apartment, he found the bedroom door locked, and he couldn't get Lori to respond to his calls, so he finally poured himself a gin and tonic, undressed, and slept on the sofa.

Still angry, Lori tiptoed out of the apartment early Saturday morning, bypassing her sleeping husband. Her best friend, Adele, had agreed to meet her at their favorite spot, the Cubby Hole Restaurant in Northfield, a good forty-minute ride north of her home. Lori arrived early, per usual, slid into a back booth, and motioned to their favorite waitress, Maddy, who came over with coffee pot, ashtray, and two chocolate donuts.

Smiling, Lori said, "Maddy, you always know what I want."

"Since you've been a teenager, you always got the same thing in the morning," Maddy said. "How do you like the city?"

"I dreamed about living in the city for so long, but now that I'm there, I miss this place," Lori replied.

"Watch it, honey. Sometimes, dreams turn into nightmares," Maddy said as she walked back to the kitchen.

Adele slid into the red vinyl booth opposite Lori and started to put a quarter in the jukebox, when Lori said, “No music today.”

“What’s wrong?” Adele asked.

Lori jumped right in after taking a sip of her coffee and said, “Jerry’s mother is driving me *crazy*.”

Adele sat in the booth with eyes wide open while Lori related the cake incident. She thought to herself, *Poor Lori.* Adele felt extremely blessed to have a loving mother and an easygoing mother-in-law. Adele had long been well aware of Lori having been brought up by a disinterested mother who was both cold and selfish. Now it sounded like Lori had to deal with a mother-in-law who was not only selfish, but a control freak as well.

Lori opened her purse and removed a cigarette from her pack of Salems. She leaned back in the booth and took a deep drag, letting the smoke slowly escape through her nose before continuing. She felt better now that she had unloaded her troubles on Adele. They went on to other topics, like who was getting married and who was getting divorced while they sipped coffee, and munched on their donuts.

Jerry and Lori never really worked out their problems with his family. They just made a truce, where Jerry went to Friday night dinner and Lori stayed home, went out with friends, or went to visit her parents when they were in town, which wasn’t often.

Her sister-in-law, Carol, became an ally in helping her understand the Brill family. Carol and Steve lived with their twins in a remodeled old house, also located in the Lincoln Park area, just a few miles from their parents. Carol, like Lori, was a teacher in the Chicago school system. The two women spent many afternoons together marking papers and visiting, especially when their husbands were busy watching baseball, football, or hockey games.

Carol and Lori spent a Sunday afternoon together in Lori's apartment when all the Brill boys were at Soldier Field watching the Bears lose a game to the Green Bay Packers.

Carol pulled a cigarette from an elegant gold case in her purse, offering one to Lori.

Taking a long thin cigarette, Lori said, "It's nice to be with someone who smokes. Jerry quit, and Adele never smoked. She is busy telling me things like how they've even banned cigarette advertisements from the television. I love her dearly, but she is so straight and proper. She reminds me of my mother."

Lori made a face, then smiled as she lit her cigarette and took a deep drag, enjoying the warm smoke as it filled her lungs. She let the smoke leave through her nostrils, which was her smoking custom.

"Look at me," Lori said, clowning, pulling back her thick black hair with both hands. "I'm literally fuming!"

Carol laughed as she made her way to the kitchen, refilled her coffee cup, grabbed a half of a chocolate chip cookie, and said, "You won't have that trouble with the Brill family. Straight and proper, huh? No way."

"Where did you meet Steve?" Lori asked.

"We grew up together," Carol recalled. "He's two years older than I am. I had a crush on him since I was five, but it took until I was fifteen before he really noticed me."

"Tell me about Caryn," Lori said. "I've been married to Jerry over two years, and I've only seen her at family gatherings, what, twice? How does Shelly let her get away with that?"

"She works and supports Joel, that's how she gets away with it," Carol explained. "He can't hold down a job. By the way, thank you for coming back to some of the family dinners. It wasn't easy being the only young woman around." Carol dipped her cookie into her coffee for a moment before popping it into her mouth. "Don't get into a war with Shelly," she warned, grabbing a napkin and dabbing at her chin and mouth. "You can't win. She rules her boys."

"Believe me, I didn't do it for Shelly," Lori said. "I hate that woman. I've been going for Jerry, and because of you."

Lori walked over to the refrigerator, opened the door, and took out a plate of food. Turning to Carol, she asked, "Do you want a turkey sandwich?"

"No, thanks," Carol said, patting her round, protruding belly. "I'm on the grapefruit diet, but I could use a glass of wine, if you have any." Carol took a few drags from her cigarette before she resumed talking. "Back to Caryn. I really think she's a depressed wine alcoholic. She and Joel were a couple in high school. They got married at eighteen, when they both graduated. She has all kinds of medical problems: back problems, migraines, and that sickness…what's it called? Where you're afraid to leave your house? I forgot what it's called." Carol pulled on her cigarette and waved her hand dismissively.

"Agoraphobia!" Lori replied from another room in the apartment. "I read about it in *Time* magazine a while back!" Lori had been walking around, opening and closing cabinets.

"What are you doing?" Carol asked.

"Looking for the wine," Lori said.

"I would settle for a gin and tonic," Carol countered.

"Funny, Carol, I can't find anything," Lori said. "I know we had merlot and several bottles of gin and Jack Daniel's. The only thing I see here is the Jack."

"Forget about it," Carol responded. "I really don't need anything." Looking up over the sofa at the wall clock, Carol said, "Actually, I better leave. My boys will be home looking for dinner." She crushed out her cigarette into a large green ceramic ashtray that sat atop a small table beside the sofa, and gathering her marked school papers, purse, and cigarettes, she gave Lori a peck on the cheek. "If you can get away any day next week, I'll be by myself. Steve has been traveling a lot. He has a special client in Michigan that needs a lot of help in her estate planning."

Lori put things back in the cabinets. She had made a mental note to ask Jerry where he was hiding the liquor, but by the end of the day when he came home, she forgot.

Steve was out of town on business, and Carol at a hockey team playoff with her boys, so Lori told Jerry to go to his mother's house alone, and she called Adele.

"Will Jim let you out alone, in your current condition?" Lori asked.

She and Adele went to a small quiet little place in Highwood called Angelo's. The two women sat in a back booth laughing and talking together about Adele's pregnancy and her plans for the baby's nursery, when all at once Adele stopped cold.

"Look" she said quietly, pointing to a couple walking out of the restaurant. Isn't that your brother-in-law?"

Lori turned in the direction of Adele's gaze. "It can't be, he's in Detroit on business this week." Lori sat and stared as Steve, Carol's husband, and some woman she had never seen before departed the restaurant.

"It sure looks like him," Adele asserted.

"Who the hell is he with?" Lori said as she sank lower on her side of the booth. *Why the hell am I hiding?* she thought to herself.

"I don't know, but it's *not* Carol," Adele said.

The woman who had her arm linked to Lori's brother-in-law had dark hair, looked to be about twenty years old, and was very thin. A waiter blocked their view, and the couple walked out.

Lori looked down. "Shit," she said. "I really thought they had a perfect marriage. There must be some explanation." She reached for a cigarette, pouting.

Adele raised her eyebrows and said, "He better have a good one, the way he was kissing that girl's neck and… and feeling her behind."

"Boy, you are observant." Lori laughed but then suddenly became dour. "Let's keep this to ourselves. I don't want to hurt Carol," Lori said, shaking her head. "It would kill me if she found out through me. That bastard."

Lori put the awkward situation out of her mind until a few weeks later, when she heard Jerry sitting in the kitchen talking and laughing on the phone with Steve. It occurred to her that Steve was on more and more business trips, and he and Jerry were becoming chummier and chummier.

She moved into the kitchen and started to make dinner. Irritated, she banged the pots and pans around, making an awful racket. Jerry hung up the phone and turned to his wife.

"What's wrong?" he asked.

"Nothing," she replied. "I'm just making dinner."

"Okay, Lori," Jerry said. "Why are you mad?"

"I want to know what's going on with you and your brother," Lori demanded.

"Nothing," Jerry replied.

"Jerry, Adele and I saw him a month ago at Angelo's with some girl other than Carol," Lori said.

"So?" Jerry responded. "It could have been a business acquaintance."

"Not the way they were acting," Lori said.

"Did you tell Carol?" Jerry asked.

"No," Lori replied.

"Steve sometimes has girlfriends, but they mean nothing," Jerry explained.

She looked up at Jerry, surprised at his casual attitude toward his brother's cheating.

"Girlfriends?" Lori said. "He's a married man, for crying out loud, with a lovely family!"

"He's always been like that," Jerry said. "Carol probably knows or suspects."

Lori pursed her lips, narrowed her eyes, and folded her arms around a large pot she was holding." What about you?" she asked.

Jerry delivered his best "little boy" look and spoke softly and earnestly. "Lori, you are the only one for me. You know how much I love you." He moved closer to her. "Listen, honey, let's go out for dinner tonight. Put away everything and get dressed into something special."

He took the pot out of her hand, put it on the counter, and pulled her towards him, kissing her passionately on the mouth while groping under her blouse for her bra hook.

She pulled away from him. "Oh, no" she said, teasing. "I've been promised a nice dinner." Lori skipped away and went into the bedroom to change, putting on Jerry's favorite blue sweater outfit. She then joined him at the door, and they went down in the elevator, to the garage, and on their way.

"Where are we going?" she asked when Jerry turned the car south and continued on past downtown Chicago to the South Loop.

"To our favorite restaurant," Jerry replied, winking at Lori.

"Oh, I know! Johnny's Steak House, on Wabash, where we had our first date!" Lori answered with a smile and a clap of her hands.

Jerry did something unusual for him: he gave the car to the doorman instead of looking for a parking space. He escorted Lori into the restaurant, resisted laughing when she opened the door before he could try to be a gentleman, bowed to his lady, and told her, “You look like a fairy princess.”

Lori responded, “And you are my Prince Charming.”

Seated, Jerry called the waiter over. “Champagne and chateaubriand for my lady.”

Lori grabbed his arm, “Honey, we can’t afford that.”

“Tonight, we are prince and princess, so we will eat royally,” Jerry assured her.

Never had steak tasted so good.

When the check came, both he and Lori had to dig through pockets to find the fifty dollars for their meal. They snuck out of the restaurant without leaving a tip. Giggling like two teenagers in love, they ran hand-in-hand to their car and drove back home. Kissing and groping one another in the elevator, they hardly made it into the apartment before shedding their clothes. Sex that night was the best they ever had.

Chapter Four

Two and a half months later, Lori was sitting in the last booth of the Cubby Hole restaurant in Northfield. She watched Adele walk in with one-year-old Sasha in her arms.

Reaching the booth, Adele called over her arm to their special waitress, "Maddy, we need a high chair."

Lori sat with her eyes fixed on Sasha as Adele put her in the chair, handed her some crackers and a toy, slipped into the red vinyl booth, and asked, "What's happening?"

Having received no response, Adele moved her eyes from Lori to Sasha and back to Lori, who just sat staring at Adele's baby, as though in shock.

Adele moved her head back and forth until suddenly she understood. She moved across the booth, poked Lori, and simply stated, "You're pregnant. Am I right?"

Lori took a deep breath and slowly answered, "Yes, and I'm scared."

"Why?" Adele asked. "You should be thrilled. Babies are wonderful." She reached across the table to grasp her friend's hands. "This is great news, Lori!"

Lori looked down at her hands clasped in Adele's, and her face broke into a mask of worry. "Oh, Adele, I'm not ready for a baby! We can't afford to go without my six thousand dollar teaching salary." Lori's green eyes were wet with tears.

Adele released her friend's hands, retrieved a clean tissue from her baby bag, and handed it to Lori.

"Lori, Lori, don't worry. I promise you, it will be great. You and Jerry, you'll make it happen. It will work out, you'll see." She looked on as Lori collected herself, wiping at her eyes and forcing a smile.

"We'll raise our children together," Adele assured her. "We'll learn all about it together."

Sasha issued her opinion by tossing her crackers, apple juice bottle, and toy on the floor before screaming.

That night, Adele approached Jim and asked, "Honey, why don't you talk to Jerry about that dental supply business idea he had?"

"Adele, you know I don't have time for it," Jim responded. "My dental office is going full guns, and I am in the process of expanding it."

"If you need money to start the supply business, take it from my trust fund," Adele offered. "Lori is pregnant, and they could use the money."

***

With a baby on the way, Lori found she was getting more and more disillusioned with the city. She wanted to raise her child in a home with a big backyard, and in a neighborhood with a good school district. Jerry reluctantly agreed. Before too long, they bought a modern, two-story, red brick, three-bedroom, tri-level house in Northfield only a half a mile from Adele. Some of its new features were a walk-in-closet, a master bedroom with a bathroom, and large patio doors opening out to the backyard from the family room.

The forty-five thousand dollar price tag was steep, but to Lori it was worth being thirty-five miles away from Shelly and back in Lori's old stomping ground. They put down thirty percent and took out a thirty-year mortgage at six and one-half percent. This adventure left them little money for furniture. They did, however, manage to buy a bedroom set with one of those new queen size mattresses.

Lori stopped packing and moved over to the expansive living room window. The sky-blue lake was filled with boaters, the beaches were swarming with people, and the roads were crammed with cars at a standstill. Police and ambulance sirens screamed as their vehicles rushed below. There was even a group of protestors chanting and carrying posters pleading to their government to impeach President Richard Nixon. The Watergate scandal was all over the papers and the news; it was replacing the Vietnam protests, and the terrorists at the Munich Olympics, as the nation's top news interest.

Lori knew there would be many things she would miss about living in the city, things like her beautiful view of the lake and the close proximity to museums and the theatre; the continuous noise, congestion, and craziness, however, she knew she could do without.

Lori planned to continue teaching for several months, even though it meant commuting to the city every day, but she was relieved of her job in her fifth month, as soon as her pregnancy began to show, as her principal felt Lori's third graders may start to ask questions. Lori felt like protesting, saying, "Why, do they still believe in storks?" but she wanted to keep her options open to return someday.

To her mother's surprise, Lori became the one in charge of paying bills and balancing their budget. Their expenses had increased and their income had slowed down now that Lori was not working. Jerry's new business venture had promise, but it would take time before it started to pay off. Jim had contributed the bulk of the initial investment. Their share had come in the form of a loan from Lori's parents. Jim handled the business end and the contacts, while Jerry was the salesman and the keeper of the supplies. Their basement was loaded with dental equipment.

Lori became involved in the business, answering the phone and mailing out packages. Adele had a hard time understanding why Lori was involved in the business, so Lori couldn't use her as a sounding board in this area. To Adele and Jim, the business was a sideline. To Jerry and Lori, the business was their main income.

At first, Lori loved being pregnant. She was the center of attention, everyone was so nice to her, and she had an excuse to eat and eat. Jerry even catered to her, doing housework and shopping. Her mom and dad came over to her house to visit, and her dad felt her stomach when the baby kicked. But by her eighth month, her enthusiasm was wearing thin, and she became uncomfortable and impatient, even with Adele, who had taken charge of preparing her for the baby.

Picking Lori up in her new Lincoln, Adele patiently listened to her friend complain about everything.

Lori put down the blue and the pink baby buntings on the counter of the Bramson's Baby Shop. "I'm really tired of looking at baby clothes," Lori said. "How can I decide what color to buy when I don't know if I'm having a boy or a girl? And I hate yellow. I have to sit down, my swollen feet hurt, my back hurts, and my tits are sore."

The petite thin cute, young salesgirl, in a fitted orange polyester pants suit came over and asked, "Can I help you?"

Adele looked at the salesgirl and asked, "Is there any place we can sit down?"

She smiled and said, "Oh yes, we have a mothers' waiting area." She walked them over to a room with large, comfortable pillowed chairs and a table with a coffee pot and asked, "Can I get you something to drink?"

"Black coffee," Adele said.

"Nothing for me. I'll just have to pee again," Lori answered sardonically. She sat down in one of the wooden rocking chairs and kicked off her shoes. Looking at Adele, Lori sighed and said, "Only in Northfield would there be a store like this."

The saleslady handed Adele a cup of coffee and walked away. Lori waited until she was well out of earshot before whispering, "Why don't they hire someone fat or pregnant instead of a beauty queen?"

Adele laughed. "Soon your baby will be here, Lori, and you'll be thin again."

"I feel like I've been pregnant forever," Lori mused.

Jerry never made it to work one particular morning in the middle of April. Sitting at the kitchen table checking the baseball scores in the morning paper, he was abruptly interrupted by a blood-curdling scream coming from the upper floor of the house. Jerry raced up the stairs and found Lori lying on the bathroom floor in a puddle of water.

"Jerry, help me, help me!" Lori screamed. "I'm having the baby!"

"Honey, calm down," Jerry said. "I think you just broke your water. Are you getting contractions?" Jerry did his best to remain calm.

"I think so." Lori looked up at him, her eyes wide. "Jerry, I'm scared."

Jerry helped Lori up and into some clothes. He grabbed her purse and the small suitcase, and he carefully maneuvered her down the stairs, through the garage, and into the car. Speeding down the street while Lori moaned, he turned onto the Edens Expressway. He immediately knew he had made a mistake; cars were at a standstill. After all, it was morning rush hour.

Lori cried, "You're so stupid! Now I'm going to have the baby in the car!"

At his first chance, he exited the expressway and sped around the side streets.

"Stop!" Lori screamed. Jerry stopped cold. In front of him was a young boy on a bicycle.

Shaken upon realizing he had almost hit the kid, he got out of the car and walked over to the boy, who was picking up his dropped bike.

"Are you hurt?" Jerry asked.

The young boy said, "No. I'm okay," got back on his bike, and continued to cross the street. People behind Jerry's car were honking their horns. Jerry got back into the car and slowly continued on, saying to no one particular, "I didn't see him. If she hadn't screamed, I would have hit a kid…"

They pulled up in front of Northwestern Hospital forty-five minutes later. Lori was put into a wheel chair and taken up to the maternity floor, and Jerry was put in the fathers' waiting room. Five and a half hours later, a nurse came into the room and called for Mr. Brill.

Smiling, the nurse said, "Congratulations, you have a beautiful baby girl. She's seven pounds three ounces and twenty-two inches long."

His lips turned down in a look of disappointment as he asked, "A girl, not a boy?"

The nurse shook her head, thinking, *These men, always looking for a boy. Don't they realize how attached little girls become to their fathers?* "Yes, a big, healthy little *girl,*" she emphasized.

"Is my wife all right?" Jerry asked. "Does she know yet?"

"Not yet," the nurse replied. "She's still out."

When Lori woke up, she was in a hospital bed next to a window overlooking Chicago's bustling downtown. She groggily noted that her stomach had deflated and everything below her navel hurt. She was happy to see Jerry sitting next to her.

"Honey, it's a girl!" Jerry said, smiling and stroking her cheek.

Lori smiled. She knew Jerry was disappointed, but she was thrilled. "When can I see her?" Lori asked. "Is she perfect? Toes, fingers, breathing?"

"I saw her through the window," Jerry said. "Yes, she's perfect. After all, she's a Brill. I guess they will bring her to you soon."

"Is the name Julie Ann, after my dad's mother, still okay with you?" Lori asked.

"We agreed," Jerry assured her. "You get to name a girl, and I get to name a boy."

After the customary week's stay in the hospital, Lori came home with her gorgeous baby girl. Jerry had painted the room a soft pink and had set up the crib, dresser, and changing table. Adele had made sure the layette, clothes, formula, and baby bottles had been delivered from Bramson's Baby Shop. A stack of gifts sat along the back of the closet.

After a few days Jerry went back to work, and the friends and family stopped coming over to see the baby. Lori was relieved to be by herself with her daughter. Now they could get to know each other. This didn't last long. After two hours of trying to calm a crying baby, Lori wished she could call her mother for help, but she knew that would be futile. Instead, she called Adele, who arrived shortly at Lori's house with her own children and a copy of a book by a Dr. Spock. Lori watched in awe while Adele nonchalantly picked up the baby and held her over her arm, while she sat her older children by the kitchen table with crayons and coloring books.

Adele looked at Lori, undressed, disheveled, and standing there with tears in her eyes.

"Okay, let's see what's wrong with Julie," Adele said. "When a baby cries, she either needs some loving, a burp, something to eat, or a diaper change." With that said, Julie burped and settled down on Adele's shoulder.

Adele tried to give her back to Lori, but Lori shook her head. Adele looked at her sternly.

"Lori, your daughter isn't a china doll," Adele admonished. "Stop being afraid of her!"

"I'm an only child," Lori explained. "I never had a brother or sister to take care of, like you did, nor do I have a mother to help me."

When Adele left, Lori walked around the cheerful pink and white room with her daughter in her arms.

"Julie, I will be a great mother to you," Lori promised. "We will play together, bake cookies, read books, go to the park, and the circus, and shopping. We will do all the things my mother never did with me. And I will tell you every day how much I love you. Our life will be perfect." She meant every word.

Chapter Five

When Julie was one year old Lori was surprised by an unexpected visit by both of her parents, who one day simply arrived at her door. She was used to her father popping in to see the baby, but her mother seldom left her own home.

"What's wrong?" Lori asked cautiously as she took their coats and led them into the family room.

Her mother, who was usually quiet, blurted out, "We're moving."

"Where?" Lori asked.

"West Palm Beach."

"West Palm Beach," Lori repeated slowly. "That's in Florida. How can you move so far away now, just when your granddaughter has come into the world?"

"Lori, we came to *tell* you, not to de*bate* it. I can no longer handle the winters in Chicago," her mother said in her cold, assertive voice.

At the sound of Julie crying, Lori walked out of the living room to tend to her daughter, leaving her parents alone. She moved into the bedroom, lips pursed, tears in her eyes. Her dad followed her. Lori watched as her father lifted Julie out of the crib and started to play with her. Julie responded by laughing and clapping her hands.

"Why, Dad?" Lori asked.

Her father turned to her and said, "Don't judge your mother too harshly, Lori. She has her reasons for the way she is." He looked down at Julie, kissed her forehead, and said, "Don't worry, we'll be back to visit, and you'll bring your family to visit us."

When they went back into the family room, they saw that Lori's mother had her head in her hands. Looking up, she said, "We better go, I'm getting a migraine."

Ignoring her mother, Lori took the baby from her dad and said to him, “I only hope my husband loves me half as much as you love Mom.”

As Lori’s parents made their way out the door, Lori’s mother felt instant relief after leaving Lori’s home. Since this baby’s birth, the headaches wouldn’t stop. The nightmares were back. Night after night Lori’s mother shuddered as the recurring vision returned, a vision of a young girl standing with open arms, pleading, “Don’t take my child, take me instead!” She kept her head straight as she sat in the front passenger seat, not looking at Lori’s home or her daughter and granddaughter at the front door as her husband pulled out of the driveway and onto the tree-lined road.

Lori parked the car on the street because there was a moving van in her parents’ driveway. She smoothed out her white sleeveless button-down blouse, tucking it neatly into the waist of her pedal pusher jeans. She pulled on her light pink jacket before pulling Julie out of the basket in the car. She knew she looked a wreck, so she tried to fluff out her disheveled black hair, but she could not spend time fussing about her appearance if she was to tend to Julie and get to her folks; house in time.

She leaned forward, holding Julie at her hip, and took a perfunctory peek into the side-view mirror and frowned slightly. Not a speck of makeup except a pale pink lipstick adorned her face. Shrugging, Lori walked through the open door into the home she had occupied from the age of twelve until twenty-six. She looked around as she made her way slowly through the empty rooms, remembering flashes of her childhood and early adulthood. She could not get herself to come to terms with the realization that this would soon become someone else’s home, someone else’s space to occupy from where they would create memories of a lifetime.

Lori's dad walked out of the bedroom, greeting his daughter warmly as he reached for Julie and held her in his arms. He cooed and smiled at his granddaughter, bouncing her lightly as he walked about the room.

Lori stood by the window, looking out at her father's garden. Rose bushes sprang up alongside apple and pear trees, while clusters of lilies, mums, poppies, and spider plants ran across the length of the white painted backyard fence. She had envisioned her dad, now retired, coming over to play with Julie and turning her yard into a beautiful garden.

Her mother came out of a room carrying a small box. Without looking at her daughter or the baby, she put the box into Lori's hands.

"I want you to put these pieces of jewelry away for your daughter, and use the check," she added, knocking on the box's top, "to help furnish your new house." She turned to her husband. "We have to get going. I heard the limo pull up." As he did not respond, she turned back to Lori, but her eyes remained somewhere beyond her daughter's eyes as she addressed her. "You need to only stay here until the van leaves." She gave Lori a peck on the cheek and walked out the door, totally ignoring Julie, as if the giggling, happy baby girl was not in existence.

Lori's dad handed Julie back to her as he watched his wife leave the room. He gave his daughter a big hug and kiss.

"Honey, wipe those tears away," he said encouragingly. "We're only going to Florida. We'll be back, and you'll visit us. We'll see one another again before you know it!"

The limo pulled away, and Lori resumed her walk through the house, taking in the emptiness of the spaces she entered. As she moved from room to room, she talked with Julie as she held her in her arms, telling her tales of her childhood.

"This was my room, where Adele and I would stay up all night long, listening to records and dreaming of who we would marry," Lori told her daughter. "Oh, Julie, I had so much fun with Adele! Maybe you and Sasha can become best friends."

After only twenty minutes, the moving van pulled away, taking all her parents' belongings with them, leaving the house, at last, truly vacant. Lori stepped outside and took one last look at the house's exterior and silently said goodbye. After settling Julie into the car, Lori drove down the street to Adele's house.

As Adele opened the door, she asked, "Are they gone?"

"Yes," Lori said, before bursting into tears.

"Come into the kitchen, I just made chocolate chip scones," Adele said as she took Julie out of Lori's arms and put her down on the family room floor next to three-year-old Sasha. Sasha immediately offered Julie her toys.

Adele went into the adjoining kitchen to where Lori was seated, poured Lori a cup of coffee, and offered her a scone.

Taking it, Lori looked at Adele with a tear-stained face. "You're my only family now, Adele, the sister I never had," Lori said as she bit into the scone. "My mother still hates me."

"Lori, stop it. It's only Florida." Adele sat beside her friend and softly stroked her black hair from her face as she cried harder. Adele knew well that Lori was crying for more than her parents' moving. It was a long time coming, this release of all the sadness Lori harbored on account of her parents' unavailability. Lori often spoke of an emptiness she felt due to her parents' inability to really nurture and love their daughter. Although her father loved her, he seemed to always be out of town. Her mother was cool and distant. Lori was mourning the loss of the kind of parents she had always wanted but never had. Now they were abandoning her once again.

"We can start going back there every Christmas vacation like we did when we were growing up," Adele offered. "Doesn't your aunt still live near my aunt and uncle in Winston Towers in North Miami Beach? You can see your parents for a few days and then continue south and join us. You know your dad will be back, and, well, Lori dear," Adele spoke softly, "you know you can't expect things from your mother now that she could never give you before." Adele continued stroking her friend's long black hair, trying in vain to comfort what could not be healed.

"I'm a mess," Lori whined, still crying and taking a quick inventory of herself. "Dirty jeans, chipped nails, hair everywhere, and all those extra pounds I can't shed. *You* should have been my mother's daughter. She liked you from the day I brought you over when we were twelve."

Adele gave Lori a big hug and said, "Stop, Lori, please stop berating yourself." She took her friend's face in her hands. "Lori, you have got to pull yourself together. It is not your fault. Your mother has problems we don't understand." Diverting Lori's attention, she pointed to the girls. "Look, Sasha is walking Julie!"

Lori sniffed and turned towards the two girls. They really did get along well, she thought, smiling wearily. Maybe they would be best friends like she and Adele were. She pulled out a tissue from her purse and dabbed at her eyes and nose, then looked around Adele's house, scanning the custom furniture, designer drapes, antiques, and traditional English paintings.

Lori tried to ease the tension and her sorrow by switching subjects. "My mom gave me a little money to furnish the house," Lori said. "Do you think your interior designer would take on a small job?"

"See, Lori?" Adele said as she smiled and patted Lori on her leg, "Your mom did come through. I'm sure Jodi would be delighted to help you."

"She comes through with money," Lori replied ruefully, wiping at her nose again. "Julie won't know her grandparents, but she will be the best-dressed girl on the block."

Steering clear of the subject of Lori's mom, Adele said, "I think the business is going great, don't you?"

"Oh, yes," Lori answered, sniffing and combing her hands through her hair in an attempt to smooth it down. "They make good partners. Jim loves the business end, and Jerry is a superb salesman." She refrained from telling Adele that Jerry seemed to be specializing in martini lunches and had been coming home drunk. There was only so much Lori could handle in one day. She turned and smiled at the children at play. Adele and Lori spent the next half hour with small talk of redecorating plans as they enjoyed one more cup of coffee and one more scone.

As Lori got up to go, Adele helped with her jacket and the baby. On the way out, Adele said, "See you at the Greenspans' party tomorrow night."

"I guess so," Lori answered, shrugging.

"What's wrong?" Adele asked.

"Jerry feels out of place," Lori explained. "He complained that living in Northfield is like living in a college fraternity. He was raised differently than we were. His way of life was checking for bargains at Goldblatt's, not buying Polo shirts at Saks."

She refrained from telling Adele that she too was having a hard time getting back into the Northfield lifestyle. In the city, she had gotten accustomed to running out of the house without make-up and wearing blue jeans, which, in this suburb was a no-no.

***

Jerry walked out of the pub with his arm around Sy McNally, an Irish Jew he had just befriended. They were both laughing and singing as they made their way to Jerry's car.

When they reached their destination, Sy said, "I'm the manager of eight dental clinics, so if my boss likes your equipment, we'll use it in all the clinics. Thanks for the dinner and drinks! You're my mate."

Jerry looked at his watch; it was already 7 p.m. Lori would be mad. *So what*, he thought. *I made a great sale, and I'm sick of going out with her fancy suburban friends. Adele and Jim are fine, but the rest of those people in that group are snobs, especially that Judy and Stuart Greenspan. Those goddamn fish eggs at his fancy country club tasted like shit.* Jerry scowled as he thought about how when he tried to be sociable, telling them some of his best jokes, and they didn't even get them. Today, Sy and his buddies had laughed and laughed at his jokes, especially the one about the brick.

Chapter Six

Lori hadn't gone to any Brill family dinners since Julie was born, so she and her sister-in-law Carol had depended on the phone to keep abreast of events. Finally, Carol made the trip to Northfield. Sitting in Lori's copper-colored kitchen, drinking coffee, and munching on chocolate cake, Lori watched the circles of gray smoke coming from Carol's cigarette.

Carol picked up the pack of Salem cigarettes and asked Lori, "Want one?"

"I'm trying to quit, now that I have a baby, but it's hard to do," Lori said. "Instead of losing pounds, I'm gaining them." Lori smirked and took another bite of her cake. "Is Shelly still ranting and raving about our move? She told Jerry I did it on purpose to keep her granddaughter away from her because she doesn't drive." Lori chewed a bit of her cake and added, "Well, it's kind of true."

"Oh, she's just angry because one of her kids moved out of the neighborhood," Carol said.

"What about Eileen?" Lori asked. "She moved all the way to California!"

"Well, of course!" Carol replied, snickering innocently.

"What do you mean, Carol?"

Carol looked stunned. "Nobody ever told you Eileen's story?'

"No," Lori answered. "I've been told to never mention her name."

Carol sat back in her chair, lit another cigarette, and unfolded Eileen's story.

"Eileen was my friend before I even met Steve," Carol began. "She was her father's favorite, and Jack Brill hasn't been the same since she left. But Shelly resented her, and they were always fighting. I watched

Shelly slap poor Eileen around many times. She treated the boys differently than she treated Eileen."

"What did her father do while this was going on?" Lori asked.

"Nothing," Carol replied. "Actually, I think Jack is afraid of Shelly too."

"Did Eileen fight her back?" Lori asked.

"Eileen was no match for Shelly in a direct fight, so she defied her by staying out late, wearing crazy clothes, bringing boys home, drinking," Carol explained. "Eileen eventually realized one way to really upset Shelly was to shirk her chores around the house. That got her into the most trouble. I can't tell you how many times Eileen wound up at my house bawling her eyes out. My mother, after all she witnessed with Eileen, was not pleased when I married into the Brill family, but I was head over heels crazy about Steve from the first day I met him."

"Boy, no one ever told me any of this," Lori said. "I thought Eileen left on her own."

"Once she declared that she was a lesbian and started bringing girlfriends home, Shelly and Jack ordered her to get out," Carol said. "It was the summer after she graduated design school. The family declared her dead and sat shiva for her." She watched Lori's eyes grow wide. "Yeah, some piece of work, the Brill family. I was surprised Shelly let Jerry invite her to your wedding."

"It wasn't Jerry," Lori responded. "Actually, after you gave me her address, I invited her." Lori couldn't help laughing as she thought about what she created by inviting Eileen.

"Well, you gave her a chance, and she blew it," Carol said. "She didn't have to come to the wedding looking for all the world like some crazy witch! Ah, well, she's a good person. Who can help but be a little crazy growing up with that kind of a mother? Eileen and I still keep in touch."

"That must be how she heard about Julie," Lori said. "Jerry and I received a beautiful pink baby outfit from an address in Los Angeles. The card was signed; *Love, Eileen and Suzanne.*"

"Suzanne is her business partner and her girlfriend," Carol explained. "She's good for her. It finally sounds like Eileen's life is turning around."

After Carol left, Lori sat shaking her head in thought. Wow, a lesbian in the family. Lori always thought of herself as a liberal, but this did kind of shock her. At Lori's wedding Eileen had warned her that she was marrying into a crazy family. Boy, was she right. Her thoughts were interrupted by Julie's crying. *Time to get Julie,* she said to herself. *That feisty daughter of mine will climb out any minute if I don't get in there. I'm lucky she's still taking a nap at a year and a half.*

Lori sat in the kitchen trying to balance the checkbook. She knew her mother and father would be surprised to learn she was the conservative one in the family, the bill payer, and the one who tried to keep their spending down. She had grown up never worrying about money. Jerry seemed to feel if it was on sale he should buy it; if it was something they couldn't use or didn't want it did not make any difference. As she was pondering the irony of it all, the phone rang.

Lori picked up her new slim blue princess phone. Jerry was on the other end.

"Lori, dress the baby," Jerry ordered. "I will be home as soon as I can to pick you up. Joel has called a family meeting at my parents' house."

"Now what?" Lori said aloud after she had hung up the phone. There was always a crisis in the Brill family. The boys liked to compete in producing lunatic schemes, with Shelly as their cheerleader. Lori figured it was Joel's turn tonight.

Jerry rushed in at 3:30 in the afternoon and hurried them out of the house, giving Lori barely enough time to grab some toys. Julie was entering her terrible twos and needed to be entertained all the time. They arrived late due to rush hour traffic. Steve, Carol, and the boys were around the table busily eating Shelly's homemade chicken dinner. Steve was munching on a drumstick and complaining after every bite.

"The twins are graduating next year," he said. "I don't know how I am going to pay for college."

Lori refrained from telling him that dropping the girlfriends would help his finances. She suspected something was going on again by the snippets of conversation she heard between Jerry and his brother.

"I know what you mean," Jerry said in between bites on a chicken leg. "Between the new house and the new business, we're also strapped financially."

Another one talking about something he doesn't know, Lori thought. *Why, he hasn't looked at a bill since we've been married.*

Joel, who was alone as usual, quickly stopped the conversation with a wallop of a statement: "That's why I called a family meeting." His wiry thin frame hovered over the table as he addressed his seated family in an authoritative tone. "No one will have to worry about money again. I have an exciting secret to tell." He leaned forward and, with a big smirk on his dimpled face declared, "Caryn's Uncle Max from Oregon died and left Caryn and me forty-million… dollars."

No one moved or said a word. Everyone sat there stunned until Joel threw out his arms and repeated. "Did you hear me, folks? Forty… million!" He savored the pregnant pause until he knew he held their attention for certain. He folded his arms over his puffed out chest and smirked as he looked at his family's shocked expressions. "That's right, folks. *I* am going to be filthy rich, and I'm going to split the money between all of us…because we are family."

Lori was the first one to speak. "Wow, that's great, Joel." Lori did nothing to mask her skepticism. "When is this money coming?"

Joel faced Lori, but his eyes quickly darted around the table to make sure he still had a captive audience. "Next week. I am going to Oregon myself to sign the papers," Joel said, taking his seat at the table. "Caryn is afraid to fly, so she signed the power of attorney over to me. Let's celebrate!"

Everyone began clapping and hugging Joel. That is, everyone but his father, who just sat watching television from his place at the table.

Lori took Carol to the side. "What's going on?" she asked. "Last year he told us Caryn was pregnant, which wasn't true, and then he bragged about being the vice president of Aetna Bank, which also was a lie."

Carol and Lori went into the kitchen and tried to call Caryn. Of course, no one answered the phone. Carol did remember that Caryn had family in Oregon, but she had never heard Caryn refer to them as wealthy. She and Lori were skeptical while Jerry and Steve were ecstatic over the millions their brother was going to give them.

Lori slowly began to believe Joel. *Perhaps,* Lori thought, *this was one lie that was just too big to pull off, so it had to be true! How can someone make up a lie this big?*

Six weeks later, Joel called and asked Jerry to drive him to the airport. As Lori needed to get some errands done, she opted to drive with Jerry and Joel, whereupon they would run errands together on the way home afterwards. They picked him up at his house, put his small suitcase in the trunk of the car, and started down the Edens Expressway to O'Hare International Airport.

"Are you going to get the money this trip?" Lori asked, turning herself around as best as she could to face Joel, who sat in the back seat.

"Oh, no," Joel answered off-handedly. "It could take a year or more. Things are in probate."

"How much money are we talking about?" Lori asked. Jerry gave her a dirty look that she did not see.

Joel's face darkened as he leaned forward. "What's the matter, Lori?" Joel answered haughtily. "Don't you trust me? You're getting me angry."

Joel affected the tone he would often utilize to create an air of arrogance. This tone was used at family gatherings when he thought he was telling everyone something they did not know. Joel liked to have the upper hand, and now with an alleged forty-million dollars at his disposal, sitting in his pocket, Joel was acting as though he had his family in his pocket as well.

"I *told* you we were going to split forty-million dollars four ways. Don't worry, Lori," Joel said as he reached out and patted her hand, which she quickly withdrew from the back of her car seat, *"You'll* get your money."

Lori kept quiet, turning her head to look out the window at the cloud-filled fall sky.

After they let Joel off at the United terminal, Lori turned to Jerry and said, "You better stop buying things and wait until you get the money."

"Lori, stop worrying," Jerry said. "This is the second trip Joel has made to Oregon. We're going to be rich, filthy rich, with ten million dollars!"

Instead of heeding Lori's cautionary warning, Jerry busied himself by shopping and planning what he would do with his millions. As Lori was the bill payer at their house, she scrutinized the bills, and her heart raced when she saw receipts for a three-hundred dollar suit, a one hundred dollar pair of shoes, new appliances, and tons of toys for Julie. When a two-thousand dollar television and stereo system was delivered to the house and charged on credit, she exploded. In the last six months, Jerry had spent six thousand dollars, the equivalent of her teaching salary for the year.

Jerry's response to her screaming was, "Lori, why are you being a spoil sport? We're going to be *millionaires*! Joel is on his third trip to Oregon to sign more papers."

"Jerry," she pleaded, "let's *get* the money before we spend it."

But neither he nor the other family members paid attention to her or Carol, who also expressed her doubts when Joel wasn't around. Jerry and Steve were busy looking at cars, boats, and exotic vacations. The family was on a high. Jerry, Steve, and friends attended champagne dinners at fancy restaurants. Coveted front row tickets to Bears and Blackhawks games were purchased. Every night, Jerry came home with toys and gifts for Julie and Lori. She kept them wrapped, as she still didn't trust Joel. Lori noticed that Shelly and Joel participated in the excitement, but not in the buying aspect. Caryn never showed up at the family parties or answered her phone—or her door.

After almost a year of stalling, Carol and Lori cornered Joel at one of the Friday night dinners, which Lori was now attending.

"Okay, Joel," Lori said sharply, walking up to him, her green eyes flashing "We want to know when we'll get the money." Carol stood staring straight up at Joel's face, her chubby face set like a stone.

"When, Joel?" they asked in unison, standing on either side of him to block him from escaping.

Joel threw his arms up in the air and screamed, "How can you doubt my sincerity, after everything I'm doing for the family?!"

"Joel, we are going broke waiting for the money," Lori said. "You haven't produced any evidence or any papers for us to sign. I think we need to talk to Caryn at her place of work."

Joel fell silent and walked out of his parents' home and disappeared for days. Shelly blamed Lori for causing trouble between her children.

A few days later, Carol and Lori went to the medical clinic where Caryn worked and demanded to talk to her. Caryn took a short break, motioning them to meet her in the employees' cafeteria. She sat with her head down, careful not to meet their inquisitive gazes. Her response to their inquiry was not surprising.

"I don't know anything about millions, ladies," Caryn said, shaking her head. Her long stringy hair that hung in disheveled strands around her small face was a mousey brown color, with hints of gray at the crown. Lori noted she was too young to have gone gray so soon. "My uncle Max died and left me twenty-thousand dollars, not forty-million," Caryn spoke in a voice that sounded as though it would crumble to dust at any moment. "Is that what Joel's been telling you?" Still keeping her gaze downward, Caryn laughed softly through her nose and shook her head, thinking, *What in hell was he up to now?* "The money is *mine*, not Joel's," Caryn continued. "He traveled to Oregon six months ago to sign the papers and receive the check because I'm afraid of flying."

"Just for the record, Caryn, how many trips did Joel make to Oregon?" Lori asked.

"Just one," Caryn replied. So many questions were left unanswered in Caryn's head for so long, she refused to move forward with this barrage of questioning. She abruptly rose out of her chair.

"That's enough, ladies. I have work to do." Caryn noisily slapped her hands on the table, then quickly retracted them and stuffed them into the pockets of her formless smock. "Please, leave me alone," she said, scurrying back into the doctor's office. Carol and Lori both sat at the table, shocked and angry.

Lori looked at Carol. "We took him to the airport three times," Lori said. "I guess he just left through the back door. Why the elaborate scheme? To what end, Carol?" Lori shook her head and noted Carol's silence as she too shook her head slowly. "I'm not surprised," Lori said. "I'm just devastated that we all fell for another one of Joel's fiascoes."

Carol patted Lori's shoulder and answered, "You're new to the family. *I* should have known better."

"It's not your fault, Carol," Lori said. You were as skeptical as I was, but please explain to me why the family puts up with Joel's shenanigans. I always thought Caryn was insane, but maybe she is the only sane one. Why does she stay with him?" Lori paused for a moment in thought. "Carol," Lori began, "what's going on with Caryn? She looks so…odd… She's going gray already."

"The Brill family, my family, and Caryn's have been in the neighborhood for years," Carol explained. "She was always quiet and a loner, but she really changed when her mom was killed in a car accident."

"Oh, my God, when did that happen?" Lori asked.

"While she was in high school," Carol explained, joining Lori as she gathered her purse and rose to go. Carol fidgeted and adjusted her skirt over her ample rump and continued. "Joel befriended her, and they married right after she graduated. Joel is actually a good guy, deep down." Carol shrugged as the two women walked on.

"Lori, where are you?" Jerry called as he moved from the front door to the kitchen.

Lori sat at the kitchen table and just stared at him, unable to respond.

"What's going on?" Jerry demanded. "Julie is crying. What's this mess? What are you doing, just sitting here?" Jerry indicated toward the pile of papers scattered all over the table.

Lori grabbed all the papers on the table and threw them at Jerry.

"JUST SITTING HERE?" Lori exploded. "Bills, bills, bills, you and your brother have ruined us! You better find a way to pay them, Jerry, before they repossess the house and the cars and your wife and daughter will be out on the street! And you'll have your brother Joel and your own stupidity to thank for it!"

Lori stormed out of her kitchen and toward Julie's bedroom, where she stayed the entire time, leaving Jerry to fend for himself for dinner.

Lori was forced to go back to teaching and to borrow money from her parents. They couldn't afford a babysitter, so she reluctantly accepted Shelly's offer to sit. Jerry dropped off Julie at his mother's house every morning, and Lori picked her up after work. She sent Jerry with a list of rules to give to Shelly, but she suspected Shelly had thrown them out. Julie, at two and a half, was a bundle of excitement most days when she picked her up, talking about the candy and cupcakes and hot dogs she had eaten.

Around Halloween, when Lori picked up Julie, she was surprised to see that Julie was covered in paint. Different shades of blue, green, yellow, and red were spattered all over the child's skin and clothes.

"Shelly, what were you doing?" Lori asked, taking the smiling Julie by the hand.

"We painted pumpkins. It'll wash off," Shelly answered dismissively, and with a wave of her hand, Shelly walked away from her.

The oil-based house paint, however, did not wash off of Julie's clothes, and it took Lori a few hours to scrub the paint off of a crying and fighting Julie.

Jerry barely made it through the door when Lori jumped on him. "I can't let your mother near Julie again. The woman is *crazy*. She used permanent paint on your daughter today!"

"Lori, cool it," Jerry responded. "Things have picked up at work, and I'm swamped. Don't bother me with these petty things." Jerry made his way to the living room and sat on the floor beside his daughter, who was leafing through some picture books. The skin on her arms was still red and irritated but clean. Jerry took his daughter and placed her on his lap and talked with her for a while.

He tried his best to calm his wife's anger by not getting into fights with her. It just wasn't worth it. It seemed that almost every time he came through the door, Lori had something else to complain about. Wasn't she happy? How hard could her life be? Julie was a well-mannered, happy child, and Lori should be grateful that Shelly wanted to help at all, considering how Lori treated her and the rest of his family when they were all together. He didn't know how to get through to his wife, but he had more important things to deal with. Wasn't she happy at how well the business was doing?

After a while, Julie had gone back to her picture books and Jerry made his way to the kitchen to speak with his wife.

"I've got some good news, honey," Jerry began, trying to cheer up his sullen wife, who was mumbling and frowning as she prepared dinner. "Jim and I are supplying the University of Illinois with instruments. All those cocktail lunches I had with Dr. Bradley paid off. See if you can last until the end of the year."

On a lovely spring day in April, the day of Julie's third birthday, Lori had been preparing things in the kitchen for the party when the front doorbell rang. Lori answered and politely thanked the mailman for the package he had just delivered. She opened the box, and Styrofoam balls fell out everywhere. Inside was a beautiful, wrapped package from Neiman Marcus. She put it down, wiping the tears from her eyes. Instead of coming in from Florida her parents had sent an expensive gift.

She had so hoped that a granddaughter would change her mother. Okay, maybe she wasn't the kind of daughter her mother wanted, but what could her mother have against her beautiful baby daughter? And her father. Oh he always told her how much he loved her, but her mother's needs always came first.

"Mommy, where are you?" Julie yelled as she came running into the kitchen. Lori's face burst into a huge smile as she picked up her bundle of joy, squeezing her tightly. *I will be a perfect mother to Julie,* Lori said to herself.

Chapter Seven

Lori's teaching career ended when she found out she was pregnant again. Even though things were starting to change with the advent of the pill, legalized abortions, and the women's lib movement, she was again asked to leave by her fifth month, just as she had been when she was pregnant with Julie. Actually, she enjoyed staying home with her daughter, who kept her too busy to be sick or bored. Three-year-old Julie was interested in everything: books, television shows like *Sesame Street*, games, swing sets—everything but the baby.

"Mommy, swing me," Julie demanded.

"Julie, Mommy can't swing you," Lori explained. "She has a baby in her tummy. Let's read a book."

"No," the child whined, hitting Lori's stomach. "Send the baby away."

"Julie, honey, soon you will have a brother or a sister to play with, like Sasha has," Lori offered.

"Mommy, I want a collie dog instead, like Joanie," Julie insisted.

In early June of 1977, three years after Julie was born and eight months after Adele had her third child, Barry Brill joined their family. His birth caused more excitement than Julie's. In the Jewish religion, the birth of a boy is celebrated with a *bris*—the circumcision. Following tradition, the bris was performed in the temple eight days after the baby's birth. Even Grandma Lil and Grandpa Ed managed to fly in from Florida for the event.

Lori's dad was especially proud of the fact that Barry was named after his father Ben. Grandpa Ben lived until he was ninety-five. He succumbed to a stroke while dancing at the Miami Beach Community Center. Good genes to pass on.

The *mohel* chosen to perform the circumcision rite rocked Barry and quietly sang to him. The happy, comfortable little baby had no idea that he was about to enter a five-thousand-year old covenant, entered between Abraham and God, which condemned every Jewish male child to circumcision.

Lori leaned over to Adele and whispered, "Thank God the women have no part in this ceremony."

Jerry passed his beautiful, dark, curly haired newborn baby boy to the mohel, appropriately named Phil Slash, who came from a long line of mohels. Phil then ceremoniously and solemnly picked up the scalpel and proceeded with the removal of the foreskin and the reciting of the prayer.

Joel turned to a cringing Jerry and softly said, "When it was your turn, Steve and I performed the ceremony on you. I'm surprised you could still have kids!"

Jerry shook his head, unconsciously moved his hand over his zippered pants, laughed and said, "I believe you."

Lori couldn't look. She turned her head away, while Adele leaned over to her with, "This is how we get even with the guys for the pain of labor."

Barry gave a kvetch, and everyone clapped. The mohel quickly quieted down the crying baby with some wine and some gentle rocking. The next kvetch was, "Let's eat!" Everyone instantly lined up at the buffet table set up in the party room at the temple. As with every Jewish event, this one was celebrated with food, except for Yom Kippur, which was observed by fasting. One end of the table was lined up with trays of corned beef, pastrami, tongue, roast beef, potato salad, coleslaw, rolls, and rye bread courtesy of Hackel's Deli and Lori's parents. The other end of the table had two kinds of kugels, chopped liver, strudel, poppy seed cookies, and an assortment of candies courtesy of Shelly's kitchen.

Jerry's family was typical as far as stereotypes went: A large, boisterous, argumentative, Jewish ethnic Chicago West Side family, originating from the ghettos of Russia and Poland. Shelly spent her time butting in line with admonitions: "Damn it, Abe, *lozn dos kinder esn ersht!*" (Let the children eat first.) Meanwhile, she followed the two teenagers and filled her own plate. Jerry's Uncle Harry walked about and cheerfully slapped everyone on the back with "*Mazel Tov*!" Some heavy-set woman in a housedress—Lori, at first, thought it might have been Rachel from Jerry's old neighborhood—gave Julie a pinch on her check, and Julie hit her. Lori smiled weakly and picked up Julie.

"Mommy, I'm hungry, and that lady hurt me," Julie said as she frowned at the plump woman, rubbing her face.

"Let's go by Grandma first." Lori smiled at the woman and took her daughter to see her Grandma Lil.

Lori had no other relatives living in Chicago. Besides her friends, only her mom and dad represented her side of the family. She smiled at her dad, who was busy congratulating Jerry's father, Jack. Lori, making her way towards her mom so Julie could spend time with her grandmother, noticed her mother sitting at the table alone. Her mother came from a very conservative, non-religious, proper German Jewish family, and Lori could tell she was feeling out of place with Jerry's family.

Lori walked over with Julie and gave her mother a kiss on the cheek. Her mother smiled at Julie but didn't try to pick her up.

"Can I get you something, Mom?" Lori asked.

Julie was whining, "I'm hungry."

Lori's mother, Lil, turned to her daughter and said, "I'll get something when the crowd eases. Go feed your daughter."

Lori went with Julie to the buffet table and turned back to see Jerry's Uncle Harry, who had just sat down next to Lil, lean his food-stained, bearded face close to her face and, in a loud boisterous voice, recite an off-color joke.

Lori watched her mother get up and quickly, gracefully, with her head held high, move towards the exit, almost catching her silk scarf in the door.

Before Lori and her dad caught up with her mother, she gave him a kiss, and said, "I understand Mom has to leave. Thanks for coming." Lori, with Julie in her arms, watched her dad walk down the steps of the temple to catch up with his wife, who was standing at the bottom of the steps, looking out onto the tree-lined street and adjusting the scarf around her neck.

Lori's dad put his arm around his wife, then turned and smiled at Lori and Julie and said, "We'll come by the house tomorrow before going back to Florida."

Lori noted painfully that her mother never turned around to say goodbye. Just another example of Lil's cool, standoffish behavior, Lori mused glumly as she turned and entered the temple. Walking back into the party area, Lori overheard Shelly telling a friend, "Mrs. Fancy Pants couldn't manage to stay around."

Trying hard to avoid a confrontation at her son's mitzvah, Lori quickly walked back out the door and onto the steps to vent before feeling she had herself under control enough to return. Her mother-in-law was right; Lori just had a difficult time accepting the painful truth about her mother. She'd had a difficult time with that truth all her life. Her mother was never there for her.

Chapter Eight

Lori walked out of the Northfield Theater with Jerry, Jim, and Adele into the warm summer night. It felt good to be out spending time with friends and catching a movie. Jerry and Lori had left Julie and two-year-old Barry with Mrs. Roy for a few hours, and Lori enjoyed a great feeling of contentment as she strolled out of the theater toward their car, chatting amiably with Adele, their heads close together in their usual conspiratorial way that sent a message to their men to butt out as they engaged in their favorite pastime of Woman Talk. The women lagged behind and continued their conversation. As they made their way through the theater's adjacent parking lot, a strange, high-pitched screeching noise was heard. Lori and Adele let out a loud scream in unison when someone jumped at them from behind a parked car. Turning around, they realized it was Jerry.

Hitting a laughing Jerry with her purse, Lori asked, "Why did you do that? Jesus, we just saw *Close Encounters,* for crying out loud! You freaked us out!"

Jim emerged from behind a car and approached the two women, laughing hysterically and asking. "Did you think he was an alien?"

Jerry joined in, "Why, she thinks little Martians live under our bed." Jerry slapped Jim on the back, and the two men enjoyed their prank.

Lori turned to him, flaring with anger, and said, "No, Jerry, that's what *you* see after a bottle of gin!"

Adele came in between them and said, "Okay, you two, we're having fun. Let's go for pizza."

Lori kept quiet as they got into the car and went to the restaurant. She thought to herself, *Adele is right. Life is good. I have two wonderful children, though that daughter of mine is a handful. I have friends, and the business is going well. So Jerry drinks some to relax. Nobody has it perfect.*

***

Lori never realized before how hard it was to raise children. Many times, she felt guilty when she thought about her teaching days when she criticized parents for not disciplining their children. Her days seemed to fly by between shopping, paying bills, visiting with friends, and watching her two kids. She was no longer needed in the business. They now had a warehouse, and several employees had been hired to do her former job.

Barry was a calm, easy-going two-year-old, and five-year-old Julie was a handful. Next year, she would be in school full time, but lately it seemed to Lori that Julie was into all kinds of mischief.

Once day, as Lori was in the living room picking up toys and snack remnants left behind by the children, she heard the sound of a thud, followed by the unmistakable sound of shattering glass. Lori raced up the stairs, fearfully anticipating injury. She ran into the first room she reached, Julie's bedroom, and found it empty. Next, she ran into her master bedroom and looked around. Empty. When she heard faint noises coming from the master bath, she quickly moved toward it, and there she found Julie standing before Lori's vanity mirror, her long blond hair askew, her sparkling blue eyes against her splotched, discolored face. Bright red lipstick surrounded the child's lips in bloody streaks, blue eye shadow was sloppily smeared around her eyes, and what could only be described as powdered clown make-up masked the rest of her daughter's lovely little face and cheeks. Lori stifled a laugh. Lying next to an open drawer on Lori's bathroom floor were open tubes and shattered liquid make-up bottles. Lori quickly checked to make sure her daughter wasn't cut before wiping up the mess at her daughter's feet. Lori then tried putting on an angry face.

"Why did you get into Mommy's make-up?" Lori asked sternly.

With a big smile exposing bright red lips and unintended red teeth, Julie twirled around the bathroom, holding out Lori's pink party dress skirt, and said, "I'm a beautiful actress."

Lori just couldn't be angry. At five, Julie was headstrong but adorable. She took her daughter over to the sink and washed her face.

"Julie, honey, if you want to play with make-up, tell me, and I will buy you some of your own," Lori promised.

"Okay, Mommy," Julie said as she smiled and gave Lori a big hug.

Lori thought that episode was behind them until a week later, when two-year-old Barry came into the family room wearing red lipstick all over his face and green eye shadow in his hair.

"Julie!" Lori screamed. To her surprise, Julie came into the room clear-faced. She looked at Barry and said, "I didn't do it, Mommy. Barry went into your make-up drawer all by himself."

This time, Lori was angry. "That's it, Julie," she shouted. "You are grounded. Into your room."

With a devilish grin, Julie tried to hug her mother, saying, "I'm sorry, Mommy. I won't do it again."

That night, when Lori went to bed, she found a big heart lying on her pillow. It said, *I love you, Mommy,* and it was signed: *Julie*. She looked at it and shook her head, thinking, *My little Jerry.*

Chapter Nine

Every Christmas vacation, Lori tried to persuade Jerry to join Adele's family in Florida. She thought she had a good argument: they could drive, it would be cheaper than flying, and they could stay with her parents in Palm Beach and then with her Aunt Tillie in Miami. Finally, one year, Jerry agreed to join Adele's family in Florida. Lori was thrilled. It had been three years since she had seen her mother and three years since they celebrated New Year's with Jim and Adele.

Lori packed a variety of games, toys, books, and snacks for the fifteen-hundred-mile drive. They had a new blue Chevrolet van, so there would be plenty of room for the kids to move around. The first part of the trip went well; weather was cooperating, no snow, just temperatures in the forties until they reached Kentucky. After the first day of driving for ten hours, everyone became tired and irritable. Julie and Barry's fighting in the back was nothing compared to the fighting in front.

"Can't you read a map? You were a school teacher!" Jerry yelled at Lori.

"I keep telling you, map reading and directions were not my best points," Lori shot back.

"Tell me something I don't know," Jerry answered with a mocking grin.

"Okay, here's something," Lori said. "You just passed the exit, we're almost out of gas, and Barry has to go to the bathroom. He keeps asking you to stop."

They stopped at a bathroom, had McDonald's for lunch, turned around, and started down the correct highway. Both kids fell asleep, lying with their blankets and pillows on the floor of the van, and Lori took out a book to read. Somewhere around seven in the evening, she became apprehensive about finding a motel and a restaurant. By nine o'clock, they were fighting again because all the motels had no vacancies and the kids were restless.

Outside of Macon, Georgia, at midnight, they found a small, unkempt motel with a vacancy sign. Fortunately, they had slept in their clothes, because at the crack of dawn they heard sirens and people scurrying around.

A policeman opened their door, and yelled, "This is a police raid!"

When he saw a family with little kids he was shocked. "What are you doing here?" he asked. Lori tried to explain. The policeman just shook his head and said, "This is no place for little kids. Get out of here."

They got in their van and started on their way, while the police were busy putting women in skimpy outfits and half-dressed men into the paddy wagon.

"Who are they?" Julie asked.

"Prostitutes," Jerry answered.

"I want to be a prostitute. Look at their pretty clothes," Julie said, peering around her mother, who did her best to hide the illicit scene from her kids.

Lori was relieved when they finally drove into the garage of her parents' condo building in Palm Beach, Florida. The kids had a great time with Grandfather Ed, playing and swimming, but by day three, Lori could tell her mother had had enough. Her mother went to bed early with one of her eternal migraines, and her dad commented, "Aunt Tillie is looking forward to your visit."

That was Lori's cue to move on.

They left the next morning for the hour and a half ride to North Miami Beach, where her father's sister and Adele's family were waiting for them. Driving down Collins Avenue, past Hollywood Beach, past the small old motels and the famous Rascal House Delicatessen gave Lori a warm, happy feeling. She was back where, a few weeks out of every year in her youth, life had been friendly, warm, and loving.

They pulled into building No. 1 in the Winston Towers complex. Aunt Tillie, her father's oldest sister, welcomed them with loving arms. Soon, Adele was there, coming from her aunt's apartment on the floor above, ready to make plans for the week.

Jerry joined them on occasion; sometimes he went off on adventures with Jim, and sometimes he took off just on his own. While they shopped, swam, played cards, and ate and ate, Jerry enjoyed exploring Florida on his own and visited all the flea markets, zoos, and museums. Florida, old hat to Lori and Adele, was a new adventure to Jerry. His family had never taken him on a vacation while he was growing up. In fact, Jerry confessed, they had never left their neighborhood.

New Year's Eve, Lori always contended, was always a hassle, especially in Miami. The restaurants were crowded and loud, and the food was mediocre and expensive. The new year promised to be different. They had become friendly with a divorced man in his fifties named Gary. He bragged that he could get reservations at the Flamingo Hotel dining room, where one of the most sought after New Year's Eve parties was held. The event was always sold out a year in advance—and even then you had to know someone to get a reservation. With some female persuasion, Adele and Lori talked their husbands into seeing the year out in style. The New Year's Eve package included a gourmet dinner, a special show, and dancing in the hotel's spacious ballroom with an open bar. Gary was able to reserve a table second row from the stage. Lori's aunt, who had lived in Florida for twenty years, could never get reservations for New Year's Eve at the Flamingo.

Adele and Lori spent more time preparing for this party than any other event they ever attended. At the Bal Harbor Neiman Marcus, Adele went straight for the lavishly expensive St. John department.

"Doesn't she look gorgeous?" the saleslady commented as Adele came out of the dressing room in a long black knit skirt, a beaded top, and black strapless three-inch high heels.

"Adele, that outfit is perfect for you," Lori enthused.

"Lori, why don't you try on the blue St. John?" Adele asked.

"Adele," Lori countered, "you still don't get it. I'm too short and fat for St. John. Let me look in one of the other departments." Lori wasn't going to say her budget didn't include St. John; she had to keep appearances, even in front of her best friend.

After searching through several stores, Lori settled for a blue silk dress and matching low heels.

On the day of New Year's Eve, it was off to the beauty shop, where a good-looking gay guy magically transformed the two women into beauties through make-up and hairdos.

After a knock on the door, Lori emerged from her aunt's condo ready to join Adele and Jim for the New Year's Eve festivities.

"You look fabulous," Jim said.

"Thanks, Jim," Lori replied.

"Where's Jerry?" Jim asked.

She answered, indicating in the direction of their bedroom. "He's having trouble getting the rented tux to fit right. Go help him move along, would you, Jim? He's always late."

Adele and Lori sat in the living room of the condo, engaging in anticipatory chit-chat and waiting for their men.

Shortly afterwards, a tall, slim, elegantly dressed Jim emerged from the bedroom, laughing. Behind him was a short balding guy in a black tux sporting a Mickey Mouse tie and matching Mickey Mouse ears.

Adele and Lori looked at each other, shook their heads, and started walking to the elevator. In the cab on the way to the Flamingo Hotel, while Lori made Jerry get rid of the funny attire, she detected the smell of Scotch on his breath.

"You're starting early, aren't you?" she admonished, stuffing the ears and tie roughly onto his lap.

He pretended to ignore her, while thinking, *Why does she continuously nag me?* Jerry tried his hardest to please Lori. He was in Florida, going to her stupid fancy party with that phony Gary, and all she could do was criticize him. So he had a few drinks; it was New Year's Eve!

They waited anxiously outside of the hotel for Gary and his girlfriend. Gary was a well-dressed, educated businessman. They expected his date to be of the same caliber. When Gary approached them with his girlfriend, Tricia, Jim and Jerry's faces lit up. Adele and Lori suddenly became apprehensive about the evening. Tricia was a bad copy of Marilyn Monroe, with her heavy eyeliner and bottle blonde hair. She was at least twenty years younger than Gary, blonde, giddy, and extremely well-endowed. In fact, she was just about coming out of the top of her skimpy red dress.

Entering the hotel ballroom, Lori was awed by the grand ballroom and its decorations. She turned to Adele, Jim, and Jerry and said, "Look at those gorgeous sparkling crystal chandeliers!"

It took a while for the men to peel their eyes from Tricia's bosom and join them in admiring the ceiling.

Adele softly elbowed Jim in the ribs and said, "The fresco painted ceiling is fabulous." Jim quickly shot his head heavenward and began admiring the ceiling too.

Jim then turned to Gary, "Wow, a ten-piece orchestra, plus a singer!"

As they were led to the front of the room, Adele and Lori started to feel better about the evening.

Gary grinned as they were seated near the stage and said, "I told you, I have connections."

Their table was behind a table of four large black-suited men; one thin, immaculately dressed older man and one sharply dressed jewelry-laden woman. They were quietly conversing, smoking, and drinking. The older gentleman seemed to be in charge of the group.

Kidding, Lori commented, "Gee, Gary, why couldn't we get the front table? You'll have to do better next year."

The band began to play. They ordered drinks, lobster and steak dinners, and joined the festive activities. That night, they went over their usual drink limit. Jerry was seated across from Tricia. They were drinking excessively, flirting, and teasing each other. On occasion, Tricia would laugh a throaty laugh and grab hold of Jerry's hand from across the table. Gary sat back, enjoying the scene. As the evening wore on, Lori became increasingly jealous and angry, and she got very close to clobbering Jerry or Tricia when Tricia leaned across the table, exposing large breasts spilling out of a very low cut neckline, the flimsy spaghetti straps struggling to keep the contents of the dress from spilling out onto the table.

"I think you need a safety pin," Jerry offered, boldly pointing at Tricia's burgeoning décolletage.

"How dare you?" Tricia angrily responded, uncharacteristically offended, and as she threw her drink at him, Jerry ducked, and the drink hit the leader of the group at the table in front of Gary and the gang.

Before anyone knew what was happening, a member of the group picked Jerry up under his armpit and tossed him violently under a table. Stunned, Jerry tried to get up and retrieve his eyeglasses from the other side of the room. It happened so quickly that the rest of them could barely move out of their chairs.

"Stay put, if you value your life," said the man who had thrown him.

The patriarch of the party's three other bodyguards stood up, ready to fight. The band played louder and faster. The emcee begged everyone to stay seated. The owner of the hotel came running over to the wet man's table. They were afraid to move. Luckily, after a bottle of Dom Perignon was brought to the table, the owner of the restaurant was able to assure the man that it was an accident.

Later they found out from the maître d' that when Tricia missed her intended target, she had hit, instead, an East Coast Mafia don.

Jerry was asked to apologize to the don by the maitre d'. Jerry pointed at Tricia and said, "But…but…It wasn't my fault. *She* threw the drink!"

Sensing the possible danger of the situation, Gary and Jim picked Jerry up, paid the bill, and hurriedly left the hotel. Jerry kept complaining about his lost eyeglasses, the exorbitant bill, and, most of all, how it wasn't his fault.

"You should be happy to be alive," Lori angrily answered, with Adele and Jim agreeing.

When the chaos at the restaurant became the major story in their condo building, they played coy. Aunt Tillie couldn't wait to tell Lori and Jerry about the New Year's Eve fiasco at the Flamingo.

"Did you see what happened?" Aunt Tillie asked. "You were probably sitting too far back. I heard there were over three hundred people there when the fight broke out on the stage!"

Lori guiltily listened without saying anything. Adele, Jim, and Lori vowed that next year they would celebrate New Year's Eve differently; a visit to the Rascal House Deli for a half a pound of corned beef and a chocolate phosphate would be perfect.

Chapter Ten

The drive back to Illinois that January following the incident that they dubbed "the Flamingo fiasco" was much quieter than the drive there. For starters, Jerry and Lori were hardly speaking, and things didn't get much better when they reached Northfield and went back to their normal life. The incident in Miami made Lori realize that Jerry's drinking was more serious than she had previously thought.

One day, when Jerry arrived home from work looking more bleary-eyed than usual, Lori decided it was time to confront him.

"Jerry, I think you better go to one of those organizations that help you stop drinking."

Lori's statement hung in the air for a few moments before Jerry replied, "You're crazy, Lori. I'm just a social drinker. Leave me alone."

The more she nagged him, the more he drank, and the later he came home.

On a typical midweek day, Lori sat at the kitchen table looking at a lone plate of cold steak, potatoes, and beans. Glancing at the clock, she noted it was nearly nine.

She picked herself up, grabbed the plate off the table, and threw plate and all into the garbage. "Damn him," she muttered.

Just as she turned the kitchen light off, the front door opened. She watched Jerry stagger in, his hair messed and his shirt half-opened. He tripped and almost fell.

"Who left this toy here? Are you trying to kill me?" he bellowed as he jumped up and down on Barry's toy airplane, leaving it in pieces.

The anger that was boiling up inside of Lori was abruptly interrupted by the appearance of her six-year-old daughter bouncing down the stairs and running to her father.

"Daddy, Daddy, you're home!" Julie screamed, clapping her hands.

Jerry bent down, picked her up, and tried to kiss her.

"Daddy, put me down." Julie scrunched up her face and pushed her father away. "You smell, and you are hurting me. I don't like you!" Julie frowned, struggling to break away from his embrace.

"I'm your father, Julie," Jerry slurred. "You can't talk to me like that!" He then threw Julie to the floor.

The child lay sprawled on the carpeted floor in mute silence, her face red and turned down in a horrible grimace, before she gulped in a lungful of air and began to howl. Horrified and momentarily stunned herself, Lori quickly gathered her wits and ran over to pick up her wailing daughter.

Jerry blocked Lori's path and looked at her with half-closed eyes. "The good mother to the rescue," he slurred with a smirk.

Julie picked herself off the floor and ran up the steps to her room, yelling, "I hate you! I *hate you*!"

Jerry, meanwhile, stood before Lori, now blocking her path up the stairway. He began pushing Lori back. "You fucking bitch," he said bitterly. Lori struggled against Jerry, blocking his unsteady legs with her leg.

Losing his already compromised balance, Jerry teetered and hit the floor hard, and Lori ran up the stairs, retrieved a sleeping Barry from his bed, and, with the child in her arms, ran into Julie's room and locked the door behind her.

She tucked the children in Julie's bed and moved to the bedroom door, her ear against the wood. She heard Jerry yell, "God damn it, doesn't anybody want to give me dinner?"

Next, she heard the kitchen door slam and the familiar sound of jiggling ice.

Lori was shaking with anger and fear, but she needed to calm her daughter, who was still crying. She made her way to Julie's bed and took her daughter in her arms and rocked her. Julie looked at her mom.

"Sometimes Daddy is nice, but tonight he is mean. Why?" Julie asked.

How could she answer? Looking at Julie, she said, "When Daddy's mean, he is mad at something that happened at work, not at you."

"Like when Wendy was mean to me at school, and I was mean to Barry?" Julie asked.

"Yes, honey," Lori replied.

"I won't be mean to Barry again," Julie said, turning to look at her sleeping brother on her bed beneath the blankets. "Will you sleep with me, Mom?" Julie asked.

That night, Lori spent a sleepless night in Julie's twin-size bed, flanked by the two things she loved more than anything in the world. All she wanted to do was protect them from Jerry and his out-of-control behavior. If she were to leave, where would she go? Were things truly unraveling?

Jerry didn't get very far the next morning, even though he left the house at six. About five miles down the road, he realized his head was exploding, and he couldn't think straight. He stopped at a small diner, called and cancelled his appointment, and then called his brother Joel to pick him up.

There were some advantages to having an unemployed brother with an employed wife. Without asking questions, Joel dropped Jerry off at his own house.

"Brother, sleep it off here," Joel told Jerry. "I'll come back for you around five, before Caryn comes home." Joel drove off, and Jerry was out like a light as soon as he touched the pillow in Joel's spare room.

Jerry came home earlier than usual that evening, roses in one hand, toys in the other, and a big "I'm sorry" coming out of his comical grin. When Lori watched her children run up to their father, hugging and kissing him, she decided to throw in the towel and hope for the best.

Jerry gave a sigh of relief when he watched Lori's turned-downed lips rise into a smile. Handing her the roses he said, "Honey, I'm really sorry. You have no idea how tough things are now, with Carter and inflation. Yesterday I lost a big sale and ended up drowning my disappointment at the bar with Sy."

Lori was tired of excuses, but she loved this man, and she knew there was nowhere for her to go with two small kids, so when Jerry grabbed her in a passionate embrace, she responded in kind.

The next morning, Lori, in her pink bathrobe and fluffy pink slippers, was standing in the kitchen, making a breakfast of blueberry pancakes. Jerry, ready for work, and Barry, dressed for nursery school, were seated at the kitchen table hungrily awaiting their breakfast. Julie was nowhere to be seen.

Walking into the front room, Lori called up the stairs, "Julie, get down here for breakfast. It is almost time to go to school."

"Okay, Mommy," Julie responded as she sauntered down the stairs wearing her pink leotard, adorned with fake fur, her pink tights, and her ballet shoes.

With an exasperated look Lori took a hold of her, and dragged her upstairs, stating, "Julie, you can't wear that to school."

"But Mommy, if I wear my ballet outfit to school, I won't have to change into it later," Julie said in a logical tone.

Without responding, Lori undressed Julie, redressed her into a yellow sweater and a plaid skirt, and stuffed her ballet outfit into a bag.

Julie had a frown on her face until her daddy picked her up and said, "I think you look beautiful."

Lori gathered coats and school supplies and started out the door with Julie and Barry.

As Julie was leaving the house, she looked back at her father and asked, "Daddy, Daddy, will you come and watch my ballet practice after school?"

"Of course I will, baby," Jerry answered.

As Lori and the kids got into the car she said to herself *Why would he promise a six-year-old that he was going to do something, when he knows he won't?*

It was Julie who got her mother out of her deep reverie by shouting, "Come on, Mom! We're going to be late!"

Startled, Lori looked up and saw her reflection in her rear-view mirror. The corners of her mouth had been turned down, and she noticed frown lines formed deep between her knit brows. Jerry and his problem had vexed her more deeply than she cared to admit, until now.

Chapter Eleven

The kids were in school, and Adele and Lori were spread across Adele's maroon and white sofa watching the 1981 wedding of Prince Charles and Diana Spencer. On Adele's new twenty-five-inch color screen television, the pomp and ceremony was spectacular.

"Adele, get a look at that dress—satin, lace, jewels, and more jewels," Lori said.

"Wow, a carriage just like in the fairy tales. Remember when we believed life would bring us a Prince Charming and we would live happily ever after?" Adele asked in a teasing fashion.

"Yes, our heroines were the fairy tale princesses, Sleeping Beauty, Snow White, and Cinderella, who waited passively for their Prince Charming," Lori recalled.

"Every girl watching the wedding must be identifying with those stories," Adele said.

"The stories all ended with the weddings," Lori noted. "We never got to see if they really lived happily ever after. I hope Diana is more successful at it than I am," Lori said, glumly.

"Her chances are much better," Adele said. "She is starting with a real-life prince, and she looks like a princess."

"Jerry is no prince," Lori mused.

"Sorry, Lori, you will never fit the role of princess. Why, you couldn't even properly pass the salt and pepper shakers." Adele laughed easily, remembering her friend's blundering during their time in charm school.

Brightening, Lori got up, went for a salt and pepper shaker, and, in her blue jeans and University of Illinois sweatshirt, she started to imitate prissy Eleanor Pratt, who had been the head of Miss Pratt's Charm School. She knitted her eyebrows and assumed a strict expression.

"Why, Lori Ann, you *must* never just *pah*ss the shakers with one hand. You could hit the person next to you. Now, take them both with your right hand, *pah*ss them to your left hand, now cross your left hand over your right and *pah*ss both to your neighbor."

Holding the salt and pepper shakers in her right hand, she grabbed a book and put it on her head. After prancing around until the book tumbled off her head, she resumed her Miss Pratt imitation while Adele kept laughing.

"Lori Ann, the object of the exercise is to improve your posture by keeping the book on your head, not on the *floor*."

Adele, in stitches, grabbed her friend. "Enough, Lori. I'm about to pee in my pants! Sit down before you fall down. Your poor mother, she tried. She really did. Why, she even convinced my mother to send me with you to Miss Pratt's Charm School."

"Oh, Adele, it's fun to feel young and silly, if only for the moment," Lori said as she plopped down on the sofa and joined Adele in a hearty laugh.

They turned their attention back to the television, and Lori looked at Adele and said, "I think we should celebrate with the Brits. How about a glass of red wine?"

Adele frowned and asked, "In the middle of the day?"

"Why not?" Lori replied. "Loosen up, my friend."

After a slight hesitation, Adele ran off and came back with a bottle of cabernet. Lori opened it, picked up two wine glasses, and poured them drinks. She held up her glass and toasted, "To Prince Charming."

By the time Princess Diana's wedding was over, Adele and Lori were having a great time, laughing and giggling like school kids instead of thirty-six-year-olds.

At ten minutes after three, Lori made a hasty exit. On her way out, Adele handed her some brochures and said, "Look these over when you're sober. I think it will be a great place for us to go this summer."

Lori barely made it the four blocks home, driving very slowly, cursing herself for going too far with the wine. Wasn't she always admonishing Jerry for this exact behavior? *Well,* she rationalized, *I needed a break. We can't be perfect all the time.* Luckily, it was Judy's day to carpool. By the time the kids came home, Lori no longer felt silly, her head hurt, and she was feeling very tired.

That evening when Jerry came home, he found eight-year-old Julie making a dinner of bread, cheese, cookies, and ice cream for her and her brother Barry.

Alarmed, he asked, "Where's Mommy?"

Julie answered, "She's in bed with a silly headache."

Jerry ran up the stairs, opened the bedroom door, ran over to the bed, and nudged a sleeping Lori. "Honey, what's wrong?"

Lori turned over in bed, gave him a funny grin, and said, "Adele and I were celebrating."

When Jerry leaned down to hear her, he whiffed the telltale smell of wine on her breath. "What were you doing?" he asked. "You smell like a bottle of wine."

"You're right," she said with a grin. "We drank a bottle of wine to celebrate Princess Diana's wedding." With that said, she fell back on her pillow and was out.

Jerry slammed out of the bedroom and thought, *What the hell is wrong with her? I've never seen her like that before.*

In the kitchen, Julie greeted him. "Daddy, I made you dinner." He looked down at the kitchen table. On a paper plate he saw cheese, strawberries, crackers, and cookies.

"Daddy, sit by me," Barry said.

Jerry smiled as he sat down and had dinner with his children.

Seeing Lori in that state alarmed and unnerved Jerry. For the next few months, Jerry made it a point to be home sober and in time.

In the morning, with her head pounding and her stomach upset, Lori couldn't imagine why Jerry enjoyed getting drunk.

Chapter Twelve

Lori moved to the door, coat and purse in hand, when Jerry stopped her.

"Where are you going?" he asked.

"To the city, to help Carol make favors and decorations for her retirement party," Lori explained.

"Oh, is she still having that party?" Jerry asked.

Lori turned towards Jerry and said, "What a silly question. She's been planning it for months. After twenty-eight years of teaching, she deserves a celebration."

Lori opened the door, walked out, got into the car, and then remembered something she had to tell Jerry and went back into the house.

Jerry, drink in hand, was on the phone. He looked up. "What's wrong?" he said?

"Who are you talking to?" Lori demanded.

"My brother," Jerry said. "Why did you come back?"

"To remind you to go to Barry's baseball game," Lori replied. "Why are you drinking?"

"It's Saturday." He then spoke into the phone. "Listen, Steve, I have to hang up."

Suspicious, Lori asked, "*Now* what's going on with your family?"

"Lori, if you are going, *go*." Jerry said. He was not in the mood for Lori and her attitude. He just wanted a relaxing Saturday.

She left, and Jerry picked up the phone and called Steve back.

Steve sat and listened to Jerry for a while, nodding his head slowly in agreement. "I guess you're right," Steve replied after Jerry had finished. "I better take care of it, Jerry."

Spring was in the air, buds were on the trees, green grass was showing through the hard bare earth, the air was calm and warm, the sun was shining, and Lake Michigan looked beautiful. Lori always took Chicago's Outer Drive to the city even though it was a longer route than the expressway. It was safer, and the scenery was beautiful.

Luck was with her that day. She found a parking space only a block from Carol and Steve's house. Lori walked up the three steps to the brick house. Carol opened the door and welcomed her with her trademark big mouth smile and a big hug. Lori took off her coat and joined Carol around the kitchen table. Carol offered her sister-in-law a plate of carrots, celery, and broccoli.

"I'm back on a diet," she said, shrugging while munching on the vegetables.

Lori looked at her chubby friend and thought, *Poor Carol, despite her many diets she is still at least twenty-five pounds overweight.*

Lori got up and walked over to the sink to get a glass of water. On the way, she surveyed the many items on the kitchen counter. Besides the invitations and decorations for Carol's retirement party, there was a stack of colorful travel brochures.

"Are you going somewhere?" Lori asked.

"Not yet. Only three more weeks of teaching, and I'll be retired. I plan to talk Steve into an exotic trip for just the two of us, maybe Bermuda or Hawaii," Carol cheerfully answered. "Maybe it'll put a little spark in our marriage." Carol smiled coyly, then shook her ample bottom and let out a loud soulful laugh.

"Oooh, Carol, that sounds great." Lori was truly happy for her friend, but she was still suspicious of Steve, who she knew had not been faithful. She only hoped it was not an ongoing issue.

Lori and Carol spent the afternoon working on invitations and party favors for the party, which was to be held at a restaurant called Myron and Phil's in Lincolnwood.

Lori left and drove home, stopping for a pick-up dinner of pizza at her family's favorite Italian restaurant, Lou Malnati's. She had an uneasy feeling as she approached her home, but all was well. Jerry had gone to the baseball game, watching Barry pitch a winning game, and she found Julie home from her day at the mall with friends.

That night, life in Carol's house was not as calm as Lori's household.

Steve walked into the house, looked at all the decorations and invitations lying around, and knew that his brother was right. It was time. He called for Carol. She came out of the bedroom in gray workout pants, a sweatshirt, no make-up, and wet hair, which she had held up with a towel, turban-style. When she tried to give him a kiss, he backed off.

"Carol, we have to talk," Steve said. "You need to cancel your party, and you need to forget about a trip."

"Please don't tell me you have cancer or something like that." Carol held her hands to her mouth in fear.

"No, it's nothing like that," Steve said.

"It's not the boys. Have you heard something I don't know?" Carol asked in alarm.

"Stop it and let me talk," Steve ordered. "I can't be at your party or go on a trip with you or do anything with you because…I'm in love with someone else."

Carol just looked at him for a moment, then relief spilled over. She tended to her hair, towel drying it as she spoke.

"Steve, are you telling me you have another girlfriend?" Carol asked. "Stop making it into a big deal. This one will go like all the others. You don't have to tell me about it. Let's just go on like always." Carol turned away from Steve and headed toward the bedroom. "I just got out of the shower. I'm going to change. Let's go out and get a nice dinner and…"

Steve knew that she knew about his girlfriends. It had been an unspoken thing between them, but this time it was different.

"Carol, I am really in love with someone else," Steve said. He watched incredulously as Carol went about getting dressed and talking about their vacation. She went to her closet and pulled out a long-sleeved red blouse and a black skirt and laid them on the bed.

"Carol," Steve said sternly, raking his hands through his hair, "listen to me. Sit down and listen to me! I…I want a divorce."

Carol sat down on the bed, took a deep breath, and said, "Okay, tell me about her." Carol looked down and smoothed out the sleeve of her red blouse. "We can weather this storm." They had been through several girlfriends, many crying nights, and several apologies and pretty pieces of jewelry. She didn't expect this to be any different, though she was upset with the timing.

"Carol," Steve said more softly sitting beside her on the bed, "you don't understand. I'm in *love* this time, and I'm leaving you. She's beautiful, tall, thin, dark, young, and she knows how to turn me on. I cannot live this way. I don't want to hurt you. She is all I think about, Carol. It's different this time."

"Turn you on?" Carol turned to Steve in anger. "Steve, for crying out loud, you're fifty. We've been married twenty-nine years. How old is she?"

Steve hesitated for a moment, then went on. There was no going back now. "I think she's twenty-one, but she really loves me," Steve said. He rose from the bed and moved to the closet, took out a suitcase and some clothes, and began putting them into a suitcase. "I'm sorry about it, Carol, but it's been going on for a while, and I don't want to lie to you anymore. I think it's best if I just leave." Steve turned his back to her and continued folding clothes into his oversized brown suitcase.

Carol ran from the bed and began pounding his back with her fists. "I won't let you go!" she screamed. "How can you do this to me right before my retirement party?"

"I'm sorry, Carol." Steve pulled himself away from her, grabbed his suitcase, fished for the car keys in his front pocket, and left the house as quickly as he could.

When Steve showed up at Lori and Jerry's house with the news, Lori left them and drove back to be with Carol.

She sat through the night listening to Carol cry.

"This will pass," Lori encouraged, though she was not certain it was true. She sat beside Carol as she lay sprawled in a heap on her bed. "Just wait it out. This is too crazy to last, Carol. Steve is probably going through something. The girl's name is Zi, and she's an eighteen-year-old prostitute, for crying out loud. She works in a *brothel* on the outskirts of Chinatown. Jerry told me all about it…"

Carol jumped up, clutching a big wad of tissue in both hands. "You're kidding," Carol managed through her sobs. "My husband is leaving me after twenty-nine years for a whore? Now I don't know who to go to first—a lawyer or a doctor."

Steve did not give up this girlfriend.

Carol and Lori met on Clark Street for lunch.

They barely had their coats off when Carol uttered, "I'm moving to Boston. My son, Danny, and his wife are expecting their first child and could use the help. I can't stay here now that Steve has made it known he intends to marry that girl."

Lori played with her pasta and said, "I can't blame you, Carol. I will miss you. I knew you were hinting at the fact that Janice was pregnant. It will be a welcome diversion. Has the therapy been helping?"

Carol took out a cigarette before answering. She was smoking again and hardly eating.

"Without therapy I would have gone over the edge," Carol explained. "Mara, my therapist, is helping me face the fact that my marriage has been over for years. She thinks Boston is a good idea. I will be near Danny and his family. I may go back to teaching."

"What about Darrell?" Lori said.

Carol continued, "I'm really worried about him. He dropped out of Harvard. His dreams of working as a lawyer with his dad have been squashed. He is so angry and disappointed with Steve. I guess I shouldn't have shielded the boys from Steve's many infidelities."

Lori looked out the window at the young adults with children and dogs casually walking along the crowded street. Since she and Jerry had lived in Lincoln Park, the area had really changed for the better—too bad they hadn't.

Suddenly, Lori blurted out, "You can't shield kids from an alcoholic father."

Chapter Thirteen

Lori accepted an invitation to a good friend's 25th anniversary party at Morton's restaurant in downtown Chicago. Jerry felt he was doing her a supreme favor by going. He hated all her North Shore high school friends, except Adele and Jim, and she hated his poker friends, especially Sy. Consequently, their social life revolved around his or Adele's family.

They picked up Adele and Jim and drove down the Edens expressway to Rush Street in downtown Chicago. Lori had schooled Jerry on the social graces for the evening, so he gave the car to the restaurant's doorman, and he tried hard to keep his fancy blue striped shirt, the one he hated because it was without a pocket, and the matching tie in place even though he was dying to open the stiff shirt at the collar.

In the restaurant's private room, which was decorated with red leather booths and pictures of celebrities, forty guests enjoyed dishes of jumbo seafood, an assortment of canapés, and an open bar while a three-piece band played.

By the time they sat down for dinner, Jerry was drunk. For his first act, he pulled the young waitress towards him, slid his hand up her short dress, and asked, "What are you doing tonight?"

Jim pulled him away and admonished, "Jerry, calm down."

For his second act, Jerry sat down, took a straw, and blew its paper wrapper across the table right into the front of a woman's low-cut dress. "Bull's eye!" he yelled. All eyes turned his way, while Lori slowly sunk down into her chair.

Three toasts praising the couple were made, and a dinner of beef tenderloin was served. The conversation at the table revolved around the stock market, travels abroad, and fashion. Suddenly, Jerry, who had been quietly stewing while listening to the blowhards surrounding him, stood on his chair and, holding a glass of wine, completed his third and final act by bellowing out, "A toast! A toast to all the bullshitters in this room!"

Lori didn't see him fall off the chair for an encore because she had already left the table during the toast and was in the ladies' room, crying.

Adele had followed her. Putting her arm around Lori, she said, "Honey, when he's drunk, he doesn't know what he's doing." She handed Lori a handkerchief to wipe her eyes.

Lori took the handkerchief, leaned against the marble sink, and asked, "Adele, why are you always giving him excuses? I will never be able to face any of those people again! I'll have to move, or go around Northfield in dark glasses. God, it's so humiliating!"

Adele laughed and said, They'll forget all about it."

"Adele, that is NOT how I want people to remember me," Lori asserted. "How are they going to forget Jerry Brill, the prize ass?"

"Come on, I'm sure Jim is getting Jerry out of the restaurant." She took Lori by the arm and led her out of the restaurant through a side door, thus avoiding the private room. Jim had already gotten the car and had put Jerry in the backseat with him. He handed Adele the keys. Lori sat in front with Adele. She was usually their designated driver because she didn't drink.

As they started to drive, Jerry suddenly perked up, grabbed Lori from behind, and whined, "Why do you hate me?"

Before Adele could react, two policemen, who were directing traffic around an accident, stopped their car. Jerry put down his back window, whistled, and screamed, "Move those damn cars."

"Jerry, stop!" Jim, Lori, and Adele collectively yelled. Adele rolled up his window, catching his arm in it. Lori turned around and punched him, and Jim tackled him against the side door. Jerry slumped down in the car seat, moaning. Somehow, they made it home and got him into bed. Jim and Adele took the babysitter home in their car.

Lori was so angry that she walked over to where Jerry lay on the bed in a drunken stupor and shook him violently. She noticed he had vomited on himself in her absence. Frustrated and infuriated, Lori shook him harder by the shoulders while screaming and yelling.

"Damn you, Jerry!" Lori yelled. "Aren't you embarrassed by your behavior? Jerry, damn you! Wake up! You are a drunken disgrace. Look at your new suit. It's ruined by vomit. You are puking all over yourself, Jerry. You are an absolutely disgusting drunken mess! Is this the way our kids and I are supposed to live? With a drunk?!"

After a while, Lori realized she was screaming to a passed-out body. Only her poor kids were listening. She left him a mess and slept in the spare bedroom, the question she asked an unconscious Jerry ringing in her ears: *"Is this the way our kids and I are supposed to live?!"*

Jerry turned over in bed and moaned. He tried to focus on the bright digital numbers on the bedside clock, but things were out of focus. He thought the clock said 2:00. He shaded his eyes from the sun coming through the window, blearily deducing that, if there was sun, it must be daytime. Something smelled awful, and it wasn't before long before he discovered the smell was coming from him. He looked down at his crumpled suit and saw he had dried vomit all over his clothes. Slowly, he managed to remove his clothing, go to the bathroom, brush his teeth, and throw on a bathrobe. The house was quiet. Maybe he would be lucky and no one would be home, he thought.

Making his way down to the kitchen, he reached for a cup of coffee, sat down at the table, and put his head down on it for a minute. Boy, did he feel terrible. He hardly remembered last night, only that he screwed up and Lori was probably ready to kill him. Thank God today was Sunday and no one was home.

His reprieve didn't last long. About a half hour later, his family came walking through the door, carrying a Lou Malnati pizza. Just the smell of it made him nauseated. Lori started in as soon as she saw him sitting in the kitchen.

"You made a real ass out of yourself last night," Lori hollered, placing the pizza onto the counter. She continued as she made her way to the cabinet to get out plates for their dinner. "I'm beginning to think you love Johnnie Walker better than your family. I've had it, Jerry. That was the last straw, and I'm–"

"Damn it, Lori, leave me alone!" Jerry said loudly, cringing at the volume of his own voice as well as Lori's shrill verbal assault. "I'm under a lot of pressure now that I'm the only breadwinner. I have to blow off steam once in a while."

"Once in a while!" Before Lori finished her sentence, twelve- year-old Julie interrupted them.

"Will both of you stop?" Julie demanded. "Barry and I are *tired* of your fighting."

Barry had already made it upstairs to his room.

Jerry slammed down his coffee cup and went upstairs to crawl back into bed. Lori brought Barry out of his room, opened the pizza, and sat down with her kids to eat.

"Why don't you and dad get a divorce already?" Julie asked as she picked at her pizza. "I'm so sick of this fighting."

"No!" Barry cried. "Can't you work it out, Mom?"

"Work what out? Dad's a drunk, Barry," Julie said.

"That's enough, you two," Lori said. "Let's just enjoy some peace and quiet and eat, okay? I can't make any decisions right now."

They ate in silence.

Chapter Fourteen

Lori knew things were unraveling at home. The kids were affected by the fighting, but they seemed to be doing all right in school, and she was grateful for their resilience. So long as they were out of the house, things were okay. Needing an excuse to get her mind off of their family problems and a reason to be out of the house herself, Lori accepted her friend Cheri's invitation to join the town planning committee. Being late for the meeting, she speedily entered the village hall, where she practically knocked over Cheri and the man to whom she was talking

As Lori apologized, they turned towards her, and Cheri said, "Josh, I would like to introduce you to Lori. She is on the town planning committee, and you will be working together on the new development."

Josh smiled at her, running his eyes up and down her body as he spoke. "Lori and I are old friends. In fact," he said, pausing and holding her gaze, "she is the love of my life."

Lori blushed as she looked away from the tall, blond, blue-eyed six-footer who happened to be her high school sweetheart. He was still gorgeous. She felt her heart pounding, and her hands flew to her cheeks as she felt the blood rushing to her face.

Before she could respond, Josh took her arm, leaned over, and whispered, "Let's get out of here and renew old friendships. Town meetings are boring."

They left Cheri staring with her mouth open. Josh ushered Lori out the building and towards his car. She looked at the car and started to laugh.

"A red Corvette convertible!" Lori exclaimed. "You fulfilled your dreams."

"Not all of them," he answered.

Still the charmer, only now he has money, Lori thought, as she checked out his Armani suit, Cole Haan shoes, manicured nails, and capped teeth. Searching for a ring, her eyes rested on his long slender fingers. There was one, but to her relief, it obviously was not a wedding band. On his pinky finger, a large brown sparkling cat eye stone surrounded by diamonds caught her attention.

His hand touched Lori's face under the chin, and she found herself close to his lips and an embrace.

Turning away at the last moment, she entered the opened car door and slid into the low comfortable red leather seat. He took the hint and moved into the driver's seat.

Trying to make normal conversation, Lori asked, "Aren't you speaking at the meeting?"

"My second-in-command will take care of things," Josh answered, as he picked up a phone, which was fastened onto his dashboard, dialed, and started to talk to someone.

"First time I've seen this gadget," Lori noted. "Very impressive. How does it work?"

"It is very new, a car phone that works like any other phone, though only when the car is running," Josh explained. "It is great for business and emergencies, but the equipment takes up most of the trunk, and each call is a fortune."

"My daughter is like you, the first one to have every new gadget or fashion item," Lori said. "What you really need is Dick Tracy's watch phone."

"What I really need… is you," Josh said.

Lori blushed and turned away, thinking, *My God, he still has the ability to seduce me.*

They headed towards Rosebud, a restaurant in the heart of town, not far from the town hall. They found seats in a booth in the rear. Josh went to the counter and came back with two cups of coffee and a piece of chocolate cake. Lori watched him as he placed the cups and plates onto the table. He had filled out some, but he still had those big broad shoulders and nice narrow hips.

"I hope you are still a chocoholic," he said as he slid in next to her, thinking to himself, *Boy, am I lucky. I thought this was going to be a boring trip. Lori still looks good. Strange to find her still in Northfield after all these years.*

"Can't you tell by my weight?" she answered, trying to keep her hands from shaking as she picked up a fork.

"You're still as beautiful as ever," Josh said. His look covered the length of her body, and he smiled approvingly. She shivered in response.

In an effort to tone down the conversation, Lori asked him about his life during the twenty-five years since they had last seen each other. Josh told her that he was now single, having recently divorced his second wife. She was secretly glad to hear his first marriage, with the girl he left her for, had failed. He and his second wife had one teenage son. Josh was a successful lawyer and real estate developer living the good life in California. Lori told him about Julie, Barry, and Jerry. She carefully left out any reference to alcohol. He laughed when he heard Adele and Lori were still best friends.

"The protector general's still guarding your life? Say hello to Adele. She will be surprised I am successful. She never liked me," Josh said.

Lori grinned at his accurate analysis of Adele.

"I am surprised that you and Adele never left Northfield," he said. Then, with a very confident smile showing beautiful white, capped teeth, he helped her up and said, "Let's take a drive around the old haunts."

Lori hesitated, looked at her watch, and said, "Josh, I better go home. It's late."

They headed back to the town hall where Lori left her car.

"Can we meet again?" he asked. "I will be working on the retirement development in Northfield for months."

"Sure," Lori said as she wrote down her address and phone number. "After all, we will be working together on the committee."

He handed her his card.

"The front is my address in California," he explained. "The back has my phone number at the Drake Hotel."

"The Drake Hotel?" Lori exclaimed.

"I always stay at the Drake when I am in town. It will always be my favorite hotel," he answered with a sly smile on his face. "Good memories there."

They parted. She headed for home shaken and confused. She thought about prom night at the Drake Hotel, where the high school days of passionate kisses ended with the loss of her virginity.

While fumbling around in her purse for her keys, Lori glanced at her watch; it was after ten. Knocking on the door, she hoped the babysitter would answer. Instead, the door flew open, and an obviously drunk Jerry greeted her. She could smell the liquor on his breath. Disgusted, she breezed right past him and removed her jacket.

"Where were you?" Jerry shouted accusatorially. He turned around quickly and stumbled a bit before righting himself.

She responded on the offensive, thinking, *How he could know*? "At the town meeting. Remember? I'm on the planning committee. Why must you always have a glass in hand? Where are the kids?"

"Upstairs in their rooms," Jerry mumbled.

"I hope they didn't see you in this condition, Jerry," Lori shot back.

He ignored her remark as he stumbled toward her, held up the glass, tripped, and spilled the drink all over the sofa. "Damn it, there was a family crisis, and I needed you," Jerry said.

"Now what?" Lori asked as she moved into the kitchen to get a sponge to clean up the mess.

Jerry grabbed the sponge out of her hand, threw it across the room, and said, "Forget the sofa and listen to me. Caryn overdosed. Joel's in the hospital."

"Jerry, you're not even making any sense, you drunken ass," Lori said. "Who's in the hospital, Joel or his wife Caryn?"

Slurring his speech, he answered, "You fuckin 'nerr lis*tenna* me. Joel left the hospital and got hit by a car. They're both in… inna hos*ppal*."

"Is Joel all right?" she asked, while trying not to provoke him further. Caryn, after not seeing her all this time, was a ghost to Lori. She was surprised to hear Caryn was still alive. Carol was in the east, and Lori stayed as far away from the Brill family as she could manage; she only joined them for Jewish holidays.

"I dunno." Jerry waved dismissively, foggy and confused and irritable. "Call my mother." Jerry stumbled back into the living room. "She's b'side herself with… with worry." He then collapsed on the wet sofa.

Lori laughed bitterly at that remark. She was sick of that whole damn family, and she really couldn't care less what happened to her idiotic brother-in-law or his deranged wife.

"Call your mother?" she called from the other room. "You're kidding. She can handle anything that creates tumult and controversy. Now Joel can make the accident into a big personal injury lawsuit. And this is the second time Caryn overdosed on drugs. If someone doesn't get her help, she will eventually succeed in killing herself."

Jerry looked up at the ceiling and mumbled, "Why d'you hate my family?"

"Because they're crazy and create their own trouble!" She stomped into the living room and stood over Jerry, who now sat with his head in his hands. The glass, with its residual liquor and melting ice cubes, sat precariously on the rug beside his socked feet. Lori looked at her husband, filled with contempt and disgust. "How much is this going to cost us?" She knew Jerry loaned Joel money. Actually, Joel hit everyone for money, but Jerry was the softest touch.

Jerry got up, staggered over to the little bar set up in the corner of the living room, and poured himself another drink, leaving his old glass on the floor.

"You're going for another drink? You can't be serious!" Lori shouted.

Jerry's eyes narrowed, and his face darkened.

"Don't you *dare* tell me what to… what to do when it involves my family."

"Hey, you managed a full sentence that time," Lori retorted acerbically. "Answer me, Jerry, how much is this situation going to cost us?"

"Damn you!"

His behavior told her he had already given Joel money, and he had clearly given himself four or five drinks. *Where did he hide this bottle?* Lori wondered. She was constantly tossing out bottles of Scotch, and he was constantly coming up with new ones. It was a game they played, but she was tired of this game and what it was doing to her marriage and her family.

"I'm going to bed," Lori said as she abruptly left the room and ran up the stairs. It had been a while since she had seen that diabolic expression on his face and the totally drunken state. She knew she had provoked him, but that was the only power she had. She could not control the money lending to his family, nor could she control Jerry's drinking. She could never control how much the Brill family infiltrated her life, so the only artillery she had was shooting remarks at Jerry—and even that backfired every time. She didn't care; it felt good to laugh at Jerry, felt good to badmouth his stupid family.

Lori walked down the hallway and checked on both kids before she locked her bedroom door, hoping he wouldn't try to knock it down again as he had a few times in the past. When the phone rang twice during the night, she never picked it up, guessing it was Shelly. Her head began to throb with a migraine. *What a crazy night!*

The next morning, Jerry was gone before the kids and Lori woke up. How he could manage to get up and go to work without having a hangover was beyond her comprehension. She guessed Jerry slept on the couch. He couldn't have driven anywhere last night.

Jerry got out of the house before anyone woke up. His head hurt, and he knew he had overdone it the previous night. He thought maybe if Lori had been home to comfort him... First he lost another sale, and then his brother was almost killed. Lori should have been home taking care of the kids. To hell with her community service nonsense! He better find something nice to bring home to them tonight.

As Lori chauffeured Julie and Barry to school, Julie asked, "Why are you and Dad always fighting? What's wrong with him anyway?"

Lori didn't know what to say to her. Barry never asked, but Julie, as the oldest and the more outgoing personality, was always commenting. Lori was still observing the "deny it, no talk" rule most alcoholic households practiced.

"He's under a lot of stress with the business," she answered.

"That's always your excuse," Julie said. "Hey, Mom, you just passed my school."

Lori stopped at the next corner. Julie got out and slammed the car door. Then she reopened the door, poked her head back in, and sarcastically yelled, "Do you think you can remember to pick me up at four? I have cheerleading practice today."

Lori watched her run over and join a group of other girls in skirts shorter than hers. She thought to herself, *The teenage years are just beginning. How will I make it through them? How will any one of us make it through?*

Barry hadn't said a word until they reached his school. He got out, turned to Lori, and said, "Thanks for the ride, Mom."

"Oh, Barry, you're welcome, honey," Lori answered sweetly. "Have a good day at–"

But Barry had already left the car. She hoped his silence was his way of coping, and she silently prayed that it would help him through this difficult time.

When spring comes and the weather is nicer, I should start making my children get up earlier and walk, Lori said to herself as she waited in a line of parents' cars moving out of the school parking lot. *We always walked to school.* After yesterday's meeting with Josh, she was anxious to see Adele, and all this traffic wasn't helping her confused mood.

Leaving the school lot, she pulled into the small shopping center in the heart of town, parked her Ford Taurus next to Adele's Cadillac, grabbed her black leather jacket, slid out of the car, and hurried into the Cubby Hole, their hide-out. Her eyes immediately darted to the back of the place where Adele always sat. Adele was busy checking the songs on the jukebox, as if they suddenly came up with new ones. Shortly, Johnny Mathis echoed through the small diner with one of Adele's favorites, *Chances Are.*

Lori tossed her purse on the table and slid into the booth. Maddy was there with coffee and a cheese Danish. With a sly grin across her face, she faced her friend and said, "Guess who's back in my life?"

Adele held her hands open in a questioning gesture and said, "From the way you are acting, it must be someone you're happy to see. Is it your mother?"

For a moment, Lori's cheerful mood changed. "That was nasty, Adele. No. Josh is back in my life."

Carefully, Adele asked, "Josh who?"

"Stop it, Adele," Lori admonished. "You know who I'm talking about. Josh Wheeler is the contractor for Northfield's retirement development. I went for coffee with him yesterday."

"Oh no," Adele declared as she leaned her left hand on her cheek and thought about what she would say. "Lori, stay away from him. He'll only hurt you again. He was a high school crush. You're married now."

Lori grinned, taking her seat. "Last night, he said, 'Adele never liked me. She'll be upset when she hears you saw me.'"

"My mother and I never really trusted him," Adele recalled. "He was too impressed with money and power, and most of all, he could turn on the charm and make people do things they wouldn't normally do."

Lori didn't say anything else. She knew what Adele was referring to: prom night 1962, when Adele reluctantly covered for Lori, who stayed with Josh at the Drake Hotel. After two years of dating, Lori had finally given in. Her memories of that night were wonderful. Josh was so romantic, tender, and experienced, knowing just where to touch her, while she was so naïve and so in love.

"Lori, forget Josh," Adele directed. "Work on your marriage. He'll only hurt you again."

Lori looked at Adele and said, "Yes, you are probably right. I was sure we would get married, but he left for college and forgot about me."

By the time Lori and Adele left the restaurant, Lori's happy mood had changed to one of sullen confusion. Her confrontation with Adele was for nothing; the very next day, Lori received a message from Josh's secretary telling her he had been called back to California.

Chapter Fifteen

Julie raced down the second floor steps. She was late, and she knew Sasha and Rachel would leave for the mall without her if she didn't hurry. Lori, stationed at the bottom of the staircase, braced herself against the railing in anticipation of another argument with her daughter.

She stopped Julie, and in the voice of a parent in control, she stated, "Julie, I can't allow you out of the house in that outfit."

With hands on her hips in a defiant pose, Julie stopped and faced her mother. "Now what's wrong?"

Lori stared at her daughter, wondering where to start. The black heels, red low-cut, V-neck top, tightly covering Julie's budding breasts, the black short skirt exposing long thin legs, the straight long blond hair, and the thick mascara surrounding her sparkling blue eyes made her daughter look years older than fourteen. She also looked like something out of the movie *Taxi Driver*.

"The skirt is too short, and you have too much makeup on your face," Lori blurted out.

Julie rolled her eyes and folded her arms across her chest. "The skirt is *not* too short," Julie whined. "Mom, I am in high school now. Get with it! It's nineteen eighty-SEVEN. Sasha gets to wear short skirts." Julie and Sasha, Adele's daughter, were best friends.

"You *just turned* fourteen. Sasha is sixteen. I still have the final word," Lori said, folding her own arms across her chest as she surveyed the skirt length again.

"Mom, you are such a prude. Keep up with the times," Julie moaned as she grabbed up her things and stomped towards the door.

Lori watched her daughter make her way to the door and wondered where she had gone wrong. She had tried hard to be everything her mother wasn't: loving, tolerant, and available when her daughter needed her.

Lori's anger suddenly turned to concern as she noted some bruising on the back of her daughter's legs.

"Julie, get back here," Lori ordered.

"Now what?" Julie responded. "Mom, I'm *late*."

"Why are your legs so black and blue?" Lori approached her daughter and bent down to take a closer look at her legs. "Have you been running into things, honey? Does it hurt?"

"I get those all the time. Forget about them," Julie said dismissively, giving an irritable shrug while holding the front door half-open.

"Maybe we should see the doctor," Lori said as she anxiously looked at two large black and blue marks on her daughter's legs and a smaller one on her arm.

"Mom! I probably ran into something like a desk or a table or something!" Julie had run out of patience.

Finally, Lori let her go, but she made a note to make a doctor's appointment for Julie.

That afternoon at lunch with Adele, Lori mentioned the bruising.

"I'm a little worried about Julie," Lori said. "Lately, she is more tired than usual, and she keeps getting black and blue marks on her legs. I don't like the way they look. I hope she isn't into drugs or with somebody who is abusing her. Can you feel-out Sasha?"

"Oh, Lori, it is probably nothing," Adele replied. "These girls with their short skirts are probably bumping into things all the time. Why would you even mention drugs? It's not the sixties, and we live in Northfield, not the West Side of Chicago. If it gets worse, have Dr. Rosenblum check her out."

"She won't go to the doctor. She thinks I'm being overprotective," Lori said. She shrugged and took a sip from her coffee cup. "Maybe I am. Who knows?"

Lori watched her daughter for signs of problems, but outside of a few more bruises, Julie was continuously on the go, until one fall Saturday morning about three months after Lori first observed the bruises on Julie's arm and legs. Lori walked into the family room, where, to her surprise, she found her daughter lying on the sofa, clutching her hands to her stomach.

"Honey, what's wrong?" Julie asked. "I thought you were going with Shawn to the football game."

Julie looked up and said, "Mom, help me. I'm really hurting."

Lori looked down at her daughter's tear-covered white face and panicked. She yelled up the stairs to her husband, "Jerry, call 911! Julie's sick!"

Jerry came running down the stairs, took one look at Julie, scooped her up in his arms, and put her in the car. Meanwhile, Lori called Dr. Rosenblum, their pediatrician, who met them at Northfield Hospital. After a few tests with no conclusive results and Julie getting weaker by the minute, Dr. Rosenblum sent her by ambulance to Children's Memorial Hospital in Chicago. Lori rode in the ambulance, while Jerry followed in the car.

"Why can't I be treated in Northfield?" Julie asked from the ambulance cot.

Lori could tell that her daughter was scared by the look in her eyes. She was also scared and a little guilty. She knew it had been stupid of her to ignore the black and blue marks, but Julie had refused to go to the doctor. Hopefully, her daughter just had a virus or something easy to cure. She must be positive.

"Dr. Rosenblum just wants to make sure he isn't missing anything, and Children's is the best hospital for diagnosis," Lori explained.

"Oh," was her daughter's response as she turned away from her mother to face the side of the ambulance.

Julie was admitted to Children's Memorial Hospital and directly taken to the oncology floor, where she was given blood tests and stomach X-rays, while her parents gave the receptionist the necessary insurance information, and then they waited in the lounge area.

After about an hour of waiting, a young, petite female doctor came to talk to Jerry and Lori. She held out her hand to them in a friendly gesture.

"Mr. and Mrs. Brill, I'm Dr. Stacy Feinberg, and I am working with Dr. Bloom, who is the head of hematology/oncology here at Children's Memorial," Dr. Feinberg explained. "Julie's blood counts are not in the normal range, and we need to do some additional testing before making a diagnosis. A bone marrow test and a spinal tap will be given after you sign the permission papers."

Jerry and Lori, still numb from the surprising journey to Children's Memorial, obediently signed the papers and stationed themselves outside of the treatment room in the parents' lounge. Lori couldn't help noticing how warm and friendly the hospital was compared to other ones. The chairs were done in bright reds, blues, and yellows. The walls were decorated with scenes of children playing in a park. She almost forgot she was in the hospital. Eyeing a picture of a boy with a baseball bat, she nudged Jerry and pointed to it.

"That boy looks like Barry," she said.

Jerry turned towards the picture and blurted out, "Oh, my God, we forgot about Barry's baseball game!"

"He'll understand," Lori answered, as the tears ran down her face.

"Stop crying," Jerry demanded. "She's only being tested. We don't know what's wrong yet. It's probably nothing."

Lori was not convinced. She fished through her purse and retrieved a wad of tissue.

"Oh, Jerry," she snuffled into the tissue and continued, "Dr. Rosenblum wouldn't have sent her to Children's Memorial if he didn't think it was serious. She has been getting black and blue marks for months."

"Lori, go call Adele and tell her to pick up Barry," Jerry said.

As Lori got up to go look for a phone, she heard screaming coming from the treatment room.

"Don't, you'll break my back! I didn't sign for this. I'll sue you!"

Lori jumped at the sound of Julie's voice. Nothing had seemed real until she heard Julie scream. She was trying to keep her emotions in check until they knew results. She felt like she was floating through a nightmare and would wake up soon.

She stopped a nurse in the hall and said, "My daughter is screaming in the treatment room. What are they doing to her?"

"Don't worry," the nurse said. "She'll be fine. These tests are dramatic the first time, but it is amazing how fast the kids get use to them."

Lori stood there frozen to the floor, thinking, *She'll get used to them? Oh, my God, what is happening to us?*

When another hospital worker asked her if she needed help, she remembered why she was standing in the middle of the hall. "Yes, I need to find a phone," Lori said.

After being directed to a phone, she found it difficult to even remember Adele's phone number. Finally, she heard Adele's voice on the line.

"Oh God, Adele, I don't know what to do," Lori cried.

"What's wrong?" Adele asked. "Where are you?"

"It's Julie," Lori explained. "We are at Children's Memorial Hospital with her."

"What's going on, Lori? Was Julie in an accident?"

Lori stood staring at the phone in shock.

"Lori, answer me," Adele shouted into the phone

Lori bounced back to the present.

"No, she was in terrible pain, and Dr. Rosenblum sent us here."

"What's the problem?"

"Adele, we don't know yet. They think it has something to do with her blood."

"Jim and I will come right down."

"No, I need you to pick up Barry at the baseball field. Listen, I'll call you later. Julie is just coming out of her tests."

Lori hung up on Adele and ran down the hall in an effort to catch up with Jerry and the nurse, who was wheeling Julie out of the treatment room. Huffing and puffing, she finally caught up with them. As they walked along the gurney to a hospital room, Julie looked at Lori.

"Mom, I'm sorry that I screamed, but it felt like a razor blade was going in my back," Julie said.

"You were very brave. We are proud of you," Lori answered as she tried to hide her tears.

Julie slept, Jerry paced up and back, and Lori sat and worried. An hour passed before Dr. Feinberg appeared.

"Please come with me," she said.

They followed her to a private office where they were introduced to the head of the department, Dr. Stanley Bloom.

Lori studied him. He sported a black mustache tinged with gray on a full round face, and he had sad brown eyes. When he offered her his hand, she was met by a powerful, steady grip. She immediately trusted him, but Jerry attacked him.

"No one has told us what's wrong with our daughter," Jerry said. "You've given her blood tests, spinal taps, and bone marrow tests. I want some answers! You've been testing her all morning."

Lori, realizing that Jerry had obviously taken an immediate dislike to the messenger, grabbed Jerry's arm in an effort to calm him down. "Jerry, please let the doctor talk."

Dr. Bloom put his arm on Jerry's shoulder and said, "I'm sorry no one talked to you. We wanted to be sure of the test results."

Pushing the doctor's arm away, Jerry shouted, "Enough with the talk. What's wrong with Julie? Is it mono?"

In a very calm voice, Dr. Bloom answered, "I'm afraid it is more serious than mono. Julie has acute lymphocyte leukemia."

The blood drained from Lori's face as she fell back on her chair. She knew leukemia was a form of cancer. Why, hadn't she cried her eyes out when Jenny, in *Love Story*, died of leukemia? But that was a movie. The next day, she had seen Ali MacGraw, who had played Jenny on screen, healthy and being interviewed. Lori had to face the fact that this was real life. Her daughter had leukemia, but her mind wouldn't accept it. It kept saying, *This cannot be happening to us. It happens to strangers, not to us*!

She looked at Jerry, who had calmed down into an almost catatonic stage. Her eyes wandered around the room, focusing on a picture of a little boy with a golden retriever. *Was it the doctor's son or grandson?* she wondered. She knew she was stalling while trying to take in the word *leukemia*.

Looking up at the doctor, Lori finally asked, "Are you sure it's leukemia? Maybe we should get a second opinion."

Dr. Bloom looked at Lori with knitted eyebrows and a sad smile. "To put it simply, her white cell count is elevated, and her bone marrow and spinal column tested positive for blast cells," he said. "There is no doubt that your daughter has leukemia."

Sitting up, Jerry asked, "What are blast cells?"

Dr. Bloom answered, "Blast cells are immature blood cells that over-multiply and leave the bone marrow too early, and consequently, they can't do their job. Here at Children's Memorial, our hematology/oncology department is one of the finest in the country, but we will be happy to send her tests anywhere. I know how difficult this is, but I need to stress the fact that the sooner she receives treatment, the better chance she has for recovery."

The shock lasted only a few seconds. Then the fear set in. Lori sat back in her chair and closed her eyes. "She has to make it. She has to live," Lori whispered to herself.

"Julie is in room 312," Dr. Bloom said. "Dr. Feinberg will meet you there."

Lori and Jerry slowly moved out of Dr. Bloom's office. On the way, Jerry said to Lori, "She won't make it. Did you hear him say she is too far gone?"

"Jerry, either be positive for Julie or leave," Lori said angrily. "The doctor didn't say that. He said it could be a difficult treatment because it was caught late."

Julie liked the young, dark-haired Dr. Feinberg. She seemed to be truthfully answering all of her questions. She even gave Julie her private phone number. Julie was a fighter, and she planned to go into full battle on this one. First of all, she needed to find out all she could about leukemia and its treatment. When her mom and dad entered the room, she realized her major battle would be keeping them from driving her crazy.

Lori threw her arms around Julie, almost knocking down Dr. Feinberg. "Baby, are you all right?" she cried.

"Mom, I talked to Dr. Feinberg," Julie replied. "We are going to battle this disease together and make it." On her bed were books and pamphlets about leukemia and about keeping a positive attitude.

Lori stayed at the hospital with Julie while Jerry went to Adele and Jim's to pick up Barry.

Before Jerry could get through the door, Barry came running up to him. "Dad, I pitched a no-hitter," Barry said. "Too bad you weren't there to see it."

"I'm sorry, son," Jerry answered. "It couldn't be helped."

Barry had heard this excuse many times from his father, but this time his father wasn't drunk. Jim had said Julie was sick. His sister always managed to take the spotlight. Oh well, he was the second child.

"Where are Mom and Julie, home?" Barry asked?

Jim looked at Jerry and answered Barry. "Your mom and sister are still at the hospital." Jim led both father and son into the living room and sat them down on the deep brown sectional that wrapped itself around the expansive room. Jerry was barely speaking, trying to pull himself together. Now Barry was getting worried.

"Dad, what's wrong?" Barry asked.

Jerry looked at his son, his eyes misting when he said, "Barry, your sister is very sick. She has leukemia." Jerry let out all the air from his lungs. He looked and felt utterly deflated as he fell back onto the sofa.

Jim uttered, "Oh, no," and sank into the space beside him.

"What's leukemia?" Barry asked, looking from his father to Jim.

"It's a blood cancer," Jerry replied evenly. "She and Mom are staying in the hospital, where she will begin treatment."

When Barry heard *cancer,* he was scared. He thought only old people got cancer.

Jim asked, "Do you want a drink?"

Jerry answered, "No, we'll go home. I have to call my family, and I really need some sleep. Where is Adele?"

"On her way to the hospital."

With a sigh that did not bring any relief, Jerry managed a one-word answer, "Good."

Julie's treatment began immediately. Dr. Feinberg and a nurse named Barbara entered the room with a large cart full of medical supplies: tubes, vials, needles, IV, and various implements.

"Mrs. Brill and Julie, I want to explain what the treatment involves," Dr. Feinberg said. "Julie, you will be given chemotherapy drugs by IV once a week for six weeks, plus daily oral medicine. If you achieve bone marrow remission by then, you will be given radiation treatments to clear your spinal column."

Julie asked, "Will I be cured then?"

Dr. Feinberg smiled and said, "No, but you should be in remission and on your way. The full regimen involves two years of treatment."

Julie's enthusiasm waned at the sound of the long treatment. She thought, *I'm a freshman in high school. I don't want to lose two years of high school. Maybe if I fight real hard, I will get cured sooner.*

She asked, "Will I be cured after the two years?"

"Sometimes there are setbacks called relapses, and we have to change the treatment and extend it," he explained. "Let's not think about that now. Here at Children's, we take one day at a time. Please don't hesitate to ask any questions you may have."

Lori's mind started to shut down into depression, while Julie kept up her questions. Lori heard words like radiation, *vincristine*, *prednisone*, and blood cancer, but all she could think about was two years and setbacks. She looked at her daughter with admiration for her courage and positive attitude.

After the doctor left, Barbara, a pretty little Irish nurse with auburn hair, freckles, and green eyes, put an IV in Julie, and her first of many treatments was underway.

Before leaving the room, Barbara told Julie, "Sometimes the medicine can make you nauseated. If you feel sick, call me."

The first treatment only made Julie tired, and she soon fell asleep. Lori looked on, feeling numb until Adele walked into the room.

Adele hugged her and walked her out to the hall, where Lori put her head on Adele's shoulder and cried.

The war against leukemia was going to be the toughest battle the Brill family ever tackled. Life as they knew it would no longer exist. Julie and Lori would call Children's Memorial home. Jerry and Barry would be displaced trying to go back to school and work.

Remission was achieved after eight weeks of treatment. Julie tolerated the chemo much better than expected. The six weeks of radiation was much harder on her. She was tired, weak, and experienced major headaches from it, but she still kept a fighting, positive attitude. Some days, she slept eighteen hours.

Out of all her problems, Julie's major complaint was the loss of her beautiful blonde hair, which started to fall out after the first three months of chemo and radiation.

Julie stood looking at herself before the mirror. "Mom, I can't go to school looking like this," she cried, momentarily turning away from the full-length mirror that hung on her bedroom door to face her mother.

"You are still beautiful," Lori cajoled. She tried to encourage her daughter through this difficult time, but she doubted it would help. She would have been devastated had she lost her own thick black hair as a teen.

"Mom, stop!" Julie turned once again to her mirror, which was becoming a mortal enemy. "I look like *shit*. My hair is falling out.." Julie burst into angry tears as she shook free from her fingers copious amounts of blond hair.

"Honey, what about the wig?" Lori asked. "You haven't worn it since we purchased it. Surely your classmates will understand."

"Mom, you don't understand," Julie replied. "I'm a freshman in *high school*. My friends are into clothes, boys, football. They can't relate to freaks like me!" Julie's face was a grimace of misery as she covered her face with her hands and sobbed.

Lori tried to hug her, but Julie pushed her away, asked her to leave, and closed the door to her room behind Lori.

At her wit's end, Lori called Adele for help. After school, Adele's daughter Sasha, plus three other girls, rang the bell. Lori sent them up to Julie's room. Twenty minutes later, Julie, in her lovely blond wig and short plaid skirt, left for the mall with the girls.

Julie had slept through the night. As Lori tiptoed into her room the next morning, she silently prayed that the outing with her friends the day before had improved her mood. Slowly opening the door, Lori was pleasantly surprised to see Julie in the closet picking out clothes. She turned towards Lori and smiled an exasperated smile.

"Mom, I have *nothing* to wear," Julie sighed. "All my clothes are too small. The drugs they are giving me have left me a bloated mess. Can we go shopping?"

"Of course," Lori said. "Where do you want to go?"

"The Gap," Julie replied.

Lori watched her throw on a pair of jeans, a T-shirt, and her recently purchased short-haired blond wig. They parked the car in town in front of a toy store located next to the Gap.

Julie stood by the window of the toy store, staring intently at something.

Lori came up behind her and asked, "What are you looking at?"

"A roller coaster," Julie said, smiling wryly. "Ever since I've been diagnosed with leukemia, I feel like I am on a roller coaster. Some days I feel good, some days I feel terrible, some days I think I will live, and some days I'm sure I will die."

She moved into the Gap, and Lori stood staring at the roller coaster with tears flowing down her face. A fourteen-year-old shouldn't have to worry about dying.

She is right, Lori thought. From the day she married Jerry, her life had been like a roller coaster ride. Only she never realized how low it could really go.

Chapter Sixteen

They were jolted out of their routine by the monthly blood tests, bone marrow tests, and spinal taps. They waited for results like a criminal in a court case. Relapse was like a death sentence. Remission was like an appeal that would eventually run out. Lori was a nervous wreck, constantly watching Julie for signs of another relapse. She checked her eyes, nails, and gums for bleeding, her arms and legs for bruising.

After three months of treatment, Lori and Julie sat outside the treatment room waiting for results. When Dr. Bloom walked into the room with a big smile on his face, Julie jumped up.

"Remission?" she asked hopefully.

"Yes, Julie, both your spinal column and bone marrow are in remission," Dr. Bloom said.

"Way to go," said a stranger in the waiting room.

When Julie turned towards him, the man gave her a high sign, and Julie laughed while asking, "Am I cured?"

"Not yet. The monthly chemo treatments and tests will continue until we reach the two-year mark. One day at a time, and today we celebrate," answered the doctor.

"Bummer," said Julie while she continued to smile.

On one of their monthly treatment trips to the hospital, Lori—sitting next to Julie's bed in the blue lounge, an unread book dangling from her hand—watched the medicine drip into her daughter's arm while Julie slept. Needing a break, she went to the oncology lounge for a cup of coffee and a donut.

Lori sat on a soft, brightly patterned sofa beside a pink Formica table laden with magazines and newspapers. Even the walls were dazzling with color. She guessed some designer had thought the room should be cheerful, but frankly its decor unnerved her. Lori watched Kay, the mother of a twelve-year-old boy dying of leukemia, lighting one cigarette after another while she paced back and forth. Noticing Lori, Kay bent down and held out an open pack of cigarettes.

"Cigarette?" she offered.

Lori looked longingly at the cigarette and said, "Thanks, but I quit years ago. Though I am thinking of starting again."

Kay burst into laughter and said, "Don't start again. It will kill you. Hey, I bet all one hundred or more of the kids who have passed through the oncology floor were secret smokers. That is the real reason so many died."

Another older woman sitting across the room said, "Welcome to the mothers' lounge. In here you can cry and talk all you want. We are all in the same boat."

"Yes, the Titanic," Kay said laughing as she sat down next to Lori.

Lori faced her squarely and asked, "Kay, how can you laugh and make jokes?"

"Honey, you have to learn to laugh in between the tears, or you will never be able to fight the war," Kay explained. "Haven't they told you the oncology floor's motto? 'Make every day count.'"

Lori found herself staring at Kay's neck. It looked like Kay was wearing a cross and a Jewish star on a thin gold chain.

Kay noticed Lori's gaze and smiled, touching the charms hanging from her neck.

"I'm Catholic," Kay explained. "My husband is Jewish. My best friend is a Muslim. I'm calling on all the gods. We light candles and say prayers in every language. Somebody up there has to come through. What about you? I could use a Chinaman's prayers! Are you Buddhist?"

Lori took a long gulp of coffee before answering, "Sorry, Kay, I'm Jewish, but not very religious. Right now, I'm very angry with God, but I could loan you my mother-in-law. She's busy praying constantly."

"My mom too, busy with her novenas," Kay said.

Lori looked at the large wall clock and got up. "I've been here almost forty minutes," she said. "I better go back. My daughter will be looking for me."

"What room are you in? I'll bring my son Jeff over. He has a wonderful attitude. Better than his mother's," Kay stated.

"Room 417," Lori answered her before leaving the lounge.

No sooner had Lori returned to the room when Kay followed with an adorable little boy. He had the chemotherapy signs of bloat and baldness, but he also had a delightful grin and large shining brown eyes. Kay motioned for Lori to leave with her.

Jeff walked over to Julie's bed and said, "Hi, Julie, I'm Jeff. I have leukemia too. How long have you been treated for leukemia?"

"Almost eight months. What about you?" Julie answered, smiling weakly.

"Two and a half years."

"Have you been in remission that whole time?"

"No way. I've relapsed three times, but I'm back in remission now."

Julie asked, "How old are you?"

"Twelve."

Julie grew silent, hesitant to speak, but she felt this little boy would be honest with her, so she took a shot. "Aren't you afraid of dying, Jeff?"

"No, I'm really an old soul reincarnated," Jeff answered solemnly. "I'm getting ready to go back for another soul."

"Jeff, you're weird." Julie cocked her head to one side, sizing up this strange little boy. She smiled at him.

"I'm going to help you get up and go to the patients' lounge with me," Jeff said.

"I can't go anywhere while this IV is in me." Julie's mood suddenly turned sour.

"Yes, you can," Jeff said. "There's a birthday party for Pasquale in the lounge. He is three today."

"Leave me alone," Julie answered. She turned her head away from him and towards the window.

Jeff wouldn't take no for an answer. He called Barbara in, and soon Julie found herself slowly walking down the hall, pulling her IV behind her just as Jeff was doing.

"Do you have a wig?" he asked.

"Yes," Julie answered.

"I like to drive people crazy with mine," Jeff said. "A good trick I use is to suddenly take it off when I am in an elevator. The surprised looks on their faces are incredible."

Julie smiled and then started to laugh. It was the first time she had ever laughed during a hospital stay.

Julie followed Jeff to the children's oncology lounge, where he introduced her to an assortment of children between the ages of three to fifteen, some with hair, some without, some bloated due to cortisone drugs, and some thin due to other chemo drugs, some on crutches and some in wheelchairs. They were maneuvering their IVs around tables set with games and projects.

Suddenly, everyone turned towards the door. Kay walked in carrying a McDonald's birthday cake and said, "Let's sing, everyone. Pasquale, come up here."

Julie joined in a chorus of *Happy Birthday.* She was too nauseated from the chemo to try a piece of cake, but she loved the idea that they could have a party in the hospital. She couldn't wait until she told Shawn and Sasha.

Jeff held out his hand to Julie and asked, "Friends?"

"Yes, friends," she answered, bringing him close to her for an angled hug around their IVs.

After that, Julie always looked for Jeff when she was in the hospital.

Adele's son gave Barry a science fiction book by Harlan Ellison to read. Though she never read the book, the title became stuck in Lori's mind: *I Have No Mouth, and I Must Scream.* It fit her mood perfectly. She knew she had to be strong for Julie, but she was so frightened. Nothing in life had prepared her for this nightmare. In charge of Julie's treatments, she had to function, but she was unable to eat, sleep, or concentrate, and she felt like screaming but couldn't.

Jerry tried to take care of the home front, but his drinking, though less than before, was interfering, and he was not making it home on time many nights. Barry, having felt abandoned for quite some time, had virtually moved in with Adele and her family.

After a year and a half of treatment, Julie was still in remission and put on maintenance, which brought life to a more normal routine. Julie's hair had grown back, she was in school almost full-time, and they were all feeling positive about the cancer. Life was almost normal again.

Then, one morning, almost at the end of the second year of Julie's diagnosis and first remission, Julie cut herself while slicing a tomato while helping Lori prepare her own and Barry's lunches before heading off to school. It was not a major cut, so Julie left the kitchen to retrieve a bandage for it. She returned with the cut covered and continued her kitchen activities. Fifteen minutes later, the bleeding had not stopped.

"Julie, I think we better take a trip to see Dr. Bloom," Lori said She became nervous and concerned, a chill running down her back as she inspected her daughter's finger, its small brown bandage soaked through. *No, God, no. It did not come back.*

"No, Mom, I'm all right!" Defiantly, Julie pulled her hand away from her mother and moved away. "It's just a cut! It's maybe deeper than we thought!"

"Honey, you've been more tired than usual and now the bleeding. I'm calling the doctor, right now." Lori moved to the kitchen telephone and began dialing a number she was sorry she knew by heart.

"Mom, my monthly tests are only ten days away." Julie took a napkin and tightly wound it around her cut finger.

"Okay, Julie, I reached Dr. Bloom on the phone. He wants us to come in." Lori moved to the living room and alerted her son to what was happening. "Barry, you need to go to Adele's after school."

"Mom, I'm almost thirteen, don't worry about me. Julie," he called out to his sister, "I hope it's nothing."

Lori and Julie made an unscheduled trip to Children's that morning. The whole ride there, Julie sat next to her mother in a stubborn silence.

Tests showed that Julie's platelet counts and red blood cell counts were very low, but there was no sign of blast cells in her bone marrow. After a blood transfusion, Dr. Bloom told them to go home and enjoy the next ten days before coming in for a series of complete tests. Lori was afraid to ask him if this was a bad sign.

Rain pounded down against the pavement. One never knew what to expect weather-wise in Chicago, especially in the fall. The sun had been shining brightly just a few hours ago. Lori left Julie in the lobby and walked three blocks to her parked car, got in the driver's side, and started the engine. Everything started up, but the car wouldn't move. It was only six months old. As she was meditating on the problem, a man knocked on her window, and she lowered it.

"Lady, you aren't going anywhere," he said. "There is a boot on your wheel. You better pay your fines at the police station."

Lori got out of the car and looked on the passenger side of her car. Sure enough, there was a Denver boot on the wheel. How did this happen? What tickets were they talking about? She hardly used the car.

Lori went back to the hospital to her tired daughter. The receptionist at the front desk let her use the phone, and she called the Chicago Police Department.

"Lady, you have exactly ten parking tickets registered to that car. The only way to get the boot off is to come down to the station and pay them by cash or certified check," the police officer said.

"There must be a mistake," Lori said. "We live in the suburbs. The car is only six months old."

Lori tried calling Jerry. No luck. She tried calling Adele. No luck.

"Mom, I want to go *home*," Julie cried from her prone position. She was tired of lying across two chairs.

Lori called a cab. Thirty dollars later, they were safely in their house. Lori met Jerry at the door when he came home from work. Her instincts told her his family had something to do with the boot. Her car had papers and wrappers in it that weren't Jerry's or hers.

After telling him about their day, Jerry said, "I'll talk to Joel."

At the mention of Joel's name, Lori lost it. For the last year, she had nothing to do with his family, but obviously now she realized they were still in her life.

"What does Joel have to do with my car?" she screamed.

"Stop yelling, Lori," Jerry said. "Joel was in a car accident, and his car was wrecked. You didn't need the car because you'd been staying at the hospital, so I let him borrow it."

"Your family means more to you than your dying daughter?!"

"Lori, stop. You're too involved with Julie. Some of us are still living too."

He then tried to hug Lori, but she pulled away. *He doesn't realize what is happening, or he won't accept that I am fighting to keep her alive.*

Lori turned towards Jerry and very calmly said, "Take care of it, or give me your fancy Lincoln. I'm going to sleep. It's been a very tough day."

Barry watched from his seat in the living room. He watched his mother go upstairs and heard the sound of his parents' bedroom door slam and heard her lock herself in the bedroom. He silently watched his father move into the living room, where Barry sat unnoticed on the sofa. He watched his father go to the bar and pour himself a drink. Barry thought about his evening at Adele and Jim's, where everyone sat down at the dining room table eating a dinner of salad, meat, potato, bread, vegetables, and dessert on china while discussing their day. He loved his family, but he secretly wished he had been born into a normal family where there wasn't sickness, drinking, and fighting all the time.

Chapter Seventeen

The blood transfusion gave Julie some needed extra energy, so she left the house to spend time at Adele's with Sasha and friends, while Barry spent the evening at a Boy Scouts event. Tired, angry, and hungry, Lori maneuvered her way through the front door and into the house with arms full of groceries. It was seven o'clock, and Jerry wasn't home yet. She was no longer certain if Jerry's absence was a bother or a blessing.

The light on the answering machine was blinking. There were two messages on the new electric wonder.

"Honey, I'll be very late," Jerry's voice said. "I have a business meeting." *Probably at the local bar,* she thought.

She hit the button for the second message. "Lori, it's Josh. I'm back in town. Can you meet me for dinner to discuss the planning committee project?" Lori's mood instantly brightened. It was the best she had felt since hearing of her daughter's remission. She had not lately had anything to boost her mood. Things were pretty normal, considering, and she allowed herself to feel a tingle of excitement upon hearing Josh's voice. She desperately welcomed a happy distraction.

Why not? Lori thought as she called Adele.

"Adele, is Julie all right? Can you pick up Barry at Boy Scouts?"

"No problem. What's up? You sound like a giddy school girl," Adele asked.

"I'm meeting Josh for dinner at the Old Hickory Barbecue Hut."

"Lori, you are being foolish," Adele admonished. "People don't change. He pulled at your heartstrings for four years and then left you for some girl with money. You are skirting a disaster."

Lori leaned against her kitchen counter, closed her eyes, and rubbed her forehead, trying to ease out a knot of tension that appeared at the onset of Adele's admonishment.

"Adele," Lori sighed, "my life is *already* a disaster. Anyway, it is just a dinner between old friends. I need a break, Adele."

"Remember you are married," her proper friend warned.

"Right," Lori replied, glancing at the clock on the oven, "to an alcoholic who never makes it home."

She stood in front of her closet like a bumbling schoolgirl, trying to decide what to wear: the black dress looked too dressy; blue knit pantsuit, too matronly; red sweater, too tight. She left the closet, took a quick shower, managed a swirl of mouthwash, and gave herself a spritz of Chanel No. 5 before returning to the closet. She finally settled on a turquoise cashmere sweater, nice fitting rhinestone studded blue jeans, Gucci loafers, and a matching Gucci purse—a casual designer look.

Lori joined Josh for dinner at the Old Hickory Barbecue Hut, a small place with wooden booths and walls adorned with pictures of rock and roll stars such as Chuck Berry and Elvis Presley. It was still a hangout for young teenagers, even though it desperately needed a remodeling job. It made her think back to an easier, simpler, carefree time of life.

"You look wonderful, Lori," was Josh's greeting.

Just the boost she needed. *God, he still has that great dimpled smile and twinkling blue eyes.* Her heart skipped a beat as he bent down and kissed her on the mouth. Her hand reached up and tousled his hair.

"Not quite as blonde, but still there," she commented.

He led her to their old booth in the back of the restaurant.

"The place hasn't changed in twenty-five years," Josh said as he reached into his pocket for some quarters. "They still have the old juke boxes. Pick out a song."

Of course she played their song, *Moon River,* from her favorite movie with Audrey Hepburn.

He looked at her with questioning eyes.

She answered, "Yes, I still have my crystal pin from Tiffany's."

He smiled and said, "Pass it on to Julie."

Lori had seated herself next to Josh. She sat playing with her salad when his hand moved smoothly over her thigh, his body leaned in towards her, and he gently kissed her neck.

"Let's take a ride," he quietly whispered. Her body trembled as Josh helped her up. She felt like a seventeen-year-old, guilty and excited.

A ride with Josh? A restaurant was safe. She was a married woman who couldn't remember when her husband and she had last been intimate. These thoughts were whirling through her head as she let Josh guide her out of the restaurant. As they started out the door, Carlos, the owner of the Old Hickory Barbecue Hut, ran after them with the phone. It was Adele.

"Julie" and "throwing up blood" were all Lori heard.

Chapter Eighteen

From Adele's house, Julie went straight to Children's Memorial Hospital. Lori drove herself to the hospital, leaving Josh at the restaurant. Jerry met them there three hours later. A platelet transfusion helped stop the bleeding. After the bone marrow and spinal tap the next morning, Dr. Bloom entered the room with a sober look on his face.

"Julie, I'm sorry to have to tell you that there are blast cells in both your bone marrow and spinal column. It would be better if you were still in remission, but we still have several treatments we can try."

Jerry and Lori sat numb while Julie took the lead in her treatment, saying, "Dr. Bloom, I've been reading about bone marrow transplants. Is that an option for me?"

"A very good question, Julie. They still have not been perfected, and if we could find a donor, they would not work in your case because of your type of leukemia, but we do have several other chemotherapy drugs, and we haven't used the maximum radiation dosages."

Lori and Julie stayed in the hospital. The next morning another series of radiation treatments were started.

The first question Julie asked the radiologist at Children's was, "Will I lose my hair again?"

"Probably." His answer was alarmingly cool and dispassionate. It was a remarkable change in attitude compared to the treatment Lori and Julie were used to at the hospital. This young doctor was all business.

Losing her hair was the least of her problems. After the radiation, Julie was put on a new chemotherapy regimen. This new aggressive treatment left her in and out of the hospital because of infections, low blood counts, nausea, and diarrhea.

The two-year mark came in October of 1990. Instead of celebrating, Jerry, Lori, and Barry sat in room 521 of Children's Memorial Hospital watching their daughter and sister moan from pain while a nurse tried to find a vein to set up an IV for treatment.

Barry turned to his dad and asked, "Why are they having so much trouble?"

Lori answered, "Because she has been stuck hundreds of times, and all her veins have collapsed."

Barry looked at Julie and said, "Sis, when I become a doctor, I am going to invent an easier way to get blood out of veins."

Julie was subdued but still alert. She answered, "I can't wait that long."

Lori turned to Barry and asked, "When did you decide to become a doctor?"

"Today!" Barry replied.

When the experimental treatment only put her in remission for four months, Julie once again took control of her treatments.

At their next meeting with the oncology department, she cried, "I will not live like a vegetable. I understand that my chances of dying are increasing, so instead of spending my last days on medicine, I want to do some fun things like travel and visit with friends. What can you do to help?"

Lori had to leave the room and head to the ladies' room, where she broke down into a flood of tears.

Dr. Bloom looked at Julie. "You are a very brave and wise young lady. Before we try any other treatments, we will put you on cortisone and blood transfusion so you can take some time off to travel. Where do you want to go?"

"Skiing, and then to Israel to pray at the Wailing Wall," Julie said.

Dr. Bloom said, "My, you are ambitious. Dr. Feinberg will talk to you about what we can do."

Jerry followed Dr. Bloom out the door, leaving Julie and Dr. Feinberg alone.

With a sheepish grin, Julie looked at the doctor and asked, "Can I ask you something confidentially?"

"Sure, Julie."

"About six months ago, when I went on the stronger medicine, my period stopped coming, and you told me sometimes the chemo does that. Well, I want to know if I can get pregnant even though my period hasn't returned."

This question caught Dr. Feinberg off-guard, and it took her a few moments to respond.

"Julie, you would still need to use protection," Dr. Fienberg said. "Tell me about your boyfriend."

"His name is Shawn, and he is gorgeous, and he has been there for me throughout," Julie said.

Watching a big smile break out across Julie's face, Dr. Feinberg felt her heart break for this precious sixteen-year-old who wasn't going to make it. She wondered how Dr. Bloom stayed in pediatric oncology for so many years. Do doctors really become immune to children dying?

She smiled warmly at Julie and said, "I would love to meet your boyfriend."

Julie replied, "He doesn't come to the hospital, but he visits me at home and takes care of me when I get to go to school."

Julie had spent more time out of school than in school. Most of her friends had drifted away. Besides Sasha, Shawn was one of the few who stuck by her. Julie was sitting on her bed flipping through a fashion magazine when Shawn came to call. Lori had let him in, greeted him, and watched him go up to Julie's room.

"Hey, Julie, I brought you some school work," Shawn said. He placed the books on a table by the doorway. He stood there for a while, unsure of what to do next.

"Thanks, Shawn." Julie got up and hugged him. Shawn wrapped his arms around Julie gingerly and then quickly stuffed his hands in his jeans pockets.

"So, will she let you go skiing?" Shawn asked.

"Yeah, can you believe it?" Julie could see Shawn wasn't in the mood to be cuddly, so she moved toward the bed and flopped down on it. "My mother, who would usually never let me do *anything*, will let me go downhill skiing. She even convinced the doctors. She'll call your mom tomorrow about the trip."

"See, I told you she's not that bad," Shawn said, keeping a smile on his face. He moved to the dresser, fidgeted with Julie's books, and then sat on the edge of her bed, looking down at his sneakered feet.

"Shawn, we don't fight anymore," Julie said. "She holds me tight with tears in her eyes, agreeing to everything. It really scares me. She must really think I'm going to die or..."

Julie realized she shouldn't have said that as she watched Shawn sit there, fidgeting. Finally, he got up and kissed her tenderly on the cheek.

"I'm glad you can go skiing with us, Jules. I have to go now to football practice." Shawn leaned in and gave Julie a quick hug, then rose to go. "See you tomorrow, Julie," Shawn said brightly as he walked out of the room.

"Okay, see ya."

As he left, Julie thought to herself, *No, death and football practice do not go together.*

Going on the ski trip was not as easy as it initially sounded. One month before joining Shawn and his family out in Aspen, Colorado, Julie and Lori spent two days at Children's.

"Okay, Julie, your mother and I are allowing you to go on this ski trip with some conditions," Dr. Bloom explained. "I understand that you are not happy that she is joining you, but we feel it is necessary that someone familiar with your treatment be there. Also, I understand you're fine with the blood transfusions but unhappy with the cortisone."

"Dr. Bloom, the cortisone makes me bloated, and I look awful," Julie said.

"Julie, one or two months of cortisone will not bloat you," Dr. Bloom countered. "It will make you feel much stronger."

"Fine, just let me have some fun in life," Julie said. "I've been treated for over two and a half years already.

They pumped her body up with some extra cortisone, administered blood transfusions, and off she went. Lori tagged along with Shawn's family. Shawn's mother, Joanne, talked Lori into taking ski lessons. Her family vacationed in Aspen every year, and she was an expert skier. Hesitantly, Lori agreed to take the lesson, though she really would have preferred to walk around and shop.

Julie learned to ski with no problems. She and Shawn took off like pros. Lori was a different story. The first day out, she ended up coming down the mountain on a stretcher. She called Jerry from the hospital.

"Julie is fine, but I broke my arm," Lori revealed.

"How did you do that?" Jerry asked. "Did you fall down? I told you to take a lesson if you were going to attempt skiing." Jerry tried to sound concerned, but he was irritated. *Can't this family catch a break? Bad choice of words,* Jerry thought.

"I broke my arm *taking* a lesson," Lori explained. "I caught the pole on a tree, and my wrist snapped."

"What a klutz. Only you could do that." Jerry tried to lighten his own mood by teasing his wife.

"Thanks, Jerry. I'm in pain, and you are lecturing me." Lori hung up, thinking, *Men!* The male instructor was no better. As she was holding her arm in agony, he was telling her it couldn't be broken since she didn't fall.

That night, her finger became swollen, and she was again in pain. Shawn's family took her back to the emergency room, where her wedding ring had to be cut off of her finger.

Sitting in the emergency room at two in the morning, Lori thought of how stupid it was of the morning staff to cast her arm with the ring still on. At that point, she felt like throwing her wedding ring away with her marriage, but Lori knew she had other battles to fight—and the biggest battle was for Julie's life.

Back from the ski trip, Julie resumed her treatments, and to everyone's delight, she went into remission. Coming home from the hospital with Julie, Lori was surprised to inhale the pungent aroma of chicken being barbecued on the grill and was delighted at the sight of clean dishes, glasses, and silverware set on the table. Her mouth watered from hunger.

"Mom, is dad cooking now?" Julie asked.

"If he is, it will be a first."

Julie and Lori walked around to the back of the house. To their surprise, Barry was standing by an expansive gas grill with tongs in hand, turning a breast smothered in barbeque sauce. A bowl of grilled barbequed chicken sat steaming in a bowl nearby.

He turned towards Julie and asked hopefully, "How were your blood tests?"

Julie gave him the high sign, indicating that they were the same. Grinning, she asked, “What’s going on here? You’ve gone domestic in your teen years?”

“It’s just temporary, until mom gets her arm out of the cast.” He indicated towards the kitchen. “Table’s all set—salad, buns, drinks. I’m just about done here.” Barry placed the last chicken breast inside the bowl and turned off the grill.

Lori smiled at Barry. “Julie, your brother has been a godsend helping with the house cleaning and the lawn. This is his first meal. Let’s try it.”

“Well, I’m still on prednisone, so I could eat a horse,” she answered as they all entered the kitchen and sat down at the table. “Oh, this looks great, Barry, thank you!” Julie said, and she started on the salad.

Barry set down the bowl and looked at his mother. “Should we wait for Dad?” He sounded doubtful, as it was unclear what time his father came home; it could be any hour of the day or night.

“He will catch up when he comes in.” Lori shrugged and put her own thoughts about Jerry and his estimated times of arrival out of her mind. She just wanted to enjoy her son’s meal and her children’s company. Soon after, the front door opened.

“Dad?” Barry called.

“No,” Adele answered as she walked into the kitchen carrying a backpack. Smiling, she handed Barry his school bag before giving Julie a hug. Turning towards Lori, she said, “Your son was so excited about making dinner that he forgot his books in my car.”

Lori eyed her warily; at this time of the evening, Adele would have sent Sasha or called Lori to pick up the books. “Okay, what’s wrong?” she asked Adele, who shook her head and beckoned her to follow her out of the kitchen.

“I’ll be right back, kids. Go on and eat,” Lori said, and she and Adele walked into the living room.

In a voice slightly above a whisper, Adele said, "Jim is at the police station with Jerry. Jerry was stopped for running a red light and then arrested on a DUI."

"God damn son of a bitch" Lori said between clenched teeth. "How can he do this to us now?! He promised to take care of the home front!" Lori yelled as she pounded her fist against the wall.

Adele threw her arms around Lori and said, "Honey, calm down for your kids. Jim will get it straightened out. Let's go back and enjoy Barry's dinner and Julie's good mood." Adele smoothed Lori's black hair from her face and smiled. "Come on, Lori, calm down."

Lori looked at Adele with loving eyes. "Thank you for always being there."

***

Walking out of the police station, Jerry turned to Jim and asked, "Can I buy you dinner?"

"Dinner? It's midnight." Jim answered. He was sick of Jerry's bullshit, tired of this guy always making everything about him. How much attention did one guy need? Why wasn't he a stand-up guy for his family, especially since it was now in crisis?

"Jim, I need to talk to someone," Jerry said, his desperation becoming more evident. "My mother… is useless. All she does is complain about Lori and cry about herself, and my brothers have their own problems."

Jim knew Jerry had nowhere to turn. He sighed and thought, *I'm doing this for Lori. I'm doing this for his family.*

They pulled into a Denny's, the closest open restaurant, and ordered coffee and eggs.

"Jim, I can't handle it," Jerry cried. "We have no life. I've lost Julie and Lori. "

"Drinking is not helping it, Jerry," Jim replied. "You've got to pull your shit together. Your family needs you. They need you to be sober and strong. You can't be strong while you're out being a drunk."

"I know, Jim, but it is my way of forgetting. Lori doesn't realize I exist." Jerry leaned in closer so as not to be overheard. "And… sex is a thing of the past. And she won't acknowledge that I'm hurting too."

Jim sat fidgeting. This type of conversation was not his style, but he tried for his friend.

"Jerry, I'm not good at this, but I'll try to get some ideas from Adele. And, Jerry," Jim continued, "while we are talking about hurting, I have to tell you… I think Barry needs some attention. We are happy to have him at our house, but he could use some time with you."

Jim thought about how the business was suffering, but he wasn't going to bring that up now.

By the time Jerry got home it was close to two in the morning. He tiptoed in, relieved that everyone was asleep. Even though he blew the evening with the family, he finally got a chance to talk to someone about his feelings. He had to talk to someone, and he was grateful for Jim being there for him and his family.

***

After getting Barry and Julie off to school, Lori went back upstairs, silently passing Jerry on his way down. She said nothing. She was done dealing with him. Her job was to take care of Julie. Before taking her shower and dressing, she made the bed and started to tidy up her room when she heard conversation going on in the kitchen. Barry was at school; Julie was sleeping. Who could Jerry be talking to? She got out of bed, put on a bathrobe, and walked downstairs.

It was Jerry's brother, Joel, about to exit the back door with a large box. When he heard someone on the stairs, he looked up and said, "Oh, hi, Lori."

Lori had not one iota of patience for any Brill. "What are you doing in my house?" she asked. "I told Jerry to keep his family far away from me."

Jerry walked in through the back door and said, "Lori, my driver's license was suspended. Joel is my driver."

She sat down and put her head in her hands. Jerry ignored her and walked out. Following him, Joel stopped and tapped Lori on the shoulder.

"Lori, I know my family has done some dumb things, but Jerry is my brother, and I love him," Joel said.

Lori looked up, tears streaming down her face, which wore an expression of pure malice. "Then get him to quit drinking," she said.

Chapter Nineteen

Julie was relentless in her quest to travel. She begged her parents and the doctors to let her go to Israel to pray. While Lori was still angry with God, her daughter was reading about the Jewish religion and establishing a closer relationship with God.

Just when Lori's arm came out of the cast, Julie relapsed and their trip to Israel was delayed another four months. Finally, after weeks of stabilizing her condition, Julie and her family boarded their El Al flight to Jerusalem.

Lori had just fastened her seat belt, leaning back exhausted and fearful when Julie banged on the back of her seat.

"Mom, I can't believe we are really on our way to Israel," Julie said. "I'm so excited!"

Lori's heart clenched in sadness as she looked into her sweet daughter's pretty, bloated face. She forced a smile, willing away a torrent of tears.

"Oh, Julie, it's really happening, honey." Lori grasped her daughter's hand, still bruised from the doctors' searches for viable veins. "You made it happen, kiddo."

This trip was taking place by sheer miracle. A month ago, Julie was in relapse mode, on heavy chemo and blood transfusions. Her doctors used some extraordinary tricks to put her in a temporary remission. One was the use of heavy doses of cortisone. Lori had paid no attention but heard through her sources about Shelly's ranting and raging about the danger of taking a sick child so far away into a country that was continuously at war. Julie wanted to go, and that was enough for Lori.

Julie was still a beautiful sixteen-year-old despite the wig and bloated body. That girl had spirit and determination.

Halfway through the ride, Jerry and Julie switched seats. Barry and Jerry slept, while mother and daughter talked.

"Mom, do Jews believe in heaven?" Julie asked.

Lori hesitated, not knowing how to answer. "Yes, Jews believe the spirit, not the body, goes to a place like heaven."

"I like that idea. I would hate to be stuck with this battered, hairless, vein-punctured body for eternity," Julie said, looking down at her chubby bruised arms.

Lori bit her lip and swallowed her tears as she turned towards the window.

"Those clouds look like snow covered mountains you and Shawn could ski on."

"More like big puffy pillows I could lay my head on," Julie replied.

Lori turned to her daughter. "How about laying your head on a mommy pillow? We have about another seven hours before we land in Israel." She put her arms around her daughter, and Julie soon fell asleep with her mother stroking her cheek and looking out of the window, thinking about the days she and her daughter had quarreled about everything and how close they had become now that their priorities had changed. Lori shared stories with Julie as if she was an adult. They debated and talked about philosophy, such as the discussion about God. Sometimes they sat outside together at night watching the stars.

After passing through Israeli customs, which wasn't easy, the Brill family looked for signs of their relatives. Spotting a sign with their name on it, they walked towards it. The man holding the sign was middle-aged with a round face and big, wide, brown eyes covered by black- rimmed glasses. He was not very tall but was still taller than the older man standing beside him, whose gray hair matched his beard and mustache and whose receding hairline exposed a large ancient scar.

The older gentleman ran towards them, and in a mixture of English and Yiddish he cried, "Lori, Lori, *eich benschn thine landsman*!"

"Uncle Dov?" she asked. He was giving Lori a blessing of a compatriot.

"Yes, yes," he answered while picking her up and twirling her.

"Dad, calm down. You'll have an attack," the younger man said as he gently pulled his father away from Lori.

Catching her composure, Lori stuck out her hand to her cousin. "You must be Michel!"

"Yes, as you can see my dad is thrilled to finally meet his sister's family." He picked up Lori's suitcase and motioned for them to follow him. As they walked through the airport to Cousin Michel's car, Lori noticed that Uncle Dov was walking arm in arm with both of her children. Already she realized that he was very different from her mother. He was warm and very talkative, while her mother had always been quiet, aloof, and secretive.

Cousin Michel insisted they stay at his home in Jerusalem, saying they had plenty of room now that his daughter was serving her time in the Israeli army. Uncle Dov, who had been recently widowed, was living with his son and daughter-in-law. Their apartment was in a modern building in the city center next to the Jerusalem hospital where Michel worked as a surgeon and his wife Sabra worked as a nurse.

Lori's mother's family treated them royally in Jerusalem. Lori learned that her mother and Uncle Dov were the only Holocaust survivors from a prominent German Jewish family. Lori was also surprised to learn her mother and father had visited Uncle Dov and family in Israel in the late 1950s. Everything involving her mother was a big secret.

The private tour Michel and the family gave them of the city was wonderful. Jerusalem encompasses an ancient world full of history, with archaeological sites to confirm it, and a modern world of shops, museums, schools, and restaurants. Their visit to the hospital was disappointing, as they had nothing new to offer them for leukemia treatment.

Yad Vashem was a very sad tour for the family, especially when Uncle Dov pointed out family names on concentration camp lists. He told Lori that most of the family spent time in the concentration camps. He escaped to Israel through the underground.

"You know your history, no? Your mother..." His voice trailed off, and he shook his head sadly.

"I don't understand, Uncle Dov," Lori said. "What about my mother?"

The old man slowly ran his wrinkled, gnarled hand over the long list of family members, looked into his niece's eyes, and said, "Your mother, Lori. She barely escaped with her life."

Lori was taken aback. Her head swam. "*My* mother? She never talked about her life in Germany." Lori looked at the names before her. She put her hands to her mouth and stifled a cry. "Uncle Dov... she never... *never* told me she was in a... camp." Lori placed her hands on the old man's shoulders and looked at him sadly. "Mother never talked about your family beyond acknowledging your existence. She reluctantly gave me your addresses when I pressed her for knowledge of our family."

The old man nodded knowingly, taking Lori's hands in his and patting them reassuringly.

"We each deal differently, dear. If it is too painful for her to recall, leave her be."

Lori vowed to confront her mother when they were back home and things improved, if ever, with Julie. She had so many unanswered questions about her mother.

Barry enjoyed Israel more than any of them. "Mom, can I ride on the camel? Did you see that topless woman on the beach? I love this food.

Are those soldiers on the bus carrying machine guns? Was Abraham really here? Look what I am collecting for Grandpa."

Barry didn't mind schlepping around a large heavy bag of Masada rocks to bring home to Grandpa Jack. Masada, a first-century fortress, high on a mountaintop, was where Jewish soldiers committed suicide instead of giving up to the Romans. It is a place of honor and inspiration.

Julie loved it even though she was sick part of the time. Jerry drank much less and enjoyed the trip, although it was apparent to both Lori and Jerry that their relationship was strained.

Lori only hoped their prayers at the Wailing Wall would produce miracles. The Western Wall, the only remnant of the Second Temple, destroyed in 70 CE, over 2000 years ago, was one of the most famous places to visit in Jerusalem. Michel left them off and went to work. They took their time walking down the large number of stone steps leading to the Wall. Lori took out the scarves her cousin Sara had provided for Lori and Julie's head covering, which was required. She watched her son and husband cover their heads with their newly purchased Israeli yarmulkes.

Visitors stuck prayers and notes in the open holes of the wall, and pious men spent hours praying there.

Lori stared at the weather-beaten white stones, and the tears came flowing down her face as she prayed to the God she had been so angry with, the God of her past upbringing, the merciful God. She begged him to spare her daughter.

Julie pulled on her sleeve. Lori turned to her. "Mom, I asked Uncle Dov to write my prayer out in Hebrew," Julie said.

Lori smiled and said, "That was a good idea. Mine is in English, so we will have all bases covered."

Barry chimed in, "Do you think Spanish would work?"

Lori smiled sadly at her son and said, "As many prayers we can put in the wall for life and health in any language will be good."

As they stood there, silently praying along the wall, they saw many men in fervent prayer. These men swayed to and fro as they held onto prayer books.

"Why are so many of the older men moving like that?" Julie asked.

"The very religious pray like that," Lori explained. "It is called shokeling. It's a tradition from centuries ago. It is said it helps with concentration."

Lori watched Julie praying and putting her paper with the prayer into a hole in the wall, as tradition dictates.

They walked awhile along Old Jerusalem looking for a café. The streets of Jerusalem were swarming with people from all walks of life. Arab women, covered from head to toe, young Jews with short skirts, male Orthodox Jews with side curls, and Christians sporting crosses walked and worked next to each other, yet as nations they couldn't get along.

"Mom, I've been to Hebrew school, but I can't read any of these signs or understand anything anyone says. Why?" Julie was filled with questions, her curiosity piquing at every turn of her head.

Lori looked at the signs all around her before answering her daughter. "In Israel, the early government decided to read and write their official language as it was written in the Torah, without vowels. In the United States and other parts of the world, the language is learned in the easier form with vowels."

Lori doubted her kids could have spoken it anyway. Israelis were a people in a hurry, speaking and moving fast. Lori was no better at it, but she could understand the elderly Jews who were speaking Yiddish, because that was the language her father's mother spoke to her while she was growing up.

Finally, they found an outdoor café and sat down on the small metal chairs and ordered a lunch of salad in pita bread and some hummus.

Julie and Lori stayed with the family in Jerusalem while Jerry and Barry took off on a tour of Tel Aviv. When they came back, Barry was all fired up about living on a kibbutz.

"Mom, Kibbutz Kadima is right on the ocean in Tel Aviv. It is beautiful, something like Miami with palm trees, only they also have camels!" He went on, excitedly, "They have many teenagers, and everyone works together. It's like going to camp."

Michel turned towards Barry. "You said you would like to learn spoken Hebrew. Many Americans spend a college semester on a kibbutz. Think about it." Then he turned to Julie. "You are invited also."

She gave him a knowing smile. "We'll see," she answered.

Lori turned to Jerry and asked, "Where else did you go?"

"Honey, Tel Aviv is unreal, a large modern city with shops, parks, cafes, and there is a bigger tech movement here than in the States," Jerry replied. "Barry and I spent hours looking over their new computers, and we ate authentic Israeli food, hummus…" His voice trailed off as he looked around him in awe.

"What about the Great Synagogue, the museums, and Tel Aviv University?" Lori asked.

"Mom, Dad and I had *fun*," Barry said.

Lori smiled. That was more important than sightseeing.

The last day of their trip was spent with their family at the cultural center watching an Israeli folklore program that brought together ancient and modern Israeli singing and dancing. The program ended with everyone holding hands and singing the stirring and solemn *Hatikvah*, the national anthem of Israel, and then lining up for the variety of food available at the different stations.

Sitting at the table, Lori and Julie nibbled on *glatt* kosher chicken, while her husband and son tried every kind of Middle Eastern flavor, including their new favorite, chickpea hummus.

Barry turned to Michel and asked, "Michel, why do you always take your medicine bag with you? Are you on call?"

"Barry, in Israel, we are always on call. Terrorist attacks can occur anywhere: the grocery store, the bus stop, or even in this cultural center." He paused and shook his head. "It's the sad state of affairs for now. I carry items such as gloves, tourniquets, antibiotics, and pain medicine."

"In America doctors won't help out because they are afraid of getting sued," Jerry said. He contemplated the dangers of visiting Israel. He looked around him. Everyone was going about his or her business, enjoying life, laughing, eating, talking. It was inconceivable that danger lurked so close at every corner.

Michel gave him a puzzled look and said, "How ridiculous. Are you saying a doctor would let someone die because of a legal matter?"

"That is the way things are becoming," Jerry answered.

Lori sat deep in her own thoughts, a smile playing on her lips. She turned towards Michel and said, "You know, Michel, like the dancing we've just seen, bringing different aspects of our culture together, *we* have brought together *our* family history and *our* future. We will continue this connection. Please come to the United States to visit so we can be your hosts."

Michel said he would love to visit, and Lori, Julie, and Barry spent the duration of the afternoon excitedly filling Michel in about all the things they would show him upon his visit to America.

Sara, Michel's wife, suddenly interrupted them. "Let them go. Security will be tight at the airport today." Sara paused to reflect and then announced, "There has been another suicide bombing at a café."

How right she was. Security at the El Al terminal at Ben Gurion Airport was unreal compared to their unchecked casual walk through the terminals in the States. They were questioned, frisked, and asked to identify and check through their luggage before boarding the plane. Jerry was almost denied boarding due to his pocketknife, which security quickly confiscated.

Back on the plane, Julie snuggled up against her mother like a small child. She looked up at her mom, and with a smile on her face, she whispered, "Thanks, Mom, for making this trip possible."

Chapter Twenty

Home only a short time, Julie, still on heavy doses of cortisone, was feeling good and planned to keep up her quest to go places and see things.

Waving a poster she had just purchased at a record store, she said, "I want to go to this concert. Bruce Springsteen is my all-time favorite. *Pleeeease* get tickets for meeeee."

Her wish was their command. Jerry was the one nominated to accompany her. He was better at inhaling the smoke and tolerating the noise than Lori was. Barry, at thirteen, wasn't interested, which was fortunate for Jerry since the tickets were a fortune and nearly impossible to get. Jerry stood in line for hours only to be turned down. Jim came through by paying an ungodly sum of money that he refused to take from them, and he bought one for his daughter so the girls could go together. For months afterward, the car radio or the house tape player was blaring music from Bruce Springsteen's album *Born in the U.S.A.*

Julie was crowding all the life she could into a few short years. Barry, Jerry, and Lori were going along for the ride, seeing and doing things they would have never done if she hadn't become sick. The slogan at Children's Memorial was: *Take one day at a time, living it to its fullest.* With Julie's lead, they tried, but by the end of her third year of treatment, it was clear to the family that time was running out.

Julie grew weaker, and the remissions were not holding. Her days at school were minimal.

Julie did not feel like taking on this fight for another year. The strong-willed, optimistic girl of the past was giving way to a very ill young woman faced with the difficulty of accepting her limited time here on earth.

One chilly day, right around the end of the school year, she sat on the steps of her high school with Shawn. Julie pulled the thick dark blue cable-knit sweater tightly around her body, and she blew warm air into her slim hands. She wore a matching knit hat upon her head, covering her blond wig. The bloat from the drugs was gone, leaving Julie very underweight and frail.

"Julie, you're acting crazy," Shawn said to her. He was not in the mood for another of Julie's sad tirades.

"No, Shawn, I *heard* those two talking about me."

"Those girls aren't worth paying attention to," Shawn reasoned. He kicked away a stone and rose to his feet.

"Shawn, don't patronize me. You're not the one with no hair and looking like a freak." Julie looked up at him, her thin face red with hurt and anger.

"Look…" Shawn was ill equipped to handle these emotions. His only defense was avoidance. "Lunch hour is over, Julie, and I have to go back to science class. Come on." He reached out his hand to help her off the steps.

"I'm not going back in there," she said, turning away from his outstretched hand.

"Julie, you can't stay out here. It's too cold. You'll get sick. Come on."

She turned to him and managed a cruel smile. "Did you forget, Shawn? I'm sick already. Didn't you hear Mara? 'Oh, Gawd, she looks terrible. I think she's going to die!' I heard her, Shawn. And you know? She's fucking right!"

"Well, you're not going to do it right now, so come on, let's go in," Shawn said.

Shawn managed to pull Julie back into the school before running off to his class. Julie went to the nurse's office and had her mother pick her up. She was done with school.

Once again, Children's Memorial Hospital became home.

Julie found herself alone one day when she absolutely could not wait until help came to visit the bathroom. So she sat up, moved her legs to the floor, and tried to stand. Her legs, however, would not move, and down she fell. Sprawled on the cold hospital floor, tears running down her face, Julie cried out for help.

Presently, Lori ran into her daughter's hospital room and helped Julie get up.

"Why didn't you wait for help?" Lori asked, alarmed at finding her daughter in such a state.

Julie's sad, tired eyes looked at her mother and Julie said, "Mom, I don't want to live like this. I can't even walk anymore."

Lori remained silent as she helped her daughter onto the toilet seat.

The new experimental treatment had not only exhausted Julie, but it had affected her bones, causing her to be in constant pain and unable to walk. Lori couldn't watch her pale, emaciated body or listen to her daughter's cries any longer. After Lori had Julie back under the covers and dozing, she ran out of the hospital room and paged Dr. Bloom.

Dr. Bloom agreed to meet Lori and Jerry in his hospital office later that afternoon.

Julie's mother and father sat in the doctor's office waiting to hear their most dreaded fear.

"As you know, we have not been able to achieve a remission for the last five months, even with the new experimental drugs, and her counts are too low to try anything else," Dr. Bloom said.

Tears spilled out of Lori's eyes, but her voice was resolute. "We cannot continue to torture my daughter. How much time do we have left?" Lori asked. She had been dreading this conversation, but she knew it was coming.

"I'm not God, but from experience, maybe six weeks," Dr. Bloom replied.

Lori looked at Jerry, who had refused to look up or comment.

"Dr. Bloom," Lori asked, sniffling, "how can we make her comfortable?"

"We'll stop the chemo, give her cortisone, pain medication, and blood transfusions, and I think you should take her home and enjoy the rest of the summer," Dr. Bloom said.

It would take almost two weeks before the effects of the experimental drug wore off and Julie would be able to spend the summer at home. Her daughter hadn't asked why they had stopped treatment, and Lori couldn't manage to talk to her about it. Julie didn't need to talk about it; she already knew.

During a visit from Dr. Feinberg, Julie asked, "Dr. Feinberg, I haven't seen Jeff here lately. Is he cured? Did Jeff get to go home?"

Dr. Feinberg put down her charts and sat down next to Julie on her bed.

"Julie, Jeff died six months ago," the doctor said softly. "That child was something else. He could organize the whole floor, and what a fighter. Just like you are." She smiled warmly at Julie and stroked her shoulder.

Julie, frail, weak, her head covered with a colorful bandana, managed a weak smile and said, "I guess I will see him soon."

Lori just stood in the doorway of the hospital room, shaking her head. No tears came this time. She just stood in awe of her daughter's strength and courage.

Dr. Feinberg had told her to rest for her upcoming trip home before leaving for her rounds. Julie waited until her door was closed, then covering her head with the pillow to hide her tears from her mother, Julie thought, *Death, take me too. I've had enough of needles, tests, nausea, diarrhea, and unbearable pain that even morphine can't stop.* She smiled as she closed her eyes and dreamed of floating with Jeff over white, soft, fluffy clouds—the clouds she saw from her window seat while on her plane ride to Israel.

Lori was busy preparing the house for the Labor Day company while Julie was upstairs sleeping. Lori had decided to try to have a party with close friends and family, even though Jerry was not in favor of it. Now she realized Jerry was right when he told her to order out. She sat down on the kitchen stool and looked around at the mess she had made: her white cabinets had stains of chocolate, her new stainless steel stove had set off the fire alarm because of spills, and her blue tiled floors were full of cookie crumbs from the burnt trays of sweets. She emptied the remnants of black and white cookies into the garbage can. Soon the flood of tears came, and Lori prayed in earnest for them to give her some relief. The phone rang, but she was in no shape to answer it.

Barry raced out of his room. It was almost two o'clock, and he was late for the final baseball game of the summer. Not watching where he was going, he almost ran into Julie, who had just walked out of her room.

"Barry, I need to talk to you," Julie said, quietly.

"Can it wait until later?" Barry asked. "I have a game now."

"No, Barry, my time is running out," Julie said. "Please come into my room."

Barry followed Julie into her room. He could barely move there. She had received so many gifts that it looked like a warehouse of stuffed animals, clothes, knickknacks, books, videos, posters, etc.

"Barry, I want you to have all my things," Julie said.

Barry wished to lighten the mood. He couldn't bear to think of losing his sister. "Julie, what am I supposed to do with your clothes and dolls?" he asked. "You keep them."

"You're not listening to me," she said. "I'm seventeen, and I am dying! I'm dying!" Julie stood in a pair of pajamas with pink and red hearts all over them. They were a gift from Adele and Sasha. On her head, she wore a pink bandana.

"I'll get Mom," Barry answered as he went for the door.

"Stop," Julie pleaded, extending her thin arm. "I'm not dying *today*, Barry. I'm still fighting. Anyway, I haven't picked the time yet. I want to go out with a bang, on a date everyone will remember. Maybe next July fourth."

"Julie, you're scaring me," Barry said, standing frozen to the floor.

She answered, "When I do die, take my stuff to Children's or burn it. Promise?"

Julie looked at her fourteen-year-old brother and smiled.

Barry held his gaze from his sister to keep her from knowing how scared he felt. Julie knew anyway.

"It's okay, Barry, I'm teasing," Julie said. "You can go. I'm tired. I hope your team wins." Julie made her way to her bed and settled in with a paperback book lying nearby.

"Okay. See ya later, Julie," Barry said as he slowly left the room. He was no longer in a hurry to get to his game. He thought about the times before she was sick, when Julie used to tease him continually and then hug him before saying she was sorry, just like today. He knew things weren't going well; Mom was crying all the time and only talking to Adele, and Dad was drinking more. What would he do if his sister really died?

Julie nestled deeper into bed and closed her paperback book. She thought she better get some rest. The next day, Labor Day, was going to be her going-out party.

Julie later woke up with excruciating head pain, and the Labor Day party had to be moved to Children's Memorial Hospital. Tests at the hospital revealed that her bone marrow and spinal column were full of blast cells. Outside of pain relief, there was little left to do. Even the blood transfusions were not holding. After several days of sitting next to her daughter's bed and watching her in a deep, drug-induced sleep, Lori decided to spend a day at home.

Upon entering her house, Lori felt like a stranger and wondered why she even came home. She walked over to the kitchen window.

Looking out the window, Lori dimly noted her surroundings. The huge old trees of Northfield produced a scenic fall as their leaves were just turning. How pretty the burning bushes looked against the yellow, brown, and green elms, oaks, and maples. The bright red cardinals and the screeching blue jays were scavenging the ground for seeds. Lori felt guilty. She knew she must go shopping for seeds. Julie, sick as hell, still reminded her to feed the birds. Would she ever get home to see them? She was trying to spend a day away from the hospital to give Jerry and Barry some of her time, but it was hard to do; her mind was on Julie the entire time.

She looked at the pile of mail on the desk and the list of phone calls to be returned. There were probably bills to be paid and well-meaning friends to call, but her heart and soul were still in the hospital, so she picked up her purse and keys, threw on her coat, and left for the hospital. Upon entering Julie's room, she was surprised to see Julie had a visitor.

"Josh, what are you doing here?" Lori asked.

Julie's face lit up as she answered from her hospital bed, "Mom, Josh brought me an autographed picture of Bruce Springsteen. I'm so excited!"

Lori was too stunned to see her old boyfriend at her daughter's bedside to answer.

After admiring the picture, Lori walked Josh out of the room and asked, "How did you find out about Julie's relapse?"

"The answers are Adele and with great difficulty," Josh replied. "When you didn't answer my many calls, I contacted Adele. She reluctantly told me what was going on."

She thought to herself, *Of course I didn't answer you. You disappeared for almost a year. Why am I even thinking about this? Nothing matters anymore, just Julie. Okay, cool it.* This was the first day in a week that Julie looked alive and happy.

"During the last year, since I've seen you, my life has fallen apart," Lori said. "How did you ever get an autographed picture of Bruce Springsteen?"

"Remember the fun we had at the Fickle Pickle, smoking, drinking, and sitting on pillows while we listened to folk singers?" Josh asked.

"Of course I do. We thought we were so cool back in the sixties. What does that have to do with Bruce Springsteen?" Lori asked.

"The owner's son is now a producer of rock concerts," Josh explained. "He was able to get the signed picture for me."

"You still keep in contact with Chris?" Lori asked. "That was so nice of both of you. Please thank him for me. Did you see how her face lit up?"

"Lori, could you leave Julie for a while and have some lunch with me?" Josh asked. "I've missed you."

Lori looked up into his beautiful blue eyes and smiled.

"Josh, I guess it was never meant to be," Lori said. "My life now belongs to Julie and my family. Thank you for making her so happy. Bruce Springsteen is her favorite entertainer."

"If I can help in anyway—money, doctors, a shoulder—please call me," Josh said as he leaned over and gave Lori a kiss on the cheek. Then he went back into the room to say goodbye to Julie.

Lori's eyes followed Josh as he walked out of her life again. A smile formed on her face; this time she was the one to tell him to leave. She had loved him once, but that was a long time ago in a different lifetime. She walked back into her daughter's hospital room.

When Josh left, Julie said, "Mom, he told me he was a friend of yours from high school. He is so nice. I really like him."

"So do I," Lori answered.

Needing a break after watching Julie sleep for the previous two hours, Lori made her way to the hospital cafeteria for some dinner. She sat at the table staring at the plate of processed turkey, corn, and boiled potatoes. How she hated hospital food. Finally, she emptied the tray in the garbage and slowly made it back up to Julie's room. Upon reentering the room, she was surprised to see her in-laws, Jack and Shelly, with Jerry.

"Mom and Dad wanted to visit, so I brought them with," Jerry said. He delivered a look of sadness and defeat; he had no fight left in him when it came to the feud between his wife and his mother.

Though Julie was propped up in bed to a sitting position and her face had a bright smile, Lori knew that she was still in major pain. Julie perked up and stopped eating the chicken soup Shelly was feeding her. "Mom, look what Grandma and Grandpa brought me," Julie Said

In her hands were a Chicago White Sox baseball cap and a gold Star of David hanging off a delicate gold chain.

“Nice,” Lori said. “Put them on, and I will take your picture with Grandma and Grandpa.” She had wanted to take some pictures because she knew they were getting close to the end of the line, but Julie had resisted because she didn’t look good.

Lori found that she couldn’t hold the camera steady, so she had Jerry take the picture.

When they were leaving, Shelly had tears in her eyes as she said, “We are praying for her.”

Lori almost gave Shelly a heart attack when she thanked her with a kiss. It occurred to Lori that her in-laws were losing a grandchild too. She really was looking for her own mother, who couldn’t come to help. In Palm Beach, Lori’s dad was dying of lung cancer, and she felt terrible because she couldn’t be there to say goodbye to him or to help her mother. Lil had phoned earlier to tell Lori that her father was getting bad. The year 1991 was becoming the worst year of Lori’s life, a year where she would lose both her father and her daughter.

As Lori walked her in-laws out of Julie’s room, Jerry asked, “Are you staying here tonight too?”

“Of course I am,” Lori said.

“Just asking,” Jerry said. “Barry hasn't seen you in days.”

"Soon he will have too much of me," she answered.

Lori sat back in the big blue chair in her daughter’s hospital room deep in thought. The summer was passing into the fall. Except for the changing colors of the leaves, it made no difference to her. This room and the hospital had unfortunately become home for Julie and her. How her priorities had changed in a short time.

In the bed next to her lay a skinny, pale, bald, sick image of her once big, beautiful, outgoing daughter. Those sky blue eyes that once sparkled with excitement were now narrow and dull looking, acknowledging the pain and detachment from this world she was experiencing. Clumps of thick, curly blond hair laid on her pillow every day, making her really look like a cancer patient.

So far, nothing had been able to clear her of those awful cancer cells. Over three years, she had relapsed three times, and the doctors managed to get her back in remission each time. This time, they gave them no hope.

Their favorite nurse, Barbara, came into the room and said, "Lori, there is a phone call for you at the nurse's station."

Lori picked up the phone expecting to hear Adele or another friend asking about Julie. Instead, Jerry was on the phone.

"Lori, we had a car accident and are at Northwestern Hospital," Jerry said. "Don't panic, we are all right."

Confused, she asked, "Who are you with, and what are you talking about?"

"Did you forget that I took the day off and went to the Cubs game with Barry?" Jerry replied.

She couldn't tell him that while she was with Julie in the hospital, the outside world disappeared. Then she remembered, yes, he was trying to do things with Barry lately. Suddenly, the words car accident registered, and Lori started to panic.

"Is Barry hurt?" Lori asked.

"He's bruised badly, and he has a broken arm," Jerry said. "They are keeping him overnight."

"Jerry, were you drinking?" she asked.

"You always think the worst of me," Jerry said. "I only had one beer. We were hit from the side and spun around in traffic. We are lucky to be alive." With that said, he hung up.

Lori felt guilty, as she never even asked about him. At the nurse's station, she asked Kathy to keep an eye on Julie. Lori grabbed her coat and caught a cab to Northwestern Hospital. It dawned on her that while she had been crying about her dying daughter, she almost lost the healthy members of her family. There are no guarantees in life and no rhyme or reason for what happens.

Jerry was shaken but otherwise fine, and Barry recovered, though he had to wear a cast for six weeks, ruining the baseball season for him. Julie was not as lucky.

For the next week, neither Julie nor Lori left the hospital. Jerry came almost every night, and Adele came several afternoons. Barry was back at school, so he only came down on the weekends. The visitors came mainly for Lori. Julie was unresponsive and semi-comatose most of the time. She never even woke up enough to talk to Shawn and Sasha.

Fullerton, the main street in the Chicago neighborhood, was busy with cars zooming by from both directions. Two young girls, probably around twelve-years-old, dressed in tight short jeans and halter tops, crossed the street with no heed to the traffic. Lori watched as they dared the cars to hit them. The old teacher in her wanted to discipline them, but that part of her no longer functioned.

The burst of yellow, red, and brown leaves falling from the trees spoke of life continuing in its cycle.

The sun set across the sky like an angry orange ball, as it did every day of the last four years. The sun and Lori were angry all the time, but it was their secret. On the outside they were stoic and beautiful.

Lori stood in the doorway, half in and half out, until a passerby tried to enter. Annoyed, the woman asked, "In or out?" Reluctantly, she went back into Children's Memorial Hospital moving slowly down the hall to the elevator. Hope had disappeared, and despair and fear had settled in her heart.

She exited the elevator on floor number three, slowly walking down the hall to the last treatment room in the corridor. She didn't need to ask Barbara, Julie's favorite nurse, anything about her daughter's condition.

In the depths of her soul, Lori knew her four-year battle with leukemia would soon be over and she would go home alone without her first born.

When Lori looked into Barbara's eyes, she saw the words she dreaded to hear.

"Is my daughter still alive?" Lori whispered.

"Yes… but not for long," Barbara said as she touched Lori's shoulder in a gesture of comfort. "You better call family members."

"How soon?" Lori asked with terror in her eyes.

Barbara answered, "Her breathing has become increasingly shallow. Maybe a day at the most."

For days, Lori had been sitting next to a daughter who could hardly talk or move, a daughter who was quickly slipping away to the other side. Her seventeen-year-old child was dying, and there was nothing she could do about it. She was a mother who could not protect her child.

Lori was desolate as she made the necessary calls to her immediate family. They needed to say good-bye, and she desperately needed their help to cope and to plan a funeral for her seventeen-year-old daughter. She glanced at the clock; it was five in the morning. She could get Jerry and Barry before they left for work and school. She would wait an hour before calling Adele, and her mother.

Her hands shook as she dialed Florida. "Mama," she cried, "My daughter is dying and I desperately need you to be here with me."

The phone was silent for a few seconds. Then Lil answered, "Lori, I'm very sorry to hear that, but you know I can't leave your father now."

"Mama, he has a caregiver," Lori said. "I need you."

"I'm sorry Lori," Lil said. "I can't help you."

Lori dropped the phone on the floor and ran down the hall to the women's restroom, where she released a flood of tears. Oh, how she missed her father. He had been deteriorating from ALS for the last six years. She knew he would have been with her if he was well. The worst part was he had lost his voice and couldn't talk to her. Why had she expected her mother to come through now, when she had never been there before? *Lori Ann, stop trying to reach her. Your mother hates you, and she will never be there for you. Get that through your head already.*

Julie died later that day, September 11, 1991, with family, nurses, and friends surrounding her. As she took her last breath, Lori stood on one side of her, held her hand tightly, kissed her goodbye, and whispered, "I love you," while Jerry stood on the other side of her bed with tears flowing down his face. A high-pitched scream then echoed from Lori's throat as her husband led her out of the room.

September 11 would be a date Lori would never forget. Barry was surprised. He had trusted his sister to last until July 4th. He remembered her words, *"I'm going to die on a date with a big blast, one that everyone remembers."* Her words made no sense.

Adele tried to hold Lori, but she pulled away, shaking her head and crying, "No, no, no!"

Jim put his arm around Barry and walked him out of the room, while Jerry just sat very still. He had no comfort to offer his wife. He felt very cold and numb.

Adele and Jim came back to the house with them. Adele made coffee and sat down by the phone to make the necessary phone calls to the rabbi, the funeral house, family, and friends, while Lori took a sleeping pill and disappeared into her room.

Somehow, Lori made it to the rabbi's study with her husband and son. When it was time to pick out a casket, Barry pulled out a folded piece of paper from his jeans pocket.

"Julie gave this to me on Labor Day," Barry explained. "It's kind of a list of instructions. And… a goodbye note." Barry handed the folded piece to his father and pulled out a tissue to wipe his tear-stained face.

Jerry took the paper from his son's hand, and together Lori and Jerry read their daughter's last request.

"Hi, folks. Well, this is a difficult letter to write, but I wanted to make sure my plans were down on paper. Hopefully, this will make things easier for you. Please bury me in a nice blue casket with my favorite stuffed animal, Eck-Eck, the monkey. Give all my stuff to the children at the hospital, and remember that I loved life and I enjoyed my years here. I love you always, Julie."

"She was more realistic than any of us. When I think of her in the ground, I'll see a frightened little monkey instead," Lori said in between her tears, though she knew she would see her daughter there and everywhere.

Lil received word that her granddaughter Julie had died. She sat on the bay window seat of her large immaculate bedroom with the phone on her lap, looking out the window, her head straight and high. She sighed, and a grimace played across her mouth as she spoke quietly to no one, "Keep watch over Julie, my Joseph. Too young…" Lil hung her head momentarily and uttered a prayer for the dead.

***

The funeral was held in the temple and the burial at Shalom Cemetery in Palatine. For Lori, most of the day was a blank. If it weren't for Barry standing next to her in the temple, she wouldn't have known who the large group of teenagers were. The only person she really remembered seeing at the funeral was Shawn. It was the first time she ever saw a teenage boy cry openly. He knew her daughter in a different way than she did, sticking by her through it all, while so many of her friends had disappeared into their own young world. Three and a half years is a long time to be supportive.

Jerry had been the one to buy grave sites at Shalom. He looked around at the new cemetery with its beautiful green lawns, manicured shrubs and trees, and nice benches and was pleased with his choice.

Jim nudged him, and he realized they had come to the part of the mourner's prayer. Jerry joined in the prayer as Lori walked up and joined him at his side.

Adele and Carol took care of everything at the house. The family officially sat shiva for three days, but family and friends stayed around through the weekend. Lori remembered loads of people—young and old, some friends and some strangers from Julie's school and doctors and staff from the hospital, and food; salads, pastries, deli trays, casseroles, cakes, fruit trays, etc. arrived at the house throughout the shiva and into the week. Later when Lori looked over the memorial book she noted that some friends from days before Julie was diagnosed had disappeared. When one or two of the missing friends would later tell her that they didn't know what to do or say, she would silently walk away from them.

Days after the funeral, Jerry and Barry went back to work and school. Lori hid in her bedroom, shutting out the nightmare with sleeping pills and pain pills. Adele was the only one she was willing to talk to, because she let Lori wallow in self-pity, never coming up with pat meaningless words. Adele just listened. Lori never understood why friends called and asked, "How are you?" What could they be thinking? Her world had crumbled, and she wanted to answer, "I wish I was dead, that is how I'm feeling!" Instead, she gave the expected answer, "Fine, thank you. Goodbye," and went back to bed. As the days passed, she just refused to answer the phone or even leave her bedroom.

Chapter Twenty-One

Two months after the funeral, Lori was fast asleep, dreaming her dad and Julie were floating together on a cloud, when she was abruptly woken up by Jerry.

"Honey, your mother's on the phone," he said.

"My dad is dead," she said to Jerry before even taking the phone.

Jerry watched her take the phone and talk to her mother. When she hung up, he asked, "Should I book flights to West Palm Beach?"

"No," Lori said as she put the phone back in the cradle and lay back down in the bed, closing her eyes.

"No?" Jerry asked. "Lori, you're not going to your dad's funeral?"

"I've already said goodbye to him." Lori's response was curt, her voice wooden.

"Lori, what about your mother?" Jerry asked.

Lori did not answer; she merely turned away from Jerry and put a pillow over her head. She had never told Jerry about her plea to her mother before Julie died.

Jerry left the room confused. He knew she was depressed, and she had problems with her mother, but…He went downstairs and poured himself a nice stiff gin and tonic, then another. Then Jerry called his mother.

About a month after her father died, Jerry walked into their bedroom, where Lori spent most of her days and evenings, with a certified letter. He walked over to the window and drew open the curtains to let the early evening light into the room.

"Lori, this came for you," Jerry said. He stood by the bed, the letter in his outstretched hand.

"I don't want it." Lori's voice came from deep beneath feather pillows and a mound of blankets.

"You don't even know what it is," Jerry said.

"I don't want it," Lori repeated from somewhere beneath the blankets.

Jerry impatiently opened the letter, handed it to her, and said, "You better look at it. It's about your dad."

Lori slowly sat up and read the letter from someone named Charlie Weaver. She looked at Jerry. "A Charlie Weaver who worked with my dad wrote about how much he admired my dad, and he enclosed information about a government insurance policy," Lori said. "There is the name of some lawyer I should call." Lori let the letter slip from her hands as she resumed her supine position, pulling the disheveled blankets around her.

"Call him, Lori," Jerry directed. "We can use the money."

"Leave me alone, Jerry," Lori mumbled. "I'm not ready to do anything."

Jerry retrieved the letter, folded it, and placed the letter in her nightstand and left the room.

The name Charlie rang a bell, but Lori did not have the energy or the will to deal with it. She had lost her daughter and her father. Lori didn't feel much like breathing right now, but her breaths kept coming, with no way to stop them. She just lay there, allowing dark and sad thoughts to roam around in her head until they were overcome by merciful sleep.

One day, Lori awoke to a loud commotion coming from somewhere downstairs. Someone was arguing with Jerry. Their voices carried up the steps and through the closed bedroom door. She turned over, put her pillow over her head, and tried to fall back to sleep. She made a mental note to purchase stronger sleeping pills.

Slowly, Lori began making out words that she heard. "...out of that bed. It's enough, already." The voice, shrill and commanding, got closer. "You've been hiding for four months." The bedroom door swung open. "You need to start taking care of your family!"

Lori tried gathering her bearings. She shook her head and opened her eyes to find Shelly standing over her bed, yelling, her face contorting with anger. Lori sat mute and glared at her mother-in-law, who stood pointing accusatorily at her.

"Now, come on, that's enough now!" Shelly yelled. "Get out of that bed and start taking care of yourself. You have a family to think about! You can't just think about *yourself*!"

Lori noted that Jerry was standing behind his mother, looking at Lori with a sad expression.

"Did you bring her here?" Lori asked her husband, ignoring Shelly's tirade.

Jerry shook his head.

Lori looked back at Shelly, her histrionics in full swing, and snapped. She rose to her knees on the bed and screamed, "Get her out of here, Jerry! I never want to see her again."

As Jerry pushed his mother out of the bedroom, Lori, through her hysteria, heard her say, "It's five months. Jerry, you get her up. She isn't the first person who has lost a child. I had a stillborn after Eileen. That selfish wife of yours needs to be more responsible..."

Lori jumped out of bed, locked her bedroom door, and collapsed onto the floor in tears. "Oh, how I hate that woman!" Lori yelled aloud. She sobbed until her head throbbed. A migraine took over. When the pounding, pressure, and razor-sharp pain attacked, nothing could move her out of her dark bedroom. She picked herself off the floor and shuffled to the bathroom for the little white pill that would finally knock her out and shut out the world. Dr. Reeder suggested her migraines were her body's way of weeping, so he gave her a large supply of pain pills, knowing Lori was in a bad state.

As far as Lori was concerned, anything that kept her from thinking was good.

A day or two later, Lori rolled over, picked up her head, looked at the bright neon lights on the digital clock, and read it was a little after ten. Someone had pulled back the curtains; perhaps she did it herself during the night? She couldn't remember. A burst of pure sunlight poured through the window, illuminating the room. *Morning*, she thought. She stumbled to the bathroom, emptied her bladder, and brushed her teeth, carefully avoiding the mirror. The pain and sleeping pills sat untouched upon the counter. In the shower, she actually enjoyed the downpour of cool water on her skin. She later stood before the closet, facing her clothes. *Maybe going out alone is a bad idea.* Then she thought about Shelly's outburst and decided to give it a try.

She recalled that Adele had visited sometime yesterday and made a point of reminding her that today was Barry's birthday. She did not remember unlocking the bedroom door to allow Adele access to her sanctuary, but she must have. *It was Adele who came in and pulled back the curtains,* Lori thought, smiling weakly. *She always knows best.* Lori decided she would go to the mall and buy Barry a present. Barry needed a mother. There was nothing she could do for Julie any longer.

It seemed like an eternity before she made it out of the front door. Outside, she stood frozen. Should she try to drive? Since Julie's death, making decisions was almost impossible. She started to walk towards the train station, taking note that it was only a short ride on the train, and then she could take a cab to the Northbrook Court shopping mall.

Lori was so proud of herself. She had managed to get to the mall to buy Barry a Polo shirt, to sit down and drink coffee, and to even answer hello to a young girl who seemed to recognize her.

Getting home proved to be more difficult. Taking a cab to the train station and entering the train was all she remembered until some man started to shake her shoulder. She looked up with a puzzled expression as the uniformed, husky man said, "Lady, wake up. We are at the end of the line. You have to get off the train."

"Who are you?" Lori asked, bewildered. She looked around. The train car was empty.

"The train conductor," he said.

"Where am I?" Lori asked.

"You are in Fox Lake, the end of the train line," he replied as he handed Lori a package wrapped in blue paper and a white bow and tried to escort her off the train.

Lori asked, "What's this?" She rose from her seat and glanced down at the wrapped box.

"You dropped it while you were asleep, I guess," he explained. "Isn't this yours?"

Lori looked down at the package again and nodded and mumbled.

"Pardon me, Ma'am?" he asked.

"Umm… nothing. Why am I here?" Lori clutched the package to her chest, gathered her purse, and looked around. Nothing was familiar. Tiny alarms began going off in her head.

"What stop did you want? he asked, urging her off the train by guiding her by the arm.

Lori's lips began to tremble and she couldn't breathe. Finally, she said, "I want to go home."

The conductor looked around for some help. Obviously, he had a nut case here, and he didn't have the time to take care of her. He left her and walked over to the cabstand.

Lori was scared. She had no idea where she was or why she was there. Nothing looked familiar. Across from the station was a car agency, and in front of it were some old buildings. Her head was pounding, her throat was dry, and she felt an anxiety attack coming on. Lori wrung her hands, trying to steady her frayed nerves.

Another man in a uniform came by and asked, "Do you need a cab?"

"Yes, oh, yes, please!" Lori cried. "Please… take me home."

"Where do you live?" he asked.

"Northfield," Lori answered as she crawled into the cab.

An hour later, Lori walked into her house, beating Barry by ten minutes. She tried to put her misadventure behind her, pulling herself together enough to hand Barry the package, give him a kiss, and say, "Happy Birthday, Barry."

The episode that was to mark the return to normal life put Lori back in bed with her pain pills and sleeping pills, where she stayed until Adele came over, one week later.

Adele walked into the dark, stuffy bedroom. Sniffing the stale air, she made a face and moved quickly to the window, pulled back the curtains, and raised the window to let in the afternoon sun and a cool breeze. Adele realized she had to do something, so she began picking up the clothes that lay about the carpeted floor. She walked over to Lori's walk-in closet and stuffed the clothes into a small hamper that sat tucked in a corner of the closet.

Turning and staring at the inert body on the bed for a few moments, she crossed her thin arms across her chest and in a soft but firm voice she said, "Lori, I love you and… this is hard for me to say. Shelly has no tact whatsoever, but she is right. You have a son who is trying *so hard* to keep his life on a normal keel while he is worried that he is losing a mother too. Let's get you out of that bathrobe, and let's go for lunch."

Slowly sitting up in bed, Lori turned her head toward the now opened drapes. Everything outside was green. The clock radio on her nightstand read 1:15. Since it was light out, she guessed it was the afternoon. The day and the date still eluded her. How long had she retreated after Barry's birthday? Adele resumed picking up clothes, cups, and papers. This was not her normal neat room. Lori maneuvered to the bathroom.

Lori looked at herself in the mirror. The image was of someone she didn't recognize. Her face was thinner and pale, her thick black hair was a mess, her green eyes were puffy from crying, and there were deep lines surrounding her mouth. She looked down and noted that her nails were dirty and chipped. Somewhere in her mind she knew she shouldn't look this way, never looked this way before, but she did not care. She felt numb.

She let Adele lead her into the shower. Then she allowed Adele to pick out clothes and put her together, lead her into her car, out of her car, and onto Northfield's main shopping street, like a puppy on a leash.

"Slow down, Adele," Lori said.

"What's wrong?" Adele asked.

"I don't know," Lori replied. "I just feel like I have to concentrate on every step… right foot, left foot, curb, step up, and step down. Like a slow motion movie."

"Let's stop for lunch," Adele suggested, sensing her friend wasn't doing well.

They went into the closest restaurant and sat down.

Adele asked Lori, "Have you even tried to get out of the house in these last months? This is the first time you have gone anywhere with me."

For some reason, Lori refused to tell Adele about her train adventure, but she did mention she managed to buy something for Barry's birthday. When Adele looked doubtful, Lori mentioned a trip she tried to take a few weeks earlier.

"I tried to go to the grocery store," Lori explained. "I walked around the store throwing things into the cart. When I got to the cookie aisle, I looked at Julie's favorite chocolate chip cookies and started to cry. I left the cart in the middle of the aisle and ran out. The drive home was the same mile I have traveled for years, but I was lost for twenty minutes."

The waitress brought menus, and Adele ordered a Caesar salad. Lori scanned the menu, looked up at the waitress, and said, "Just coffee."

Adele leaned over the table, took hold of both of Lori's arms, looked into her sad face, and said, "Honey, you had the worst loss anyone can endure. It won't be easy. You, Barry, and Jerry need professional help. My friend Bobbi is a wonderful therapist specializing in this area. I will make an appointment for you."

"I guess I am getting too much for you to handle too," Lori mused.

"No, Lori," Adele responded. "I will always be there for you, but you need more help than I can give you."

Adele took Lori home and then called her friend Bobbi Weissman, a grief therapist. Two days later, Adele picked up Lori and drove her to the therapist's office in Highland Park, a few miles from Northfield. She planned to pick Lori up from the office about an hour later.

Lori walked into a warm and cozy room. She sat on an overstuffed maroon sofa with an abundance of pillows, while Bobbi sat next to her on a padded, straight-backed, blue chair. Tea, coffee, and cookies sat on an adjacent marble table. Bobbi was in her forties, about five feet tall, with short straight brown hair, and she was dressed in jeans and a soft navy sweater.

Lori was comfortable with her immediately. She had a steady, even-toned voice and soft, compassionate brown eyes. In their first session, Lori talked a little and cried a lot. She began seeing Bobbi twice a week.

"I only want to see and deal with the friends and family that have shared the four years of pain and joy," Lori told her during one session.

"I want to scream every time a person asks me how I am. After being hit by a ton of bricks, how *should* I be?"

Bobbi took off her large, black-rimmed glasses, leaned in towards Lori, looked directly into her eyes, and said, "I am a therapist, and I can't possibly imagine what you are going through."

"Do you have kids?" Lori asked.

"Yes, two boys, six and nine," Bobbi said and quickly continued on, as she couldn't possibly imagine losing them. "With other people, do what makes you feel comfortable. Most acquaintances will be reluctant to go near you, because they don't know what to say. They are horrified at the death of a child."

"Yes, neighbors avoided me like the plague," Lori said. "It seemed like only little kids and dogs talked to me, and when I walked into a room full of people, all conversation stopped."

Bobbi put her glasses back on and leaned forward, tenderly touching Lori's hand. "The hurt and pain you are feeling can be compared to a wound," Bobbi explained. "It's open and raw in the beginning. The wound will heal slowly, but the scar will stay forever. Feeling numb, leaving shopping carts, crying, forgetting things, those are all part of your depression. It will take time."

Adele picked her up after her first four sessions. Following Lori's lead, she refrained from asking questions until she couldn't keep quiet any longer.

"Okay, how is the therapy going?" she cautiously asked.

"Good, you were right," Lori said. "I do need to talk to a professional, besides my friends. This one is too hard to tackle alone."

Adele smiled. She was relieved her friend was getting the help she so desperately needed.

"Lori, you *need* to go shopping," Adele noted. "Your clothes are falling off of you, your hair needs styling and coloring, and you need a manicure." Adele put her hands on Lori's shoulders, smiled, and said, "That's therapy too, you know!"

Lori actually started to laugh. For the first time in her life, she had lost weight without trying. Amazing what pain and depression can do to you. She did manage to buy a few things at Pizzazz, a small boutique owned by their friend Fern. When Fern and Adele brought out five blue outfits, even Lori had to relent and try them on.

Next, under protest, Adele walked her into Chez Paul. Upon their arrival, Paul, her gorgeous gay hair stylist, ran over and hugged Lori.

"Lori, I haven't seen you in *years*!" Paul enthused. "I am so sorry about your daughter. She was a great kid. A natural blonde." Paul pulled away from their embrace, and he took a good look at Lori. "My God, your hair has no shape, and it desperately needs color. Don't worry, I will fix you up, good as new."

"You can shape it, Paul, but the gray stays. It is my badge of…" She couldn't finish the sentence as tears streamed down her face, and she collapsed onto Paul's shoulder. He consoled her the only way he knew how: by giving her a big hug, by styling her hair, and putting make-up on her face.

He stood back, handing Lori the mirror, and asked, "Now, don't you feel better? You look gorgeous. Remember, we never say *gray*. The color of your hair is rich, lustrous, shining silver. The salt-and-pepper looks good on you," he said encouragingly. "Very sophisticated."

Lori took the mirror from Paul and scrutinized her reflection. *I look older*, she thought. The majority of her hair still shone black and luxuriant. The thin ribbons of gray throughout had a rich luster she liked. It reminded Lori of what silver might have looked like embedded deep in the earth. Lori looked deeper and noted tiny lines surrounding her bright green eyes. *These eyes cry every night,* she said to herself, quoting a popular song of days gone by. She had to admit, she did look older, and her eyes held a sadness she was not sure would ever fade. Who could come out the other end of such loss unscathed? As a whole, the chin-length bob cut was sophisticated, polished, and Lori liked the effect it had on her. Her heart felt lighter.

She spoke silently to Julie, "I hope you like the new look, kiddo."

Lori smiled as she thanked Paul. Before Adele drove Lori home, she told Adele, "It does feel good to get out of the house. Thank you for dragging me out and making me live again. I couldn't do it without you."

Adele hugged her and watched her as she walked up to her door, then drove away.

Jerry greeted Lori at the door and said, "I was worried about you. Hey, you look great. Glad to see you back." Jerry smiled warmly at his wife and moved in and embraced her.

"I'm working on it," Lori answered, hugging her husband, while thinking, *I look better, but I feel like a hollow shell. I just don't know if I'll ever be the same again.*

"Welcome back, honey," Jerry said softly.

"What have you been doing while I was out of it? Who has been paying the bills and taking care of the house?" Lori asked Jerry.

While Julie was sick, Lori did those jobs like a robot, getting very little sleep, but once Julie died, she quit everything.

The warmth Jerry had just felt for his wife chilled a bit, and he stepped back from her, replying, "Lori, I'm not an imbecile. I took over the bills, and my mom helped with the house. Though, at first, the bank sent back things I signed. You must have been signing my name for years."

She laughed at the bank story and cringed at the thought of Shelly taking care of her house.

The sound of her laughter brought hope to Jerry, hope that Lori was truly on the mend.

"I will try to take back my jobs now. Thanks for being there," Lori replied.

That night, Jerry assumed she was ready for everything. She tried to accept his advances, as he was being tender and thoughtful, but she still needed some time to release her emotions. Rejected, Jerry pulled away from his wife, rolled out of bed, and walked down the stairs. Lori craned her neck to listen and frowned as she recognized the sounds of Jerry fixing himself a drink at the living room bar. Her heart sank anew as she realized he hadn't given up his drinking at all, just slowed down for Julie. The day was overwhelming. She dropped back down on her bed and fell right to sleep with no help from pills.

Jerry turned the television on low, sat down on the sofa, and slowly drank his gin and tonic. He thought, *Okay, how long does she expect me to go without sex? It's been almost a year.* He took a swig from his drink and swirled the glass, looking intently at the ice cubes within. *At least she is getting out and starting to act somewhat normal.*

Lori's ability to concentrate was gone. As her therapist had explained, she had shut down part of her mind. Maybe that was why she could sit for hours in the house just staring off into space. Her thoughts ebbed and flowed. Wryly, she thought that maybe it was time to find a guru to help her learn to meditate. Einstein insisted that God doesn't play dice with the world. Maybe Julie was part of a master plan. What kind of a plan could there be where one part dictates a young woman must die? Lori desperately wished she could believe in something. Her father's family's religious beliefs were no help now. She refused to talk to the rabbi. God had become her enemy when he took her young daughter. She could take Jerry's approach and drown herself in alcohol. Obviously, his hiatus from drinking during Julie's illness was over. Why should she stay sober and bear the brunt of his outbursts?

At one of their sessions, Bobbi asked, "How is Barry doing? Was it hard for him to go back to school? High school kids can be insensitive."

"I don't know," Lori replied honestly. "He won't talk about it, and truthfully, I haven't been much of a mom lately. I had an heir and a spare, and I should have had several spares, because the pressure is too hard for my son to suddenly fill the shoes of the first born, and be the only child in a now dysfunctional family."

"Think about trying to be a mother to Barry again," Bobbi advised.

"Oh, Bobbi, it is so hard to be a mother when I need one so desperately," Lori said as she reached for her glass of water and swallowed hard.

"Lori, someday we need to explore your relationship with your mother, but not now," Bobbi said. "Barry may need some help, Lori. Here are the names of two very qualified therapists for Barry and for your husband. Can you read yet? If so I have some books I would like to recommend."

"Not really," Lori replied. "I did read Ellie Wiesel's *Night.*"

Bobbi swallowed hard before saying, "That is a tough book for you to read now."

Lori answered, "There is a quote in the book that hit home, 'When a child dies he takes stars and trees and meadows and leaves behind a question mark.'"

Bobbi just smiled, and they sat quietly for a few minutes.

"Lori, have you thought about volunteering at Children's Memorial Hospital?" Bobbi asked. "You could be a great help to other mothers."

Lori put her head down before answering, "Bobbi, I was once very optimistic, working diligently for the cure of cancer, soliciting merchants and individuals for money, by phone and in person, as a member of an organization for cancer research." Lori then started to laugh. "Oh, Bobbi, today I am so pessimistic I would only injure parents and kids who still have hope. Maybe someday in the future."

She opened her purse and took out her calendar and marked the date for her next session. Nowadays she couldn't remember anything without saving it on paper.

Lori left wondering if anyone who hadn't been in the same place could really understand.

The Cubby Hole lunches with Adele were a good part of her therapy. Leaving Bobbi's office, Lori drove over to the restaurant and slid into the booth opposite Adele. She was hungry and opted for a burger and fries, just like high school days.

"Bobbi and I think Jerry needs to see a therapist, and he won't," Lori blurted out.

Adele answered with a knowing grin, "Look at his family, Lori. To them, therapy would be a sign of weakness."

"More coffee?" Maddy asked.

Lori turned to the waitress and said, "Maddy, you've been around a long time. What can I do with Jerry to convince him that men need to talk things out too?"

"He don't need a therapist, he needs AA," Maddy disclosed, pulling her face down to a half-frown. "I'm sorry to say it, honey, but you asked."

Adele stopped nibbling on her salad, looked up at Lori, and said, "She's right."

Lori just shook her head and said, "I know, Maddy, I know. It's just… he won't go there, either."

Maddy poured them coffee and walked off, telling them she would be back in a moment to take their order.

"What about Barry?" Adele asked.

"I didn't give him a choice," Lori said. "He's seeing Dr. Reston in Lake Forest once a week."

"Good choice of doctor," Adele noted.

"That's what I thought, but Barry won't talk to me, and so far Dr. Reston hasn't broken through," Lori said. "Does he talk to your son Jonathon?"

"Jonathon wouldn't tell me," Adele said. "Around my house, Barry acts fine, but he was never one to show his emotions. Sasha may need to talk to someone. She is having a hard time accepting Julie's death."

"They were best friends," Lori said thoughtfully. She had not thought of how Julie's death affected anyone else, and it made her sad to think of Sasha missing her best friend at a time in her life when she would have needed a best friend most of all—changing schools, going to college, growing up, and becoming a woman. What would she have done had she lost Adele during those critical years? "Therapy may be a good idea before she takes off for college," Lori added.

Jerry tried to bond with his son. They went golfing together and attended some baseball games. Lori was an excellent cook, but now Jerry put something together, or took Barry out, because he was afraid if Lori tried she would burn the house down. Jerry and Barry were now missing two family members.

Lori was haunted by guilt. It is a parent's job to protect her child, and she had failed at her job. Realizing she had another child to protect, she became paranoid towards Barry, watching him for signs of leukemia, and when she did interact with her son, she found herself restricting his activities in fear of accidents. He was now their only one. At times, she wanted to shout out to him and say, "Son, grab whatever you can and enjoy yourself, because there may be no tomorrow."

When Barry entered the kitchen and saw Lori making breakfast, he swiftly tried to take over, saying, "That's okay, Mom, I can do it. I've been making my own breakfast for a long time."

Lori looked up at him, smiled, and said, "Please, Barry, let me try to be a mom again. You are over fifteen, and before I know it, you will be going away to college."

He sat down, smiling, and said, "Pancakes will be great. Its Saturday, so I have all morning to really enjoy them."

As she tried to concentrate on making a full breakfast of pancakes, eggs, juice, and fruit, she carefully asked Barry about his life.

"Do you have a baseball game today?" Lori asked. "Maybe I can watch it."

"Mom, I'm not in baseball anymore," he replied. "There is too much to do in high school." Barry grabbed butter and syrup, but his mother told him to sit down and relax. "I've got the rest, Barry," she said.

Lori walked over to her son sitting at the kitchen table and placed glasses and a pitcher of orange juice down on the table. She looked over at him and suddenly realized he had grown quite tall and had lost his boyish looks.

"Honey, are you in any other sports or clubs?" Lori asked as she went about setting a place before him and serving hot pancakes.

"Not really," Barry replied, reaching for the pitcher of juice. "I'm still serious about my plans, you know, of becoming a doctor, so I have to concentrate on my grades." He took a big gulp from his juice glass, then started toward the pancakes. "These pancakes are awesome," he said, smiling, his mouth stuffed with warm, gooey goodness.

"Thanks," Lori said. "I wasn't sure if I remembered how to make them."

Over breakfast, Lori spent time getting to know her son again and easing into some semblance of normalcy.

Barry enjoyed a leisurely breakfast of apple pancakes, talking with his mom about daily issues that concerned him and his plans after high school. It felt good to talk to his mom again.

"Just… take time to enjoy life, Barry. Do everything you can," Lori said as she smiled sadly at her son, who nodded knowingly.

"I know, Mom, I know," Barry said. "We never know how long we have, do we?" This was a theme his mom drilled into his head constantly. It was so hard to be a kid in his home now.

A loud car honk came from the driveway, and Barry turned towards the door.

"Mom, I have to go," Barry said, shoveling the rest of his pancakes into his mouth. "Jonathon is waiting for me," he mumbled with a stuffed mouth. "Thanks for breakfast. It was really good."

"Jonathon drives?" Lori asked, surprised.

"Mom, he's over sixteen," Barry said, chewing his food as quickly as possible. Barry bent down gave her a syrupy kiss on the head and moved out the door.

Sitting back, she wiped at her forehead with a napkin, then sipped her hot coffee and played with her plate of pancakes. She thought about how much she had neglected Barry in the last four years and how little she knew about his interest in medicine. Barry had grown up in her absence. He was the child who never complained, just adapted. Would he always be like that, or would he someday explode?

Her thoughts were interrupted when the doorbell rang. Lori walked to the front room, and opened the door. She was startled to see an official looking man standing on her front porch, holding a badge. In his other hand, he held a manila envelope.

"Mrs. Brill?" he asked.

"Yes?" Lori replied. She kept her screen door closed and slowly went for the latch to lock it.

"Ma'am, I'm John Denning, from the U.S. government," he said. "May I come in? I would like to talk to you."

A chill ran through her as she said, "My son, my husband, has something happened to them?"

Smiling, he answered, "No, I'm the bearer of *good* news."

Realizing they were still standing at the door, she apologized, led him into her front room, and said, "Please come in. Please sit down." She motioned towards the sofa and added, "We haven't had much good news lately."

"Mrs. Brill, we've been trying to contact you for months," the man said, taking a seat on the sofa. He waited until Lori settled into one of the wine-colored occasional chairs that sat opposite the matching sofa. "As you may know, Mrs. Brill, your father worked for the United States government."

"I did not know that, Mr. Denning," Lori said. "I have to confess that I never knew what my father did for a living, not exactly. Do you know?"

"Yes… well," Mr. Denning stammered, then cleared his throat before speaking. "When he died, he left you his insurance policy, totaling three-hundred thousand dollars." Mr. Denning handed Lori the manila envelope and continued, "You need to sign these papers so we can send you the money."

"That's a lot of money," Lori said. "But…what about my mother? She's still living. Doesn't this money go to her?"

Mr. Denning answered, "Your mother is well taken care of too. She's receiving your dad's pension. You were on his insurance policy."

Mr. Denning smiled while pointing to a spot for Lori to sign the papers. It was not until he left that Lori, sitting in the living room in stunned silence, realized he, like her mother, never answered her question about her dad's job.

She thought to herself, *In normal circumstances, I would be ecstatic about receiving this much money, but nothing can help now. Well, we will be able to send Barry to college and maybe retire.* She thought it best to let Jim help her invest the rest and, more importantly, keep it away from Jerry and his family.

The next week, Lori met Jim for lunch at the same restaurant she had been meeting Adele at for so many years. Over lunch, Jim suggested investing in computer businesses.

"Lori, it's the nineties, and with the advent of the Internet and this burgeoning computer age, computer companies like Microsoft, Apple, and Cisco are the way to go," Jim explained. "Call my broker, and he will help you."

Chapter Twenty-Two

The sessions with Bobbi were helping. Lori was now down to once a week, getting her own coffee, and sitting on a straight chair away from the Kleenex box.

"Bobbi, I can't find any meaning to the world anymore," Lori said. "Are we good guys sentenced to death for a crime we haven't committed, like in that Woody Allen movie, *Love and Death*, or are we souls sentenced to a number of years of life on earth for a crime we didn't commit, as Isaac Bashevis Singer reasons?"

Bobbi smiled and answered, "A question that makes me believe you are doing better. You are actually coming to with some intelligent thinking again." Bobbi leaned forward in her chair toward Lori. "From what you've told me about Julie, she was never doom and gloom. It sounds to me like her philosophy was: *Make every day count.* We may live eight minutes or eighty years. It is what we make of that time that is important."

Lori became silent, and her look became distant. Bobbi reached for her hand.

"Try for Julie," she said.

Lori's eyes met Bobbi's, but her voice could not respond.

Lori did try hard to function in the world again, but things like Julie's eighteenth birthday threw her back into a full depression. Neither Jerry nor Barry acknowledged the date, busying themselves at breakfast and leaving for work and school without a word, even after she brought it up. When the phone rang, Lori knew it would be Adele.

"Lori, we need to meet today and talk about Julie, but I can't meet you until one o'clock," Adele said. "Jonathon broke his tooth, and I have to take him to Jim's office. How about meeting me at the Cubby Hole?"

"Right, Adele," Lori said. "Thanks for remembering."

"How could I possibly forget?" Adele said.

After about forty minutes of staring at the clock, Lori realized she had to get out of the house before she fell apart. She threw on a pair of blue jeans, a sweater, and sneakers and got in the car with the intention of going to the grocery store.

She remembered switching lanes because she needed to slow down and concentrate on where she was going.

The sound echoing through her head sounded like a train racing by or maybe a ton of horns passing by, interrupted by the bang of a drum. Suddenly, she became aware of a man's nose in her face and a body leaning through an open car window beside her.

"What the hell is wrong with you, lady?" the man yelled. "The light turned green ten minutes ago, and you are just sitting in the middle of the street with your car idling!"

Lori looked up into a black bearded face on a large man wearing a green baseball cap. "Where am I?" she asked.

"Oh, shit, why do I always find the nut cases? Move over, lady," he said as he reached in and opened her driver's side door. He motioned to the driver's seat. "Listen, if you move over, I'll move your car into that shopping plaza parking lot over there so I can get my truck by. Don't panic."

Lori obediently and numbly moved over to the passenger seat. When the nice man left, she looked around the shopping center, trying hard to focus. Her breathing was shallow, her hands were shaking, and she was in a panic. She did not move until she heard Adele's voice.

"*There* you are," Adele said, leaning into Lori's open car window. "I've been sitting in our booth waiting for you."

Lori grabbed on to Adele, crying her name over and over.

As Adele helped her friend out of the car and into the Cubby Hole, she panicked, thinking, *What should I do? I thought she was doing so much better. Why didn't I pick her up?*

Handing Lori a cup of coffee, Adele asked, "Do you want to talk to Bobbi?"

"Now that you are with me, I'll be all right," Lori said in a small, quivering voice.

Adele waited until Lori took a few sips of black coffee and was visibly calmer before hitting her with questions. "What happened?"

Lori took a deep breath and answered, "All I remember is that I went into Sunset for some groceries before meeting you, and then I was in the car crying, and this nice man moved the car into the shopping center."

"Forget it, Lori," Adele said. "It's the day. How can you possibly concentrate on anything today when you should be celebrating your daughter's birthday?"

The jukebox suddenly rang out with *Happy, Happy Birthday Baby.*

"Did you put that song on, Adele?" Lori asked.

Adele shook her head and said, "No."

They looked around the restaurant. There was only one other occupant, an older man. They shrugged and sang along with the song in between tears.

Adele followed Lori's car home and helped her get undressed and back into bed.

"You just rest, Lori," Adele said. "Today was a rough one." Adele leaned forward and kissed her friend on the forehead. "I'll call you tomorrow," she said as she closed Lori's bedroom door.

Later that day, Jerry walked into the bedroom, turned the lights on, walked over to the bed, and shook Lori awake.

"Tell me, what's wrong now?" Jerry asked. "You're back in bed, there is no dinner, and a box of Dove bars is melted all over your car seat."

Lori just stared at him.

Barry was standing in the doorway. Jerry turned to him and said, "Your mother is nuts. Come on, let's go to McDonald's."

"Dove bars… Dove bars..." Lori repeated, trying to piece together what Jerry had been saying. Now she remembered. Dove bars were Julie's favorite ice cream bar. She remembered leaving her cart in the middle of the store and running out. She must have run out with the box of Dove bars still in her hand. She off-handedly wondered what would have happened if she were arrested for stealing a box of ice cream bars. She would tell the authorities that the bars were for her daughter, and then she would begin to cry. *They would think they had a nutcase on their hands,* she thought. "Maybe they'd be right, Jules," Lori said aloud.

After ordering food inside the nearby McDonald's, Jerry sat with his son while they waited for their order. "I thought your mother was getting better, Barry," Jerry said. "I wonder what set her off again."

Barry looked quizzically at his father for a moment, then answered, "Julie's birthday, Dad."

"When?" Jerry asked.

"Today, Dad. Julie's eighteenth birthday is today. Man..." Barry slammed his hands down on the table and got up to retrieve their dinner at the front counter. "Get a fucking clue," he mumbled to himself.

In the fall of 1992, a year after Julie's death, Lori tried to get back into the social life in Northfield, but she couldn't handle it, as former acquaintances seemed uncomfortable to be around her, and Lori's priorities had changed.

At a mahjongg game at Adele's house, she felt like getting up and leaving as she listened to Judy, one of the players.

"Look at this Prada purse," Judy said. "The zipper broke, and the company refuses to fix it. Why, this purse cost me *five hundred dollars*. I'm thinking of suing them."

"How long have you had the purse?" Susan, another player, asked.

"That is not the point," Judy asserted. "I am one of their best customers, and I expect to be treated with *respect*."

Adele looked at Lori and held up her hands, asking her to ignore it. She then looked at Judy and said, "Let's play."

Lori listened to the conversation, feeling lost. She didn't care about Prada. How could she be worried about fashion or restaurants or what car she owned after what she had gone through? She looked down at her Target blue jeans and the chipped nail polish on her nails and smiled to herself.

Volunteering at Children's Memorial or soliciting funds for leukemia research was not working for Lori either. In fact, the first time she walked into the oncology patients' lounge with boxes of toys, she burst into tears and ran out of the hospital and did not stop running until she reached her car in the hospital's parking lot.

At the annual cancer fundraiser luncheon, instead of being honored, she felt like a freak when she was called up to accept some kind of plaque in memory of Julie, especially when everyone at her table then choked on their kind words.

"Lori, we are really sorry," they uttered, looking everywhere but at her.

Yes she thought, *they are really sorry that I'm ruining their fun. The old saying is true, dammit. When you laugh, the world laughs with you, and when you cry, you cry alone.* Somewhere in one of the books she read, it said, acquaintances give you a week to get it together; friends, two weeks; and family, three.

One day, Lori phoned Kay, the mother of Jeff, the twelve-year-old boy who had died from leukemia. She had kept Kay's number all this time, and she realized she hadn't summoned the courage to phone her and tell her about Julie. This time, she called to try to meet with another mother who had lost a child. She was surprised to hear Kay's husband answer the phone in the middle of the afternoon.

"It's Lori Brill, a friend of Kay's from Children's Memorial," Lori said. "Is she home?"

"I'm sorry, she's gone," he replied.

"Do you know when she will be home?" Lori asked.

"Listen, I don't know," he said. "She's somewhere in California. After our son died two years ago, she just up and left."

Before Lori could respond, the receiver went dead. Lori just held the phone for a few minutes before hanging it up. *Time to see Bobbi again,* she thought.

Bobbi was able to squeeze Lori in at her last appointment of the day.

"Adele is the only one who will mention Julie's name," Lori said. "It drives me crazy to be with people who are tiptoeing around it. I want to scream, 'Please say her name and let me talk about Julie!'"

"Why don't you?" Bobbi responded.

Lori let out a big sigh and sank back into the overstuffed chair. Most times, the size and softness of the oversize chair was comforting to her; today, it felt like it would swallow her whole. "Bobbi, It wouldn't help," she said. "Everyone including my husband and son will shrink back and look at me like I'm crazy."

Bobbi didn't respond. She turned away from Lori and searched through her files in her filing cabinet.

"What are you looking for?" Lori asked, slightly miffed at Bobbi's inattentiveness.

"Give me one moment, Lori… Ah, here it is," she said as she turned to face Lori and handed her a sheet of paper with a poem on it. "Please read it and keep it."

"Read it? Now?" Lori asked.

"Yes," Bobbi directed.

"Aloud?" Lori asked.

"Yes, Lori," Bobbi calmly replied.

Lori looked over the printed words before reciting the poem she had never read before.

"*The Elephant in the Room,* by Terry Kettering," Lori spoke softly.

"Louder, please, Lori," Bobbi directed.

Tears filled Lori's eyes, and her speech became hoarse. She shook her head and continued reading silently until she came to the end of the poem.

"We talk about everything else—except the elephant in the room."

Lori stopped reading and stared at Bobbi, who said, "Keep the poem. Every time you read it, substitute Julie's name. Realize that other people are not mean; they don't know how to deal with the elephant in the room."

Lori sniffled and swallowed hard. "This poem tells all. I've heard the saying but never read the poem before. It identifies my life now. Sometimes, besides Julie, I am the elephant in the room. When I walk into a room, all conversation ceases. I can only talk about Julie with ease to Adele. My husband and my son won't talk to me about Julie's life and her death.

"Oh, Bobbi, will this terrible pain ever go away?" Lori asked.

Bobbi left her chair and walked over to Lori. With a hand on Lori's shoulder, she said, "No, Lori, but in time it will ease, and you will learn to live with it for your family, your friends, yourself, and Julie."

Bobbi stood patiently as torrents of tears tore through her client. Lori held her head in her hands and sobbed loudly, engulfed by a great rush of sorrow and grief.

Chapter Twenty-Three

Barry quietly crept up the stairs and opened the door to Julie's room. He surveyed the interior. Nothing had changed in the last three years. All his sister's clothes and possessions were still where she had left them. He plopped down on the pink bedspread, with the heart shaped pillows. He slowly picked up Pepper, the soft brown and white stuffed dog and turned it around in his hands, raising it close to his face. The sweet familiar scent of his sister was still mixed into the animals fake fur.

Barry missed Julie. He wanted his sister back in his world. Back in his world as an equal, not as a cancer patient. He felt abandoned by the sister he had known the first ten years of his life, the one who would tease him, chase him out of her room, and call him a wimp among other things, not the one who stayed in bed most of the day crying in pain.

He was a stoic child, his mother had once said, one who didn't cry easily. But he knew now if he didn't get out of Julie's room quickly, tears would come, and he couldn't let that happen. He couldn't let his parents see him crying, especially his dad.

His mother was so fragile since Julie had died he feared she would fold up if anything happened to him, so he walked on ice, afraid to do anything that would get him into trouble. He had to get out of the house and go away someplace far for college.

He stared at the setting sunlight bouncing off the musical decals on the window. Bright orange, purple, and blue colors produced a stunning rainbow. Maybe it was a sign from Julie. He shook his head and smiled thinking, No, it is just light reflecting—a scientific fact.

Right after hearing the sound of the remote control raising the garage door, he heard his mother's soft voice echoing through the house, "Barry, where are you?"

As he lay Pepper back on the bed, he thought of Eugene Field's poem *Little Boy Blue,* and wondered how long his mother would make Pepper and the other stuffed animals wait for a Julie who would never come back.

Barry, in his high school graduation cap and gown, looked around the football field for his parents. When he caught sight of them, his eyes focused on the tears running down his mom's face, and he thought, *In the last three and a half years since Julie died, all Mom does is cry, whether it's a sad or a happy occasion.*

He had never really felt safe in his home. First there were the fights over his dad's drinking, then the silence after Julie died. He wasn't sure which was better. Julie had been so bright he had felt the need to keep up his grades. Now it was paying off. He would finally get away.

His dad reached him first. Lightly punching his shoulder, he said, "Great job, son, graduating with honors. Why, your old man was lucky to get out of high school."

His mom just surrounded him with her arms, reluctant to let go until Jonathon came running over. Barry always felt like she was going to smother him. It was hard to suddenly become an only child.

"Hey, man, good job. Can't wait until you join me at UCLA in the fall," he said while giving Barry a high five.

The summer flew by, and before Barry knew it, they were packing for college, and then he was on his way. Barry sat back in the car, watching the kids line up at his old high school bus stop. Dad was driving him and his mother to the airport. His dad was repeating a theme he had been on for a month.

"Lori, why do you have to go with him?" Jerry asked.

"Jerry, it's his first year," Lori replied. "I want to help him get settled."

"Jonathon is there," Jerry said. "He can do it. I still don't know why he has to go so far away. There are plenty of great schools in Chicago."

Barry tuned them out. Through the last few years, he had learned to not listen to their bickering. He used to think they would get divorced, but not anymore. They enjoyed torturing each other. He really didn't mind his mom coming with, especially since she was staying with his Aunt Eileen. He thought it odd he had an aunt who he had never met in seventeen years.

Lori talked throughout the flight, while Barry acted like he was listening. Jonathon, in his gold Honda, was a welcome sight at the L.A. airport. While the two boys sat in the front, busy catching up on events, Lori sat in the back, taking in the scenery.

It was her first trip to California, and she quickly fell in love with the fantastic weather and landscape, especially once they left the expressway and began climbing up a winding road to the top of a large hill overlooking the city and the ocean. The burst of yellow covering the sky as the sun set among the abundant low green shrubs, tall palm trees, and beautiful red, blue, and pink flowers got her thinking about retiring out west.

Soon, Jonathon stopped the car in front of a magnificent old house that was painted in multiple colors. Lori looked around in awe while the boys carried her suitcase and packages up the wooden steps to a large columned porch holding several white wicker chairs and an enormous old swing. A warm breeze scented by lilacs from the full purple bush just left of the large wooden door greeted them.

A tall, slim woman with bright green eyes greeted them at the door. Dressed in black tailored pants, green silk blouse, and sporting a short reddish-brown hairdo, the woman opened her arms in a warm welcome.

"Lori, Barry, what a thrill to have you here," Eileen said.

Lori stood frozen to the porch before she broke out in a smile and said, "Eileen! I would have never recognized you."

Eileen burst out laughing as she recalled Lori's wedding, the first and last time they had seen each other, and asked, "Did you expect a witch?"

The boys looked at each other with puzzled expressions.

Lori laughed too as she recounted the events of a day so long ago. "I heard comments like, 'Oh, my god, could that be Lori in that black get-up? A black wedding dress and hat? What, no black veil?' " Eileen burst into laughter once again as Lori continued, "She looks like a witch. Is this a joke? Why is the groom's mother running down the aisle?"

The two women laughed and laughed, and the two young men just smiled and shrugged, not entirely getting the joke.

Eileen was still laughing as she led them into the house.

"Why did you do it, Aunt Eileen?" Barry asked.

"To get even with my parents for kicking me out of the house," Eileen said.

Jonathon, asked, "Why would your parents kick you out of the house?"

"Because they found out I was a lesbian," Eileen replied.

Both boys, with eyes wide open, asked, "Really?"

Eileen's eyes wandered for a moment before answering, "Yes, I had discovered that I preferred girls, and I still do, but it was the early sixties, and things were much different then."

Lori thought to herself, *Back then I had no clue what a lesbian was. I wonder how Jonathon and Barry think today.*

Barry put down the suitcase and said, "Aunt Eileen, my friend Jonathon is getting anxious, as we are due to help out at a fraternity party across campus."

"I was young once," Eileen said. "After you give me a kiss, you can get going. I'll take good care of Mom until Monday. Then I'll bring her to join you at orientation."

Barry gave Eileen a hug and kiss, and Jonathon shook her hand before they took off.

Taking Lori's suitcase, Eileen led her up a winding wooden staircase to one of the guest bedrooms. Pointing to a broken, scuffed step, she said, "Suzanne and I just moved in, and the place is a mess. We have great plans for restoring this painted lady to her grandeur, so don't make any judgments from this visit. Unpack, clean up, but be quick, Suzanne is working, and I want this day to be ours, to finally get to know each other."

The tall, sophisticated woman that walked out of the room was nothing like she thought Eileen would be, but then again, Eileen possessed some of the Brill traits. Her tall, slim build was like that of her father, Jack, and actually, now that Lori thought about it, Eileen had Shelly's take-control attitude. In the few minutes she had been in the house, Eileen had issued orders in her deep voice, but somehow she wasn't annoying like Shelly; she actually made Lori feel welcome and comfortable.

Over a bottle of white wine and a broiled salmon dinner on the patio, Eileen questioned Lori about life with the Brill clan in Chicago. After Julie died, Eileen had called, and she and Lori had established a friendship by phone and e-mail. Now, they were finally talking face to face. After about an hour of talking, Lori turned the tables.

"Eileen, when… how..." Lori hesitated. She wasn't sure how to ask her question.

Eileen rescued her. With a mischievous grin, she answered, "Design school was where I found my first love, Tammy. In the early sixties, Illinois was way behind California in its tolerance for gay people, so I took off for the west coast. After a year of odd jobs, I landed a job at Miriam Rose Interiors, working under her top designer, Suzanne Davis."

"Suzanne is your *friend* now," Lori said, hesitatingly.

Eileen shook her head, smiled at Lori's attempt to understand, and said, "Suzanne is my *love*. You will meet her tomorrow. We just clicked, even though we are very different. She is a short, blond, Southern dynamo, organized and punctual, while I used to be disorganized, artistic, and always late before she became my teacher, taking me under her wing, teaching me how to dress and act like a successful designer."

"It seems like the two of you have done very well, a successful business and partnership," Lori offered.

"Yes, we bought out Miriam Rose Interiors and expanded into one of the best design firms in Los Angeles," Eileen said.

Lori stifled a yawn, looked at her watch, and said, "Eileen, it's been a long day, and I think I need to put my head on a pillow."

Chapter Twenty-Four

The thump, thump sound of a hammer woke Lori up from a deliciously deep sleep. This was the first time in many, many months Lori had slept without the use of sleeping pills or painkillers. She brought them along on her trip to California just in case, but in her exhaustion, she completely forgot to engage in her nightly ritual of taking a few pills before lying down for the night.

Amid the noise, she showered, dressed, and made her way downstairs. She stopped a moment to take in the sunlight bouncing off the multi-colored floral stained-glass window and the magnificent wood carved banisters. Workers who could achieve such beauty were scarce today.

Upon entering the kitchen, she quickly came to the realization that this morning, Eileen's partner, Suzanne, was in charge. In the midst of the construction chaos, there was order. Vases full of pink and violet flowers adorned a table set with delicate china. A perky little blond Southern belle greeted her the moment Lori stepped off the steps.

"Pleased to meet you. I'm Suzanne."

Handing Lori a generous plate of steaming, golden, pecan pancakes loaded with butter and syrup, she motioned for her to sit down at the table.

"I'm famished, and these look wonderful," Lori beamed, taking a deep whiff of the aromatic food before her. There was a pitcher of orange juice, some sugar cookies arranged neatly on a plate of delicate china, and a fresh steaming pot of coffee.

"Coffee?" Suzanne asked as she started to pour some from where she stood at the kitchen counter.

"Yes, please. It's nice to meet you too, Suzanne. I'm Lori."

"Oh, I know that!" Suzanne said with a giggle, and she smiled sweetly. "Eileen has told me a lot about you. Cream and sugar?"

"No, thanks."

Worried after scanning the area, Lori asked, "Where's Eileen?"

"Don't you start fretting," Suzanne said as she walked over and placed a pretty white china coffee cup before Lori. "She will be back in time to get you to Barry's appointment at the university. Our business is crazy. Some clients just think they own us, lock, stock, and barrel."

Putting her hands on her hips, she looked Lori in the eye.

"I am so plum pleased that Eileen has finally found some family," Suzanne said. "She has been hurting for years, and when she hurts, I hurt. Now it is your job to get the rest of them to talk to her."

Lori looked at her and smiled. "I'll see what I can do, but frankly, I think she has been the lucky one all these years." Lori leaned in conspiratorially. "That family of hers is *crazy*."

Suzanne let out a hearty laugh and said, "All families have crazies among the good ones. But family is family!"

Chapter Twenty-Five

Jerry rose from his hard plastic seat as he saw Lori among the throng disembarking from the afternoon L.A. to Chicago flight.

"How did it go?" he asked, draping his arms round her shoulders as they made their way to retrieve her luggage.

"Great," Lori said, leaning into Jerry as they walked on. She felt comforted by his presence. "Barry is going to have a wonderful four years, between the fantastic school, Jonathon, and spending time with your sister. I just hope he has time to study." Lori pressed her hand to her husband's chest and paused their walking.

"Jerry, I just have to tell you… your sister is wonderful," Lori said. "Why have you and your brothers cut her out of your lives? I can understand your parents being old-fashioned and not accepting her lifestyle, but…"

"Lori, you don't understand what went on in my house with her." Jerry shook his head and walked on.

"Tell me!" Lori yelled after him. She quickened her steps to keep up with Jerry's pace. "Then tell me! How can I know what went on if you don't tell me anything?"

He turned and looked at his wife with angry, narrowed eyes, and said, "Leave me alone, Lori. I don't want to discuss it."

They walked on silently, their brief tender moment of reunion shattered. Lori watched as Jerry grabbed Lori's single blue suitcase from the luggage carousel and frowned.

"You do what you want, Jerry," she said as he approached her, "but as far as I am concerned, she's my friend."

While life in California was going great for Barry and Eileen, life in Northfield for Lori and Jerry was disheartening. Instead of improving, they were falling deeper into depression and falling further apart from one another. Barry had now been at college for two years, and Julie had been gone for six years. Most of their family and friends had gone back to living and expected them to do the same. Even their best friends and business partners, Jim and Adele, were having a hard time dealing with them.

One cold, bleak winter day, as she moved into the family room with her cup of coffee and paper, Lori realized she hardly paid attention to Jerry anymore. She was peripherally aware that he was sitting somewhere in the family room, nursing his third—or was it his fourth?—Scotch shortly before noon, still in his pajamas. Lori stole a glance his way. Jerry looked pathetic, slumped in his chair, looking down at his glass, lost to the world. Lori never nagged him anymore. There were times lately when she was tempted to join him. Instead, she had showered and dressed early before coming downstairs to make herself some toast and a strong pot of coffee. Jerry, she pondered ruefully as she made her way to her favorite overstuffed chair, favored something much stronger in the morning. *Better to be prepared for the day, whatever it brings,* she thought. This was a far cry from the half-conscious state she had been in during those bleak months directly after Julie's death, but she had made a promise to herself and to her daughter that she would do her best to move forward.

Lori had been sitting enjoying her coffee for only a few minutes when someone broke the quiet sounds of papers rustling and Jerry's ice softly clanking inside his tumbler by knocking on their front door.

Upon answering it, Lori was surprised to see Jim on a weekday morning. When she tried to make small talk, he curtly responded, "I need to see Jerry."

"Be my guest," Lori replied glumly. "My Prince Charming is in the family room." She pointed in the general direction of the living room. Jim passed by her and quickly moved into the family room.

He looked at Jerry with a disgusted smirk and said, "Jerry, I brought the proposal for the dental school in Wisconsin. You left it in the office, and I thought you might need it for your appointment with the dean this afternoon." Jim placed the folder that contained the proposal on the coffee table that sat in the center of the room.

Slurring his speech, Jerry looked up bleary-eyed and answered, "Yeah, yeah, Jim."

Jim looked at him and said, "Look, Jerry, today is my day off, but *I'll* take the appointment."

"Stop being a hotshot, Jim. I can… I can do my *own* job," Jerry said as he struggled to raise himself from his chair.

"Like hell you can, Jerry," Jim said, raising his voice. "Look at you. You can't even stand up." Jim turned to go but stopped and turned around. "I don't claim to know what you've been through, Jerry, and I know it's been rough, but I do know one thing." Jim paused and waited for Jerry to look at him while he spoke. When Jerry did not, he continued, "I know that Julie would be disappointed in you. She wouldn't want you throwing away your life this way."

Getting no reaction from Jerry, Jim took the proposal from the coffee table and headed towards the door. He stopped by Lori, who stood in the foyer, her arms tightly folded around her body.

"I'm really sorry, Lori," he began as he embraced her, "but *something* has to be done with Jerry. There are some good rehabs we could get him into."

Lori took this moment to lean into Jim for support, and she embraced him and said softly, "I know, Jim, I know." Jim, clean-shaven, wearing his classic Polo shirt and pants, smelling of clean, woodsy cologne, gave Lori a peck on the cheek and a nod as he walked out and got into his silver Lexus, while Lori turned back into her house to face a ranting, raving, drunken husband.

"He has no right talking to me like that!" Jerry yelled as he leaned forward from his chair and pounded his fist on the coffee table. Now that Jim was gone, it was safe for Jerry to react to his friend's admonishments.

"Oh, for the love of God, Jerry!" Lori cried. "Stop your histrionics! Jim has every right as your friend *and* business partner to put you in your place! You are in no shape to go to any appointment this afternoon, you drunken fool!"

Jerry dropped his tumbler of Scotch, rose unsteadily off his chair, and wobbled toward the fallen glass. As he did so, he lost his balance and fell forward, his head narrowly missing the edge of the coffee table. Lori watched in disgust as Jerry just stayed where he lay, face down on the carpeted floor, his glass tumbler just out of reach. Suddenly, Lori realized that they were just tumbling down and down. She felt as though she could not look at her husband another moment longer, and from somewhere deep inside her, she knew what she had to do.

"Jerry, I'm done," Lori said as she tried to choke back her sobs so she could sound stronger. "Barry is at school, and Julie is dead. Either you go to a rehab to sober up, or I'm gone too. After Julie fought so hard to stay alive, how can I let us take life so lightly?"

Lori moved to the foyer closet, put on her coat and hat, and walked out the front door, locking it behind her. Jerry, stunned, struggled and rose up from the floor of the family room, slurring and crying, "Lightly, Lori? My life… I take my life lightly, Lori?" Hearing no response, Jerry stumbled into the foyer and, failing to unlock the door, shouted at the closed door before him.

"Lori? LORI! Don't go, damn you! Lori, help me, please help me, for Julie's sake!" Jerry pounded on the front door until, exhausted, he slumped onto the floor of the foyer, calling out to Lori and Julie intermittently between loud, bitter sobs.

Chapter Twenty-Six

After Jerry finally agreed to go for help, Lori called Jim, who got Jerry into one of the better rehab places in the country. Before Jerry had time to think about it, they were packed and on a plane to Arizona. As they left the plane and walked out onto the tarmac, Lori removed her winter coat and basked in the seventy-five degree temperature. She looked at Jerry and reality set in. He looked thin; his face was gaunt and haggard as he pulled out a package of cigarettes from his pants pocket and lit a cigarette with nervous, shaky hands.

"Lori, I'm not sure if this is a good idea," Jerry said. "I'm not that bad. I could try to quit on my own."

"You tried before when Julie was sick," Lori responded. "It lasted only a month. Actually, it was a forced refrain from alcohol when you got a DUI driving ticket, and Jim was able to turn it into community service." Lori lost count how many times she and Jerry had gone over this argument; it was in the several dozen range, she was certain.

"What a waste of time, cleaning roads!" Jerry mumbled.

"Hey, you kept your license and stayed out of jail," Lori reminded him.

"Well, I'm ready to go back to Chicago," he said, taking a deep drag off his cigarette.

"When did you start smoking again?" Lori waved the smoke away from her face and walked across the tarmac and on towards the building that held the luggage carousel.

"If I'm going to give up alcohol, I need a substitute," Jerry said.

A man holding up a sign with their name on it approached them and asked, "Are you Jerry Brill?"

"Yes, we are the Brills," Lori said.

"When you get your luggage, there is a waiting van outside," he noted. They picked up their luggage and walked outside to the waiting van. One other couple joined them. Nobody talked during the one and one half hour ride from the Phoenix airport to the Ranch, located just north of Scottsdale in the McDowell Mountain area.

When the van pulled into the area, they were surprised to see a vacation setting instead of a hospital scene. It was a rehab for the wealthy and famous, with beautiful grounds surrounded by cacti, flowers, and mountains. One building had hotel-type rooms, surrounded by a swimming pool; another building held offices, a dining hall, lecture halls, and a workout room. A smaller building in the back held a medical facility, with bars on some of the windows.

The two couples were led into the main hall and then into a reception room, which was decorated with cheerful colors of yellows, greens, and oranges. The facility looked great, but the occupants didn't. They were from all walks of life: men, women, black, white, Latino, Jewish, Christian, rich, poor. Most were thin, lethargic, and silent. Some sat, their hands shaking, and several were standing around smoking cigarettes. They all had one thing in common: they were alcoholics, drug abusers, or both.

Lori was led out of the main facility, and Jerry was taken inside a building before they even had a chance to say goodbye. She had the urge to run back for Jerry, but she obediently followed her guide into a small office.

Seated in a comfortable office overlooking the grounds, she listened to Brian, Jerry's supervisor and her only connection to Jerry while he was at the Ranch.

"Mrs. Brill, you do understand the rules," Brian said. "You can only have contact with Jerry on Sundays. The Ranch, as we call it, does not allow phone calls or communication with the outside world. You are not allowed to stay on the grounds. You cannot bring him anything. Everything he needs will be provided. Call me with any questions you may have," he said, as he handed Lori his card and a brochure about the Ranch.

"How long do you think it will take?" Lori asked.

"A lifetime, Mrs. Brill. A minimum of six weeks here," he answered. "Be prepared for setbacks." Brian was a big, confident man with a baritone voice. Lori developed an instant dislike towards him, or maybe, she thought, towards the message he was giving. She had hoped for a quicker solution.

Jerry was taken into an office, where he filled out endless paperwork and answered what he thought were stupid questions. Then he was given a tour of the facilities and led to a nice but sparsely decorated room containing a bed, chair, nightstand, and a private bath.

Before he had time to open his suitcase, there was a knock at his door. Upon opening it, he was greeted by a large muscular man with a baritone voice.

"Jerry, I'm Brian Piekarski, your supervisor and link to everything that goes on during your stay," Brian said.

Jerry shook his hand and asked, "Is this place like jail, or am I allowed to come and go as I please?"

Brian laughed and replied, "I'm sure you didn't read all the papers you signed, but you agreed to stay on the grounds and only leave accompanied by one of us. Anyway, we're going to be keeping you busy. Tonight is free, but tomorrow, after breakfast, you will have a complete physical and sociological exam. Then you'll start on your schedule, which includes AA meetings, lectures, therapy, and workouts."

"Do we have any free time?" Jerry asked.

"Of course you do," Brian said. "There's a TV room, a card room, and a relaxation room, plus a swimming pool and our beautiful grounds.

Of course, there are no liquor, drugs, or gambling allowed. Direct all questions to me. Here is my phone number."

Lori stayed at a small, modern motel about a mile from the Ranch. She treated herself to a Mexican dinner of tacos and salad and a margarita before she retired to her room to tackle some of the books she had brought along.

That first week, Jerry thought the medical doctor appointments were a waste of time, and the lectures on things like diet, exercise, and the evils of cigarette smoking were no better. He was only there to stop drinking. He walked into the doctor's office for test results, sat down, and hoped he could get out right away and join his new friend, Roy, in a game of pool.

A Dr. Lorado walked in to speak to Jerry. "Sit down, Jerry," he said. He then put several radiology scans and X-rays on the screen. Taking out a file, he looked at Jerry. "We know that you have messed up your life sociologically and emotionally. Well, now I have to tell you that your drinking has done a pretty good job on your liver and your heart. How old are you?"

"Fifty-eight," Jerry said.

"Do you have any grandchildren?" Dr. Lorado asked.

"I better not," Jerry wisecracked. "My kid isn't even married."

"Well, Jerry, if you want to live to see grandchildren, you better start taking care of your body," Dr. Lorado said. "No more alcohol, no more cigarettes, no more junk food, and you need to start an exercise regimen."

"Jesus, Doc, if I have to give up everything, there will be nothing left to live for," Jerry said.

"Sex, Jerry, and it will be much better without booze," Dr. Lorado said. "I know, I've been in both places."

Jerry laughed.

The doctor got up, turned towards Jerry, and said, “You’ve said you’ve been off of alcohol for a week. How are you doing?”

“No problems,” Jerry said confidently. “I could do it on my own, but my wife insisted I come here.”

“Good,” Dr. Lorado said with a sly grin.

Lori was allowed to visit on Sundays. First she had to check with Jerry’s counselor, Brian. His job was to give her an outline of Jerry’s general progress and to answer her questions.

Lori tried to emphasize to Brian that Jerry really needed to deal with his overbearing mother and the death of his daughter.

Brian asked, “What about his father?”

“He had nothing to do with raising the boys,” Lori said.

“Every parent, involved or not, has an effect on his child. I’d like you to go to the Alcoholics Anonymous sessions for families of patients. Here,” Brain said, handing her a sheet of paper, “this is a schedule of meetings.” He also handed her a book to read about the Alcoholics Anonymous program Jerry would be on. Lori looked at the title: *The Twelve Steps Program*. She had heard about it, but she never thought they would be living it. She cringed, thinking how embarrassed her mother would be if she knew. Leaving Chicago for treatment afforded them some anonymity, though after Julie’s illness and death, nothing should bother her.

“Jerry is waiting for you in the next room. Encourage him,” Brian suggested, bringing her back to the present.

Lori entered a small sparse room with a table and chairs. It had been one week exactly since Jerry had been admitted. He looked the same. His conversation resembled someone detached from the place.

“How are you, Jerry?” she asked, not really knowing what else to say.

"I'm ready to leave." Jerry looked nervous, crossing and uncrossing his arms, and his crossed leg jiggled incessantly the entire time Lori visited with him. "Most of the people here are really fucked up between their taking drugs and drinking. They are real addicts, Lori, not me. I can stay away from alcohol on my own," he responded in his usual cocky manner.

Lori's whole body tensed up as she said, "I'm proud of you for coming here. I expect you to finish the program, Jerry," she answered.

She had been listening to his counselors, so she refrained from telling him that this was the last straw for her, that if it didn't work, she was gone.

Lori attended an AA meeting for spouses, where she had to acknowledge her husband was an alcoholic. Standing up and telling a large group of people that her family was not perfect gave her an odd feeling. She realized she had never helped the situation by hiding behind the old warning: *Never hang out your dirty laundry.*

Lori listened intently to the lecture that followed that first meeting. She learned things she had never considered before. They were told alcoholism is a disease that should be treated as a sickness, like an ongoing pneumonia, and until your whole family accepts that and stops treating it as a terrible family secret, there will be no hope of recovery.

They were told to never argue with an inebriated person; only talk to him when he is sober. Lori kept repeating that advice in her head as she thought back to the many times she did the opposite. In order to help an alcoholic recover, one must be patient and understanding. The road to recovery would start when your spouse admitted that he or she was an alcoholic. Lori learned that only a very small percentage of people stayed off of alcohol for life.

Another revelation was that most alcoholics had a genetic disposition to alcohol or had been raised in a home with a drinking parent. It was unlikely in Jerry's case. *But who knows,* Lori thought, *maybe Shelly kept a hidden bottle around.* Lori left the meeting encouraged and interested to do her part. So far, she had been reading novels, swimming, and shopping. She went back to her room and read *The Twelve Steps Program* plus all the other brochures she had been given.

By the end of the month, Jerry wasn't his usual cocky self. He had been experiencing withdrawal symptoms such as the shakes, nausea, and headaches. He readily stood up at the meetings and admitted to being an alcoholic. He hated to admit it, but the prospect of dying of a failed liver helped keep him fighting his addiction.

On Sunday, visiting day, he walked into the lounge, spotted Lori, and walked over to her.

Lori stopped in her tracks as Jerry approached. He was pale, thin, and unsteady. *Why, he looks just awful,* she thought.

His hand shook as he reached for hers. "Let's sit down," he said. Turning towards her, Jerry said, "You and Jim were right. I'm an alcoholic. I am in detox, and it's hell going without a drink for this long, but I'm going to make it."

Lori got up, gave Jerry a hug and a kiss, and said, "Jerry, I'm very proud of you, and I know you will make it." According to her meetings, once he admitted to being an alcoholic, he was on the road to recovery.

"Lori, I'm meeting some very unusual people here," Jerry said. "We can only use first names, and we aren't allowed to probe into backgrounds, but there is a famous basketball player and a popular musician going through the program." Jerry felt that gave him a bit of security; even famous people had this disease. Somehow, it made him feel better about himself. He felt the group therapy was helping him get better with each session.

Chapter Twenty-Seven

At the next AA meeting Lori went to, they were paired into groups with other spouses or family members. Stephanie, the first woman to talk, put her hand up to her forehead to brush away long strands of hair, exposing a black and blue eye and a swollen lip.

"This is two weeks old. My husband had a choice: rehab or jail," she said.

"Did you give him the choice?" Darlene, their group leader, asked.

Stephanie looked at her and then put her head down on the table before resuming her story. Finally, she looked up and said, "No, I was too chicken, always afraid to talk back to him. My brother and his wife threatened my husband after they saw my face and my six-year-old daughter's broken nose."

"Honey, I lived with the same type," another woman volunteered. "Before we came here, he broke my arm because I wouldn't give him anymore drink money. I had to send the kids to my mother's before he hit them again."

Another girl answered, "My husband never hit us, but he put us into debt. We had a big house on the mountain that we lost. I never knew what was happening in our life, living in a dream world, until the finance companies started coming around taking back everything: house, cars, TVs, furs, jewelry." She paused, thinking back on her recent past before continuing. "He is a happy, funny drunk, who is much nicer to everyone when he is under the influence, so I never complained."

"You're lucky. Mine is a mean, angry son of a bitch when he drinks too much," lamented a skinny little woman.

A man quietly confessed that his twenty-year-old son, hooked on drugs, was finally found on the streets of San Francisco after a three-year search. Lori thought about Steve and Carol's son, Darrell, who had managed to pull himself out of the mire and make something of himself. *Sometimes there is a happy ending,* she thought to herself.

The counselor spoke up, saying, "As you can see, there are many kinds of alcoholics." He indicated to each woman who spoke. "There are mean ones, funny ones, pathetic ones, angry violent ones. Also, there are differences in the way they treat their victims. Abuse does not have to be physical. I'm sure all of you have suffered some type of emotional abuse. I want you to think about why you have stayed with your alcoholic family member or friend."

Lori pondered it and answered, "Because of Mark Twain."

"What?" the counselor asked.

" 'You can't reason with your heart. It has its own laws.' "

Most of the people in the group looked at Lori like she was crazy. One woman, however, dressed in Southwestern Indian garb and festooned with fine turquoise jewelry finished the quote. *" '. . . and thumps about things which the intellect scorns,'* compliments of Mr. Twain."

She was a striking woman with thick, wavy, black hair flowing down to her waist and long slender legs on a thin frame.

She turned towards Lori, offered her hand, and said, "My name is Rain. I believe we have a lot in common."

As they spent more time together, learning more about one another, the women were amazed to discover they shared more in common than they initially thought: alcoholic husbands, a love of literature, the same religion, and hidden family secrets. Though Rain was unique: a Southwest Jewish sixties hippie turned American Indian in order to hide her true identity.

Lori was drawn to this unusual woman. She was witty and charismatic, and although she kept much of her past under lock and key, she was real. Her green eyes, with the long black lashes, were captivating.

When she talked, everyone stopped and listened. Rain lived in Arizona; her second husband was at the clinic with Jerry, and she and Lori immediately formed a bond, spending a lot of time together outside of meetings.

***

Jerry woke up, took the covers off, moved out of the bed, and headed to the bathroom. On the way, he looked down, held his hands out, and smiled. For the first time in nearly two months, they were steady. He took a shower, dressed in shorts and a T-shirt, and looked out the window. *This Arizona is not bad*, he thought. *Seventy-five degrees in February and no humidity.*

He walked into the cafeteria and started to get in line when he heard someone calling, "Hey, you! Jerry, isn't it? Come over 'ere."

Jerry followed the voice to a large table in the back. A tall, muscular, older guy with a full head of black hair motioned. "Sit down." In a thick New York accent, he said, "I'm Tony. I seen ya at the lecture. You look familiar." The man leaned forward on his metal chair, which creaked ominously like the creaking of a coffin in a B-horror movie. "Where ya from?"

The large swarthy Italian man next to him said, "Hey, Tony, we're s'posed to be anony… anonno…"

"Anonymous," Jerry said, ending the sentence.

"Fuck dat shit," Tony said. He waved his thick hand dismissively like he was waving away a fly. He then turned to Jerry. "Where ya from, what's your name, and who do you work for?"

Jerry answered, "Jerry Brill, from Chicago. I have my own business, dental supplies."

"Chicago, Chicago, that's my kind of town!" Tony started to sing, then in the same breath, he grew serious. "Ever serve time?"

Jerry started to get nervous as he looked at the two bouncers sitting with Tony.

"No," Jerry answered, wiping the sweat off his hands along the length of his khaki shorts and swallowing.

"What about Miami?" The chair groaned once again.

Jerry tried to get up. Suddenly, Tony, with a hand the size of a bear paw, pushed him back down. "Stay put and don't ya move," Tony said in a menacing, low voice, "if ya value yer life."

At those words, Jerry turned beet red as a memory of a night in Miami a long time ago came into his memory.

Tony's deep-set, dark eyes all but disappeared under the folds of his lined face as he squinted in a grin. "That's it, Miami." He turned to the guy next to him. "Ya see, Fats, I'm right. I never forget a face. Hell, kid, I saved your life, didn't I?"

Fats asked Tony, "Whaddya you talking about, Tone?"

Tony looked at them and grinned before unfolding his tale. "Must be twenty years ago. I'm guarding for Resko, the New York boss, may he rest in peace." He looked at Jerry. "It was New Year's Eve in Miami, right, kid?"

Jerry nodded. Tony continued with the story.

"We're sitting at the front table with Resko and his wife. Resko arranged to have a beard, Gary Senesi, bring his girlfriend, Tricia, and sit at the table right behind us. This way he can see her on New Year's too. This kid, Jerry, starts flirting with Tricia, and she throws a drink at him. It hits Resko. Now Resko don't give a shit about that, but he wants to kill the kid for flirting with Tricia."

Jerry's mouth fell open for a moment before he gathered up the courage to speak up. "It was a set-up? Gary worked for Resko? Oh, my God."

"You didn't know?" Tony asked.

Jerry shook his head, and all three guys started laughing.

Tony said, "No wonder you acted like a dumb shmuck. Hey, kid, you owe me a drink!"

Jerry got up and came back with a tall glass of orange juice. Tony gave him a friendly pat on the back. Now Jerry was required to have breakfast every morning with the boys.

At Lori's third Alcoholics Anonymous session for spouses, a newcomer named Samantha gave them a sad laugh when she was called upon to tell her story.

"Most of you have spouses here," Samantha said. "My husband does not have a problem, but my seventy-seven year old mother is an alcoholic. She has been kicked out of two retirement homes and one assisted living place for abusive behavior. The woman, in a wheel chair, was throwing things at nurses who took away her Jack Daniel's. She also was soliciting a worker. Sex for alcohol. She has made my life *hell*. My father and my sister cut out years ago."

Lori looked around for Rain, but she wasn't at this session. Lori followed the others into the lecture hall. They were going to hear one of the lectures given to the patients. They were told that the addict is really never cured. He or she must learn how to live with the disease. Just one drink can ruin everything, causing a relapse. The speaker emphasized that it was important to remove all bottles of alcohol and to solicit friends and family members to help keep triggers away. Ultimately, it was the patient who had to learn to live in a world full of forbidden items, but it was always good for him to have help in his fight.

Lori left there with mixed feelings. It bothered her that Jerry's alcoholism was always referred to as a disease. To her, a disease was something you had no control over, like Julie's cancer.

By the end of the second month, Jerry looked much better. He spent their two-hour visit telling her about the 12 Steps and Friends of Bill. Lori mostly let him talk uninterrupted. She realized AA would be a part of their lives for a long time.

"How are the therapy sessions going?" Lori asked.

"It's difficult dealing with family and alcohol at the same time," he answered.

Lori couldn't help but blurt out, "Dealing with Shelly could take a lifetime." She thought about all the messages she had received from Shelly. Shelly couldn't call Jerry at the clinic, so she tried hard to get Lori on the phone. At some point, Lori would have to call her back. *Maybe,* Lori thought, *Adele would do me a favor and call her.*

"You're wrong, Lori," Jerry said. "Brian, my counselor, feels that my father's indifference has caused more problems for my brothers and me. My mother at least gave us attention and interaction. From an early age, my mother encouraged competitiveness between my brothers and me. Being the youngest, I was always on the losing end. I was fourteen when Eileen was banished from the family. Never understanding why caused me to have nightmares that I too would be banished. I then tried hard to be liked."

"What did your parents tell you about Eileen?" Lori asked.

Jerry was ready to open up and let Lori into an ugly part of his life he never wanted to revisit. He remembered hearing screaming and yelling coming from Eileen's room one Saturday night. He heard his mother shouting, "Get out and never come back!"

Lying in his bed, Jerry had been woken up plenty of times by Shelly and Eileen's screaming matches, so he didn't think much about this particular fight until the following morning, when he woke to find, instead of a house full of people eating bagels and lox in the kitchen, his mother and father sitting in the living room praying aloud the prayer for the dead.

"Ma, Pop, who died?" Jerry had asked as Joel and Jerry had just come into the living room, still in pajamas, still sleepy from the night before.

"You no longer have a sister," Shelly turned and told them flatly. "You will not talk to her or see her as long as you live in this house." The boys' father said nothing to them, but he just sat there, repeating the prayer for the dead: "*Yisgadal, vay yiscadash…*"

Joel and Jerry never saw their parents like this. What had happened? Frightened, the two boys went in search for their big brother, Steve.

Steve already knew the situation and explained it in plain simple terms. "Mom caught Eileen with a girl last night," Steve said as he sat on his bed, reading a magazine. Their parents' lamentation prayers could be heard in the distance.

"So what?" Jerry said, settling down on his big brother's bed. "Eileen has many girlfriends."

Steve rolled his eyes, kicked at his younger brother, and said, "How dumb are you? Eileen *likes* girls. Get it? They kicked her out for now. Don't worry, she'll be back."

Steve was right on one count. Jerry was naïve and had no idea what Steve was talking about, but he was wrong about Eileen coming back.

"The next time I saw Eileen," Jerry explained to Lori, "was over ten years later at our wedding. I was surprised when Carol gave you her address. I thought she was really dead. I thought my sister had died. How could they just cut her off like that?"

"No wonder you never tried to contact her. Don't be hard on yourself for not knowing about what was going on, Jerry," Lori said softly, trying to console her husband. "It was the late fifties or early sixties, and we were all kept in the dark about homosexuals. Is that when you started to drink? You couldn't have been more than about, what, Jerry, fourteen? Who knows about that stuff at that age?"

Jerry shrugged and frowned, recalling the darker parts of that incident, the screaming, the histrionics, the confusion, and the fear he felt about one day having a sister, then one day not, and never hearing her name spoken again, as though she never existed. Jerry remembered thinking, would he be next? What if he did something his parents did not like? Would he be cast out of the family next?

"I only remember you social drinking when we first got married," Lori offered.

"I started to drink a little in high school because it helped me to be someone else," Jerry explained. "I wasn't drinking a lot in the early years of our marriage. After you quit working and the children came, I guess I couldn't take the pressure of being the sole breadwinner, competing with your friends in Northfield. I became depressed and drank more." Jerry felt uncomfortable talking about it all, but he knew from what was taught at the sessions that he was better off getting used to divulging and expressing his feelings.

"Why didn't you talk to me?" Lori asked.

"I didn't know all this, Lori," Jerry said. "I was just angry, and the alcohol helped. You expected me to take care of *everything*. Then Julie got sick, and the world fell apart. I couldn't believe how strong you were throughout her illness."

"I had to be for Julie, but… when she died, I fell apart afterwards," Lori said. Jerry grasped Lori's hand as she spoke. Little by little, the facts were falling into place.

As Jerry kept talking about his sessions, Lori began to realize that she never really knew him. Under that friendly, outgoing, fun loving guy she married was a lonely little boy trying to fit in and be noticed. The road to recovery would be long, but at least they were on their way.

By the end of the second month, it was obvious Jerry was going through some serious changes. There was intensity and a seriousness that Jerry had not felt before and that Lori had not seen before. During a Sunday visit, he sat and looked more pensive than usual. He looked across the table and into Lori's eyes and said, "Lori, *please* forgive me for all the hell and torture I've put you and the kids through."

Lori searched for the proper response. She knew he meant it. She wanted to hide the anger. Her stomach was in knots as she recalled all those years of sadness and pain. Was one apology supposed to heal all the wounds or make up for every hell she had experienced?

At a loss at how to sum up all she felt in one answer, Lori opted for the good wife's answer and said, "If you are willing to reform, Jerry, I will stick by your side."

On the way home, Lori fretted over this one fact: Jerry was telling the truth about his feelings; Lori was not.

Lori walked into the clinic, met Jerry in the lounge, and they sat down as they had for several weeks now. They sat silently for a few moments, facing each other. Lori was nervous. Jerry had been in rehab for two and a half months, and he was going to be released from the program in three weeks. She worried about their reunion, and she had an idea he might not like. She stood up straight and took a deep breath.

"Jerry, I've had it with Illinois, the weather, and the people," Lori asserted. "I want to move to Arizona. I've talked to Jim, and he would be willing to sell the business. In fact, he would be thrilled to slow down, and with our investments, thanks to Jim, we could possibly retire, and…"

Jerry interrupted her and said, "Slow down, Lori. You're rambling on. Sit down, will you? This is serious stuff here." Jerry waited until

Lori composed herself and took her seat across him before he spoke again. "Lori, I think that's a *great* idea."

Lori let out her breath, got up again, gave Jerry a big hug, and said, "Do you really? I'm so relieved. God, I was so nervous! I think I need a drink—whoops, I mean a coffee."

Jerry got up, walked over to the counter, and poured them both some coffee, and he picked up a couple of cookies. Lately, he needed sweets to substitute for the alcohol.

"Actually, *I've* been thinking along those lines too, Lori," Jerry said upon his return. "A few of the people here have given me the names of retirement communities in the area. Why don't you go looking with that new friend of yours?"

Lori called Rain when she got back from her visit and told her, "He loves the idea. Pick me up, and we will go looking."

Rain picked Lori up in a Jeep. She looked at Lori. "Girl, when you go with me, you need to wear blue jeans and boots, or at least closed shoes. Those sandals won't work." Lori went back to her room to change out of her shorts and open-toe shoes.

"That's better," Rain said, as Lori, now dressed in a pair of dark blue jeans and closed-toe sandals, mounted the Jeep and sat herself next to Rain. They moved north, pulling up a winding mountain just north of Carefree. All Lori could see for miles were mountains, cacti, and brush until they pulled into an Indian reservation consisting of a few teepees, a few small casitas, an apartment building, a general store, a schoolhouse, and a large factory-type building.

Lori turned to Rain. "I don't think I can sell Jerry on moving *here*."

Rain smiled. "This is where I live and work." Suddenly, the Jeep lurched to a stop at the edge of a mountain. Lori held onto the roll bar overhead with all her might, sure she was going to fly out of the vehicle and over the mountain. Rain, unperturbed, got out and motioned Lori to follow. Shaking, Lori got out of the car and walked over to Rain.

Rain pointed to a valley full of houses, swimming pools, and assorted buildings, and said, "I hate that they were allowed to build so close to the Indian land, but you'll love it. It's called Ventura. It's a six-hundred acre retirement community with predominately middle-class residents from the east coast or from Chicago."

Rain walked Lori over to her casita, greeting various Native American women and children as the two women made their way around the reservation. She lived in a small two-bedroom stucco house where beautiful Indian artifacts such as rugs, feather headdresses, painted jars, painted pictures, wood furniture, and silver and turquoise jewelry were tastefully displayed within. Lori was in awe.

"Rain, where did you get all these things, and why are you living here?" Lori asked.

"We'll talk about it another time," Rain said, changing the subject. "Let's go down and look at Ventura."

Lori loved Ventura. It didn't take her long to pick out a new house and put it on hold, pending Jerry's approval. The home she chose was much smaller than their current home in Chicago. It was a two-bedroom ranch with large open spaces. The kitchen was furnished with new stainless steel appliances, granite counter tops, and ceramic tiles that Adele's remodeled kitchen had, and the master bath with its Jacuzzi and rain shower was large and luxurious. The house backed up to a majestic mountain with desert views of giant saguaro cacti, brush, and blue skies, far from the city center, adjacent to Rain's Indian reservation.

Too her surprise, Jerry told her to take care of everything and have it ready for him when he left the Ranch next month. Working with Rain, who seemed to know everyone in the area, Lori soon found herself the proud owner of two houses—and two mortgages. She quickly called a broker in Chicago, who told her house prices in Northfield were soaring. It was 1998, and she put their house on the market for three hundred and fifty thousand dollars. The retirement place cost less than half of that amount. If all went well, they would be in good shape.

The hard part would be telling Adele and Jerry's family. She thought Barry would be thrilled because they would be closer to California. She was wrong. Upon phoning her son with the good news, Lori was informed that Barry had just been accepted into the medical school at the University of Illinois. He was going back to Chicago, and his parents were moving west.

"But, Barry, I thought you were applying to medical schools in California!" Lori said.

"Well…I *was*," Barry explained, "but Anne really wants to live in Chicago, next to her family."

"Things are that serious, huh?" Lori said. "Are you planning to get married soon?"

"Not until I finish medical school," Barry said.

"Why didn't you tell me?" Lori asked.

"Mom, you've been busy with Dad," Barry said. "By the way, how is he?"

"He's doing great," Lori said. "In fact, he gets out in three weeks."

"That's great, Mom," Barry said. "I'm glad things are going well for you both."

Barry sat silently on the phone, expecting to hear some form of congratulations regarding his news about medical school. Instead, he listened as his mother went on about their new home in Arizona and how things were changing for her and his father. She discussed the improvement of his father's health and how excited and nervous she was about their recent decision to move.

After a while, Barry begged off the phone, saying, "Mom…I have some things I have to do. I'll, uh, talk to you later. Bye."

They hung up, and Lori sat down on the bed in thought. She was going west and he was going back to Chicago. This bit of news kind of put a damper on her enthusiasm. Even Barry seemed less than enthusiastic over the phone. She called Adele and spilled her guts, like so many times before.

"Lori, he will be in medical school and wouldn't have any time to see you anyway." Adele was always the voice of reason, the calming of the waters. "Sasha is in dental school," Adele went on to explain, "and we *never* see her. We'll talk when I pick you up later at the airport. Give me Barry's phone number so I can congratulate him on getting into medical school!"

Lori hung up, suddenly horrified. She hadn't even congratulated her son. She quickly called him back, but he was already gone. She heard a honk, grabbed her suitcase, and went out to the waiting Ranch van.

Chapter Twenty-Eight

Lori hadn't seen Adele since she picked Lori up at the airport three days prior, nor had she even left the house in three days when Adele knocked on the door. She came in lugging a grocery bag.

"Lunch from Max and Benny's, corned beef sandwiches. Do they at least have a good deli where you're going?" Adele asked.

"I think Phoenix has one," Lori said as she pulled out the sandwiches and prepared a space for them at the kitchen table.

Adele looked around at all the boxes and things throughout the house and asked, "How's it going? You look frantic."

"Truthfully, Adele, I'm looking for a bag of dirty clothes and hoping I didn't just give it away to the Salvation Army truck," Lori said.

"You'll find it," Adele said as she looked in the give-away box sitting next to the table. "Did Jerry really keep his seventies bell bottoms and leisure suits? Remember the sideburns that went with them?" Picking up the rice cooker, she smiled. "I bet you never used this thing. I remember when he dragged it home on the plane." She then picked up a gourmet cookbook and burst out laughing.

"What a joke!" Adele exclaimed. "You actually tried to serve French cooking to Jerry, a Brill. He tossed it out and then went through the garbage when he heard how much you paid for quail."

Lori took the book from Adele, moved her away from the boxes, and said, "Let's eat lunch. You aren't helping me get rid of stuff. We're downsizing to a place half this size, with no basement. It's really hard to toss out things that evoke memories."

Adele refused to comment. She would miss Lori terribly, but she knew her friend needed to get far away in a new environment to start healing from her awful loss. It had been eight years since Julie's death, and Lori was still in mourning. To date, she had never touched anything in Julie's room, leaving it like a shrine.

Lori pulled out paper plates from the cabinet, and said, "My china now."

Adele took two Cokes out of the refrigerator, and they sat down to lunch.

"You're welcome to store some things in our basement," Adele offered.

"Thanks, Adele," Lori replied. "I'll take you up on it. Barry asked me to let him sort through his own things when he moves back to Chicago for medical school."

Adele smiled and said, "Barry will make a wonderful doctor, one who thinks of others—a rarity today. Jonathon can be his lawyer."

"And he is a definite perfectionist," Lori said. "No instruments will be left in his patients after surgery. Remember when we took the kids apple picking and then made pies? I can still see Barry measuring every cup of sugar and flour to the exact amount."

Lori laughed as she thought about how Barry sliced those apples to perfect size while the rest of them had a mess going.

She turned to her friend and said, "Thanks for remembering that. Sometimes I tend to forget the fun times and only concentrate on the pain."

The doorbell rang. When Lori opened it, she pulled back. "This is not a good time," she said when she was greeted by her real estate agent and a nice looking young couple.

The agent pulled her aside and said, "Mrs. Brill, the Feldmans saw the house already and love it. They just want to check out a few things."

Lori, standing there with no make-up and in torn jeans, shook her head and said, "I'm a mess and so is the house."

He pleaded with her and said, "I think we could have a sale. Their mother is sitting for the baby."

Adele appeared, took Lori's arm, and said, "Let them in. We can hide in the backyard. The sun is out."

An hour later, the agent approached Lori and said, "We have a sale, for $329,000, if you can get out in a month."

"So fast…" Lori said with panic in her voice.

Adele spoke up and said, "She can do it."

When Adele left, Lori sat down and cried. She wanted to move, but not so fast. After all, she had spent most of her life in Northfield, forty of her fifty-four years. She called Jerry, hoping he would tell her to wait, but he thought it was a great idea, especially when he heard the sale price.

Lori hardly left the house once she had a month's deadline to get out. One week before the moving van was due to come, Lori tackled her hardest job. Adele volunteered to help, but Lori knew she had to do it herself.

She walked into the room and looked around. Everything had been just like nearly a decade before, as though this were some sort of a time capsule. Lori walked over to Julie's bed, sat down, and looked around. It was then she realized she had been holding her breath since she had turned the knob of the bedroom door. The afternoon sunlight shone through the half-open shade, and Lori watched as tiny dust particles danced lazily in its beams. Lori breathed deeply, trying to detect a lingering scent of her daughter, just as she had done so many days and months after her death, but now, after all this time, the room merely held the scent of something deprived of fresh air, of life itself. Julie's earthly essence—the perfume she wore, the flowers she would bring into her room, the patchouli incense she burned, the pure and fresh teen-age smell of her—had faded, and Lori found that fact painful as well as comforting. She took one more deep breath and slowly blew it out.

"You've moved on too, Julie," Lori said softly. "I don't blame you, honey. Time is starting to close the wound for me, but the scar will never leave. I can now see you as a baby and a little girl, instead of only seeing the daughter that was sick."

It was time to move forward. Lori rose from the bed and began carefully sorting through the dolls and stuffed animals, keeping some and packing most into boxes to be sent to children's hospitals. Julie had been into all the new fads. Her room had the first Apple computer. She took computer lessons when the programmers were teaching students how to make software and the computers took up a whole desktop. Every wall was plastered with posters from rock groups and, of course, the Boss, Bruce Springsteen.

Why hadn't Barry taken them in his high school years? she wondered. In the corner of the room was a jar of pennies Julie had collected in the eighties, when the newspapers announced there was a copper shortage.

Going through her daughter's clothes was the hardest job. Shutting her eyes, wiping out the world around her, it was here that Lori could smell a trace of Julie's special fragrance, and she could hear her voice, sometimes coy and soft, other times very loud and demanding, like a typical teenager. Every outfit brought back memories of joyful and tearful occasions. Most of the things she ended up putting in the box were drawings, poems, stories, letters, and schoolwork from both her children.

One of the hardest parts of the move was leaving Julie alone at the cemetery. No one in Illinois would visit Julie every week like she did. She vowed to at least fly back to Illinois to visit her daughter every

September 11, the anniversary of her death, until Lori was buried next to her.

She walked out around the back of the house. A warm breeze scented by lilacs from the full purple bush just left of the back door greeted her. She would miss Illinois's lush vegetation. Then she went back inside for one last look. Lori stood in the kitchen surveying the stainless steel appliances, the wide-planked hardwood floors, and the granite countertops. She recalled the major fight she had with Jerry until he finally gave in to remodeling the kitchen. She took a deep breath and smiled, thinking how her priorities had changed. Once you are run over by a truck, you think differently.

After the moving van left with the last of their things, She gave a final look around before closing the door.

Lori jumped when Joel came up behind her. He always seemed to be sneaking up on her.

"Hey, sister-in-law," he said. "I'm here to say goodbye and pick up the car."

She turned around to face him. He never seemed to age; he was still thin, with a full head of sandy colored hair, so different from his two brothers.

Jerry had asked her to give his car to Joel. It was a six-year-old black Lexus, and they planned to buy two smaller, unimpressive cars to go with the casual lifestyle in Arizona.

"The car is still in the garage, Joel," Lori said. "I forgot to check and see if there are any of Jerry's things still in it." Lori took the keys out of her purse, opened the garage door, and they walked over to the car. While Lori checked the glove compartment, Joel checked the trunk. When she heard his laughter, Lori walked to the back of the car.

Joel held up a half-empty bottle of Johnnie Walker Scotch. He handed it to Lori and said, "Found it in the tire well. My brother was clever."

Lori looked at the bottle and thought, *No wonder I could never figure out where those bottles magically disappeared to after I had checked everywhere*.

She handed it back to Joel and said, “It’s yours, with the car. Jerry is dry, off of all alcohol now.”

Thankfully, Adele pulled up and broke the tension. She looked as fresh and classy as anyone Lori had ever known as she rolled down her window and just smiled at Lori. Her black hair was in a perfect bob cut; her clothes were crisp, fashionably casual, classic upper-middle class. Adele beamed with happiness and self-assuredness; Lori envied her that. Lori said goodbye to Joel with a dismissive wave of her hand and happily left with Adele.

At the airport, Adele and Lori had a tearful goodbye.

“We’ll be back for visits, and you will come out,” Lori said as she hugged her best friend.

“Of course,” Adele answered assuredly. “Why wouldn’t we?”

Once Lori got seated on the plane, she slept for the full four-hour ride.

Chapter Twenty-Nine

Lori sat on the front steps of her new home in Ventura, soaking in the peaceful, restorative magic of the early morning sun and taking stock in her life. She had always taken care of the bills and paperwork in their marriage, but she and Jerry had always shared the big decisions. This time, Jerry had left her with all the jobs while he worked at pulling himself together for the next phase of their life together. She had sold the house and the business in Illinois. Well, she mused, she wasn't entirely alone; Jim had helped a great deal. But she had to give herself credit; she was not the naïve little girl who moved out of her parents' home and into a marriage. She was learning just how independent and strong she was when pushed out of her comfort zone.

These were tough lessons to have learned, with enough trials and tribulations to test the strongest mettle, but she was surviving. She looked forward to doing more than just surviving but thriving in her new environment. For now, she sat and waited for the moving van to pull up to the new home she had picked out herself and purchased in the retirement community.

With the help of her new friend, Rain, Lori decorated the small, two-bedroom ranch house in warm Southwestern hues. Coming on the moving van would be treasures from Chicago that wouldn't fit in, like Jerry's antique marble-topped desk, her grandmother's antique Chinese carved chair, a mahogany china cabinet, and Julie's computer table and dresser. These things held memories, and she could not yet part with them like she could with the rest of the furniture. It would take a while to shed all layers of comfort. As she eased into her new life and created new comfort zones in this new place, at this new time, the old would fall away eventually.

At the Ranch, a heavier, tanner Jerry greeted Lori with a big smile. He was definitely on a high. Before putting his golf bag into the trunk of their rented car, he pointed proudly to the clubs.

"Ping, sent to me from Jim and Adele," Jerry said.

Ping, shming, Lori thought. She didn't play golf, so she didn't know what he was talking about, but she acted impressed anyway.

"Nice gift," Lori said, nodding approvingly. "They are getting you ready for retirement. Have you heard from anyone else?"

"Lots of cards from friends, and both Joel and Eileen called," Jerry said.

They avoided mentioning other family members. They both knew Shelly was furious at them for moving, but they had to move on for the good of Jerry's health and the health of their marriage. Shelly, in her usual habit of avoidance, had never even acknowledged that her son had a drinking problem; she found hiding everything worked for her, but it was slowly killing Jerry.

As they drove to their new home, Lori tried to be on a high also, but it was hard to believe all would be well. Emotionally drained, she nevertheless tried to be encouraging. She put her hopes in their attempt at rebuilding their lives.

As Jerry looked around their new home, she stood back in anticipation.

"The place looks great," Jerry said cheerily. "What did you do with all the other things we had?"

"Adele has some things in storage, but I had to sell or give away a lot because we don't have a basement," Lori said.

Lori stood back waiting for the "Where are my…" questions or the angry explosion.

Surprisingly, they never came.

Instead, Jerry pulled her towards him, and with an old familiar grin he said, "Lucky *I* wasn't there. I would have never been able to get rid of anything." Jerry embraced her warmly, holding onto her for a few moments before releasing her and saying, "Show me the complex."

"Let's start with our backyard," she said, as they walked out the sliding doors to survey the view of the majestic mountain with desert views of giant saguaro cacti, brush, and blue skies.

"Looks like heaven. Where's the golf course?" Jerry asked as he pulled Lori towards him once more and kissed her deeply. Lori returned the kiss before she led him down the path. They stopped at the swimming pool, which was surrounded by magnificent floral arrangements, green grass, large palm trees, and comfortable blue vinyl lounge chairs occupied by many over-fifty residents. The adjacent clubhouse and restaurant had golf carts that could be signed out and used for transportation. Seated on a golf cart, they toured the rest of the complex, which included a small shopping center, two more pools, and an eighteen-hole golf course.

Jerry surveyed the area, shook his head admiringly, and said, "This place is just great, Lori. Are you sure we can afford it without going back to work?"

"Hopefully, yes. We made money on the house, the business, and our stock investments." Lori couldn't believe she even knew about stock investments, but it was, again, a new arena in which she found herself standing. "Mainly the tech ones, the ones Jim's broker put me in, have doubled. That is some good news, huh?" Lori smiled at Jerry's approving grin.

"You did great, Lori!" Jerry said.

They tried using one car, Jerry's new gold Honda, and a golf cart, but it didn't work out, especially since Jerry had daily Friends of Bill meetings to attend, and Lori needed some freedom.

Lori opted for her neighbor's used silver six-seat General Motors van. The van came in handy when company came to visit.

Anxious to explore Arizona, Jerry and Lori started out on a driving trip. When Jerry handed her a map, she said, "No way am I directing. Those days are over. You know I have no sense of direction, especially now that old age is creeping in and the wires are getting rusty."

Jerry took the map back and laughed, saying, "You're not that old, Lori. You've got time before I'll accept that excuse. You know," he offered, "I read that soon they will be able to put directional devices in the cars."

Lori smiled and said, "Think about how many marriages those devices will save."

Jerry drove on, becoming pensive and quiet. "You know, Lori," Jerry began, taking hold of his wife's hand, "while I was at the Ranch, I realized if I didn't sober up, you would probably leave." He paused and then said, "No, I'm sure you would have, and I would not blame you."

Lori felt the truth was the best thing she could offer Jerry. There was no reason to cushion any hard truths.

"You are right about that," Lori replied, her face pulled down to a frown. "I've been through too much already, Jerry. I just don't think I could stand it if you began drinking again. Keep that in mind, Jerry," she said, patting his hand, "especially when you are tempted to go off the wagon."

Jerry nodded and let silence move between them as they drove on. He later pointed to a multicolored painted mountain as they drove into Sedona. Lori was in awe of the scenery, especially with the terrain and climate changes. They passed through desert, farmland, odd-shaped colorful mountains, with plants and animals totally foreign to the Midwest, with names like mule deer, cacomistle, kangaroo rat, cholla, and the hundreds of names for the desert snakes. Opting to find different hotels on the way, they traced through forgotten Route 66 and stayed at a charming old Fred Harvey hotel called La Posada.

On the beginning of the trip, Lori was totally defensive, watching Jerry like a hawk for signs of alcohol consumption and trying to block out memories of other disastrous car trips with the kids. By the middle of the trip, she actually relaxed and enjoyed her new husband. She knew this could be just a fairytale time and that she would have to take reality checks often, as only a very small percentage of alcoholics stayed sober.

They stopped by an overlook, taking in the clear blue sky and the majestic mountains. Jerry pulled Lori close to him, gently kissing her neck. Nestled in his arms, Lori wondered. She had fallen in love with the man who could laugh at himself, the man who could relax her and make her heart jump at his touch. That man was hiding for years, and only now was he resurfacing. Would he stay? Lori was afraid to hope, but she wanted him to stay. She wanted to stay and be Jerry's wife again.

After their second honeymoon trip around Arizona, they settled into their new life in the Ventura retirement community. Jerry made friends with everyone, easily remembering names and personal information. After a few AA meetings, he found several buddies to hang out with and a mentor for support. He was much more social with strangers in Arizona than he had ever been with family and friends in Chicago. Maybe being away from his family and Northfield's competitive nature was helping.

Lori, however, for all her planning and spearheading their new life, was having a harder time. She missed Adele. So far, Rain was the only one she had connected with. Walking outside along the back patio between the cacti and brush, Lori suddenly felt very alone. She missed her house with the green grass, trees, shrubs, multicolored flowers, the shrill chirping of blue jays, and the melodious singing of the songbirds. She missed what was familiar and comfortable. She wondered how long it would take before she was used to the slithering snakes, scurrying lizards, and howling coyotes that came with Arizona's beautiful scenery. She had to admit the weather was fantastic—blue skies, little rain, and no snow, even in February.

She thought about the morning when she ventured into the community center for a lecture on the desert environment. After the lecture, she had sat down with some of the women, drank coffee, and engaged in lively conversation with her new acquaintances.

The conversation was going well until one of the women asked, "How many children do you have?"

It had been years since she had to face that question. She hesitated, took a deep breath, and answered, "One now, a son. My daughter died eight years ago."

Silence. She had created an awkward moment. Two of the women at the table looked elsewhere, and the other one sat twisting her hair around her finger before responding, "How awful to lose a child. How did she die?"

After briefly answering, "Leukemia," Lori excused herself and went back to her empty house. Jerry was at an AA meeting. Needing a friend, she started to call Adele, then changed her mind and called Rain. She needed someone in Arizona.

"Rain, I need someone to talk to," Lori said.

"Hi, Lori," Rain replied. "I'm about to take a hike in the mountains. Do you think you are up to joining me?"

"I'll try, if you promise to take it slow," Lori said, thinking about the exercise class she had taken with Rain where felt like she almost died.

"Exercise is good therapy for whatever bothers you," Rain said. "Wear long pants and good hiking shoes. I'll pick you up in ten minutes."

Lori looked through her closet. She put on jeans, a T-shirt, and hiking shoes, grabbed sunglasses, and hurried out the door to Rain's honking horn.

Rain looked at her through the Jeep's open window and told Lori, "Go back for a jacket and a hat."

"Rain, its eighty degrees out," Lori argued.

"Lori, its three in the afternoon," Rain said. "The hat is for the sun, and the jacket is in case we stay into the late afternoon when the sun goes down. I have enough water, and I've got a compass."

Lori stopped and stared at her friend with the toned, muscular body, and said, "I better forget it. I'm just a weak Jewish girl from the Midwest."

Rain got out of the car, opened the door, and gently pushed Lori into the Jeep, saying, "Get in. I'll have you back for dinner."

They drove out of Ventura's gated entrance, making a right turn into the Indian reservation, past the homes, schools, and shopping area to the open spaces. Lori closed her eyes, grabbed the seat, and held her breath as Rain twisted around the narrow mountain road in her open automobile. It made her think of her high school days with Josh. About halfway up, Rain stopped the car, grabbed her backpack, and motioned to Lori.

"Let's go," Rain said.

After only fifteen minutes of hiking, Rain whirled around to the sounds of her friend's screeching.

"Help!" Lori cried. "Snake!"

They had just begun their hike; was it possible they were already in trouble? Quickly, Rain grabbed Lori's arm and pulled her to the side.

Lori shook with fear, stomped her feet, and said, "A rattlesnake almost bit me!"

Rain surveyed the ground for a few moments then sighed, releasing her own tension.

"No, Lori, see that?" Rain pointed to the snake making its way from the two women. "That's a coral snake, Lori. It's *not* poisonous. Calm down. Snakes are a part of the desert. You have to watch for them." She took Lori's hand and walked her along the mountain path. "You're going to have to know your environment if you want to survive in the desert. Whether you're hiking or not, you must get to know your friendly and unfriendly critters. It's a matter of life and death."

"Yeah, that seems to be the theme these days," Lori said pensively as she made her way carefully along the path, mindful of where she put each footstep.

Rain heard the change in tone and remembered Lori had called her to talk, and it sounded serious. "Now, what was wrong when you called me?" Rain asked.

Lori shook her head and said, "Nothing as bad as the snake."

Rain turned and gave Lori a half smile. She would be ready to listen whenever her friend decided to talk. "See, Lori, I told you exercise was therapy for everything," Rain said.

They walked in silence, with Lori's gaze glued to the ground, when suddenly Rain stopped in front of a group of low cactus with purple fruit. She took out gloves and a bag and started to pull off the purple flowers.

"What are you doing?" Lori asked.

"We make a wonderful drink and a great jam from the fruit on this prickly pear cactus," Rain explained.

"What about the saguaro?" Lori asked as she surveyed the tall cactus plants lined up along the mountains.

Rain stood tall and lean against the mountain ridge. Turning to Lori, she said, "Did you know it takes fifty years for saguaro cacti to grow an arm? The saguaro can grow fifty feet and can live up to two hundred years. The natives use the pulp from the fruit to make cakes and the seeds to make butter."

Lori smiled at her friend and said, "You sound like a *National Geographic* special."

Rain let out one of her full hearty laughs before continuing with the conversation. "Lori, you have to learn about your surrounding environment so you don't feel so 'out-of-place Jewish girl from Chicago 'out in the desert!" Rain turned to the cactus and marveled at the size of the majestic plant. "You know how you have birds that build nests in trees back at ho– back in Chicago? Well, small animals and birds call the cactus home."

Rain and Lori resumed their walk along the path, and Rain looked about her for a moment, scowling as she spoke up again. "I'm so damn upset about all this new construction that is threatening their existence, especially the casino," Rain said.

The volume and tone of her voice increased into an angry, emotional lecture, as did her speed of travel. Lori was huffing and puffing in her effort to keep up with her.

"Rain, you're going too fast," Lori said. "Please, can we stop? I need a rest."

Rain tempered her anger long enough to lead them over to a group of rocks overlooking the valley below. Handing Lori a bottle of water, she said, "Sit down and take a drink of water."

Lori gratefully sat down upon a rock, took a drink, and looked across the ridge. She could almost picture the wagon trains being ambushed by Indians, a scene she couldn't describe to Rain, who was obsessed with how the white man treated the Native Americans.

Rain was still on her lecture: "The natives' land was taken from them by deceit, cruelty, and murder. Brave warriors were turned into alcoholics. Today, the white man is using Native Americans to create gambling casinos."

Lori tried to change the subject to ease the tone the day was taking on. "Coming from Chicago, I can't believe we are enjoying thirty days of gorgeous sunshine without a drop of rain," Lori noted.

Rain bent down and picked up a handful of dirt and sand. She held it up to Lori's face.

"The land is *dying,"* Rain asserted. "Without rain there will be no water for the crops, the plants, or the desert animals." Her whole face lit up in anger. "You imported Northerners will not notice or even care until you can't fill your swimming pools!"

Lori shrank back, her eyes wide. "Sorry," Lori replied. "I'm still learning about the desert. It's a shame this beautiful land can't be preserved as is, though I could do without the scorpions and the snakes. Phoenix is starting to look like L.A. and Scottsdale like Highland Park, Illinois."

Rain's face softened, as she took a moment to reminisce. She turned towards Lori. It wasn't Lori's fault the desert land was going to shit. She had just left Chicago; she couldn't really know the state of affairs in Arizona. Rain made a concerted effort to not come down so hard on Lori.

"How right you are," Rain said. "When I left the Midwest in the sixties, I lived on a commune near here. It was so different then: open ranges, abundant wild life, no concrete or artificial, brought-in vegetation."

"Where did you live, Chicago?" Lori suspected Rain was from Chicago from her accent and things she had said before.

Rain avoided answering the question directly but turned to Lori and smiled and said, "The past is past, Lori." She got up and brushed sand and dirt from her behind. "Let's go back. It's getting hot."

As Lori exited the Jeep, Rain handed her two books. One was titled *Living in the Arizona Desert,* and the other was *Women Through the Years.*

"Happy reading," Rain said, smiling.

Lori thanked her and went indoors, grateful to have such a friend. She wondered why Rain had been so elusive about her past. "Everyone's got a story," Lori mused aloud alone in her home. "I guess some of us would just rather not tell it."

Jerry was still at his meeting, so Lori went back outside and curled up on a patio lounge with her books and a tall lemonade. As Lori felt tired from her hike under the hot sun, she wasn't sure how much reading she would get done, especially books regarding ponderous issues from her liberal and ecologically conscious friend.

Chapter Thirty

Spring was in the air, and the tourists were descending upon their little town. Lori usually loved to soak in her Jacuzzi tub after her morning walk. This morning was different. She grabbed a bagel with cream cheese and a cup of coffee and ran out to the car and headed towards the airport. Today, Adele would arrive. In a t-shirt, shorts, and sandals, Lori raced through the terminal, making it just in time to greet her cosmopolitan friend as she stepped off the plane.

"Adele, I am so glad to see you!" Lori said excitedly as she gave Adele a big hug.

After grabbing her Tumi suitcase, Lori scanned Adele's elegant coral Chanel suit, with matching high heel shoes and leather purse. *Oh, God, does she look out of place,* she thought. Adele's hair was, as always, a perfect, shiny, chin-length black bob.

"What's with the dressy outfit, Adele?" Lori asked. "How on earth can you still wear three-inch heels, in fashion or not? Jesus, Adele this is the desert, not Northfield. Dress here is very, *very* casual."

Irritated, Adele stopped in place, hands on her hips, and scowled at her friend. "Well, it's nice to see you too, Lori," Adele said, oozing sarcasm. "You told me we were going directly to a show at your friend Rain's club. I take it this is too dressy?" Adele indicated to her upscale outfit.

Lori tried hard not to laugh as she thought about Rain's club.

"Sorry I didn't explain her better. Rain is a *free spirit*. Her club is on an Indian reservation." Lori hooked her arm in her friend's arm and walked her along as she spoke. "We'll swing by the house and re-dress you, and you can take a quick look at our new place."

With a disapproving gaze, Adele fixed her eyes on Lori's casual island look and on her now almost totally gray, unkempt hair. *How could she let herself go like this?* Adele thought to herself. *Perhaps Arizona has changed her.*

Lori dropped Adele's suitcase in the back of her van, opened the door for Adele, and quickly drove them to her home, pointing out sights to Adele. They only had time for Adele to change into something casual. Adele delivered a half-smile to Lori's admiration as she handed Adele a pair of blue jeans and a dark green baby doll halter shirt.

"Wow, Adele, you almost look like a native!" Lori said as she handed Adele a pair of sneakers.

Adele took a look at her reflection in the bedroom mirror and laughed, thinking, *I'm dressed for garden work!*

"Why must we be in such a hurry? I'm tired from the trip," Adele said as she tried to sit down in Lori's kitchen to put on her friend's sneakers.

"You'll rest later, Adele," Lori spoke excitedly. "I promised Rain we would be there in time for the entertainment."

Reluctantly, Adele got back into the van, thinking, *I've come all this way to see my friend, and all she can talk about is some Indian's show. Well, I better see what she got herself into. After all, forty years ago, I promised to take care of her*. Adele slipped on her friend's white canvas sneakers as Lori chatted happily as she drove along.

The show was on the adjacent Indian reservation. Covered booths were set up where native crafts were displayed for sale. All at the show were dressed in shorts or blue jeans except the entertainers and Rain, who was busy displaying her jewelry and talking to guests. She was dressed in a white embroidered blouse tucked into a brown suede skirt. Around her neck, she wore antique silver adorned with turquoise.

As Lori introduced them, Adele gave Lori that look that clearly said, *Casual? You made me dress casual while she is dressed like Pocahontas?*

Rain quickly sized up Lori's friend. She had heard so much about her, and Rain could see Adele was feeling out of place. This was not her speed, to be sure.

"I hope you enjoy your stay here, Adele," Rain said, smiling warmly.

Ignoring Adele's look, Lori told Adele, "Rain is into making jewelry. She has teamed up with some of the Native Americans, and they are making beautiful modern designs out of turquoise and coral stones. She actually has a warehouse and small factory. Today, the natives are having a craft show with entertainment, and she is in charge of it."

Walking along Rain's booth, Lori asked Rain to show Adele some of her jewelry.

"What a stunning piece," Adele declared as she tried on one of Rain's handmade coral necklaces. Lori knew Adele would like the jewelry.

Rain handed Adele a long heavy turquoise and silver beaded necklace and said, "This one will fit you better. The green toned turquoise brings out the color of your eyes and goes with your personality. You are a Capricorn, right?"

Adele knitted her eyebrows and asked, "How did you know?"

Rain just smiled as she watched Adele try on the necklace.

"How much is it?" Adele asked.

"All the money above my cost, which is $250 on this one, goes to causes like schools, health clinics, and recreation centers for the natives," Rain said. "You decide what you want to pay for it."

Adele wrote out a generous check.

Lori sat back in her chair and watched her two friends try to understand each other for her sake. Having them together heightened her awareness of their uncanny differences. Adele protected her like a trusted older sister. Lori was comfortable with Adele, divulging secrets and revealing innermost thoughts. Adele was a great listener. Rain shook her up, challenged her, and took her into undiscovered territory.

Adele was impressed with the work and left the show decked with Indian jewelry and a black suede beaded coat. Lori knew Adele could have done without the Native entertainment in the hot sun, but they couldn't leave and insult Rain's friends. They sat on the few chairs lined up in between the blankets, facing the makeshift stage. Plates of Southwestern Indian food, plus juice from the prickly pear cacti, were passed to them.

The same teenage boys and girls she had seen milling around the reservation in blue jeans and t-shirts were magically transformed into 19th century Navajo Indian dancers. The boys wore deerskin loincloths, beaded moccasins, and full feather headdress, and the girls wore beaded suede outfits, moccasins, bells, and exquisite turquoise and silver jewelry. They danced to the beat of ancient drums.

When Lori and Adele left the Indian reservation, the first words out of Adele's mouth were, "Please, may we go somewhere and get some *normal* food?"

Smiling, Lori said, "I watched you playing with the corn mush and vegetables, trying to be polite."

"Don't you agree that food was horrible?" Adele asked. "And eating outside in the heat didn't help. Was I really that obvious?"

"Come on, Adele, if the menu doesn't have tuna, steak, or a salad, you are lost," Lori said.

As they walked into the Cheesecake Factory, Adele gave Lori a sly smile and said, "Sometimes I eat pasta too."

They leaned back in the comfortable chairs, enjoying the air conditioning. The waitress came over with menus. Adele didn't need one, saying, "Caesar salad with chicken and a diet coke with lemon."

Looking at Adele, Lori said, "I actually ate at the reservation." She turned to the waitress and said, "Just black coffee."

"You're not getting cheesecake?" the waitress said.

"I'm getting too fat," Lori replied. Then, rethinking the situation, Lori called the waitress back and said, "Bring me a piece of strawberry cheesecake." They caught up while they enjoyed their lunch.

As they left the restaurant, Lori glanced down at the plates. Adele had only eaten half the meal, while her own plate didn't even have a crumb left. No wonder she couldn't lose any weight and Adele was still the same size eight.

"What do you know about Rain? Where did she live before?" Adele asked as they entered Lori's house. Jerry was wisely out of sight.

"She won't talk about her past life," Lori said. "I met her at rehab. She is in the process of divorcing her second husband because he won't stay sober. I know she's very smart, loyal, and fun. She's very spiritual, and she is teaching me how to tune in to nature. My sleeping pills have been replaced by yoga and meditation. Since I can't have you every day, it is good to have her around."

"She reminds me of someone," Adele answered, musing.

"You sound like Ogden Nash when he said, 'Middle age is when you've met so many people that every new person you meet reminds you of someone else.'"

Annoyed at the age crack, Adele asked, "Is she joining us tomorrow?"

Their friendship went back so far that they spoke to each other in a form of shorthand. A word or certain look was instantly interpreted. Adele's knitted eyebrows, pursed lips, and carefully worded question told Lori she didn't approve of Rain. Lori tried her best to hide it, but she was truly disappointed. She should have known they were from different worlds, and these two worlds were bound to collide.

Great, she thought, *I'm finally starting to relax and have some fun, and the two people who are closest to me are giving me a hard time. Jerry is always complaining about my hippie girlfriend who lives on an Indian reservation, and now Adele is on the case as well.*

Lori sensed the tension leave Adele's body when she answered, "No, it is *our* day. Massages, facials, and pedicures have been booked at the Camelback Spa for us."

"Terrific," Adele said. "I want to see the resort area my friends are always talking about."

Scottsdale was becoming more and more like the North Shore suburbs of Chicago. The hotels, restaurants, and shops were catering to the high maintenance crowds flocking to Arizona from Chicago and California. Camelback Spa was no different, catering to an upper class clientele that expected the best. Adele felt right at home there and fell into place in her role as the pampered housewife on holiday.

"The atmosphere here really beats Elizabeth Arden in downtown Chicago," Adele commented lazily as they lounged in the Jacuzzi, surrounded by palm trees and water fountains.

"John has golden hands. What a massage he gave me," Lori swooned.

"Lori, you let a guy massage you?" Adele asked. "What is happening to you out here?"

"Why not?" Lori replied. "They are so much better than the women. Most are gay anyway."

Just then, an attendant offered them towels and led them to their facial appointments.

Lori gave her a knowing smile.

After their day in the spa, they shopped a little and then left for Lori's home.

Driving to Lori's house, Adele said, "You hardly ever talk about Jerry exploding. Has his temper eased now that he isn't drinking?"

"Oh, Adele, he has mellowed like a fine wine," Lori said.

"Funny you would compare him to a wine," Adele replied. "I remember when you used to say in his old age he would become fermented like an aged bottle of whiskey."

They looked at each other and laughed.

The next day, they shopped until they dropped. Adele found stores Lori never knew existed.

By the time Adele left for Chicago, Lori was exhausted from shopping, eating, and staying up nights talking.

On the way to the airport, Adele turned towards Lori and said, "Come to Florida for New Year's."

"I couldn't handle another New Year's Eve celebration in Florida," Lori said. "Anyway, we usually stay home New Year's. It is too hard a night for Jerry. You know what I mean. Why don't you and Jim come here?"

Adele hesitated before answering, "I'll talk to Jim about it."

Lori could tell it wasn't going to happen. Adele was a creature of habit.

Lori missed Adele while Jerry took to retirement and Arizona. His days were very scheduled with his AA meetings, health club visits, stock market watching, golf games, cleaning the house, and tending garden. Jerry had graduated to running the community, becoming a director on the board of their retirement community.

Lori looked up and saw Jerry entering the house, sweat beading down his face as he dropped a large basket of oranges, grapefruit, and tomatoes on the kitchen counter.

Lori's anger flared immediately. "How did you get tomatoes to grow here?" she demanded. "What is our water bill like? Why have you become a gardener in the desert?" Her questions came rapidly and accusatorily.

"I have time now. So what?" Jerry said as he scowled at his wife and shrugged. "Stop watching everything I do." He stomped around the kitchen and prepared himself a glass full of ice and poured himself water from a pitcher. "If you don't mind too much, I'm going to use *more* water and take a shower before dinner. It's nearly a hundred degrees out there."

Lori watched Jerry leave the room. She went back to preparing dinner. Before she had finished cutting the large red home-grown tomatoes, the shrill sound of the phone echoed through the room..

Anticipating the caller, she swallowed hard to keep the tears back as she picked up the phone off the kitchen wall. "I've been waiting for your call," she said.

Adele answered, "I've been thinking about you all day, but I was busy babysitting."

Adele's daughter Sasha had a three-month-old baby boy. Lori wondered, *Would Julie be married now?* After all, it was 1999, and Julie would have been twenty-five years old.

She turned back to the phone and said, "Adele, you always remember, thank you." They chatted for a while. Lori smiled happily when Adele said, "Barry and Anne were at my house for our Labor Day picnic. She is such a nice girl. Have they been talking about marriage?"

Lori answered, "Barry is determined to wait until he gets his doctor's degree. Meanwhile, they are living together. A new world."

After they hung up, Lori put down the phone and stared out the window of their living room, where the lit yahrzeit candle sat on a nearby table on a small stand. Lori had lit it the sundown of the day before, on the eve of the anniversary of her loved one's death, as custom decreed.

It was hard to believe eight years had passed since Julie had died, and equally hard to believe Lori was functioning. It did not surprise her one bit that as soon as she had let the wound reopen again, she broke down into uncontrollable weeping.

Jerry appeared in the kitchen doorway draped in a large beach towel. He looked around when he heard weeping and found Lori sitting on the sofa in the living room, crying and looking out the stretch of windows that revealed the dusky mountain scenery that lay before their new home. The sun had set, leaving behind various shades of brilliant pink and deep purple smeared across the expansive sky.

"What's wrong?" Jerry said. "Who called?"

"Adele," Lori said softly, tears spilling freely down her face. "She remembered… today is September 11th, the day Julie died. I lit the candle last night, but you weren't here…"

He glanced at the still flame of the commemorative candle, then looked at Lori sadly for a moment before he replied softly, "Call me when dinner is ready. I'll be on the patio." He turned and walked out of the living room toward the bedroom to dress.

Lori looked after him with tears streaming down her face. She really couldn't understand him. Maybe it was different for a mother than for a father. Even though it was eight years since Julie died, when that date or Julie's birthday or the holidays came around, she still felt like the wound was being stabbed open.

Chapter Thirty-One

After a day of Christmas/Chanukah shopping in seventy-five degree weather, Jerry and Lori were happy to get home. After dropping the packages down on the table, Lori made her way to the refrigerator for a cold drink while Jerry checked the answering machine for messages.

The first message on the answering machine was from his brother Joel.

"Call me right away," Joel said in his message. "Something terrible has happened."

As Jerry rushed to dial Joel in Chicago, Lori tensed up and thought, *Here we go again.*

Jerry's face was ashen white as he hung up the phone. "My mother died," he said.

"Shelly is dead?" Lori repeated it to herself. "I don't believe it. She always seemed so strong."

"She wasn't sick," Jerry said in a low mumble. "She had a heart attack in her sleep. Please start packing and call the airlines." Jerry slumped into a chair, held his head with both hands, and cried uncontrollably.

Lori put her arms around him and told him she was sorry. Then she left him alone and proceeded to make arrangements and phone calls.

On the plane trip the next morning, Jerry put the seat back and laid there with his eyes closed. Over and over he said to himself, *I'm so guilty. I haven't been home to see her in a year, and she was afraid to fly out. Why didn't I visit her? Why? Because life was so much easier without my mother and Lori fighting. Oh, God, I can't believe my mother is dead!*

When Lori and Jerry exited the plane at O'Hare Airport, Jerry's cell phone rang. Joel directed them to go straight to Weinstein's Funeral Parlor in Skokie. Exiting the airport terminal, a gust of cold wind and white wet snow greeted them. Buttoning up her coat and covering her head with a scarf, Lori shivered as they boarded the bus to the Hertz terminal. After renting a car, she realized she was the designated driver when Jerry got in the passenger's seat.

The drive was awful. Snow, fog, sleet, ice, and a seat that wouldn't move forward made Lori scared and nervous. She couldn't believe she had lived in Chicago fighting the winters for most of her life. Arizona was looking better and better. Shelly had to die in the winter. Jerry was no help. He just sat back on the seat, eyes closed and not saying a word. She hoped she wouldn't get them killed driving the expressway in the bad weather. When they pulled into the parking lot of the funeral home, she gave a sigh of relief.

Lori happily sat in a back seat in the Weinstein's Funeral Parlor conference room, drinking coffee while the Brill siblings fought over the details for Shelly's funeral: casket and casement type, newspaper announcement, graveside service or not, flowers, what the rabbi should say about her. Their father Jack said nothing until they discussed the number of days they would sit.

"Shiva is seven," Jack said. "We will sit seven days."

What a day to have a funeral. A fierce wind blew snow everywhere. They huddled under the canopy praying the rabbi would be brief. Lori shivered as her mind drifted back to thoughts of her Aunt Tillie. In Lori's youth, every time they picked up her dad's sister at Midway Airport she would say, "Florida has thinned out my blood, and I can no longer tolerate Chicago weather." When Jerry's brother Joel asked the rabbi to let him say a few words, Lori thought she would kill him. She was so cold that her hands and feet felt numb, and she could hardly breathe. She looked up at the sky and whispered, "Thanks, Shelly."

When it was Barry's turn to throw the dirt over the casket, as was tradition, he took out a box whose label indicated that it was from Israel, and he removed earth from it. Earth from the Holy Land is considered to possess atoning power.

Turning to Jerry, she whispered, "Did Barry do that for Julie?"

Jerry gave her a puzzled look as he answered, "How can *you*, who can't let go of Julie, not remember her funeral?"

"Truthfully, I remember every detail of those four years up until the day she died," Lori confessed.

Jerry looked at Lori with newfound concern and said, "Yes, Barry did use earth from Israel, and the rabbi thanked him."

Lori absolutely couldn't recall Julie's funeral.

Looking around at the large number of people at Shelly's funeral, Lori was amazed that she had so many friends willing to stand in a cold snowstorm to pay their respects. Suddenly, she realized those years of conflict with Shelly were now over. Lori didn't feel relief, just numb.

As they trudged through the snow-covered cemetery away from Shelly's resting place, Lori confessed, "Jerry, I'm sorry that I had so much controversy with your mother. I know it was hard on you."

Jerry shook his head a bit and sniffled, saying, "Well, Lori, I'm not gonna lie. Life's been pretty difficult for me with so much hostility between you and Mom."

"Jerry, I could never get you involved," Lori explained. "It frustrated me to no end."

"Involved?" Jerry stopped and shouted, "What the hell is that, Lori?" Jerry looked around, making sure no one heard them fighting, at a funeral of all places. He watched the funeral mourners make their way quickly to their cars to escape the bitter cold. "I *was* involved, Lori, but you didn't know it or you did not see it. I was involved with Mom, when she talked to me, giving her side, and I was involved with *you* while you talked to me, giving your side, and who in hell did *I* talk to? I talked to the bottle. No one else would listen to me!"

"Are you trying to blame me for your drinking?" Lori shouted. "Is that what they tell you at your fucking meetings?"

Lori moved away from Jerry, but he caught hold of her coat and pulled her back.

"Wait a minute, Lori!" He held onto her tightly and said, "God, you have no idea what I went through trying to keep you two *from killing each other*!" He spoke softer now, pressing her to him. "Mom had a hard time understanding you, Lori, but she knew how much you meant to me."

Lori and Jerry held one another for a few moments before walking in silence through the snow to their car. Once inside the car, Lori broke the silence.

"I guess we were both just fighting for your attention. Now that I am older, I look at it differently," Lori said. This time, she let Jerry drive, and she sat back in her seat.

"Now that my mother's dead, you mean," Jerry corrected, turning on the car and blasting the heat. "Things will look different now that she is gone."

"Actually Jerry, since Julie died things have looked different," Lori said. "I now realize what is and isn't important.

They ended up staying at Jerry's mother's house for the traditional shiva—seven days of mourning. Neighbors and friends brought in trays of kosher food daily. Lori, along with Barry's girlfriend, Anne, had her first experience with a traditional Orthodox Jewish shiva. The mirrors in the house were covered to prevent vanity, and those in the house sat on hard stools, and for the first time in that house, conversations were conducted in whispers. Most of the people that came to pay a condolence call were strangers to Lori. There were relatives that remembered their wedding and neighbors that asked about their children and their life in Arizona. When the rabbi came for the evening service, he talked about the charity work Shelly did at the synagogue. They sang praises of a woman Lori never knew. She wondered why Shelly had never shared this side of herself with her daughter-in-law. She wished she could have talked to Adele, but she and Jim were out of town, and Lori couldn't wait until they were able to head back to Arizona.

Lori perked up when she suddenly saw Eileen walk in. She had missed the funeral, but she was in time for the shiva. When she walked into the house, all eyes were on her father Jack. Eileen walked over to him and spoke into his ear. To the congregation's surprise, Eileen's father stood and gave Eileen a hug, uttering only, "Sha." Everyone let out a collective sigh of relief and returned to their soft-spoken conversations and their eating. Then Eileen's brothers ventured forward and greeted her.

"Lori, so good to see you again," Eileen said as she sat down next to Lori. "Where's my boy?" Eileen asked, wiping her nose with a napkin. It was apparent she had been crying.

Lori answered, "He was at the funeral, but he had to go back to the hospital. He will be here later."

After everyone left and the boys put away the chairs and heavy things, Eileen and Lori worked on clean-up. Walking into the living room, Lori found Eileen busily scrubbing a spot of food off the carpet.

She pointed to the spot and looked up at Lori, "My mother is going to kill me for allowing people in the living room."

"Eileen," Lori said, shaking her head sympathetically, "I'm sure she'd understand. It was quite a crowded, bustling funeral." Lori helped

Eileen off her knees and then led her to the plastic-covered flowered sofa.

"Sit down, and I will get us some coffee," Lori said. Coming back with two cups of strong coffee, Lori sat down on one of the red mohair armchairs, placing the cups on the coffee table next to a large assortment of small figurines her mother would call *tchotchkes*. She turned towards Eileen.

"Tell me about your mother, Eileen," Lori said.

Instead of talking, Eileen spent the night sobbing and getting out all the hurt caused by being estranged from a family she loved, and spurned by a woman from whom she desperately needed nurturing, but who gave her only either a cold shoulder or flat-out rejection.

When Lori had retired late that night, she realized the reason she felt such an affinity toward Eileen: they had both missed out on the nurturing love of a mother. Lying below Jerry's slumbering body on the lower half of the bunk bed in Jerry's old bedroom, Lori silently wept for the loss of her own mother, although she was still very much alive.

Jerry decided to stay in Chicago another week to help his dad, but Lori wanted to get out of there. Lori found Jerry alone in his old bedroom. She sat down next to him on the lower bunk.

"Are you all right?" she asked, playfully ruffling his hair.

"Yeah, I guess so," Jerry said, shrugging. "I will really miss talking to my mother."

"Since we moved, how often did you talk to her?" Lori asked.

Jerry's silence meant more than she realized. If she talked to her own mother once a month, it was a lot. It was impossible to even converse with her mother now that confusion had taken over—not that it was ever easy conversing with her in the first place. Here they were, Jerry grieving for the loss of a domineering, overbearing mother and Lori grieving for an aloof, distant mother she never really knew. The doctors said it was not Alzheimer's but depression and withdrawal on her mother's part. A visit to see her mother was on her mind now, so she asked Jerry if he would mind if she left for Florida and met him at home in Arizona.

"No," he answered. "It will give me time to sort things out with my brothers." He turned to her and kissed her gently on the forehead, saying, "It looks like we both have some mother issues we need to take care of, huh?" He kissed her forehead again. "I know you never had a great relationship with your mom, Lori. I think it's great you want to visit her, for all it's worth. Just don't expect much. It hurts less if you don't expect much."

Silently, Lori pulled her husband beside her to lie down on the single bunk bed, and there they remained for a while holding one another, trying to heal each other's wounds.

Chapter Thirty-Two

When it became too hard for Lori's mother to live alone after Lori's father died, Lori tried to get her to retire in Arizona, but her mother insisted on staying in Florida. Her mother had always been stubborn, but she never interfered with her life like Shelly.

Lori packed her bag, said goodbye to the Brill family, stopped at Chocolate Potpourri, her mother's favorite candy store, and headed to O'Hare Airport. It was much easier going to Florida from Chicago than from Arizona.

The temperature in West Palm Beach was in the eighties, much more to Lori's liking than Chicago's twenty degrees. The ride from Fort Lauderdale airport was easy. Her mother was now residing in an assisted living home in West Palm Beach. As Lori entered the small two-room apartment, she was surprised to see her all dressed up. In her eighties, her mother still had a beautician come to the assisted living home once a week. Still slim, dressed in a Chanel suit, sipping wine, she looked so out of place. Lori had noticed most of the women sitting in the halls or lounges were in bathrobes or pants outfits.

As Lori bent down to kiss her mother, she caught a whiff of her familiar perfume, Chanel No. 5. She handed her the box of toffees, hoping she wouldn't notice the two missing pieces Lori had devoured on the plane. Lori didn't inherit her mother's figure or her willpower.

Lori looked at her mother and wondered how a mother who still looked and acted like a princess at eighty-five could have a daughter with gray hair, unpolished nails, and dressed in sloppy jeans and sandals. *If only she could have had Adele as a daughter,* she mused.

Her mother was acting odd, like the socialite she always tried to be. She handed the box of candy back to Lori and turned towards the door as if she was expecting someone.

"Thank you, dear," her mother said. "Tell Marie to serve them after dinner."

Humoring her, Lori mumbled, "OK." Marie, she gathered from other references to her through the years, must have been one of her mother's German household cooks or maids.

Gently, Lori moved to her mother, and holding her hand, she told her, "Mom, I heard from Israel. Uncle Dov died."

Her mother looked puzzled. "Who?" she asked.

"Mom, your brother, Dov."

"I have no family. They all went up in flames."

"Would you like to tell me about it?" Lori tried to find out about her mother's past life, but she would never talk.

"Terrible," her mother said as she pointed to the window.

"What is terrible?" Lori asked as she moved over to the window and looked out on a beautiful, manicured golf course. Turning back to her mother, who was talking gibberish, Lori became confused.

"They cut down all the beautiful trees. The fox has no place to hide."

Not understanding her comments, Lori decided to ignore them and once again opened the subject of her childhood and their relationship.

"Mom, why did you and Dad travel so much without me?" Lori asked.

"Are you starting on that theme again? Dad worked for the State Department and had to travel. We were old and set in our ways by the time you were born. My God, you had a wonderful childhood—a nice home, nannies, toys, designer clothes, whatever you wanted. You were a very lucky child."

The designer clothes never helped Lori become the sophisticated daughter her mother had wanted. She was too short, heavy, and clumsy to qualify. She did, however, have a knack for picking elegant, classy friends like Adele. Lori really wanted to tell her mother that the major thing she lacked growing up was her love and attention, but once again, she dropped the subject and retreated, letting all the unspoken words between them disappear into thin air. She remembered her husband's words to expect less, as it hurts less. She wondered if she ever could.

"I'm tired," her mother said. "Tell Marie to clear the table and turn down the bed."

Lori knew she was dismissed. She kissed her mother goodbye and went down the hall. The doctors had told Lori that her mother did not have Alzheimer's but that she was slipping away into the past, to a happier time. There was very little anyone could do.

Leaving her room and passing through the halls, sadness engulfed Lori. Some women were busy knitting, some playing cards or bingo, and others were sitting like lost souls. Her mother didn't fit into any of these groups; in fact, throughout Lori's life, she never fit into any group. Lori really didn't know her mother, and she guessed she never would. Lori had to admit to herself that her mother's memory and bouts of confusion were getting worse. Lori got into her rented car and drove to the Fort Lauderdale airport. She wanted to be back in Arizona before Jerry came home from Chicago.

Back home, Lori was already in a state of anxiety from her visit with her mother and from the fact that she was worried about Jerry's reaction to his mother's death when she was awoken in the middle of the night by a howling sound. The piercing reverberation sent shivers down her spine. She got out of bed and moved towards the open window. The sky was dark except for the full moon peeking out of the mountains. Lori could see no animal. She guessed the howling must have come from coyotes. A strange foreshadowing fear encompassed her. Up until now, Lori had felt peaceful in the desert.

***

Jerry sat on the plane and stared out the window. He couldn't believe his mother was dead. He was fifty-eight, yet at that moment, he felt like a lost little boy. His mother had always been there for him, and now he was feeling guilty for having moved away. If she had been alive, she would help him with his pending problem of how to tell Lori about Joel.

"Wine with your meal, sir?" a stewardess asked him. He was traveling first class thanks to a nice agent.

"No, thank you," he replied. "Well, wait… Okay, maybe just a little."

Chapter Thirty-Three

Lori picked up Jerry at the Phoenix airport. They drove north on the freeway, getting off on Pima Road for their trip to Carefree and home. Contrary to what she expected, he was full of life and busy teasing her. She became suspicious.

"What's going on Jerry?" Lori asked. "Were you drinking?"

"Of course not," Jerry said. "How can you ask that?"

"You are coming from your mother's funeral," Lori replied. "Why are you so happy?"

"I'm happy because we are going to be rich," Jerry said.

"Oh, really?" Lori immediately sensed Joel's stink all over Jerry's incongruously jocular mood.

"My brother Joel is really onto something now," Jerry said. "Inflation is coming. With inflation, the price of gold is going up. Joel has an in on a new gold mine."

Before he could finish, Lori gripped the steering wheel and screamed, "No, no, nooooo!"

"Stop!" Jerry yelled as their car slammed into the car in front of them.

"Son of a BITCH!" she screamed as she got out of the car to meet the driver in the car in front of her.

A gray-haired elderly gentleman looked at his car and then at Lori. "I was stopped for a red light," he said. "Didn't you see that it was red?"

"I'm very sorry. It was my fault," Lori countered while thumbing through her wallet for her insurance card.

The man went back to his car, took out a piece of paper, and wrote down her information. Looking up at her, he said, "Don't be so upset.

It's just a little nick. I'll trust you to report it. The police take so long nowadays." He handed Lori his card that said: *Retired investigator*.

"Thank you," Lori said. When she got back into the car, she pulled it over to the curb, turned to Jerry, and said, "Okay, tell me what's going on with your brother. Let's get it over with."

"You want to talk about this *now*?" Jerry asked.

"Jerry," Lori said, impatiently, "just tell me."

"Well, okay." Jerry let a pregnant pause linger between them before he spoke up again. "For just forty-thousand dollars, we can become one of the primary owners of a new gold mine. Lori, you won't believe who the other investors are: Tony Veneti, the actor, and Bob Fields, the owner of the Diamond Jets."

Looking Jerry directly in the eyes, Lori narrowed her eyelids; her words squeezed out between pursed her lips. "I don't care if the President of the United States invested," Lori said. "If Joel is in on it, it will fail. Don't you know that by now? Jesus, Jerry! Sometimes I can't believe you have a master's degree in business."

Jerry looked away and didn't say anything. Lori grabbed his shoulders and pulled him towards her. "Please don't tell me you already gave him a check!"

From the look on Jerry's face, she knew he had already given Joel some of their retirement money.

"Maybe I can cancel the check," she said aloud to herself as she put the car in gear and quietly drove them home.

Lori did not have to wait long before she saw Joel had cashed their check from their money market. *I'm now the proud part-owner of a shitty gold mine*, she thought ruefully.

Lori called Adele. "Do me a favor, call Joel and tell him you are interested in his gold mine."

"Oh no."

"Oh yes."

"Another Joel scheme, huh? 'Adele asked.

"Uh huh."

"When will Jerry learn?"

"When we're penniless and living in a cardboard box along the side of a road."

A few days later, Adele called back. "After three tries, I finally got a hold of Joel. When I asked for a proposal on the gold mine, he told me it was too late to invest. By the way, he has been seen driving a red Porsche."

"Thanks, Adele." Lori hung up the phone and sat down at the kitchen table, running her hands through her thick peppered gray hair. Her stomach sank.

Bye-bye, forty... thousand... If we live too long, we will run out of money, and at this age, I couldn't go back to teaching. She was grateful for her father's life insurance money that she had tied up in stocks and in an account of which Jerry knew nothing. She knew Jerry was a soft touch. *God forbid he ever found that money, it would all end up in Joel's pocket.* Shelly was dead, but the Brill family was still haunting her.

The ringing of the doorbell diverted her. She got up and opened the door to the UPS man.

"Miss Lori, a package from far away: Israel," he said.

Lori smiled and said, "Thanks, Nate. I needed a lift this morning."

She took the package, turning it over and over as she walked back into the kitchen. Taking a knife, she quickly opened it.

Chapter Thirty-Four

Jerry opened the front door and walked into the kitchen. Lori was sitting sorting through a stack of papers and pictures. She looked up and asked, "How was the meeting?"

"Actually, I was shopping," Jerry said. "What's on the table?"

"I received an unusual package from Israel," Lori said. "My cousin Michel was going through his late father's things, and he found pictures and letters his father exchanged with my mother from as far back as 1945."

Jerry sat down on a chair and reached for some of the letters. "Wow, they must be interesting," he said.

Lori looked up and said, "Actually they're all in German, so I have no idea what they say. I was thinking of putting them together and flying to Florida with them."

Jerry was now standing by the kitchen counter, pouring himself a cup of coffee, when Lori asked, "By the way, why haven't you been going to your meetings lately?"

Ignoring her, he said, "I think you should get the letters translated before you take them to confront your mother. My bridge instructor is German. He may be able to help."

Holding up a picture of her mother as a teenager sitting on a boat, she told Jerry, "That's a great idea. Would you ask him?"

Jerry left Lori and went looking for his bridge instructor. About an hour later, he walked into their kitchen with a thin, bald, salt-and-pepper-mustached, proper-looking gentleman.

"Lori, this is Gustav Meyer," Jerry said. "He is from Berlin, speaks fluent German, and is willing to translate your mother's letters."

Lori retrieved the earliest dated letter from 1945 and handed it, with a stack of others, to Gustav.

"My mother never told me anything about her life before coming to the United States. I'm hoping these will give me some insight. Can I get you something to drink?" Lori asked as Gustav sat down at the table and started to look over the letters.

"A cup of tea would be nice," Gustav said.

Lori put tea and some cookies on the table and waited patiently as he read several letters, making notes on a sheet of paper from time to time. Finally, leaning forward on the table, he looked up directly at her.

"You are from one of the wealthiest and most prominent Jewish families in Germany," Gustav said. "The name Brune was considered akin to Rothschild. They were in banking and government. I was just a child, but I believe your grandfather was one of the negotiators after World War II."

"Mother always acted like a duchess, and the kids in the neighborhood liked to tease me by imitating her," Lori said.

Gustav replied, "Well, she really was one. In pre-war Germany, the name Brune was respected."

"Do the letters talk about her life in Germany?" Lori asked.

His eyes narrowed and his tone changed. "No, they are very sad, from right after the war," Gustav said. "I will read you one, and I will then write out a translation of the others. Some of the papers are worn and torn, so it will not be totally accurate."

"I am grateful for any information you can give me," Lori said.

He took out a paper and began reading:

Oct. 16, 1945

My dearest Dov, my beautiful little brother,

Thank God (if there still is one) I have found you. I've been told you were with the resistance, helping fellow Jews get to Israel. As far as I know, the only family left is Cousin Gertie, who is in a camp in Poland. If you have found other family members, please let me know.

Father, along with my dear husband Siegfried, was arrested at the beginning of the war when we were still in Germany, too dumb to leave when we could. I know Mother, grandmother, and our poor sister Katrina died in Dachau. I was in Dachau with them. I watched them being marched into the crematoriums. Why I survived I will never know. It's really due to a wonderful young American, whose unit liberated the camp. He took special interest in me, transporting me to the hospital and visiting me daily. I am broken of mind, body, and spirit. This is all I can write now, as I am still recuperating in the hospital. Please write me. You are all I have.

With love,
Your sister, Lillian

"If I could take these home, I will be able to type out translations for you," Gustav said. "I live in Ventura, in the next development."

"I would be so grateful," Lori answered.

After he left, she sat at the table and cried. She looked up toward the ceiling and shouted, "Mama, why? Why were you so secretive? Why didn't you tell me any of this? Things would have been so different!" She wiped away her tears with a napkin and quickly composed herself. "Jerry, I'm going to Florida. I need to talk to my mother."

Lori got on the phone and booked a ticket for the following week, when all the letters would be translated. Calling the assisted living place, Lori found that her mother had taken to her bed and wasn't responding to anyone. The doctor had been about to call Lori. Hanging up, Lori decided to change her ticket to the next day. In the morning, she left the house with a small suitcase containing a few essentials. Something inside of her told her to hurry. There were no direct flights from Arizona, so it took Lori over six hours before she found herself in Florida.

As she left the Hertz area in the small blue Toyota, crazed by the turn of events, she cursed the car as clouds gathered into a dark mass and pouring rain soon bombarded her window, and she couldn't find the right button to turn on the windshield wipers. Finally, she calmed herself down, found the wipers, and slowed down, curving around a downed tree. It was September and hurricane season, not the typical Florida sunshine she was used to.

Lori raced into the home two hours later and stopped cold when she saw a crowd of medical personnel walking out of her mother's room.

One doctor moved over to her, and putting his arm around her shoulders, he said, "I'm so sorry, Lori. Your mother's heart gave out. We did everything we could."

Lori sank into his arms and sobbed, "I knew she wouldn't wait for me."

Lori walked around her mother's last residence, which was just one room with a private bath, not the mansion of her youth. Everything in that place was in perfect order: spotless floors, uncluttered tabletops, clothes folded and lined up within a millimeter of each other. She looked around at the small room and the meager amount of things her mother had at the end of her life. She remembered being annoyed when her mother tried to get her to take most of the knickknacks and household things in the condo she was leaving.

Lori had told her, "I don't want anything. Get rid of all of it." Now she was sorry. Julie had died only a year earlier at that time, and Lori was still angry. Now that her mom was dead, she would never be able to find out about her early life in Germany, nor would she be able to make amends with her over their strained relationship.

Lori's father requested to be cremated. This was not a Jewish custom, though many Reform Jews had recently adopted it. Today's generation no longer visited the cemetery as people did in years past. She remembered her grandmother dragging them to the cemetery regularly.

Since her mother had no family in the United States, they had the funeral service in Chicago at their old temple in Northfield with Barry, Jerry's family, and a small group of their friends. They sat shiva for two days at Barry's two-bedroom, downtown Chicago condo.

Being Reform Jews, no mirrors were covered and the house was full of noisy people instead of a quiet, whispering crowd. Trays of abundant food came from Ashkenaz Delicatessen instead of the homemade kind at Shelly's funeral. Lori just felt numb through all of it. She tried, but the tears never came, even when Adele and some other friends reminisced with her about their high school days.

When their friend Evie said, "Your mother was one of the last dignified prim and proper ladies," everyone agreed.

When Lori asked, "What about me?" they all laughed.

Lori's cousin Michel sent his condolences, and Lori promised to send him copies of the translated letters.

After the funeral service at Shalom, Lori dragged Jerry through the cemetery to visit Julie's grave, plus other family members' graves. Jerry went along to appease her, but he never felt comfortable visiting cemeteries. He gleaned no comfort from the visits; the idea of loved ones left out in the cold, alone, and having well meaning, living people standing over their bodies just depressed him. Lori brought along a camera and took pictures of the grave markers. After reading the letters from her mother, she thought about putting together a family history for future grandchildren. She guessed dates and names would be accurately carved on the stone markers.

"Jerry, why do the Jewish stones only record the name of the father? Look at Julie's stone," she said, pointing. "In Hebrew, it says: *Julie Brill, daughter of Jerry*. Years from now, my descendants will have no record of my name."

"How should I know?" Jerry responded. "It's traditional."

Angrily, she answered, "Yes, I guess it *is* traditional to disregard the women."

"Lori, please," Jerry admonished, "we are in a cemetery, quiet down. Get off of Rain's soapbox."

She only kept quiet because she didn't want Julie to think they were still fighting.

After the two days of shiva they went to O'Hare Airport and finally home to Arizona. Upon entering their house, Lori went right to bed—her escape mode from dealing with her mother. Lori awakened to a quiet house, but a very bright sunny one. She got out of her king-size bed and went into the bathroom. She washed her face, brushed her teeth, and entered the kitchen.

Next to the coffee pot was a note from her husband: *Honey, I've gone to an AA meeting. Please take it easy, and don't get too depressed. Remember, your mother was eighty-six and lived a full life. I'll be thinking of you.*

She smiled as she reread the letter. He was worried about her. Yes, she was depressed and sad, but it was a different feeling, nothing like her depression over Julie's death. The doorbell rang. Lori opened it, and Rain walked in.

"I'm sorry to hear about your mother," Rain said as she walked over to the kitchen counter and poured herself a cup of coffee. "Were you able to talk to her about the letters before she died?"

Lori put down her coffee, spilling some of it on the table, and said, "No, I honestly believe she somehow felt that I was coming to confront her."

"The spirits can do strange things. I know from my life with the Navajos. Here," Rain said, handing Lori a paperback book. "I brought you Elie Wiesel's book *Night*. It's probably the best short but very dynamic account of the camps."

The next day, an envelope from Gustav, her own personal German translator, arrived in the mail. Lori cuddled on the sofa with coffee, a bag of cookies, and the letters.

March 10, 1946

My Dear Dov,

I am finally feeling well enough to leave the hospital. I know you want me to join you in Israel, but I have another interesting opportunity.

The young American soldier who has befriended me has asked me to marry him. He is seven years younger but a very capable young man. He comes from a Jewish family that has connections with the government, so I believe he will be able to get me into the United States.

Do I love him, you will ask? At this stage, I don't know what I feel, only that life must go on. He can never replace my beloved Siegfried and little Joseph, but I must have been spared for a reason.

Lori wondered who little Joseph was. Could Lori have had a half-brother who died in the camps? Could he still be alive? Was that why her mother wouldn't talk to her about Julie? She had blamed her mother's attitude on her father's death. How awful to not know for sure and to not be there to comfort your child in passing. Her Julie had been surrounded by family and friends. She shivered at the thought.

Though none of her mother's letters described her stay in Dachau, she was now reading Elie Wiesel's *Night*, again courtesy of Rain, and crying through the whole one hundred and twenty-seven pages. This time she looked at it through the eyes of her mother. She had also re-read *Catcher In The Rye,* now seeing it thru the eyes of a brother longing for a sister who died of leukemia.

June 05, 1946

My Dear Dov,

I am now Mrs. Edward Weinberg. We were married yesterday in a civil ceremony and are sailing for his home in Chicago. We will have a religious ceremony with his family for their sake. I'm not sure if I still believe in God. I will write from the USA!

With Love,

Your sister, Lillian

The next letter in the grouping was ten months later, written in March 1947. Until this letter, Lori had felt detached, as though reading a novel.

March 14, 1947

My Dear Dov,

On March 10, I gave birth to a beautiful brown-eyed, brown-haired, plump baby girl. She is truly a miracle child. In the camp, we girls never bled, so I thought my production years were gone. I am naming her Lori, after our mother Leah. I wanted to call her Leah, but she deserves an American name.

My new life is truly wonderful. Ed and his family are treating me like a princess. We live in the city overlooking Lake Michigan. He is doing some kind of government work. I am trying to put the camps and my former life out of my mind, but the nightmares will not go away. Maybe the new baby will help.

Tell me more about your young lady.

Your Sister, Lillian.

Now that Lori was in the picture, the people in the letters felt more like family. Too bad that from the beginning, her mother had thought she was too heavy—plump baby girl!

Lori put the letters down and called Adele. Adele listened, interrupting with an occasional, "You're kidding." Finally, she said, "You must pursue this further. Did you know your mother was married before meeting your father? You may have half-brothers and sisters."

"I doubt it," Lori said. "If they survived, she would have mentioned it in the letter. No wonder she couldn't deal with Julie dying. In fact, she couldn't deal with any children, including me."

"What did she tell you about the camps?" Adele asked.

"Adele, I am trying to tell you that I knew nothing," Lori responded "You grew up with me. I would have told you. I knew she came from a wealthy family in Germany and the only family living was in Israel. She indicated that she lost family during the war, but she wouldn't talk about it."

"My God, your mother lived with ghosts from the past," Adele said. "Do you remember your mother having a number on her arm or hand?"

"I never saw her naked, and she always wore a girdle and a nice dress." Lori stopped a moment to think. "You know, actually… it was always a long sleeve thing, or she wore a sweater with it."

"Your mother was so prim and proper that no one expected her to wear shorts or pants outfits when they became popular with the other mothers." Adele said.

When they hung up, Lori felt much better. She wanted to call Israel, but she would have to wait until later due to the time difference. She was exhausted from trying to absorb all she had learned about her mother. She vowed to pursue her family history, going to Germany someday in the future. For now, she put the envelope safely away in her desk drawer. If she knew what she was doing, she could look things up on the Internet. The damn computer, a gift from Barry, sat silent and unused. She vowed to take some classes. She needed to be current. Maybe when Barry had a break from school he would help her; after all, it was his history too. But for now she felt she had better get back to living.

Chapter Thirty-Five

Dragging herself home from exercise class one night, Lori slowly opened the front door and was greeted by a very arrogant Jerry, who was sitting in the living room with his brother Joel. When Lori approached the two, Jerry sneered at her and waved a check in her face.

"Look at this!" Jerry said. "One thousand bucks from my brother Joel, and you doubted the gold mine. Six months isn't even up, and he personally brought me my dividend."

Lori turned to see Joel wearing a big grin on his face, and she said, "Isn't that nice? When you give us back the other thirty-nine thousand out of our forty thousand, Joel, I will be a much happier believer."

"Keep knocking him," Jerry said, chuckling. "Joel is onto something big this time. My brother is hobnobbing with the likes of the actor Tony Veneti. In fact, he's going to his house in Beverly Hills next week. Right, Joel?"

"Joel," Lori asked, never once taking her eyes off the face of her smug brother-in-law, "what happened to your winning race horses?"

Joel merely glanced Lori's way, not attempting to make eye contact, and reached for his beer can sitting on a lamp table next to him. "Lori, that's ancient business," Joel said. " I'm onto bigger and better things now."

"Did Eileen invest in the gold mine, or did she lose enough when your horse, *Fancy Pants*, had to be put down?" Lori asked.

"Come on, Lori, that wasn't my fault," Joel replied. "The trainer gave the horse too much water before the race. Come on, sister-in-law," Joel said, attempting levity as he motioned to the couch with the can in his hand, "stop acting so tough. Kick back. Sit down and join us."

Lori looked down to the cans that sat beside the two men on the matching coffee tables.

"Is that beer?" She knew it was; she simply couldn't believe it was in the house. Once again, like in the past, Lori's urge to strangle her brother-in-law became almost too strong to contain.

"Do you want one?" Joel took a swig off the can and smiled. "It's Coors, from Colorado." It was then that Joel raised his eyes to meet Lori's. He challenged her gaze and smirked at the outrage he was certain bubbled just under the surface of her cool demeanor. *Pompous, stuck-up bitch*, he thought to himself.

Ignoring Joel completely, Lori turned towards Jerry and asked, "Are you drinking?"

The previous week, she had found an empty bottle of vodka and had ignored it because Jerry drank Scotch. Suddenly, she remembered being told many alcoholics revert to vodka because you can't smell it on their breath.

She looked at Jerry's pathetic, smug expression and knew what had to be done. Knowing her next move in the face of certain destruction was a comfort to Lori.

"You gave all our money away, and now you're drinking again," she said as she walked away from her husband. "I've had enough." She walked into the kitchen, grabbed the remaining beer cans off the counter, and whipped them at the floor. "I've had enough!" she repeated, then stormed out of the kitchen toward the bedroom.

Lori was pulling clothes out of her closet and stuffing them into her opened suitcase atop the bed when Jerry walked in.

"What's going on, Lori?" Jerry said. "I had just one beer. Beer isn't the same as Scotch. It's not anything to get upset about." Jerry waited for Lori to reply, and when she did not, he continued talking. "It's Joel, isn't it? Don't worry, Lori, he will come through this time."

Lori stopped packing and took a few deep breaths to calm down and just stared at Jerry. At that moment, all she felt was anger and resignation. Anger for all the days and years she believed him, trusted him, feared him, and put him before everyone, including her children, and resignation that Jerry was never going to break any bad habits—not the habit of getting suckered by his brother, and not the habit of drinking. She said to herself, *You are done making noise and not taking action.*

Within seconds, Lori had zipped shut her suitcase, walked past Jerry without a word (she did let the suitcase smash him in the leg as she left the bedroom), grabbed her purse and keys in the kitchen, and walked out the front door.

Chapter Thirty-Six

Jerry just stood in the kitchen among the smashed beer cans that sat fizzing and oozing all over the floor and watched Lori leave. Joel came up behind him.

"Don't worry, Jerry, she'll be back, especially when the money from the mine comes through," Joel said. "Why don't you come with me to California?"

He stood watching through the kitchen windows as Lori got into the car with her suitcase.

"I don't know, Joel," Jerry mused. "In all these years, she's never walked out on me. She's always stayed—through Julie, through my drinking."

"Forget her," Joel said. "Come with me to California. Veneti will line you up with beautiful young girls."

Jerry turned towards Joel and said, "Go yourself. You've caused enough trouble here."

When Joel left without another word to his brother, Jerry picked up the phone and called his mentor Sy.

"Sy, I need help," Jerry said. "I've *fucked up*."

Lori pulled her car up the mountain road, parked in front of Rain's casita, and knocked on the door. From within, Rain answered, "Come in."

"Rain, can I stay with you for a few days?" Lori entered her friend's home and put down her suitcase, hoping the sight of it would convince Rain of the gravity of her situation.

Without looking up from the book in her hand, Rain responded, "I was just leaving in a few minutes." Rain closed her book and left it beside her place on the couch and rose to greet her friend. "Grab your coat and toothbrush and come with me."

They were in the Jeep for almost an hour. Lori thought it odd that Rain had never once yet asked her about her suitcase.

"Where are we going?" Lori finally asked.

"Vegas," Rain replied. "I have a jewelry show there."

"Aren't you curious about what happened with me?" Lori sounded hurt and wanted an answer.

Rain turned to her friend and smiled. "Lori, really. I was married to one too. It's not hard to figure out, but you know, I think you should have left long ago. He's an alcoholic who has relapsed. You're insane to stay." Rain said it so flippantly that it brought Lori out of her self-pity.

Lori thought to herself, *No, this friend is not Adele. My mother maybe!*

They pulled into Las Vegas and went straight to the town's main convention center.

"Lori, this is a working vacation," Rain explained. "Grab that large case in the back."

She spent the weekend helping Rain to set up the show and demonstrate her jewelry. She watched her organize hundreds of people, butting heads with the CEOs of corporations and the union workers, and her admiration for this dynamic woman grew.

Lori was preparing for bed after a long weekend, thinking about Rain's comments, when her cell phone rang. Her son was on the other end of the phone.

"Mom, what's going on?" Barry asked. "Dad called. He thought you were in Chicago."

"Don't worry, Barry," Lori replied. "Dad and I had a little disagreement, and I took a ride with Rain. I'll call him."

Lori wanted to ask Barry if Jerry sounded drunk, but she didn't want to worry him, as he sounded upset enough. Lori called Jerry, but before she could say anything, he started to yell, so she hung up.

Since he didn't know how to call her back, she waited a few minutes and called him back. She had turned off her cell phone.

"I will hang up for good if you can't speak calmly," she told him while she was looking through her make-up bag for something to calm her nerves and put her to sleep. She knew she had packed sleeping pills; it was just a matter of finding them.

Jerry said, "Lori, I don't think you care if I do or don't drink. In fact, I don't think you care about me anymore."

"Jerry, stop it," Lori said. "It's your choice. I will not live with an alcoholic ever again. When you can prove to me that you are free of alcohol, we will talk."

Lori hung up. Surprisingly, she felt fine, not scared or shaky, and Jerry didn't try to call her back. Rain was right; speak with conviction, act like you really mean it, and be prepared to follow through was her advice. She took some sleeping pills and settled down in the big cushy bed.

The next day, she helped Rain load the Jeep, and they took off for Arizona. Rain seemed pleased with her sales from the weekend show.

When they arrived home, Lori decided to stay with Rain a little longer. Her place was perfect. Jerry would never come over, as Rain intimidated him. He didn't know what to do with strong, opinionated women.

Lori loved visiting Rain's place and felt very comfortable in her friend's home. Decorated with Native American artifacts and beautiful oil paintings, Rain's home made one feel like you were in another century. The weirdest part of her home, Lori noticed, was the absence of personal photographs or things. It was like she was trying to wipe out her history.

At first, Jerry kept calling Lori's cell phone.

"Lori, stop this nonsense and get home," Jerry ordered.

"Jerry, I am done," Lori responded. "I will not live with an alcoholic. When you've proven the drinking is over, I will talk to you."

Jerry started to use Barry and Adele to intercede. Lori was right to stay with Rain. One evening, Jerry tried to see her, and Rain wouldn't let him in.

"Jerry, when Lori is ready to see you, she will let you know," Rain told him. "You will not harass her while she is staying at my house!"

Lori didn't hear his answer, but she could imagine what it was. When he left, she felt better, thinking he must be sober, otherwise he would have broken the door down.

The next day, before Lori even took her morning shower or managed a sip of coffee, the phones started to ring.

"Mom, Dad wanted me to let you know he is back at the Ranch," Barry said.

"Barry, don't let him get you in the middle," Lori directed. "Things will work out if he has taken that important step. Your dad was doing so well for years that I couldn't let him throw away his life by drinking again."

The phone rang in the den, and Rain answered it. She entered the kitchen and handed it to Lori.

"It's Adele," Rain said. She handed Lori the phone and walked back into the den to give Lori her privacy.

"Lori, Jerry called Jim," Adele said. "What is going on? I'm worried about you."

Interesting that he called Jim, Lori thought. Jerry usually worked things out with a family member. Then again, he knew how Lori felt about his family.

"Adele, I called and told you about his drinking again," Lori said.

"I understand," Adele replied. "You needed to leave for a while to teach him a lesson, but why would you go live with Rain instead of coming to Chicago?"

What the hell difference does that make? Lori thought, fuming. She was not in the mood to start an argument with Adele, so she gave her a calm answer.

"I needed to do my thinking where I live now," Lori said.

"Do you want me to come out and be with you?" Adele asked.

"Thanks, Adele, but I'm all right," Lori said.

"Well, if you'd rather," Adele said coolly. "Just keep in mind that Jerry needs and loves you."

Adele's jealousy was not lost on Lori, but she thought it was better not to address it with her. This problem could wait. Lori's immediate crisis was with Jerry, and she had to handle it her way.

She brought the phone back into the den and put it on its cradle.

Rain looked at Lori and asked, "Problem with Adele?"

"Not really," Lori said. "She just doesn't understand what life with an alcoholic is like, and she always defends Jerry. It is strange, because she and Jim were with us during some of Jerry's worst drinking episodes."

"Adele hates change, and she desperately wants to keep your foursome together forever," Rain said.

Lori took a seat on the deep brown leather sofa and stared off into space, stunned at Rain's analysis. She was right. Adele never let go of anyone or anything, while Rain dispensed with people one, two, three if they didn't measure up to her expectations.

If Jerry was really back at the Ranch and religiously going to AA, Lori would have to make a decision soon.

Lori stayed on the reservation for another month, becoming a participating member of the community. Hair in a ponytail, clad in jeans and moccasins, she stood outside Rain's door on the cliff. To her north were mountains lined with cacti and shrub, to the east were buildings: Rain's jewelry factory, a school, apartment building, tents, casitas, and a small outpost. To the south was the 20th century: modern roads, shopping centers, and developments like Ventura.

Rain called out to her, "Let's go."

Lori followed Rain and a group of about twenty Native American women as they hiked up the mountain. They were carrying blankets and baskets of supplies. The head of the group, Little Sister, approached Lori, patted her on the back, and said, "Good, you are coming."

They walked for almost an hour, finally settling in an area of caves and mountain ridges, overlooking a river.

The group gathered in a circle around a fire, holding hands and chanting ancient songs to the sound of drums. One younger woman turned to Lori and explained, "We believe everything needs the help of the spirits, and everyone here will call upon their own individual spirit."

An older woman smiled, displaying several missing teeth, while she handed Lori a blanket and said, "Sit, hear the land. You need not explain anything to anyone here. Do your own thing.".

Lori sat on the blanket, closed her eyes, and listened. At first, all she heard were the drums, but soon she could hear the rush of the water flowing down the mountain to the valley below, and then the sound of small animals scurrying about.

"I love the sound of the drums," Lori said aloud to no one particular.

The girl sitting near her said, "Gee, thanks for saying that. I forgot to turn off my cell phone. If it rings, it will kill the mood of the gathering."

"How did that make you think of your cell?" Lori asked.

"Drums were our telephones in the past," the girl said.

Dishes of corn meal, fruit, water, and deer meat were passed around. A drink called peyote, made from cactus, was handed to her. Before she drank it, Rain appeared.

"Lori, you better forget it," Rain said. "It can induce hallucinations in those who are not used to it. Have you ever tried LSD or even coke?"

Lori shook her head no.

Rain took the peyote from her and said, "Just drink the water."

The women gathered in groups, discussing everything. A tall, thin, dark-skinned young girl with long, braided hair approached Lori.

"You live at Ventura, right?" the girl asked.

"Yes," Lori said, suddenly recognizing her. "You're Jean?"

"I work at the Cactus Club, where they call me Jean, but I am Navajo, and my Navajo name is Little Wolf," she said. "You need a Navajo name. Think about it."

All eyes turned towards Rain, who was standing in the middle of the circle speaking about how Native American women needed to be more independent. When she sat down, another girl got up and read a poem.

When two older women dressed in native costumes of buckskin, feathers, and beads entered the middle of the circle and started to dance to the beat of the drums, Lori realized the middle of the group was considered an open circuit, something like Bughouse Square in Chicago, where anyone could get up and speak.

The moon was full and the coyotes were howling as the group spent the night outside around the fire and beneath the expanse of stars overhead. In the morning, all the women joined hands in a friendship circle before moving down the mountain and back into the fast-paced world in which they were forced to live.

Lori's head was whirling from the incredible experience, and she hardly talked for the rest of the day. Sitting outside of Rain's house, she suddenly saw Mother Nature's work, like the falcon nesting on the mountaintop, the assortment of desert plants, and the small animals and birds living in the cacti.

Chapter Thirty-Seven

Lori was reclining on a lounge chair out at the pool near the community center waiting for Rain to finish giving a lecture on the Native American culture in the area. She was contemplating her next move while listening to an old Sonny and Cher tune playing on the radio. Poor Sonny had died in a ski accident. *Rich or poor makes no difference, trouble still gets you,* she thought.

Rain came out of the community center and approached Lori.

"Lori, come join me inside," Rain said. "You were a great help at the show. Maybe I can put you to work making jewelry."

"What beautiful beads," Lori said. "Do you really think I can make them into a bracelet?"

"Jewelry making is a precision job," Lori said. "We will start out with a simple project and then move on to a bracelet."

After picking out a combination of different sized and colored beads, Lori sat at a long wooden table and tried to follow Rain's instructions, but it was hopeless.

"You picked out a beautiful combination of beads, but you still don't have the hang of stringing them. Here, let me help you," Rain said as she moved towards her.

Lori looked up and somehow managed to drop the whole tray of fifty-some-odd beads.

"Oh, no! I'm a klutz! I guess my mind is better than my hands," Lori said as they crawled beneath the table and around the room, picking up beads.

"That's not saying much," Rain answered as they both burst out laughing.

After a good laugh, they put the beads away, poured themselves cups of coffee, and sat down on the chairs in the center's television room.

With a sly grin on her face, Lori said to her friend, "It's good to hear you laugh. You're always too serious."

"I'm too serious, and you are like an old fifties wife, always catering to your husband," Rain said. "Weren't you involved in the independence movement of the sixties and seventies?"

"Rain, I'm five years older than you," Lori said. "When I went to college in the mid-sixties, our goals were still set at getting that Mrs. degree by graduation. We were actually *trained* to be old fifties wives. While you went around braless, barefoot, and stringing beads, I was cooking, cleaning, diapering babies, and putting up with a controlling mother-in-law."

"Don't get hostile," Rain soothed. "I'm just asking. It's a good thing you weren't braless," Rain teased, sizing up her buxom friend. "Have you always been so well-endowed? I'm jealous!"

Lori looked down at her chest and shrugged, then turning to her friend, she said, "Tell me about your adventures in hippie-land."

"I told you about the commune in Arizona," Rain began. "We went to Woodstock in '69 to hear the music and to protest the war. Twenty of us drove in two VW buses. We heard it was going to be big, but half a million people on three hundred acres was beyond our imagination. A spirit of communion and a feeling of being connected to something powerful engulfed us. Every popular and semi-popular rock and country musician was there playing beautiful music. The songs are still playing in my head." Lori watched as Rain's seriousness slipped a few notches and she reveled in her reminiscing, gesticulating wildly with her hands, pausing to reflect pensively or smile in between the telling. Lori admired her for being an expressive storyteller.

"We partied all day and all night, Lori," Rain continued. "Along with the music, there was anything you wanted in the drug and sex department. At Woodstock, I was tripped out on acid for three days. I almost died. The last thing I remembered was walking over to listen to Timothy Leary's Psychedelic Prayers. Three days later, I came out of an acid trip lying on the grass, wearing nothing else but someone else's jeans. My blouse was gone.

"Never locating my friends, I eventually bummed a ride to New York with one of the Grateful Dead's crew. When I reconnected with friends weeks later, they said they were told I died while on acid. I suddenly realized I was traveling with a great group of friends who never bothered to look for me, dead or alive. I think I was actually happy when my dad found me and made me go back to school.

"I was really young then," Rain said. "After the sixties, I became involved with causes for the underprivileged and neglected people in our society, especially the Native Americans."

"Are you still trying to change the world?" Lori asked her.

"Actually, I'm beginning to feel too old and too tired to keep up the battle," Rain said.

"So am I," Lori said.

"Please be quiet, I'm trying to listen to the news from Chicago," said an elderly women sitting on a chair close to the television.

Just as Lori turned towards the woman, she heard the name Joel Brill coming from the television, and she leaned forward to listen.

The newscaster was announcing that entrepreneur Joel Brill had been indicted for selling bogus gold mines. Lori collapsed back onto the chair. What had Joel done now? This was the first time he had involved anyone outside of the family. Lori's face quickly lost its smile. Getting up and grabbing her purse, she started to leave the community center.

"I better find Jerry," Lori said. "Joel is his brother."

"Let him deal with his brother," Rain said casually.

Lori looked at Rain and said, "You don't understand the Brill family. If his brother is indicted, so are *we*."

She ran all the way to her house. Jerry was already packing.

"Don't go running to your brother's side!" Lori pleaded. "Don't get involved!"

He looked up, waved a paper towards her, and said, "I am already involved. I've been subpoenaed. He listed *me* as a director."

"I'll come with you," Lori said.

"Jumping on again, just before the ship sinks!" Jerry said. "Not very smart, Lori."

"You might need help bailing out the water," Lori said.

"The plane leaves in an hour and a half, so move it," Jerry said.

Lori ran to answer their door to find Rain standing there. "Lori, keep me informed," Rain said. "I may be able to help."

Jerry, who had followed Lori to the front door, ignored her. Under his breath he uttered, "Great, maybe she can get the tribe to do a rain dance for us."

The trip to Chicago was awful. Jerry slept or acted like he was sleeping. He refused to talk to Lori. They rented a car and drove to the Federal Building, where they bailed Joel out of jail. He must have been in shock, as he just sat there quietly while they tried to find help. Steve was useless, and they refused to involve Jack or Barry. Finally, Lori called Jim, who found them a lawyer. They immediately went from the jail to the lawyer's office.

Byron Green's office was on the sixth floor of the lawyer's building on LaSalle Street across from City Hall. Joel perked up when they walked into a beautiful modern leather and marble office.

Spreading himself out on a cushy chair, Joel sighed and said, "This is where I belong. How could that judge let me stay in that cold, small, concrete cell overnight?"

"You're lucky you weren't in county jail," Lori said.

All eyes turned towards the door, where in walked a middle-aged gentleman who looked like he was an ad for Jack Linn, the men's clothing store located on the first floor of the building. He had on a blue pin striped long sleeve shirt, a blue matching tie, a navy suit, and probably a salt and pepper hairpiece.

Pointing to Joel, he said, "I guess the arrogant one is my client." Then, turning towards Lori and Jerry, he said, "I'm Byron Green, and you must be Jim's friends." He then walked to the back of his enormous desk and punched a button. "Fay, bring in coffee." Looking up from the desk, he asked, "Anyone, cream or sugar?"

When Fay served coffee, Byron reached into a desk drawer and pulled out a container of cigars, offering them to Jerry and Joel. Joel took one and rolled it around his fingers, inspecting it.

"Cuban," Joel said admiringly. "You really know how to live."

Lori stayed silent and glowered at her brother-in-law. She wanted him to fry. She rethought her involvement in bailing this pompous ass out of jail.

Byron looked back at him, grinned, and said, "Some people feel that you are also living the good life, but on their money instead of your own. Do you agree with them?"

Joel jumped up and immediately began defending himself. "Tony's crazy lawyer is causing all the trouble. When we went down to see the mine instead of enjoying the trip, that lawyer started asking too many questions. I need to fly to California and talk to Tony."

Lori jumped up, faced Joel, and said, "You're not going anywhere on my bail money."

Byron said, "Both of you sit down. Joel, you are out on bail and can't leave Chicago. If I'm going to represent you, I will need you to tell me the absolute truth, and I need everyone to only answer my questions for the time being."

Lori sat back down and continued glowering. Jerry sat still, his eyes on his shoes.

"How much money did you raise?" Byron demanded.

"Five-hundred-thousand dollars," Joel said. "I have some guys that have pledged more money, but I don't have it yet."

"How much do you have left?" Lori asked.

"Three-hundred thousand." He turned to Jerry and said, "I was really trying to make it up to you for the time the family didn't get Caryn's uncle's money."

"Stop the bullshit!" Lori yelled, losing control once again. "I'm ready to kill you and your whole family." She turned to Jerry. "If he's telling the truth, it's not as bad as it could be. But who knows with Joel?"

Byron smiled and said, "I get to ask the first question. You still have some of the money, that's good news. Do you have files outlining where the other two-hundred thousand went?" Byron asked.

Lori gave Joel a dirty look and said, "You better sell that new Porsche, pronto, and hang on to the money for your defense."

"Is Steve being sued also?" Jerry asked, finally looking up and speaking.

Byron answered. "Steve drew up the papers, but he didn't sign anything." Byron turned to Jerry. "Maybe you can talk to your brother Steve."

"I just called him," Jerry stated, his voice wooden, "and he refused to turn over any of the papers or to help us. He kept saying he had nothing to do with it. Joel stated on paper that he paid him twenty-five thousand dollars in cash."

Byron put up his hand, and turning to Joel, he said, "Here is the major question. Is there a working gold mine?"

Joel looked around the room but didn't answer. Lori gritted her teeth and seethed. Byron repeated the question.

Joel's answer was, "Well… I was looking at mines, but I didn't actually purchase one yet."

Byron sat back in his chair and said, "That's not good."

"How bad is the evidence against Jerry?" Lori asked, unable to contain her silence a moment longer.

"He didn't sign anything as a director," Byron said. "I hope we can keep him listed as an investor that is losing money. I don't know… since he is Joel's brother, I will try to make an out-of-court settlement with the investors. Tony Veneti initiated the lawsuit, so he and the other investors may be happy just to get some of their money back. I just hope the feds stay out of it. This is going to take a while. Go home, and I will keep in contact."

Jerry and Lori visited Barry at the medical school and then left for the airport the next morning. Besides the gold mine problems, they had their own personal lives to sort out.

They kept in daily contact with Byron while he tried hard for an out-of-court settlement. Unfortunately, the press was having a good time with the case because of the celebrity investors.

Jerry didn't touch alcohol the whole time they were in Chicago. Lori moved back into the house, against Rain's advice. At first, Lori moved into the guest bedroom, then she moved back into their room, but their relationship was still strained.

"Are you back for good or just until I go to jail?" Jerry asked.

"I'm here as long as you stay off of alcohol and treat me with respect," Lori shot back. "If I have to leave again, I'm not coming back. You won't go to jail. I will, because I am going to kill your brother."

The call came two months after they were home and trying to get back to a normal life. It was from their lawyer, Byron Green.

"We need a conference in Chicago," Byron said. "Just when I thought I had a settlement with the investors worked out, the federal government stepped in. Because the mine and the majority of investors are from out of state, it is a federal offense. The prosecutor wants to make Joel a guinea pig."

Lori was not surprised. Adele had sent her some Chicago papers where the swindle was on the front page.

When Rain opened the door to Lori's house and saw her packing, she asked, "Where are you going so soon after coming back?"

"Chicago," Lori replied wearily. "New problems with the gold mine trial." Lori then dropped the sweater she had in her hand and collapsed on the bed, crying. Rain moved to her side and comforted her until her crying subsided.

"After all the years of heartache, things were finally looking up," Lori said, sniffling. "Jerry had actually gone back for treatment, and he has been off of alcohol, but now I have to worry about…about spending all our money on lawyers, or even worse, Jerry could end up in jail!" Saying it out loud only caused Lori more pain, and she began crying once more. "Oh, Rain," Lori sobbed, "I feel like every time I take a step forward, I'm knocked back down. My life is like riding a roller coaster."

"I've been following it," Rain said, sitting beside her friend, holding her.

"You've been following the roller-coaster?" Lori said. "I'm some wreck, huh?"

"No, silly," Rain explained, "the Chicago papers just stated it was a federal case. Who's the judge?"

"Jason Cohen," Lori said.

Rain flinched, letting her arm slide off her friend. "Jason Cohen?" Rain rose from the bed and began walking about the room. "I thought he'd be retired by now." When Rain caught Lori looking at her strangely, Rain sat back down on the bed and took one of her friend's hands in her own and spoke slowly.

"Tell me everything you know about the case, Lori," Rain said. "I swear I'll do my best to help."

"Why?" Lori asked, slightly comforted by her friend's concern. "Do you know him?"

"You're my friend, I want to know, and I may be able to help," Rain said as she smiled a half-cocked smile.

Something about her unusual reaction told Lori to answer but not ask too many questions.

Jerry and Lori barely spoke during the flight on the trip and had made separate sleeping arrangements; Jerry would be staying with his brother Joel, while Adele and Jim offered Lori their guest room, knowing of their visit and their strained relationship.

Once they arrived at Byron Green's office, he wasted no time in telling them their current situation. Byron felt they could use an additional lawyer, one who specialized in federal cases. They were now considering legal fees tripling the initial ten thousand dollars, and they were looking at the possibility of jail terms for Joel and Jerry. Byron suggested they stay in Chicago for a while.

Lori picked up her purse and jacket, closed the door to the lawyer's office, and followed Jerry onto LaSalle Street. It was a beautiful spring day, and even in the downtown area of Chicago, yellow and red tulips were making their way up through still-hard winter soil. She turned to

Jerry, who looked worn and thin and, worst of all, absolutely lost. Her pity got the best of her, and she locked her arm in his as they walked on.

"Honey, we'll get through this one," Lori said. "Nothing matters except the fact that everyone is alive and healthy."

Jerry merely looked at his wife and held her tightly. "Your mouth to God's ear, Lori. There are going to be tough times ahead," he warned. "We'll just do the best we can." He looked in his wife's eyes and said, "Lori, can't we both stay in a hotel or at Joel's? I'm not sure you should stay at Jim and…"

Lori waved him off and said, "Jerry, the stress of this lawsuit alone is killing us, and I can't promise I won't harm your brother. Let's just spend some time alone, okay? I don't want to stay at a hotel. God knows how much this damn lawsuit will cost us. Besides, Adele is thrilled I'll be staying with them during this whole thing. Maybe some time apart is what's best."

Driving to Adele and Jim's house, Lori looked out the window at her precious Lake Michigan with the joggers, bike riders, and the clouds overhead. She thought she saw Julie sitting on one of them.

Jerry kept driving, thinking about paying all the bills, thinking about this damned lawsuit, and also about a recent conversation he had with Jim just before flying out to Chicago.

Chapter Thirty-Eight

Lori reached into her purse for a tissue. The air always smelled different in Chicago—wet, from the humidity and the lake. Already her nose was dripping and her eyes were watering.

No longer used to the big city traffic, the trip seemed to take them forever. They pulled into Adele's driveway and rang the doorbell. Jim answered, and they walked into an unusually quiet house.

"Where is everyone?" Lori asked. She was accustomed to Adele's house full of grandchildren on the weekends.

Jerry walked over to Jim, gave him a warm hug, and said, "Hey, friend, how are you?"

Jim hugged back and nodded silently.

Lori looked around the empty house. "Are they giving you two a break this weekend?" she said, smiling.

Jim took a deep breath, placed his hands on Lori's shoulders, and said, "Lori, Adele's been diagnosed with breast cancer."

"What?!"

"She's upstairs, Lori," Jim said. "Go and talk with her. She needs you now."

Lori's mind raced as she made her way up the stairs. *This isn't happening, not to Adele. She's the strong one.* It occurred to her that Adele had always been the strong one helping everyone else.

Upon entering the bedroom, she found Adele lying in bed. Lori just walked over to her, sat herself on the bed, and embraced her friend tightly.

"When did you find out, Adele?" Lori asked frantically. "What is going on?"

Adele sat up and smiled, accepting her friend's tight embrace, and said, "Thank God you're here. I had a biopsy three days ago, and the doctor called this morning. He wants to schedule surgery for next week."

Lori broke the embrace but stayed seated beside her friend. "How come you didn't tell me, me your *best friend*?" Lori grew angry now. "I tell you everything, Adele! I want to be there for you too! You have to tell me these-"

"Lori, stop!" Adele interrupted. "You've been tied up with all this gold mine mess. I never thought it would be anything, so…I didn't want to worry you. You've got enough on your plate."

"But I won't be in the way here?" asked Lori.

"NO!" Adele shouted. "I want you to stay. Please, Lori. If it's not too much trouble, please stay here while you're in Chicago. I know you've got that mess to deal with, but I… think I'm going to need my best friend. I don't know if I can handle all this without you."

Lori threw her arms around her friend, held her, and said, "I'm here for you, Adele. We'll get through this together." She pulled away from her friend for a moment. "Besides, I'll be damned if I'm staying with that bastard Joel in his house," said Lori, attempting levity. "I guess you've got yourself a houseguest."

"Thank you," Adele whispered, resting against her friend's chest, fighting a torrent of tears.

Lori took a deep breath, got to her feet, and said, "Okay, first we need to do a few things, like check out all the options now available, and I know they've done wonders with breast cancer treatment. We've got to get you the best help available, do some research, and…"

She could tell she had lost Adele in the midst of her tirade. Adele was clearly not in the mood to discuss options and treatment. She looked frightened and lost. There was too much sadness and despair in the faces of two of her loved ones, and she had seen it all in one day. When would it end? Lori changed her tack. "Actually, we will make that the second thing. First things first. Get dressed. Jerry and I are starving. The four of us need to go to dinner."

"Now you're talking." Adele got up, gave Lori a kiss, and went to her closet to find some clothes to put on. She looked out from the closet and said, "Let's go to Paissano."

"Sounds great!" Lori said as she walked over to the window and looked out so Adele wouldn't see the tears in her eyes. She knew her friend well enough to know Adele did not want to sit around discussing options, bemoaning her diagnosis. She had to be strong as long as Adele needed it. She had said all the right things to Adele even though past experience made it hard to believe. Another loved one with cancer. She wondered how she was going to handle it. It really put the gold mine fiasco in perspective.

Lori and Adele descended the steps, walked into the kitchen, and looked at their two guys, who were silently sitting at the table drinking coffee.

In a loud jolly voice, Lori said, "Hey, you two lugs, get up. Your women are ready to go to dinner at Paissano and not some fast food place."

Jim looked up and smiled at Adele, who gave him a reassuring nod. "Just give me a minute to shave and put on some clean clothes," Jim said.

The four of them got into Jim's Lexus and turned onto the Edens Expressway towards Chicago's Lincoln Park area.

"How did you come up with Paissano?" Jerry asked. "We haven't been there in years."

Lori answered, "It was where Jim and Adele took us on our blind date. Adele and I thought it would be fun to celebrate our forty-five years of friendship."

They turned off on Clark Street, found a parking space, and entered the small, intimate Italian restaurant. To Lori and Adele's delight, Paissano looked the same, with its red covered booths and walls depicting scenes from the owner's village in Sicily. Tony Paissano had passed away, but his wife, Marie, was still there, in the kitchen supervising everything, while their son ran the place.

Lori intercepted Marie, who had come out of the kitchen with a bottle of wine for the foursome. "No wine, but I would love your homemade lasagna," Lori said.

Adele piped in with, "Me too."

A day that had a bad start had a good ending for the four of them. Walking up the steps to the bedrooms, Jim stopped Lori. "Thank you," he said with tears in his eyes.

Lori took his hands in hers and said, "Jim, you've always been there for us. Of course we'll be here for you."

The next morning, Lori woke early, made coffee, and checked the phone book for some numbers.

Jim, dressed and ready for work, came into the kitchen and grabbed a cup of coffee and a banana. Lori hung up the phone.

"I heard you say, 'Thanks, Dr. Feinberg.' What's that all about?" he asked.

"Dr. Feinberg was one of Julie's doctors," Lori said. "About five years ago, she changed her specialty from pediatric oncology to gynecological oncology. She confirmed that Adele's doctor is one of the tops in the field."

"Good to have you on the team, Lori," Jim said. "Especially today." Adele was scheduled for a slew of pre-surgery tests that day.

"Hey, Jim, my favors don't come cheap." Lori smiled wide to lighten the mood. "How about cleaning my teeth?"

"Come on over, and I will personally take care of you," Jim said as he smiled his usual charming smile, tinged this time around with worry and sadness.

They didn't see Adele walk in, and Jim jumped when Adele said, "I won't let him clean my teeth. He hasn't done that in over twenty years. Wait for his hygienist, Melissa."

Chapter Thirty-Nine

By the time the surgery took place, Lori was drained from consoling Adele, Jim, and their three children. She tried being strong for her best friend, but the impending trial and Jerry's drinking issues had pulled her in too many directions. She tried hard to focus on her friend's health, but it reminded her all too well of the pain and anguish surrounding Julie's treatments and time spent in the hospital. Still, Lori was present for Adele's surgery.

Lori, Jerry, Adele's family, plus Adele's good friend Vicky sat silently in the hospital waiting room, thumbing through magazines or pacing back and forth to and from the coffee pot, or the information desk. Time seemed to hardly move.

All eyes turned towards the door as Dr. Yuki, Adele's surgeon, entered the waiting room.

"I've got good and bad news," Dr. Yuki said, but he did not wait to hear how they wanted the news doled out. "It's stage three cancer. We did a mastectomy of her left breast, and we removed several lymph nodes, and biopsies of the tumor and the nodes are underway. The initial findings show no metastasis, but we must wait a couple of days for all the test results. Her prognosis for recovery is good."

The group gave a sigh of relief as they clung to his last statement, even though they knew stage three was not good. The wait for Adele to come out of recovery seemed endless. By the time they were permitted to see her, she was sitting up and asking for her lipstick. She was so stoic, never breaking down, never complaining, and never hinting that her world wasn't perfect. Everyone used her as a sounding board. Lori wondered if she really knew Adele after all those years.

Adele looked around the room at her gathering of family, friends, cards, and flowers. When she spoke, it was though she was addressing a congregation of devoted followers.

"Thanks, all of you, really, for sitting here all day," Adele said. "You don't know what it means to me to know you all care. But now we all need to rest, so let's break up this party." She was proud that so many people loved and cared for her, but she really wished they would all leave so she could have a good cry over her lost breast. She wanted to be alone to contemplate this new fear of dying. She vowed to be strong for all of them, and especially for the memory of her mother. She stared at Lori with a newfound understanding. She wondered how Lori kept it all together, how she stayed sane.

On the morning of the day Adele was released to go home, Dr. Yuki came into the room.

"Good morning, Adele," he began, walking over to where she sat on the bed. "Here's what we found. Three lymph nodes were cancerous, which means the cancer has spread past your breast. Now, that's not too bad a number, considering how many lymph nodes we removed, but we don't want to take any chances. We will have to put you on a more extensive regimen. We want to make certain we get all those cancer cells. In two to four weeks, we will start chemotherapy, and then, further down the road, radiation." Dr. Yuki gave Adele a pat on her hand and a tight smile. "Do you have any questions?"

Adele's tortured mind remained snagged on the words "cancer has spread" and could not take in much more information.

"I'm sure I have a million questions, doctor. You'll forgive me," Adele replied, stunned by the news, "but I can't think of a one right now. Could you… could you…"

"We will have plenty of time to talk, Adele," Dr. Yuki reassured her. "Give yourself some time to heal. Once we are able to remove your drain, then we can begin the chemotherapy. We'll talk later when you're ready. Write down any questions you may have, and we'll try and answer them the best we can."

"Can I go home?" Adele asked.

Dr. Yuki smiled, nodded, and said, "Rest up at home. We'll see you in about two weeks."

When the doctor left, Adele sank down in the hospital bed and cried.

***

Lori rose from Adele's kitchen table and poured two cups of coffee. She had dropped by to make sure Adele had everything she needed at home upon her return from the hospital. Adele had asked Lori to look in on Jim as well. He was heading out to pick up Adele from the hospital, and Lori wanted to make sure she was there for her return.

Lori walked over to Jim and set his full coffee mug before him. She watched as Jim sat at the head of the kitchen table, his eyes staring off into space, a grim expression on his face. *Oh, God,* Lori thought, *don't have her come home to see this.* Jim always was immaculate with his clean-shaven face and perfectly manicured nails, even though he loved to tinker with an old car or two. It was due to the fact, he once explained when the girls were teasing him for being so fastidious, that he had become a dentist before gloves were required, and hand grooming became a sort of habit. That morning, when Lori found him sitting at the table with a newspaper, she noticed his nails were dirty and he was sprouting a beard.

"Growing a beard?" she asked, taking her seat at the other end of the table.

"Yeah, thought it would go with retirement," Jim said.

"Is your daughter taking over the office full-time now that she graduated?" Lori figured engaging him in conversation would help them both, but Jim was slow to answer. "Jim?"

"Huh?" Jim asked.

"Your daughter, is she taking over the office now that…"

"Now that Adele is sick?"

"Well, no… I meant now that she has graduated dental school."

"Yeah." Jim sighed, looking beyond the kitchen, beyond walls, beyond the confines of the house. "Thinking in that direction."

"Jim, Adele will bounce back," Lori said. "She is one tough lady."

She held her coffee cup with a firm grip as her hands shook. She tried to act natural and not let Jim realize how hard it was for her to deal again with cancer in a loved one.

Jim looked up, faced her, and said, "Lori, I want to thank you and Jerry for being here while I go and pick up Adele."

Lori laughed as she swung her arms around in a circle, looking to her left, then her right.

"Jerry?" Lori said. "What Jerry? Do you see Jerry? He's a worse coward than you are. He's off somewhere with his family."

"Well," Jim replied, moving his coffee mug a fraction of an inch, "thank you, then, for being here and making sure she has what she needs. Those… those, uh, pajamas that you got her…"

"You know her, Jim," Lori said. "You think she'll even wear them? She'll come home and, boom, she'll be dressed in her best Chanel. I have to teach that woman how to lounge! I got her a lounging outfit. Think she'll wear it?"

"I really don't know what she'll do, Lori," Jim replied sadly. "I don't know what's going to happen…"

Lori watched helplessly as her best friend's husband broke down in tears. Quickly, she put down the coffee cup and rushed to his side.

"Jim," she said softly, squeezing his shoulders, "Adele is going to need your help and support. You *can't* fall apart. I know it sounds impossible right now, Jim, and it's so cliché, but, but you have to be strong."

Jim left Northfield and drove to Northwestern Hospital, where Adele was waiting for him. Adele got in the car and kissed Jim on the cheek, and in a noncommittal tone of voice, she told him about the test results and her conversation with Doctor Yuki.

"I've been told the chemo treatments are easier now that they have new drugs and anti-nausea medicine," Adele said.

Jim reached for his wife's hand and squeezed it reassuringly. He hoped it would help reassure himself as well.

Adele looked over at her husband and smiled. *Thanks for being so brave*, she thought to herself. "I'll do fine, they say," Adele said out loud. "In each of our lives, there are periods of trouble." She squeezed her husband's hand and said, "We'll get through this, Jim."

Back at home, Adele and Lori holed themselves upstairs in Adele's bedroom for some alone time and "girl talk." This was unexpected girl talk, Lori mused silently as she watched her friend get into the Capri pants that were part of the light tan loungewear outfit she had bought for her. She couldn't imagine what losing a breast would do to her as a woman.

"Do you like it?" Lori stood beside her friend, assisting her into her top. Adele's chest was bandaged and taped up at the surgery site, and her left arm had limited range of motion from the deep incision and lymph node removal. "I got it at Lord and Taylor."

"I do," Adele replied, buttoning up the tan cardigan top. She glanced at her unbalanced chest, how one breast obviously protruded from her chest where the left side was egregiously flat. Adele took in a deep breath and turned to her friend. “I look a little lopsided, Lori.” Adele said, frowning as she fidgeted with her top.

“Well, you can hardly notice,” Lori said.

“I notice,” Adele said. “Once I get the drain pulled out and I’m healed more, I can go for those prosthetics or a padded bra. I haven’t decided which one to do. Maybe I’ll look into reconstructive surgery.”

“Oh, great, you can get that boob job you’ve always talked about,” Lori kidded.

“Ah, that’s the silver lining to all this,” Adele replied.

“Well, it looks like you are ready for the lounging part of your recovery, anyway,” Lori said.

“I’d rather go to lunch,” Adele said.

“We‘ll go in a few days, once you’ve got your strength back,” Lori assured her.

“We‘ll have to go shopping for another one of these outfits,” Adele suggested.

“Oh, I’m so glad you like it so much, Adele!” Lori said.

“Did you pick up a matching one for yourself?” Adele asked, moving toward her dresser to pick up a brush. Lori beat her to it and began brushing her friend’s hair. Her hair was black and shining and fell into the perfect bob she always wore.

“I didn’t think of it. Should I?” Lori asked.

“You’ll have to learn to lounge in style with me, Lori,” Adele joked. “I can’t be seen convalescing with the likes of some bedraggled Arizona hippie!”

Lori laughed, shook her head, and said, “Only you would care enough about not only how *you* look during chemotherapy, but how your visitors look!”

Adele winked at Lori, grateful for some levity, and said, “Just keeping up appearances, my dear. It’s a must!”

The two women laughed until Adele grew quiet, taking the brush from Lori's hand and inspecting it. "It's going to fall out, they told me," Adele said.

"I know, honey," Lori said. "Julie lost… It happened to Julie too."

"How did she get through it?" Adele asked. "How did you get through it?"

Lori took the brush from Adele, placed it back on her dresser, and said, "There are great, expensive, real hair wigs you can get, and pretty scarves too. You'll see, it will grow back. It's not permanent, and we can have fun picking things out for you, just like we did for Julie…"

Lori looked at Adele. She could see her upbeat tone was not helping her friend at all. Why should it? It never did a damn thing for her when people were disgustingly cheerful around her as her world was crumbling.

"I'm sorry for the bullshit lines, Adele," Lori said. "I don't know what to say. I don't know how we managed. We had no other choice. You just have to take it one day at a time."

Adele walked over to her window and looked down at her flowers in her garden. "Lori, I am so depressed," Adele said. "I've never been sick before. How can I handle these treatments, the loss of my hair?" She turned to her friend.

"Oh, Adele," Lori said as she walked to Adele's side. "Adele, why don't you cry, scream, or yell? Life is unfair, and you should be angry. Cancer is shit. You don't have to hold up for everyone. You have a big family and many friends. Let us help you."

Lori quickly thought of something, then moved to her purse that sat on the bed and looked inside. In a moment, she had pulled out a yellowed piece of paper.

"I've carried this around for years," Lori said. "It's a poem given to Julie by a twelve-year-old leukemia patient. I believe he and Julie are looking down at us from heaven." Lori unfolded the paper and began to read:

> " 'Julie, from Jeff,
> To live is not to be free as a bird.
> To live is to fight every day to stay alive
> Take the good as it comes
> Try to leave the bad behind.' "

Smiling, Adele took the poem Lori handed to her, slipped it inside the pocket of her new cardigan top, and said, "So she had a Jeff besides a Shawn."

"He was only twelve, but they were good friends," Lori said. "I expect to get the poem back when this stage of life is just a memory and you are back to normal."

Chapter Forty

Lori tossed off Adele's granddaughter's pink princess blanket and fumbled for the ringing phone. Opening her eyes, she forgot where she was, although it already had been almost two weeks that she had been staying at Adele and Jim's place. She quickly recalled she was not home and there wasn't a phone on the nightstand, and the phone call probably wasn't for her anyway. She was wrong. Jim appeared at the door of the guest room a few moments later.

"Lori, Jerry's on the phone," Jim said after he knocked.

"Come on in, Jim," Lori said.

She yawned and reached out for the phone. She waited until Jim left the room before she spoke to Jerry. Jerry had stayed at Joel's house, so it could either be important or another of his brother's *mishegoss*.

"Lori, Byron called," Jerry began. "The judge has set up a meeting with all the investors, lawyers, and us at eleven. Meet us at the Federal Building."

"Today?" Lori asked.

Hanging up the phone, she glanced at the clock radio on the nightstand and saw it was only seven o'clock. That gave her some time to spend with Adele before leaving for downtown. She entered the bathroom, brushed her teeth, showered, and dressed in the only nice outfit she had brought with: black pants and a pink cashmere sweater.

She was able to avoid the morning rush hour and arrived early. She parked her car in the underground parking lot and took some time to admire Buckingham Fountain before she walked over to the Federal Building on Dearborn. Turning the corner, she saw, to her surprise, a swarm of reporters around the front of the building.

As she pushed by them, they approached her, asking, "Are you with the Brill case? Do you know when Veneti is coming?"

Lori held her head down, shielding her face from photographers, and hurried into the building and up the elevator to Judge Cohen's chambers.

Lori was led into the chambers and directed to a seat around an enormous table. So far, neither the actor Tony Veneti nor Fields, the owner of the Jets, was in the room, just Lori, Jerry, Joel, and a bunch of lawyers drinking coffee, nibbling on sweet rolls, and thumbing through papers.

She was looking around in awe at the walls covered with many autographed pictures from celebrities when a tall dignified gray-haired gentleman entered the chambers. He was only about five-foot-nine, but he appeared to be much taller due to his judicial robe and the confidence with which he carried himself. When all in the room started to stand, he motioned that it wasn't necessary.

Addressing the people seated around the table, he said, "I am Federal Judge Jason Cohen, as most of you already know. Believing that it would just be an unnecessary expense and feeding frenzy for the press, I have met with the three lawyers involved in this case, and we have worked out a settlement." While he was talking, his bailiff passed out documents.

"I'm calling a half hour recess for everyone to look over the final settlement," Judge Cohen continued. "We will then come back for a discussion and a settlement or a date for a court trial. I'm assuming each lawyer has already consulted with their client and has their proxy, so a half hour is sufficient time."

Lori was fuming as she realized Joel and Jerry must have agreed to a settlement without telling her when the bailiff approached her and said, "Lori Brill, the judge would like to talk to you."

"Why me?" Lori asked as she followed the man into Judge Cohen's private office.

Judge Cohen signaled for her to be seated in the cushy leather chair which was located across from his desk. Her body quivered as she sat down. She felt insignificant compared to the powerful judge and his imposing chambers.

The walls inside this office were filled with pictures from presidents and foreign dignitaries.

"Very impressive pictures," Lori ventured nervously, as she was about to ask him why he wanted to see her alone. Before the words came out of her mouth, he spoke up.

"They mean nothing without my daughter," Judge Cohen said. "I understand you and Renee are very close friends. How is she? I hadn't seen nor heard from her in twenty-five years." The judge grew silent, his eyes misting over. "You must be very special to her, Lori. When she called, she promised a reunion if I would help you and your family."

Lori sat there confused for a few moments. Then it dawned on her.

"Oh my G… You must mean Rain," Lori said. "She never told me you were her…"

"Yes."

"Are you her father?" Lori asked.

The man just nodded and said, "Rain?" He smiled and shook his head. "I didn't know Renee went by that name. How does she look, Lori? Is she well?"

The dignified, powerful, older federal judge was about to break down. Lori promptly answered him, regaling him with glowing accounts of Rain's life in Arizona.

After a few minutes of discussing his estranged daughter, marveling at her adventures, he quickly pulled himself together and gave Lori a very judgmental stare. She sat up very straight, anticipating a lecture.

"Now, young woman, what your husband and brother-in-law did was very stupid," Judge Cohen said. "I have tried to help your family by organizing a conference and an agreement for Renee's sake. This will be between us." Before Lori could thank him, he asked, "By the way, are you related to Captain Edward Weinberg?"

"Yes," she answered, "he was my dad. How did you know my maiden name? Did you know him?"

"When I'm involved in a case, I obtain a file on everyone concerned with it," Judge Cohen explained. "I met your father when I was with the FBI."

"Your Honor, I believe you are mixing him up with someone else. I don't know what you're talking about," Lori anxiously answered.

"The Ed Weinberg I knew was a Jewish captain about my height, with curly dark hair," Judge Cohen said. "He became one of our most valuable spies after World War II and through the Cold War and the Middle East crisis."

Lori turned white as she slumped back into the chair and said, "I… I knew nothing about it. Nobody ever told me what my dad did for the government."

Judge Cohen brought her a drink of water.

"You and my daughter will have a lot to talk about," he said. "Sit awhile. I need to go back to the conference."

"Mister Cohen, I am glad I met you, and I'm awfully glad you will be reconnected with Rain… er… your daughter," Lori said.

"So am I, Lori," the elderly gentlemen said, smiling softly. "So am I."

Lori realized how ignorant and protected she had been throughout her young years. Once she was picked up at school by a State Department car and taken to a hotel two hours away. She and her mother had stayed there for a week with a friend of her dad's from the State Department. She never questioned why, because she had a great time. Now she realized they were probably holed up in a hotel miles from home because they were in danger of being found.

Still in shock, Lori remained silent as they left the courthouse. She barely even glanced at Joel, the bane of her existence. Joel, Jerry, and the lawyer were ecstatic. Veneti and Fields, through their lawyers, had agreed to not prosecute.

They accepted a fifty-percent return of their money. They really didn't want the publicity a trial would bring. The feds, due to Judge Cohen's persuasion, agreed to bar Joel from all financial dealings and to put him on three-year probation instead of a jail term. Jerry was represented as an investor who agreed to take his forty thousand dollars as a full loss so Joel would have more money to settle with the other investors.

Walking with the men down Michigan Avenue to their cars, Lori was in her own world, a world of shock and disbelief. She really wanted to hear Rain's story. On the drive back to Adele and Jim's place, Lori told Jerry what had happened in the judge's quarters.

"I'll be dammed," he uttered. "I thought Rain was a deadbeat, maybe hiding from the law. I will have to apologize to her."

Lori delivered Jerry a dirty look that he missed, having turned his head at the right time.

Deadbeat, fumed Lori to herself. *Why, Jerry, because she's independent and strong-willed? Because she isn't a fucking drunk?* Jerry sure knew how to rile her without really trying.

Lori didn't know how to thank Rain for stepping in the way she did. It really was beyond the call of duty.

Renee, alias Rain, joined Lori in Chicago one month later, as promised, to see her father after twenty-five years.

Lori recalled how Adele had thought Rain looked familiar, so when Adele and Rain encountered one another again over lunch, Rain's familiarity grew stronger. Lori wanted to hear her story, but she would have to wait for the right time to hear it.

On the day Rain was to meet her father, Lori was picked up from Adele's home by limo and brought into the city to the luxurious Drake Hotel, where Rain was staying during her visit to Chicago. Upon meeting Rain, Lori was all compliments.

"I like your hair up, Rain, and that jeans outfit looks nice on you," Lori said.

Rain gave a hearty laugh as they made their way into the limo and said, "Jesus, you're being careful—but not very subtle! Were you afraid I would show up in my dad's chambers dressed in full Navajo gear?"

Rain patted her over-sized purse that she placed on the seat beside her and said, "Just in case, I brought some jewelry along." Lori and she were then driven to an upscale café downtown, where the two women took a leisurely lunch.

Lori was grateful they were not staying to eat at the Drake; there were too many memories there.

They entered the café and were seated at a table near the windows so they could enjoy a view of the city.

"Wow, this city is still lovely and bustling," Rain said, looking out the window at the building surrounding them. "So much has changed…"

Lori waited until they each ordered their lunch before she jumped in. "Okay, we have about two hours before you meet your father for you to finally tell me your story. You know mine, a drunk for a husband, a daughter lost to leukemia, and a Holocaust survivor mother."

Rain looked at her friend, sizing her up. She guessed it was quid pro quo time. She took a sip of water from her glass and began.

"Okay, before I became Rain, I was the daughter of Jason Cohen, a federal judge, and Irene Cohen, a wealthy and prominent socialite," Rain explained. "I grew up with everything handed to me. I went to the best private schools and followed my father into Harvard Law School. My life was not my own. My father mapped it out. In law school, I met a handsome, wild, charming, nonconforming student. When my parents refused to accept him, claiming that he was a gold digger, we did the rational thing: we eloped.

"I soon found out that Josh had married me for my money," Rain continued. "He enjoyed the good life and insisted we join my parents in their social events. He soon became their ally instead of my rebel, encouraging me to finish law school.

"After five years of following the script, I realized something was very wrong. My mother had died of cancer, and I truly hated my life. When I found out that Josh had a mistress, whom he was keeping at an apartment that I was paying for, I flipped. I took my dog Princess, a large suitcase, and all the cash I could get on short notice and started to drive. Unconsciously, I headed back to Arizona. You know all about my time in Arizona—that was my early hippie indoctrination. Well, by this time, my commune was gone, things had changed, and I was soon out of cash. Not wanting to be found, I accepted lodging with a kind Native American woman named Little Sister."

When Rain mentioned the name Josh, the blood rushed to Lori's face. She was afraid to ask his last name. *It can't be Josh Wheeler. It couldn't be.* Why was she feeling so strange about it? She quickly shook it off, blaming it on her overactive imagination.

The waiter, dressed in a sharp white shirt, black tie, and black trousers, came with their drinks.

"Here is your Riesling, ma'am," the waiter said, placing the glass of wine before Lori.

He placed a tall glass of iced tea in front of Rain and left.

"Wine?" Rain asked.

"Yes," Lori quickly answered, gulping down nearly the whole glassful.

"Lori, I've never seen you drink like that before," Rain observed.

"Well, I'm not near Jerry, so it's all right. Rain, what was your last name when you were married?" Lori asked, ignoring that niggling feeling in her stomach. She took a deep sip of wine, thinking it would calm her nervous stomach.

"My first husband's name was Josh Wheeler."

Lori choked a bit on her wine, Rain slid a glass of water toward her friend, and said, "You may do better with some water. Have some."

Lori gazed at Rain's large green eyes, her natural long black lashes, her thick, shiny, wavy hair, and her slim body. *What an attractive, sexy woman, even at fifty. No wonder Josh fell for her. All these years I conned myself into thinking he was bewitched by some girl's money only.* Lori summoned the waiter and took another glass of wine and drank it down as quickly as she had the first.

"In fact," Rain continued, eyeing her friend as she gulped down another glass of wine, "you might know him. He grew up in Northfield. Isn't that where you lived?"

"Yes, the name is *very* familiar." Lori felt as though the restaurant was spinning a bit. She closed her eyes to calm herself.

"Are you all right?" Rain asked. "You look pale."

"I guess I'm hungry," Lori said.

"Well, wine won't fill you," Rain said.

"I drank too fast," Lori said.

"Let's order some appetizers," Rain suggested. "Get something in your stomach."

Lori felt lucky she didn't end up with Josh after all. Her dad had him pegged too.

"I really don't want to talk about that anymore, if you don't mind, Lori," Rain said. "It was a long time ago, and the past is the past."

Lori was profoundly grateful and said, "Whatever you want, Rain. I was just curious."

The handsome young driver greeted them as the two women made their way out of the café and whisked them away in the waiting limo.

Lori felt like a tourist in her own city, light-headed on the wine and giddy from being driven about like royalty. Is this what being the daughter of a prominent judge is like? She thought she could get used to this kind of treatment.

Like a tourist from another world, Rain was glued to the window.

"I can't believe how this city has changed!" Rain frowned a bit, looking up at the sky. "Even though it is built up and beautiful, the cold dreary atmosphere cannot compare to Arizona's clear blue sky and bright sun three hundred and sixty days a year. I could never again handle Chicago's noisy streets and thousands of cars and people hurrying along."

"How long have you been gone?" Lori asked.

"About thirty years," Rain said.

As they exited the limo, their driver said, "The judge is waiting for you on the fourteenth floor room…"

Rain cut him off with a smile and a wave of her hand and said, "I know where his throne is located!"

Standing in the awe-inspiring chambers, dressed in normal street clothes, her long hair up in a bun, light make-up, and a scared expression on her face, she was suddenly transformed from haughty and confident Rain, Queen of the Desert, into intimidated, little twenty-year-old Renee Cohen.

When a distinctive, thin, silver-haired figure in full judicial robe entered, Lori slowly exited, wishing her friend good luck. Rain followed her to the door.

"He's a great man, Rain," Lori said in a whisper as she exited the room. "And he misses you a great deal."

"Thanks for coming with me, Lori," Rain said. "I'll see you in a few."

Lori sat outside the chambers in an adjacent courtroom trying to read her book she had in her purse, but the image of Josh Wheeler kept creeping into her thoughts.

Renee and her father stood silent, facing each other. Rain broke their gaze and looked around at the walls filled with impressive documents and signed pictures of famous people.

"Not much has changed here," she said.

Her father moved towards her, but she wasn't ready to embrace him.

"Mind if I sit?" she asked, making her way to a chair across from his enormous mahogany carved desk. He moved behind the desk and sat down on his burgundy leather chair.

"You're looking well, Renee." His voice was firm as he sat straight against the back of his chair, his fingers pressed before him in the shape of a steeple. "You remind me of your mother right before she came down with cancer." He stopped and a quick smile shot across his face, then it was gone, replaced by a serious one. "She was a beautiful woman too."

"Is that a compliment or a curse?" Rain asked, leaning back onto her chair, trying to be just as tough as the formidable man seated before her.

Judge Cohen sunk down at his hands. "You must really care for that Lori girl," he said. "She must really mean a lot to you, otherwise you probably could have gone another twenty years without ever returning to Chicago."

"She has stood by me, Dad," Rain said. "She's been my friend, allows me to be me."

"And who is that, exactly?" Judge Cohen asked, his voice almost grumbling in his chest. "Does she too run around the desert in support of the natives? Making jewelry, spouting off subversive literature?"

"No, she runs back and forth, supporting a drunk, like I used to," Renee shot back, "before I came to my senses and realized he was just another man trying to control my every move."

"He was a man in trouble, Renee," Judge Cohen said. "Perhaps he was only doing what he saw was just…"

"Don't stand up for him, Dad!" Renee shouted. "It was okay for him to treat me that way because he was wealthy?" Rain shrank back in her seat as her father glowered over her. "And for God's sake, don't speak to me about what is just," she continued, her voice more subdued. "You tried to control me, and I got out. I got out from under your thumb, and you couldn't stand that!"

Her father delivered a long stern stare before speaking up again. "We've all had our share of heartache and tribulations, Renee. No one is immune. I did what I thought was right. And I *was* right, you'll recall. Josh…"

"I don't want to hear about how right you were about Josh, Dad," Renee said, her voice growing louder. "Jesus! Is it so wrong I grew up and made some mistakes? Isn't that how we learn?"

"What were you going to learn, running around with that gold digger?" Judge Cohen asked.

"What will I learn now, digging up the past, dragging around memories of these men, like so many dead bodies?" Rain asked. "I'm through."

"Through with me too, I gather." Judge Cohen's voice was softer now. He placed his hands on his desk and cleared his throat before speaking again. "Renee, I… I was hoping you had used this opportunity to help out a good friend as an opening to come back."

"Come back to what, Dad?" The softness with which he spoke cut her deeper than any yelling they could have engaged in, and her voice caught in her throat as she continued. "To let you control my life again?" She raised herself up in her seat and spoke. "I'm sure with your FBI resources you've realized that I've made a good, productive life for myself back in Arizona, so... You know, I've no reason to stay here. Look at us, we've been together for, what, five minutes? Already we're fighting." Renee's emotions threatened to overcome her if she stayed in the office another minute. She got up in an effort to leave.

Judge Cohen moved around the desk and stopped her. "Renee, *please.* I'm eighty-three years old. I don't want to fight. I just want you to let me be a small part of your life before I die. I've missed you so much, Renee." Judge Cohen's emotions got the better of him. He slumped onto her chair and put his head in his hands.

Though she tried to fight them, the flood of tears burst forth and streamed down her face as she bent down and laid her head on the shoulder of her father while he pulled her close to him.

"I've missed you too, Daddy," she said.

"I did a lousy job of protecting you," he admitted. "I drove you away. I know that now, Renee. Please forgive an old man. Please don't leave."

"Funny," Rain said, sniffling and patting her father's balding head. She managed a wry smile and said, "*You* asking *me* for clemency."

They spent the next twenty minutes talking about everything, tentatively mending a bond that had been stretched beyond endurance. Then Rain poked her head out of the chambers and invited Lori in.

The judge offered Lori his hand, and with a pleasant smile on his face, he said, "Thank you for bringing my daughter back to me."

Lori could tell the man had been crying, as his eyes were rimmed with red, almost as red as his daughter's. She thought it best not to ask any questions.

As they left the chambers a while later, Rain turned to Lori and asked, "Is the Walnut Room still open for lunch? Let's go have tea."

By the time they walked over to Marshall Field's seventh floor Walnut Room, Renee was Rain again, self-confident and mysterious. She had taken her hair out of its austere bun and let it cascade down her back, and she had once again adorned her outfit with some of her stunning jewelry. Lori watched the heads of the other diners turn towards her with admiration and wonder.

Sitting down at a table overlooking the famous Christmas tree while savoring the warmth of her aromatic tea, Lori asked, "How did the reunion with your father go? It looked like things went well…"

"My father!" The expression on Rain's face changed, and she hesitated before continuing in a slow, measured speech, which was totally against her nature. "All I can say is I still love, fear, and hate him."

Lori answered, "He has that power over everyone. I felt it the first time I met him. Why, he scared *me* half to death. The title Federal Judge helps, but it's really something about him."

"Yes, when I was young, people who knew I was his daughter treated me differently," Rain said.

"You have that power too," Lori said. "You may have been successful in avoiding him for all these years, but, lady, you can't run away from the genes he passed on to you. As Queen Elizabeth the First said," Lori said, affecting a booming English accent, "I am my father's daughter!"

Renee gave Lori a sly smile, sat up straight, and turned back into Rain. "I've seen enough of Chicago today. Let's go visit Barry and then try to get on an early flight home."

"I thought you wanted to see a buyer at Neiman Marcus," Lori said.

"I can talk to her on the phone," Rain said. "Chicago is haunting me with too many memories."

When they walked out of Marshall Field's, a limo pulled up near them, and the same good looking young man approached.

"What's your name?" Rain asked as they entered the limo and gave him Barry's address.

"James."

"Are you with the Bureau?"

He smiled but didn't answer.

She tried again. "Will you be following me to Arizona too?"

"No, ma'am."

Rain turned to Lori and said, "I grew up being shadowed and watched. In my teen years, I played hide and seek with poor Tony. Before my dad went into politics and the courts, he worked for the FBI. Did you know that, James?"

My God, Lori thought. *So the judge really knew my dad. I bet he worked with him at one time.*

No answer from James. The limo stopped in front of Barry's house, and James helped them out. He handed Lori a card with a phone number.

"Call if you want to leave earlier than the scheduled pickup for the airport," James said.

The door opened and immediately barking was heard, along with the squawking of a parrot.

"Welcome," Anne said, and the two women tried to enter, but they were run over by a black and white tabby cat that magically appeared out of the bushes and scurried into the house before they did.

"Is this the Brill house or the city zoo?" Rain asked, laughing.

"The Brill Zoo," Anne answered with a hardy laugh.

Rain, who never minced words said, "When are you and Barry going to get married and have kids instead of animals?"

Anne smiled and replied, "As soon as my love graduates from medical school."

Chapter Forty-One

Lori parted with Rain, who left in the limo on her way to the airport after dropping Lori off at Adele's. Aside from the gold mine muddle, she had been with Adele constantly during her stay at Jim and Adele's these past weeks. There were many changes in the treatment in the last decade, but the chemicals were the same and still brutal. As much as she loved Adele and wanted to be a good friend, she couldn't accompany Adele on all her chemo appointments. It brought back too many memories, and Adele respected this fact. She assured Lori that she had plenty of Chicago friends and family members who were a great support system, so Lori knew Adele would not be abandoned.

Jim had given Lori her own spare key, so she opened the door without ringing the bell. Adele was now in the middle of her chemo treatments and no longer looked perfect, nor was her house in tip-top shape, even though they had a cleaning service come in once a month. It was now Lori's turn to get her out of the house and back in shape.

"Lori, I can't go out. Look at me—no hair, and look at my arms!" Adele pushed back the sleeves of her sweater and revealed arms peppered with black and blue bruises. Her face looked bloated from the medication. "I am becoming Kafka's insect!"

"Not with me around," Lori said. "Where did you hide that outrageously expensive wig? I want it when your hair grows back so I can trick Jerry into thinking I dyed my gray hair black again."

"It's yours," Adele said. "I hate that thing."

Lori ran her hand over Adele's bald scalp.

"Hey, good news… I can feel fuzz, and I can see short gray hairs."

"They won't stay gray for long," Adele vowed. "As soon as my hair grows back, I'll be at the beauty shop."

Wig in place, they drove to town, parked, and walked past the beauty shop and stopped in front of Joseph's Shoe Store.

"Get a load of the three-hundred dollar bowling shoes passing as leather sneakers," Lori commented.

"I bet you still have yours from the seventies when we bowled," Adele answered.

"Yes," Lori slyly answered. "They're still stored in your basement."

"We were terrible bowlers, weren't we?" Adele sighed.

"How about stopping by Pizzazz for some lingerie?" Lori asked.

"Not until I get my other surgery," Adele said.

Dummy me. I forgot she needs reconstructive surgery to replace her breast, Lori said to herself.

They stopped in at the Original Pancake House, where they savored the aroma of fresh brewed coffee, ordered eggs and pancakes, and continued their conversation.

"Mmm, I'm glad my appetite is back today. I have to take advantage of the days I am not nauseated," Adele explained as she dug her fork into her warm stack of pancakes.

Lori looked around and commented, "Funny, so many landmarks like Marshall Fields, Carson's, and Eli's Steak House have disappeared from Chicago, but Northfield never seems to change."

"Not true," Adele countered sadly. "The Cubby Hole is gone." Adele leaned her head on her left arm.

"Don't remind me," Lori said. "We were so busy, we hadn't even gone in these past few weeks."

"You were busy, and I was too damn sick," Adele said.

"Why did it have to close down?" Lori mused.

"It became old, disfigured, and useless, like me," Adele answered, looking down at the table.

Lori stirred her coffee with her spoon, thinking, *What happened to my optimistic friend?*

"Adele, restaurants can be replaced, but people like you can never be replaced," Lori said. "Your children, grandchildren, friends, Jim, Jerry, and I all love you for what is inside of you, not for your looks, which are still perfect. Well, maybe you're a little too thin."

Adele smiled wanly and sipped her black coffee. "Almost as good as the Cubby Hole," she announced.

"Jim hasn't complained about your lost breast, has he?" Lori asked. "If he has, I'll take care of him."

Adele laughed and said, "No, he's been wonderful. I'm the one that's having a bad time."

They were interrupted by a few of Adele's friends, who had stopped to wish her well. The waitress came over with the check. Lori picked it up and helped Adele with her coat.

Looking straight into Adele's eyes, Lori said, "Remember what they always told us at Children's: Take one day at a time."

In the car, Lori thought about the Cubby Hole. "The good old Cubby Hole is really gone, demolished, with our history in those walls."

Adele thought and then said, "I forgot about the notes we stuck in the walls behind the juke boxes."

"All our hopes and prayers were on those notes," Lori recalled. "God, the dumb things we prayed for, like make him take me to the prom."

Adele shook her head. "You would have been better off if he left you home."

"Why do you hate Josh so much?" Lori asked.

"Because he hurt you," Adele said.

"Jerry has hurt me more, and you always defend him," Lori said.

"Jerry loves you dearly," Adele said. "He has a problem he can't control. Josh continuously cheated on you, but you were blind to it."

"With whom?" Lori asked.

"Everyone," Adele replied. "Why, he even tried with me, but I didn't jump, because he was your love."

"How young and naïve we were," Lori recalled. "No more. Now I've taken charge of my life. I want to take my turn before it's too late. Enough of that good girl stuff."

"Watch out, world!" Adele said, laughing.

"Adele," Lori's voice grew serious, "Rain and Josh were married. He left me for Rain."

"What?! Oh my God, Lori! How long have you known this?"

"Not long," Lori replied. "She told me a bit about her past when she came to Chicago to visit her father."

Lori unloaded the juiciest bit of gossip to date. It felt good talking about it, and as she continued, the shock of it wore off.

"Well, like I said before, you are better off without him. He proves me right at every turn," Adele said.

"I have to admit, I was sick with jealousy when she told me," Lori said. "I was so angry."

"What for? You're better off," Adele scoffed.

Lori thought a moment before speaking. "Doesn't anything get you angry, Adele? What about the cancer?"

"Yes, Lori, I am angry, and I'm worried that I won't make it, but I'm going to do the best I can to try," Adele said. "Thanks for letting me talk about it. Now, please watch where you're going. I want to get home. Driving with you is almost more dangerous than cancer."

Lori slowed down and laughed. It was her last night in Chicago with Adele, and she wanted them both to get home in one piece.

Chapter Forty-Two

The next day, Lori called the airlines to check on her flight back home to Arizona. Finding that it was delayed, she spent extra time with Adele before parting with her, promising they would see one another soon. Lori then left Adele's house in her rental car and haphazardly drove around her old neighborhood, stopping in front of a small, green-painted, brick and wood house on Willow Street. She stared, amazed that her old house was still standing after all the teardowns in Northfield. It was built in 1955, a year Eisenhower was president and the world was at peace.

In the yard, the evergreen Lori's father planted in his attempt to garden had grown to enormous size, looking like a fantastic Christmas tree, but the rose bushes he had spent hours caring for were gone. She remembered a strange conversation she had with her dad when she was around ten. He seemed to be babbling on about weeds being the enemy, and it was Lori's job to help him eliminate them. Then, just before he left on a long business trip, he held her arm tightly and said, "Remember, while I'm gone, you must eliminate the weeds."

He was gone for two months that summer, and she tried to pull weeds, but honestly, she couldn't tell the difference between the weeds and the good plants. She now realized that for him the weeds were the Hitlers of the world. For Lori, the weeds represented the bottles of alcohol and the cancer cells she had been fighting all her adult life.

The one-car garage was fine for them, as her mother did not drive. Why hadn't she questioned the fact that they were the only family in the neighborhood to have a driver from the government at their disposal? Probably because everyone else's father was at home all the time. She sat in the car a long time while the memories of her youth came flooding back. She thought of her friendship with Adele, how she was the only friend she allowed close to her.

I can't lose her now. The tears Lori had been holding back came in torrents.

"Do not go gentle into that good night," used to be Lori's favorite line in a Dylan Thomas poem before she had a clue to its real meaning. After watching so many friends and relatives fight their way through chemo, going out gently would be a blessing. Shelly, of all people, did it perfectly: healthy one day, heart attack in her sleep, and gone the next day.

Still in her memory mood, she decided to take the long way to O'Hare Airport. Lori focused on the clear blue sky reflecting off a winding Lake Shore Drive, as the car stretched and wound around like a snake. Birds hovered across the lake hoping to catch one of the jumping fish.

From the airport, she called Jerry to give him the state of the union in Chicago and to tell him her plane would be late. She suggested he call Jim and give him some support.

"Jim and Adele were there for us," Lori said. "Stop hiding. Call Jim, and when I return to Chicago, you are coming with me, Jerry."

"Okay, I hear you," Jerry said.

On the plane ride home, Lori thought about how weird life was and how important it was that loved ones know how much you cared about them before it was too late. She dismissed the thoughts about her mother and their hurtful relationship before the old ache took over. She could hear her father's gentle approving smile and feel her mother's uncaring stare.

Instead she told herself, *Maybe I need to be nicer to Jerry; after all, he is trying to reform.*

Food was replacing alcohol and cigarettes for Jerry. Meeting Lori at the airport, his first comment was: "Did you bring me a frozen pizza from Uno's?"

"Of course, wasn't that the reason I went to Chicago?" She opened up a shopping bag she had been holding and revealed three frozen pizzas tightly wrapped in clear plastic.

Smiling approvingly, Jerry kissed his wife tenderly. "Okay, now tell me how Adele is doing."

Lori leaned back in the car, very happy to let Jerry drive them home. Her mind floated back to a time when she would clench her teeth and hold on tightly to the seat, anticipating the inevitable accident due to his intoxicated state. Instead of answering his question, she fell asleep.

"Wake up, we're home," Jerry said.

After entering the house, Jerry grabbed the shopping bag and was preparing to pull out one of the pizzas when Lori grabbed it from him and put it on the kitchen counter.

"Hey, handsome, the pizza can wait. I need you now," Lori said as she flirtatiously led him to the bedroom, where he hungrily undressed her, and they made passionate love.

That night, she was willing and responsive to his caresses, reverting back to her younger days of teasing and seducing him with kisses over his whole body and moaning with pleasure as she yielded to his advances. The touch of tongues, the sweet taste of a mouth void of alcohol reopened an emotion that had been dormant for years.

Later that night, while they enjoyed the pizza for dessert, Lori told him, "Since you quit drinking, you have become a wonderful lover—slow, romantic, and a master with your hands and mouth. We have many wasted years to make up for."

He grinned and led her back into the bedroom, but alas, now their age interfered with a repeat performance in the same night.

"Honey, this is taking too long," Lori said. "You are crushing my bones, and I have osteoporosis. I think once was enough tonight. You are huffing and puffing. We better stop. Mr. Goldberg had a heart attack during sex last month, and he is two years younger than you, and..."

"Lori, will you shut up?"

Chapter Forty-Three

When the time finally arrived, Jerry and Lori paid for half of Barry and Anne's wedding, as Jerry had promised. Lori's friends gave Anne a shower at Wolfgang Puck's Spago. They were involved in the plans for the rehearsal dinner, which was held at the Pump Room, and Lori and Jerry chose the rabbi. The double ceremony with Rabbi Simon and Father Franklin was very touching. The two clergy had become a team doing the main intermarriages in the area. Lori especially liked the program they all put together with Anne's parents, explaining each religious custom and identifying the members of the wedding party.

The wedding colors were black and white, enabling Lori to hide her weight in black and refrain from dieting. Adele helped her pick out a black sequined knit dress from her favorite designer, St. John. Lori felt honored when Anne asked her to give her opinion on a wedding gown she had picked out. Lori was afraid that her big mouth had gotten her into trouble weeks earlier when her mother Mary suggested Anne wear the 1960s wedding gown she had worn.

"Oh, Mary, every girl wants her own dress," Lori had uttered without thinking.

It turned out Mary's size ten, which was considered a perfect size back thirty-five years ago, needed too many alterations for Anne's size four.

When Lori met Anne and her mother at the bridal shop, Anne took her aside and said, "Thank you for saying something to my mother. I wanted my own new dress, but I didn't want to hurt her."

Lori thought of her mother and of Julie, two missing loved ones as she saw Anne, resplendent in her wedding gown, walk down the aisle.

She let the tears flow freely, figuring most people would think she was joyfully crying over the marriage of her only son.

The room at the Drake, Lori's favorite hotel—recently remodeled, but still elegant with its massive sparkling chandeliers, traditional furnishings, and formal balcony—made a perfect setting for a wedding.

Lori did a good job of getting family and friends together. Jack looked especially handsome in his tuxedo, but he seemed lost without Shelly. Joel was dancing with everyone and bragging about his current position as a vice president of Chandler Financial, which may or may not have been true. Steve and Zi were invited, but they never made an appearance. However, a lovely young teenager dressed in a tight pink silk Oriental dress appeared at the entrance to the ballroom. She identified herself as Barry's cousin, and the wedding consultant found her a seat. By the time Lori looked for her, she had departed.

Steve's ex-wife Carol was there with her new husband, Phil, her twin sons, Danny and Darrell, and her three grandsons, who had taken a fancy to Adele's five grandchildren. Watching Adele taking care of her grandchildren, Lori realized why her efforts to get her best friends to retire in Arizona were futile.

Rain and her father seemed to be back to their old habits. "Dad, I'm telling you, in the next election we will elect a woman for president."

"Renee, you're still dreaming," he said. "This country will never elect a woman, or a black man, for that matter."

Joel appeared at the table. He gave Judge Cohen a pat on the back, and in his most confidant voice he said, "Your honor, you did the right thing giving me a light sentence. Wait until you see the great things I'm going to do for Renee's jewelry business." He held out his hand to Rain. "Dance?"

Joel and Rain had gotten chummy during Joel's recent visit to Arizona, despite Lori's very vocal protestations. Finally, Lori decided to let it go. Rain had a mind of her own, and her father would, once again, have to come in and save her from herself.

Rain got up and joined Joel in a dance. "It looks like you and your dad are having a great reunion," Joel whispered in her ear as he pulled her close to him.

"Mmhmm," she answered skeptically. "He's still a stubborn old goat."

The judge watched them dance. He shook his head, saying to himself, *She is still a naïve little girl, especially if she has hired that shyster.* He got up and walked to the bar for a drink.

Eileen picked up her Jack Daniel's from the bartender and started to walk back to her table when she stopped cold and stared out on the dance floor, where her father was dancing with her partner Suzanne.

It's that Southern charm, y'all, Eileen thought, laughing to herself.

The evening was winding down. Barry and Anne had quietly slipped away to the airport for their honeymoon in Hawaii. Lori was looking for Jerry. She had asked the bandleader to play their song, *Sunrise, Sunset.* She snuck behind him and asked him for a dance. He looked so handsome in his black tux that she was falling in love with him all over again. Lori put her head on his shoulder and enjoyed the slow dance. Afterwards, they walked over to the dessert table. Jerry told Lori he wanted to make sure they boxed everything so they could take home the leftovers.

Lori smiled and replied, "What else can we do? Your mother isn't here with her shopping bag."

Before Jerry could answer, Anne's father was at their side and said, "It's time for us to pay the bill."

Lori took his arm and said, "I'll go with you. I'm the bill payer in the family."

Jerry stood looking at the table, thinking about his mother, when his old drinking buddy, Sy, walked over with a gin and tonic in hand.

"Boy, Jerry, you really did change," Sy said. "You haven't been near the bar all night, not even a toast for your son. You know, me and the guys really worried about you when your girl died. Didn't think you would forget her."

"How could I forget her, Sy?" Jerry responded. "And why would I? I don't ever want to forget Julie."

After settling the bill with Tom Wilson, Lori sat down in the ballroom and took off her shoes. Most of the guests were gone or starting to leave, as it was past midnight.

She looked around the room for Jerry, Adele, and Jim. She and Jerry planned to stay at their friend's house until the following afternoon, when they would head back to Arizona and home. Thank God all had gone well. She would have to let Jerry know how proud she was of him.

"There you are," Adele said to Lori, "Thank God I found you."

Startled, Lori looked up at Adele. "Oh, Adele, I…" Lori did not like the look on her friend's face. "What's wrong?"

"Jerry's by the bar, and… "

Lori didn't wait for Adele to finish the sentence. In her heart, she knew the answer. She ran over to the bar. Adele picked up Lori's shoes and ran after her.

As she got closer to the bar, Lori yelled, "Oh, no!"

Jerry turned towards her with one of his old, inebriated smiles and said, "Don't worry honey, I'll be fine." In his hand was a bottle of Johnnie Walker Red. "I'm just celebrating my son's wedding."

Jim appeared with coats in hand. He took Jerry by the arm and said, "Come on, buddy, we're going home."

"Jim, boy, leave me alone," Jerry ordered. "Sy and I are just starting to have fun."

Jim grabbed hold of Jerry and dragged him out of the ballroom and over to the elevator.

Adele, with her hands full of coats and purses, said, "Come on, Lori, let's get him out of here."

"You're right, Adele, I would hate to have the Wilsons see him drunk." Lori moaned.

Chapter Forty-Four

The next day, late in the morning, Lori and Jerry walked out of Adele and Jim's house and kissed them goodbye.

"Thank you for letting him sleep it off, you guys," Lori said. "I'm sorry about last night."

Adele hugged her friend and said, "He just did a little too much celebrating, that's all."

"We stayed up most of the night talking, Adele. I kept you up all night after we got back from the police station."

Adele shrugged it off and said, "Jim and I have a light schedule today. You can both sleep on the plane."

Jerry and Lori thanked Jim for, once again, getting Jerry out of trouble, said their goodbyes, and silently drove in a cab to the airport. Jerry's head was still hurting as had been years since he had woken up drunk. Lori was tired from only having had three hours of sleep, drained and disappointed that Jerry had ruined their mitzvah.

Lori boarded the plane, sat by the window, put back her seat, and stared out as the plane took off. Soon, the plane was past Chicago's beautiful skyline and the clear waters of Lake Michigan. Large, billowy, fluffy clouds appeared. Lori stuck her head close up against the window. She blinked once, then again; sitting atop a billowy cloud outside her window was a beautiful teenage girl with long blond hair, twinkling blue eyes, and a big smile exposing straight white teeth. She whispered, "Julie, Julie."

Lori looked around the plane. No one else was staring out their windows or seemed surprised. As she turned back to the window, she heard Julie's voice shouting out, "Mom, it's time to let go."

Lori whirled around to face Jerry. "Jerry, look out the window. Julie is over there sitting on a cloud."

Jerry looked out the window, then at his wife. "Lori, are you all right? There's nothing out the window but clouds."

Exasperated, Lori raised her voice. "Jerry, she's right there." Lori stabbed at the window with her finger.

The stewardess came over to her and asked, "Is there a problem?"

"No," Lori said, looking out at the now unoccupied clouds. She rested back in her seat and closed her eyes.

Jerry looked at her, thinking, *Boy, is she in bad shape.*

The stewardess glanced out the window, then at Lori, frowned a bit, and said, "Well, if you need anything, let me know," she offered, then walked down the aisle.

Lori and Jerry disembarked from the plane, picked up their luggage, and walked out of the Phoenix terminal, where two men greeted them.

"Hi, Jerry," the larger of the two said.

Surprised, Jerry looked at him. "Brian, what are you doing here?"

"Lori called me from Chicago," Brian said. "Lori and I think you could use some time at the Ranch, but it has to be your decision."

Jerry turned to Lori and said, "Honey, I don't *need* rehab again. I was celebrating my son's wedding. It was just one slip in three years."

With a most determined look on her face, Lori looked Jerry in the eye and said, "Jerry, that one drinking episode landed us in the police station. I will never live with a drunk again. Either you go with Brian, or I'm gone for good."

Jerry put down his suitcase and looked at Lori with pleading eyes. She just stared back at him in a very determined stance.

Jerry turned to Brian and said, "I guess I'm yours." He knew she meant it this time. She hadn't really talked to him since the police station.

Why doesn't she realize that I also lost a daughter too, only I'm a man and can't deal with it the same way she can? He guessed these issues would have to be dealt with in therapy sessions and not at the bottom of an empty Scotch bottle.

Lori watched Jerry leave with Brian. She picked up her suitcase and walked towards the parking garage thinking, *It's 2001 and Lori Brune Weinberg Brill is no longer afraid to take a stand in life. She has weathered too many storms in the last thirty-one years, and because of them, she has become a stronger person. She now knows she can make it alone if Jerry doesn't get it together and stay sober.*

Chapter Forty-Five

The letter came while they were celebrating Lori's divorce; at least Rain was. Lori was just sitting on her kitchen chair tightly holding the final decree and staring at it. Rain was pouring more red wine in the crystal stemware the ones she took out for the celebration. She was trying to convince Lori that she was lucky to finally be rid of Jerry.

"Lori, you deserve a medal for staying with that jerk for so long," Rain said. "These last six months were a nightmare for you; the lies, the promises, the fights, and then when he struck you."

Lori looked up and quickly responded, "He didn't hit me on purpose. I took his bottle of Jack and emptied it in the sink. He went after the bottle and knocked me down." Lori looked down and sighed, "Oh what's the difference. After my son's wedding and then when he left rehab, I was done."

Lori raised the glass to her lips and took a sip of wine. "Rain, what really did it was the thought of grandchildren. I am guilty enough for letting my children be embarrassed by their alcoholic father. I won't do that to my future grandchildren."

Rain gave Lori a disgusted look, grabbed her own glass of wine and gulped it down. "You still have a soft spot for Jerry," Rain said. "Thank God he moved back to Chicago, otherwise I might be tempted to shoot him."

Lori broke out in laughter, mainly because she knew Rain was capable of doing it. Rain was tough, not like Adele, who always found an excuse for Jerry—and for everyone else.

"Rain, I'm really tired. Thank you for always being there for me," Lori said as she rose from her post, leaving the divorce decree on the table.

They parted company with a hug, and Lori fell into bed feeling a combination of relief and sadness.

The morning sun bounced off the glass windows, producing a rainbow effect. Lori stretched her arms and legs out and slowly rose from the bed. She still felt a little tipsy. Funny, last night she drank too much celebrating her divorce from an alcoholic! Life would be different now. At least her son was settled with a wonderful wife and a profession. She won't have to worry about him. It was her turn to find a new life—alone.

She inhaled the strong, pungent smell of coffee brewing. *Bless those new timed pots* she thought as she made her way into the kitchen. As she poured the coffee in to the tall blue and white mug she noticed the certified letter sitting on her granite counter. Lori remembered Rain had answered the door and signed for it, and then they had dismissed it as another lawyer's letter.

She picked it up, turned it around in her hand, and knitted her eyebrows in wonder. The return address was Berlin, Germany, and the name was Brune, her mother's maiden name.

She opened the envelope and stared at the official looking stationery. The body of the letter stated that one Baron Joseph Brune believed that Lori Weinberg Brill was related to him, through her mother Lillian. If she was this person it was imperative that she came to Berlin immediately since he was now on his deathbed, and there were many family matters to discuss.

After several phone calls to check on the information in the letter Lori decided to go to Berlin.

The answer to her problems with her mother may lie in Germany. The ache in her heart may finally find meaning, and easement, and the timing for her was perfect. A time to think and a new adventure.

Baron Brune had secured a first class seat for her, so she was able to board the plane early. She sat down in seat 2A next to the window.

She was ready to get her life back. She had spent over thirty years trying to live with a man who was bent on destruction. Now she was on her way to Berlin to learn more about her mother's family, the Brune family.

She welcomed the glass of wine in first class. She was nervous, as she had no idea how Baron Brune was related to her. It was nice to find out that not all of her mother's family perished in the Holocaust.

Lori turned away from the window when large dark clouds obstructed her view. Her seatmate was an elderly, blue-eyed, thin-haired, German gentleman. Their conversation was polite and generic: about the weather, sights she should see in Berlin. His perfect English was tinged with a light accent. She couldn't help wondering if he, as a youth, or if his parents were members of Hitler's SS. Never having been in Germany before, she hoped to do some sightseeing after her meeting with the baron, to get a feel of the Germany her mother's family had lived in for generations. She wondered, *Did our past really direct our future?*

After a change of planes in Chicago, a ten hour flight across the ocean, an uneasy sleep, and an airplane breakfast, she finally arrived in Berlin.

I'm in Germany, she said to herself, *Germany, the country responsible for wiping out six million Jews, including most of my mother's family*. Then she thought, *I'm here today because my mother survived. But did she really survive?*

To Lori, her mother was an empty shell, never showing any emotion. She was really in Berlin to solve a mystery, because now she had a clue that there may still be Brunes in Germany.

Lori pulled her red suitcase off the carousel and moved towards the exit sign. She chuckled to herself as she caught the meaning of some of the German words; she didn't know any German, but she still could interpret Yiddish from the days her paternal grandmother cared for her.

How strange that the languages were so alike, almost as strange as the fact that Germany, a highly civilized and proper country, became the home of the Holocaust.

After passing through customs, she spotted a gentleman holding a sign with her name on it. Sighting a tall, thin man with a trim salt and pepper goatee, dressed in a tailored black suit, holding a sign saying *Brune/Brill,* she approached him. The man gave a slight bow and, in a heavy German accent, introduced himself.

"Herr Schmidt. Mrs. Brill, I presume?" He took hold of her suitcase and directed her to follow. She followed, though slowly, due to her limp, to a waiting ancient Rolls Royce. He put her luggage in the trunk and opened the passenger's side for her. They drove north for forty minutes with no more conversation than, "I hope you had a pleasant flight, and the baron is anxious to see you."

Off a busy street in a fashionable Berlin neighborhood, they drove through wrought iron gates down a tree-lined road back about a mile to an enormous old white stone mansion. Schmidt turned to Lori.

"When the Brune family built this house some two hundred years ago, this area was country," Schmidt explained. "When the baron reclaimed his property, only twenty of the three hundred acres were left. The rest had been sold off and developed into homes, roads, and shops. As you can see, we are now in the heart of the city."

They stopped in front of the building. Herr Schmidt helped Lori out of the car, over the cobblestone front walk, and up one step to the door. The door, heavy and wooden, held within its frame a beautiful stained-glass pane with pictures of bluebirds and crimson flowers. On the right side of the door was a small *mezuzah*. Lori put her hand to her lips and then touched the mezuzah, as was their ancient Jewish custom.

After they entered the house, Herr Schmidt excused himself.

"I'm sorry, but we no longer have a chauffeur," he said. "Be comfortable, and I will return shortly." He left her suitcase by the front door and left with the car, presumably to park it in the six-car garage they had passed on the way to the main house.

Lori found herself standing in an enormous room with little furniture but wall-to-wall paintings. She gravitated to one particular painting. It was of a small boy with light brown hair, dressed in a white shirt, royal blue short pants with knee socks, and an Eton jacket. He was in the house, looking out a floor-to-ceiling window that was covered on one side by a heavy gold drape. Even though one hand was pulling a very elaborate wooden horse on wheels, his attention was on something outside the window. It was easy to see that the little boy was very excited by what he was viewing out the window. His eyes were lit up, his face had a broad smile, and his other hand was pointing to the outside. Outside in the background was painted a very dense green forest, within whose shadows hid a bright red bushy-tailed fox behind a wide tree. The large bright black eyes of the fox seemed to make a connection with the boy's face.

Lori could not keep her eyes off the picture. Was this the brother she never knew? She thought about Julie, who had died in her arms after they had tried everything possible to remove the cancer from her body. At least she was with her daughter to the end, easing her last days. Her mother's son, Lori's half-brother, died a tragic death at the hands of the Nazis, without his mother. Lori swallowed hard. All these years since her daughter died, she had felt guilty about surviving. Her mother must have lived with terrible guilt.

Her eyes shifted from the boy to the fox. The animal looked healthy with a very vibrant red coat, and even though the tree trunk hid part of the fox, the animal looked comfortable in its surroundings. Something about the fox was familiar to her. She closed her eyes and worked on her brain to retrieve a story about a fox from her past.

As Schmidt returned, he watched Lori intently. Finally, he walked up behind her.

"Do you recognize the boy in the painting?" he asked.

"No. I recognize… There is something about the fox." She smiled, as her mind floated back to a scene with her mother. Here, in vivid reality, was her mother's fox.

"What do you mean?" Schmidt asked.

"The last time I saw my mother, I visited her in an assisted living home," Lori explained. "She insisted that I look out the window. She told me she was very upset because the trees had been cut down and the fox had no place to hide. I thought my mother had gone mad, because she was in Florida, next to a golf course, where there were no trees or foxes. I never saw her again. She died shortly afterward. Maybe she felt like the fox in the picture during the years after she was taken from this house."

"Take a look at the boy in the picture," Schmidt said.

"He is a very sweet little boy," Lori observed.

"He is your brother, Frau Brune," Schmidt said.

"He *was*, you mean," she answered, frowning as she gazed at the painting, at the little boy's face. "He was killed in Auschwitz, and my mother never recovered from it."

"You are mistaken, Lori Brune," Schmidt said. "Joseph Brune escaped going to the camps, and he lived."

Lori whirled around, facing Herr Schmidt. "*What?* How?"

"I will let him tell you," Schmidt said.

"He is *here*?"

"Follow me."

The rooms were enormous, windows floor to ceiling, marble floors, and walls decorated with oil paintings done by the masters, but sparsely decorated and dimly lit. She felt as though restless spirits of her ancestors filled the open spaces, felt overwhelmed by the size and breadth of the rooms, as though they would swallow her up. As she saw more of the house, she felt sadness, heaviness, a lack of color, a lack of life.

She followed Herr Schmidt to a sizable library with mahogany wood paneling and expansive, towering shelves of books, polished dark wood floors, and again, little light. She walked close to one wall of books. From a distance, many of the books looked ancient, and close up she could see several still had linen covers and gold rims. Herr Schmidt's eyes met hers, as if he understood her thoughts.

"Yes, most of the books are rare first editions," he explained. "The baron spent many years refurbishing the library as it was before the war. This is the baron's favorite room, though he hasn't been able to read in years."

They moved on to the far end of the room. Sitting in a wheelchair by a large window was a distinguished but frail old man. She couldn't see his lower body because a tan wool blanket covered it, but the white dress shirt covering his upper torso seemed to hang on a bag of bones.

He turned his wheelchair around to face them, his eyes kind, his face lined with deep fissures carved into his soft, doughy skin. He motioned to Lori to sit down on the high-backed crimson velvet chair opposite him.

Turning to Schmidt, he said, "Pour the wine, then leave us be."

Lori accepted the glass of red wine, thanking Schmidt, as she took her seat on the velvet chair. The man in the chair stared at her for a long time before speaking.

"How old are you?" he asked in a strained but strong voice.

Lori fidgeted with her purse. What a strange question for someone who may be her long lost half-brother. She answered, "Fifty-six."

He smiled, and a faint sign of dimples that once dotted the corners of his mouth further softened his look.

"You don't look it," he said. "My mother had me when she was twenty. So I guess she bore you when she was thirty-five, probably in 1947, right after the war. You were most likely an accident. Was she married before or after you were born, in the camps or in the USA?"

Lori's body tensed at the thought of her being an accident. Perhaps her mother wasn't able to love her like she should, but Lori hated the idea of her mother thinking the child inside her was an accident. This conversation made her heartsick. He looked fairly kind; perhaps he was just being careless, as the elderly often are. She tried to brush it off.

"May I call you Joseph?" Lori asked.

"That is my name," the old man replied, nodding.

"Yes, I suppose I was a surprise *and* a nightmare to our mother," Lori said. "She never got over her time in the camps, nor did she ever recover from them, believing that you and your father had been killed. I never knew about her early life until I became an adult."

"Tell me about our mother," Joseph said.

Lori hesitated. Then, after taking a deep breath and putting her folded hands in her lap, she decided to tell her half-brother about the good mother, not the mother who stayed in bed for days with migraines, or the one who hardly talked to Lori, or the mother who never told Lori that she loved her, or the mother that refused to be a grandmother, moving to Florida the minute Lori's daughter was born. When she thought back, she found that all her fond memories were with her father in the picture, try as she might to come up with tales of birthday parties and dinners that her mother had thrown together for family. She relied, instead, on stories of her Grandmother Weinberg's get-togethers.

"Did she still play bridge?" he asked. "Mother loved parties, the opera, and she was an expert bridge player. She and her partner, Fraulein Gerber, played in tournaments. I always wished I could tell her that I became a master bridge player."

Lori pressed her lips together and frowned before speaking. "Joseph, the mother I knew never played any games, not even Steal the Bundle." She grew quiet and stared at Joseph. Here sat a sick old man who must be remembering his first ten years with a mother he believed had died forty years before she really did. How sad.

Lori slumped in her chair, now guilty at how she had misjudged her mother's behavior. She wanted to know about the mother Joseph mourned.

"I have so many questions for you," Lori said.

"Yes, but I am an old, sick man holding on by a thread, so we will go slowly," Joseph said.

Schmidt came into the room. Joseph took a raspy sounding breath, turned to Schmidt, and said, "Make sure my sister finishes her wine and dines on some of Mrs. Schmidt's good cooking."

He then turned to Lori. "I apologize, sister, but I must retire. We will talk in the morning."

Lori caught her breath and rose up, as Schmidt wheeled him out of the room.

Lori sat alone, thinking, until a plump young girl dressed in a black uniform with a crisp white apron approached her. The girl, whose dark hair was severely pulled back in a bun, couldn't speak English, so she pointed to Lori and, using her hands, simulated putting something into her mouth and chewing. It took only a moment for Lori to gather that she was being asked if she would like something to eat.

Lori responded, "*Ikh veln keyn shlof,*" which was Lori's German/Yiddish version of, "*I want to sleep*."

The girl looked at Lori strangely before asking, "Sleep?"

Lori gave an unplanned yawn before answering, "Ya."

"*Gut,*" the girl said, as she motioned for Lori to follow her up the curved wooden staircase to a high second floor, through a slightly warped oak door, and into the very bedroom that held her suitcase.

Lori smiled and shook her head in a confirmative gesture.

The girl smiled back and said, "*Gute Nacht!*"

The bedroom was large but depressing. Lori was exhausted, so she went right to bed. She spent a restless night among the heavy furniture, drab burgundy drapes, and howling wind. Opposite her canopied bed was an elaborately carved white stone fireplace. Even though she doubted it had been used in years, she could still smell the smoked timbers. A large, dark-colored tapestry of castles with waving flags and forests filled with stags covered the wall above the small writing desk. A small metal-framed window shared the opposite wall with a small picture of a black shepherd dog next to a magnificent brown and white horse.

If she believed in ghosts, she would have to say she felt her mother hovering over her all night. The heavy air, the distinct scent of Channel No. 5, and the shadows that scurried around the room, but never fully formed, kept waking her.

In his own bed, Joseph Brune, although exhausted, was plagued by flashbacks of his past, memories of the last time he saw his mother.

It was March of 1943, right there in the same room. Even though the world was falling apart around them, Joseph was oblivious to it then. After all, he was only ten years old and a member of the wealthy, privileged Brune family of Berlin.

***

Joseph yawned as he climbed down from his bed. As he glanced out the window, he was surprised to see that the sun was just peeking through the trees in the distance. There was so much noise coming from the first floor that he believed he had overslept and missed school. He remembered thinking that couldn't happen, as his trusted Nana Elsa would have woken him up. He grabbed his robe and his slippers, left his room, and started down the stairs. He stopped cold when he saw three policemen from Hitler's Nazi party talking to his grandmother. He recognized the swastikas on their sleeves. He hid behind the banister, spying on the scene downstairs.

Grandmother Sarah, dressed in one of her long black silk dresses with her silver gray hair wrapped into a bun, was arguing with one of those Nazi policemen. Her long white pearls were swinging back and forth as she became more agitated.

"Mother Brune, please calm down. I think we better do as they say if we want to see your sons and our husbands again," Joseph's Aunt Inga was saying.

He saw his mother just standing there, very quiet, while the officers eyed her. She was so beautiful that everyone stared at her. She was very tall and slim with long black wavy hair. She had on long black leather boots showing through the bottom of her ankle-length black silk, lace embroidered dress, and she usually had an infectious smile on her face, but not today.

One of the officers walked over to her and said, "We would like to make this peaceful. There is a car waiting outside to take you to see your husbands before they are detained for hiding Jewish money from the party. Please explain to Mrs. Brune that if I have to use force, I will."

Then Joseph, from his hiding place, saw the policeman with a gun pointed at his grandmother, mother, and aunt, shoving them out the door, while his grandmother shouted, “How dare you?! I am the matriarch of the Brune family!”

Before he could scream for his mother, a hand covered his mouth, scooped him up, and ushered him out the back door of the house and into the iceman’s truck. Joseph stayed quiet and obedient because the hand belonged to his trusted Nana Elsa.

He lay in the back of the truck in between the layers of ice cubes, shivering for hours until the truck finally stopped. Elsa picked him up and took him into a very small stone house and wrapped him in blankets. He looked at Elsa with questioning eyes.

“Nana, where are my mother and father?” Joseph asked.

She sat down on the bed. “Joseph, dear, there is a war going on, and it is not safe for Jewish people in Germany now. I promised your father that I would hide you until the war is over.”

“What about my cousin Bruno?” Joseph asked. “Is he here too?”

“No, Joseph, the policemen took him before I could get to him,” Elsa said. “They took him somewhere safe.

She handed the boy a cup of tea and said, “Here, dear, drink this. You are still shivering. After the war, everyone will get back together. But for now, we will stay here on my family’s farm.”

Elsa had a boyfriend named Heinz who worked the farm. Joseph became his helper on the farm. A year later, Elsa and Heinz had a little girl they named Marie.

***

Joseph drifted off to a deep, restful sleep, his thoughts no longer ravaged by painful childhood memories, as his dreams became happy images of fat red foxes gamboling in the dense forest.

Lori was glad to be awakened by Schmidt's knock on the door "*Guten Morgen.* Breakfast is being served."

Lori walked into the small adjoining bathroom. Looking for another towel for her bath, she opened the linen closet and stopped and stared. All the towels and washcloths were not just neatly folded; they were precisely folded with a care that illustrated an anal retentive attention to detail and order. A smile came to her face as she remembered failing folding no matter how hard her mother had tried to teach her.

After dressing in a brown tweed skirt and a tan cashmere sweater, she peered out the small window onto a thick forest of ancient trees situated at the back of the mansion. A knock at the door interrupted her thoughts. She opened the door and was met by Herr Schmidt.

"I hope your room was satisfactory," he said. "I'm sorry I couldn't put you in one of the more luxury rooms, but most of our sleeping rooms are under sheets."

"What?" Lori asked.

"Sorry. As you can see, only the baron, three house servants, and myself live here now, and we seldom have guests, so we no longer need fifteen working sleeping rooms. When I first came to work for the baron, we had twenty servants caring for the house."

"It took twenty people to take care of this house?" Lori asked. "What did they do?"

"Most of them took care of the garden and stables," Schmidt explained. "Heinz, the baron's personal groomer, was with us for years. In fact, I believe your mother was a horsewoman. Her name is etched above a stall next to the name of a horse that was called Chesney."

At the mention of a mother she couldn't identify with, Lori's body stiffened and her tone changed. She asked, "Do you believe in ghosts, Herr Schmidt?"

His eyes met hers in a questioning gaze before nodding and answering. "There are many ancient residents that roam these halls."

They walked on. The silence between them was finally broken when, in an effort to change the subject, Lori asked, "How long have you worked for Joseph?"

"At least twenty-five years," Schmidt said. "I was his secretary and traveling companion. I even went to your country with the baron." He was silent for a time. Then his voice changed from confident to defensive. "The baron is very special to me. He took me in when I was young and faltering."

Lori turned towards him and said, "You've done a great job of taking care of him. Thank you."

Herr Schmidt bowed slightly and then stiffly walked on towards the dining area, where he directed Lori to a green velvet chair alongside an enormous baroque table that could hold at least twenty dinner guests. Fruit, yogurt, fish, meats, cheese, and toast were served on silver trays and china plates. She sat there alone for several minutes, sipping juice and feeling strange, noticing that the large gold jeweled candelabra was really a Jewish menorah.

The warmth she had missed from Joseph the night before appeared in the morning. Upon entering the breakfast room, Joseph wheeled his chair over to her, and held his arms open. "*Shvester, gebn mir ein arumnemen.*" (*Sister, give me a hug.*)

Lori bent down and kissed Joseph. Tears streamed down her face.

"Why has it taken us so long to find each other? I hated being an only child, envying my friends with siblings. Oh, Joseph," she said, sniffling, wiping away her tears with the back of her hand, "our mother would have been a different person had she known you were still alive."

Joseph nodded sadly. "We weren't looking for each other. After the war, I was told all my family had died in the camps, so I stayed on the farm until middle age, when I had my named changed back to Brune and set out to restore the family fortune and help prosecute those responsible for the Holocaust."

Lori sat herself down right next to her brother, never letting go of his hands.

"My dear sister, even though I was only ten when I was separated from my family, I remember much about life in Germany before Hitler," Joseph recounted. "I remember laughter and joy in this house and in the one in Munich. We were more German than Jewish. We were from centuries of Jewish Germans. Rich, powerful, proud, for centuries, we were too arrogant to think anything would happen to us, like the American Jews of today. Our family could have easily left Germany in the thirties when the Nazis were afraid to touch us.

"I remember riding in father's huge open topped Rolls going to parks, festivals, restaurants, theaters, and Christmas parties at the homes of prominent gentile Germans. We ate ham and shrimp and only went to synagogue on Rosh Hashanah and Yom Kippur."

Lori sat on the edge of her chair, listening attentively, only releasing Joseph's hands when he removed his glasses to rub his eyes.

"Had cataract surgery and now I can't see a thing," Joseph said.

Joseph was quiet for a few minutes, and Lori respected it. They moved to the table and ate in silence for a while, each with their heads full, brimming with thoughts and emotions.

While Joseph ate his breakfast, he thought back to that time, visualizing a small white frame farmhouse with chickens, goats, and many cats running around, catching mice or lounging in the sun. He saw Marie, a small, longhaired little blonde girl wearing a red gingham dress, handing him nails as he built a new chicken coop. His hands were calloused in those days, his heart happy.

"In the seventies," he began, breaking the silence, "I left the farm and relentlessly went after restoring the Brune name and fortune. My first job was with a commodity firm. Good with numbers and experience on a farm, I soon made a great deal of money that I invested in real estate. When I was able to obtain this house and some of our land, I invited Elsa and Marie to come live with me, but they preferred to stay on the farm, so I supported them there." Joseph slumped down in his chair and was overcome by a succession of deep, rumbling coughs.

Herr Schmidt appeared from the back of the room with some water and a box of tissues, one of which he used to clean up Joseph's mouth. He bent down and said to Joseph, "I think you've had enough."

Helga the cook entered and refilled the silver coffee pot and carefully removed the breakfast dishes and any tiny crumbs left on the table.

Joseph shook his head, clearing his throat once more, and said, "Helga, dear, I should like some hot tea for my throat."

"*Wie Sie wünschen, Joseph*," Helga replied, and she took her leave.

"Forgive me," he said to Lori, and he grew silent, waiting for his coughing fit to subside. He took a few sips of water and took a few labored but deep breaths before continuing.

"Lori, please keep talking with me. I want to get to know you." Lori hesitated. She looked at Herr Schmidt, who said, "Master Joseph has made his request."

"Well, Joseph, I want to get to know you too," Lori said. "Did you ever marry or have any children?"

"No, I then donated the rest of my life to redeeming the Brune property and to keeping the memory of the Holocaust alive," Joseph said. "I would have gone to the ends of the earth to find her had I an inkling that my mother had survived the Holocaust. Her name was on the death list from Auschwitz."

At first, that sounded strange. Then Lori thought about the fact that her mother never acknowledged that she was in Auschwitz, so she probably never checked the lists. Two people who survived the horrors of the Holocaust couldn't live their lives because they never found each other. She couldn't imagine the pain Joseph was feeling now, but she knew it hurt her to find a lost brother only when he was on his deathbed. She felt tears welling up in her eyes.

Joseph slumped down in the chair once more. Lori got up and went to his aid. His face was pale, and his hands were ice cold.

Schmidt, who had been standing in the back of the room, came forward and said, "I think you've had enough for the morning, Sir. It's time to rest. Your solicitor will be here this afternoon."

Joseph took a deep breath and looked up at Schmidt. "I must finish this conversation before my solicitor comes. Please leave us for now. Helga will be in momentarily with tea."

"Joseph, we can continue later," Lori said. "I can stay here longer."

He waved his hand at her. "*Ja, mein lieber*, but I cannot. Just listen. I am a very rich man who is dying of cancer. All the money in the world can't help me now. My solicitor is coming here specifically to put some changes in my will. I wanted to turn this house into a Holocaust museum, but the city will not allow it. Do you want the house?"

"No, Joseph, I don't want anything in Germany," Lori said. "I know the house is full of memories for you, but for me, it will only have hauntings."

"Then I will leave it as planned to the Brune Holocaust Memorial Foundation," Joseph said. "Schmidt will show you around, and we will send anything you would like to own."

Lori smiled. "I would like to have any personal things you have of our mother's, and the picture in the hall of the little boy and the fox."

"Did you realize that's a picture of me when I was a little boy?" Joseph asked, smiling weakly but impishly. "It took me twenty years and half a million dollars to find and redeem the painting. It was painted by Hayward." He took off his glasses and wiped tears from his eyes.

"We had a family of wild foxes on the estate that I loved to watch," Joseph said. "One pup hid behind a tree, while the other came out in the open. Unbeknownst to me, they were feasting on the hens in our chicken coop. Hans, our man in charge of the coop, shot the more aggressive male. I cried for days. I wanted to keep the other one as a pet, but my father said we must let her be free. She disappeared shortly after her mate was shot."

"Did you ask for the fox to be put in your portrait?" Lori asked.

He nodded.

"Joseph, Mother made reference to the picture the last time I saw her," Lori said. " 'They cut down the trees,' she said, 'and the fox has no place to hide.' I didn't understand, and I thought she was hallucinating."

He smiled and let the tears flow freely down his old, wrinkled face. Schmidt appeared again, taking the box of tissues and offering them to the old man, bent down to tell him something, and then resumed his place at the back of the room.

Joseph regained his composure, sniffling and wiping at his nose. He leaned forward. "When my solicitor arrives, I plan to leave you, your son, and granddaughter each twenty million dollars, and some to the family in Israel, and the rest to the hired help, a few friends, and charity. Lori Brune, you have the right to contest my will as the closest living relative, but I think it will cost you more than it will be worth." The old man smiled at his sister. "It pleases me to no end you were able to make the trip to see me.

Joseph then turned towards Schmidt. "Heinrich, please give me the jewelry bag."

Schmidt stepped forward and handed Joseph an old red velvet bag and left the room. The material was slightly faded and worn, but it was in good shape, given the years. He opened it and pulled out a gold mesh bracelet.

"This bracelet is twenty-four carat gold," he said as he handed it to Lori, who turned it over in her hands, inspecting it.

"Open the locket, Lori," Joseph urged in a whisper.

Opening the locket cover, which was round, with tiny pearls surrounding it, Lori revealed a small painted picture of a young girl.

"Mother?" Lori asked, her hands and voice trembling.

Joseph nodded. "Turn the locket over. My father gave it to our mother as a gift." The name Brune and the date 1930 was inscribed on the back. "I want you to keep it in the family. There are other precious family jewels in this bag for you to pass on or to do with as you please."

"How were they hidden from the Nazis?" Lori said.

"Lori, the Brune family lived in Berlin for over two hundred years, working in banking and government until 1943, when all family members, except me, were taken to the camps by Hitler's lunatic regime," Joseph said. "My nanny, Elsa, a German Christian woman with no Jewish ancestry, saved me by taking me to the country and raising me as her own child.

"In 1974, I left my adopted family and went out to recover my family's holdings. I was aided in my pursuit by an event that happened in 1943 right before my world collapsed."

"About two days before the Nazis pounded on our doors and marched off my whole family, I was awakened in the middle of the night by a strange scratching sound under my window. Believing the servants must have left one of the dogs out, I went downstairs and looked out the den window that faced the back of the house. I was shocked to see my father, with shovel in hand, digging in the backyard. Afraid to disturb him, I watched silently. He put his shovel down, lowered a metal box into the earth, and then covered it with dirt. With barely a sound, he entered the house after looking in all directions.

"When he saw me, he put his finger to his mouth. Not understanding what was happening, I stood very still. He pulled me to him and explained, 'Joseph, I've buried a time capsule.'

"I asked him, 'Father, why didn't you let Hans bury it? I've never seen you digging in the yard before.'

" 'Because I want to keep it a secret. Only you and I will know about it. You must not tell anyone about it for ten years, when we will open it together. Remember, it is our secret.'

"Yes, father," I said. Then my father, who wasn't very demonstrative, did something strange. He picked me up and carried me upstairs to my bed, where he gave me a hug and a kiss before leaving my room. I never saw him again.

"We did not open the capsule together, but I never forgot about it. In 1974, at the age of thirty-seven, I went back to our house, which, luckily, was located in West Berlin. The house was still standing, but instead of being in the country, surrounded by hundreds of acres of farmland and forest, it stood by a development of houses, stores, and parks. The house had a "For Sale" sign on it.

"I brought a shovel, went in the backyard, and dug until I found that metal box. Inside it were documents yellowed with age, but as clear as could be. They were titles to all the Brune family properties, bills of sale, and IOU notes, plus paper hundred mark bills, diamonds, and gold coins. The paper money was useless, but the diamonds and coins provided me with some money to exist and fight for what was rightfully ours.

"It took me close to ten years to retrieve the house, some property, many paintings, and holdings from Swiss bank accounts. I didn't have the help of schooling, but I had inherited my ancestors' genes. Thus, I became a very successful stockbroker and businessman," Joseph concluded.

Lori's bottom lip quivered and her eyes teared as she listened to her brother's story.

"Thank you," was all Lori could manage, as Herr Schmidt re-entered the room with Joseph's cup of tea and said in his very commanding voice, "Mrs. Brill, eat your breakfast. It's getting cold." He then wheeled Joseph out of the room, one hand still holding the tea cup, explaining to Joseph how he can have his tea in his bedroom, and Lori silently finished her breakfast while holding on to the bag of family treasures.

This time, she would be very cautious with the money Joseph was leaving her. After covering her family's needs, she would continue his quest to keep the memory of the Holocaust victims alive, for Joseph and for her mother. Something in Chicago in her mother's name, and something in Israel in Uncle Dov's name would be good.

Chapter Forty-Six

Two days passed without any news from Joseph or Herr Schmidt, and no one would let her see her brother.

"He's resting," Herr Schmidt told her. "He gets excitable when you are near, wants to keep talking, but he needs his rest."

Lori watched doctors come and go, with Schmidt, the cook, and the housekeeper going about, taking care of the house. They tried to make her comfortable, but the smell of boiled cabbage and heavy German cooking soon became bothersome, and her nerves were tense from their whispers and stares. She guessed they wondered whether she would take over the house. She walked the rooms and sat in the garden.

She called her son Barry, and her friend Rain reporting all her new found information. Adele was the one she really needed to talk to because Adele had known Lori's mother, but the cancer had returned and Adele was back in treatment, and difficult to get to. The time difference also made it hard to get ahold of anyone. E-mail had been her best way of communicating.

When Lori approached the doctor on the third day, she was told the situation was dire, and there was no longer any hope for the baron to recover. She was no longer kept from his room, but every time she tried to see him, he was sleeping.

An uneasy stillness permeated the house. Lori tried to imagine the house alive with her mother a brother, and their large extended family

She felt an invisible thread connecting her and Joseph. She wondered if her son Barry still felt a thread connecting him to his deceased sister Julie.

There was a knock on her door. She opened the door to Herr Heinrich Schmidt. She braced herself for bad news, but instead he said, "I'd like you to come into the library. When you first came here and informed Master Joseph that his mother survived the Holocaust, he asked me to find anything I could about her time in the camps. Are you aware that your mother participated in one of the first Spielberg *Shoah* interviews?"

"No," Lori answered. But there was a lot she didn't know about her mother.

"Lillian requested that it not be included in the archives until her daughter died. That explains why we never found it. In order for us to see it, you must sign this notarized permission form."

Lori sat there and just shook her head. She would never understand her mother. Finally, she picked up the pen and signed the form. She looked up at Herr Schmidt, "Will Joseph be able to see it?"

Schmidt shook his head. "This isn't the time for him to see such things. Besides, I know he will be pleased that you will get some understanding of what your mother went through. May I bring you anything to drink before I put it on?"

"Yes, a gin and tonic, please," Lori said.

"Are you sure?" Schmidt asked.

Lori nodded yes, and she sat back in the chair as Herr Schmidt turned on the video.

A young man appeared on the screen.

"My name is Neal, and I work for Mr. Spielberg. Today, we are honored to interview one of the most prominent members of our Jewish community. We are in an assisted living facility in Florida where Lillian Brune Weinberg resides. Lillian is a member of the Brune banking family of Germany. Her family lived in Germany for over three hundred years. They were prominent in the government and all social aspects of both Germany's Jewish and gentile families. They could have easily left

Germany in the early years of the war, but they chose not to because of their many connections."

Lori gasped as her mother appeared on the screen. She looked just the way she did on Lori's last visit. She was sitting in a chair, not her wheelchair, her hair was done into a nice short style, and the gray was really shining silver.

She had her characteristic red nail polish and her black silk dress with that beautiful long 10-millimeter strand of pearls around her thin neck. Lori took a drink of her gin and tonic and swallowed hard.

The interviewer started to ask a question when her mother turned to him. *"I don't want any questions. I will tell you what I feel like telling you. Then we will be done.*"

Lori just shook her head and laughed, lifting her eyes heavenward. If only Adele were here to see this. She turned back to the screen.

"The young man has told you who I am. My father-in-law with his two sons, one of whom was my husband, ran banks in Berlin, with branches in other cities. Our bank helped finance the German government, even Hitler when he first appeared. By March of 1943, we had been stripped of our banks and of our investments in Germany. Right after my father-in-law died, my husband Joseph and his brother were arrested. Two days later, the SS came to our home and told my mother-in-law that they would take us in a waiting car to see the men."

Lori's mother continued talking in an unemotional voice, like she was reading a tax form. Lori just stared at the screen.

"The car that was waiting for us was our own Rolls Royce. One officer was sitting in the driver's seat, and he was trying to figure out how to run the automobile. The three of us were literally shoved into the automobile while my mother-in-law, in her commanding voice was explaining to the officers that her late husband, Alfred Joseph Brune, had helped finance the war and had been an ear*ly supporter of Hitler, the now owner of the Brune empire.*

"My sister-in-law and I were wedged in the back with an officer. He kept rubbing his hand against my skirt. We had been told that they were taking us to headquarters to join our husbands, but instead, the car sped across town to the Berlin train station. Before we knew it, we found ourselves shoved onto a third-class train car seated on dirty wicker chairs with guns pointed at us. As I looked around, I realized the train was crammed with other women, and they had their children with them. My mother-in-law stood up and said, 'I will not stay here. I have never traveled anywhere but in first-class and with my trunk. Where are my sons?'

"That is when one of the officers pointed his gun at my mother-in-law's head and pulled the trigger. He shot her dead. From somewhere in the back of the train, I heard a woman scream, 'He shot Mrs. Brune. There is no hope for any of us.' The women were hysterical. And there was my mother-in-law's body, lifeless on the floor of the train, blood everywhere. What could we do? Nothing.

"Then there was shouting and screaming all through the train until an officer, he lifted his arm in the air, like this, and shot into the air. 'Who wants to be next?' Of course, the train quieted down after that.

"My sister-in-law Inga and I were stunned with fear, especially when the train started to move, and the officer, he opened the train car and he just kicked my mother-in-law's dead body down to the tracks. Like she was a sack of old bread. We sat quietly sobbing. We didn't want them to hear us crying, thinking this was the worst thing that could ever happen to us."

Lillian turned to the interviewer. "You have enough reports of the condition of the camps. I refuse to deal with it. All I will say is, to the best of my knowledge, only my brother, who migrated to Israel, survived the Holocaust. All other family members died."

The interviewer asked, "I believe you had children..."

Lillian shot daggers at the interviewer. "Yes, I have a daughter, born after I came to the United States. On that day, in 1943, let's go back to that, the SS went back to our house in Berlin and cleaned it out of all living inhabitants. Children, pets, servants—all were killed, but they kept anything of monetary value."

"Herr Schmidt," Lori spoke up, "can you please put it on hold for a few minutes?" She got up and went into the bathroom, where she spent ten minutes crying and shaking. Her mother had mentioned having a daughter so casually, without any feeling, as though she had mentioned she owned a pair of brown shoes.

When she returned, Herr Schmidt had a cup of tea and a cake sitting on the table near the chair. He asked, "Would you like to take a break for some refreshments?"

"No," she answered. The tape continued.

'Could you at least tell us how you ended marrying Captain Weinberg and coming to the United States? You were in Dachau, right?"

"Young man, bring me another glass of water now." Lillian took a drink from the glass handed to her, then she began again.

"It was the spring of 1945 when the SS announced we would be evacuating the camp. Our group of twenty women was herded to the railroad station. Overhead, we heard and saw planes, Allied planes. We were told to enter the cars. Inga and I looked at each other and shook our heads. 'Not another car,' I said. Suddenly, an American bomb dropped on one of the cars full of people. The smoke and the fire clouded around us, and we ran in between the Allied bombs and the German guns. We didn't know where to run. I was holding Inga's hand when another bomb went off. I looked down, making sure she was still running with me, and all I had left of Inga was her right hand." She paused for a moment. "I screamed and collapsed." Lillian paused and drank from her glass before continuing.

"Later on, I opened my eyes to find myself being carried in the arms of an American soldier. I put my hand by my head and found it covered with blood. I closed my eyes and heard him say, 'Please don't die. The war is over. Tell me your name,' he asked.

"I tried to say my name, but all I could remember was my number. I held up my arm to show him. He looked so sad at me. I tried to thank him, but my face was just bones, no muscles left. It was impossible to talk. I think I fainted after that.

"He looked into my eyes, 'Don't worry,' he said, 'I am going to take care of you now. Just ask for Captain Weinberg if you need anything.' He was a very nice man.

"When I woke up, I was in a makeshift hospital. I remember dreaming about food, but I couldn't get anything down. The doctors, they later told me I weighed fifty-three pounds. You can see, I am a tall woman. I am five-foot-seven. They put me on intravenous feeding and ice water. I had been hit in the head by a piece of shrapnel, from the bomb that killed Inga," Lillian explained, looking down and touching her head with her hands. "I've had headaches for the rest of my life."

Lillian then turned to the interviewer and said, "I've had enough," waving her hands dismissively. "Tell Anna to come and get me. Here, young man. Take your water."

Lori thanked Herr Schmidt, and rising, she headed towards the garden for a much-needed walk.

As she walked out, Schmidt told her, "Lunch is in twenty-three minutes."

She smiled, thinking of her German mother who never lost that aspect of being exact.

Chapter Forty-Seven

After three days of waiting, and no change in her brother's condition, Lori left her mobile number with Herr Schmidt and escaped from the house, first taking a cab to the Jewish Museum on *Lindenstrasse,* where Joseph contributed a large sum of money to finance an exhibit about the Jews during the Nazi occupation. The newer addition of 2001, a sprawling, ultra-modern museum shaped like a giant, silver-gray lightning bolt, sat alongside the older, Prussian Baroque-style building, the *Kollegienhaus*, which was the former courthouse.

The museum's exhibits journeyed through the years Jews had lived in Berlin, dating all the way back to the fourth century, contributing vastly to the city's intellectual, cultural, spiritual, and economic history. The exhibits awed her and humbled her. The extreme angled stairways and hallways, with its incongruous and jarring beams jutting out and crossing from one narrow wall of stairway to the other, made her feel uneasy, disjointed, giving her a sense of a loss of equilibrium. The museum wasn't meant to be comfortable and cozy or intellectual and safe, after all; its visitors were welcome to experience a sense of fragmentation and unease on a visceral level.

Lori read from the museum's pamphlet that the architect himself had designed the museum to possess the aspect of, in his words, "…a compressed and distorted star, the yellow star which was so frequently worn on this site." One exhibit in particular moved her tremendously: artist Menashe Kadishman's installation called *Shalechet*, or *Fallen Leaves*, located in the central part of the museum called *The Voids*. Visitors were encouraged to walk along this cold, concrete corridor atop ten thousand open-mouthed faces cut out of circles made of iron. As Lori made her tentative way across the flat iron faces, the loud, echoing clanking emanating from her feet and those of fellow visitors walking along the long concrete corridor reminded her of hundreds of shackles locking, of hundreds of prison doors closing. She looked at her feet and gazed upon hundreds of faces, their mouths opened in anguish and terror, their cutout eyes empty, devoid of hope, expressing an endless cry, an endless sorrow.

Lori didn't know how much more she could stand. She could not move any faster through the exhibit, afraid she would slip on the large iron plates and come crashing down upon the faces that represented the millions of fallen men, women, and children. Panic seized her as she looked up at yards and yards of solid concrete overhead. The clanking continued, reverberating against the odd-angled walls of the concrete path. Sobbing silently, she plodded through the exhibit. With the sound of crashing metal ringing in her ears which each step she took, Lori cried for the lost millions; she cried for her mother, her father, and her brother. She cried for herself as a little girl, as a young woman, who only wanted the love of a mother who was too distant, too damaged by her horrible past to open her heart.

"God damn this war, God *damn* it!" Lori said quietly, fishing through her purse, producing a tissue with which to wipe her tears. Her fellow travelers were solemn, some in tears, their heads hung down in contemplation. It seemed that no one went through this exhibit unscathed.

With all that she had experienced on this trip, she wondered if it was a good idea to have come here at all. But how could she not, when her own brother was a major financial contributor?

And what was her momentary discomfort and sorrow, comparatively?

Lori made her way out of the strange and sad museum, allowing herself to breathe deeply only when she broke through the exit doors and the sun shone fully upon her. She was free. She was emotionally exhausted. It had felt good to cry; it was a relief. She said a silent prayer, promising to visit again when she had the strength to endure that kind of experience. For now, it was enough.

Lori had come to Berlin prepared to hate the city of Hitler. She had to admit to herself that Berlin was a large, bubbling, open, fascinating, modern city with a population of close to four million people. It also had a strong Jewish community of over twenty-five thousand people. What sense is there to live in the past?

She took a cab to Bebelplatz to see the Hotel de Rome, which was located in her family's original Dresdner bank building. The ornate, classical architectural splendor of the 1889 building overwhelmed her. She walked on the nearby shopping street and listened to the foreign chattering of tourists who were enjoying their spring vacation. She realized Berlin was a city like every other cosmopolitan city: cars raced by only to be stopped by the traffic, police and ambulance sirens screamed, cell phones rang, and men, women, and children bumped into each other on their way to shops, offices, and restaurants.

She cautiously maneuvered her way around a crowded outdoor café until she found an empty table. In the guttural sound of the German language, a sandy brown-haired, blue-eyed middle-aged waiter spoke to her in English. "May I help you?"

"Coffee and a pastry, please," Lori said.

"May I suggest a *schlagober* and a *linzer* tart, *gnädige Frau*?" he asked respectfully.

Lori smiled and nodded yes, though she had no idea what she had ordered.

It turned out to be delicious, a cup of black coffee topped with whipped cream and a powdered sugar-covered, apricot-filled butter cookie. She was enjoying herself when a group of teenagers sat down at the table next to her and three out of the four took out cigarettes. As she unwittingly inhaled the putrid scent of cheap tobacco, it reminded her of a time when at least seventy-five percent of her family and friends smoked. Now in the States, smoking was outlawed in most places, and just a handful of people still smoked cigarettes. She was surprised that so many young people in Europe were still smoking. She hadn't smoked in over forty years—that is, if one didn't count the time she tried smoking marijuana with Rain.

She smiled as she remembered that night sitting under the stars on her patio one late night, her friend trying to convince Lori of the spiritual qualities and benefits of partaking in smoking the drug.

"Native Americans have been smoking peyote for centuries, using herbs to cure all sorts of ailments!" Rain enthused.

"Spin it however you want, Rain, you hippie. I know you just want to relax and get high," Lori had teasingly admonished her friend.

"I never said I didn't," Rain said, taking a long, deep drag off her slender, colored glass pipe and holding the smoke deep within her lungs for half a minute before exhaling again. "I'm just letting you know the properties, that's all. What's from the earth can't hurt. It's natural!"

"Poisonous mushrooms are natural too; so is lava," Lori replied, taking the pipe and sucking a small amount of smoke into her lungs, then blowing it out seconds later.

"Well, I'm not asking you to eat poisonous mushrooms, nor am I asking you to smoke molten lava!" Rain said.

Lori didn't know if it was the effects of the marijuana or just their plain silliness that made them laugh so hard into the night.

She quickly ate, left, and hailed a taxi for Joseph's house. Even though she was enjoying the city, she felt compelled to stay nearby in case her brother asked for her.

On the fifth day, she was summoned. The expression on Herr Schmidt's face was deeply etched in pain as he directed Lori to Joseph's room. Lori opened the door slowly, hesitating at the doorknob. Inside, the room, empty save for its one occupant, was dark except for a faint stream of light showing through an open window drape.

Lori approached the oversized dark wooden baroque bed. Pale and emaciated, Joseph looked like death had already visited him. In a barely audible voice, he tried to communicate to her as she leaned her head in to listen.

"Lori, go home… to your family," Joseph said. "My life is now fulfilled. I am happy we met, sister. Don't wait for me to die. Remember me alive."

Lori pressed her hand to Joseph's cheek and answered, "I need to stay. I just found you."

The old man moved his face closer to her hand and smiled weakly. *"Auf wiedersehen, liebe schwester.* Goodbye, sweet sister."

She had turned for a second to seat herself in a chair beside Joseph's bed, when she heard a very low vibration. Some movement at the foot of his bed caught her attention, and she froze.

At the foot of the bed, just inches over Joseph, hovered the young mother Lori had seen a few days ago hovering around her bed in the upstairs bedroom. Her hair was long and black, and she wore an all-white dress with short sleeves. Her arms, void of any tattooed numbers, seemed to grow as they encompassed the bed and finally wrapped around all of Joseph in a loving embrace. Her eyes concentrated on Joseph, and her face beamed with unbridled joy.

Lori thought, *Lillian is happy now that she is finally reunited with her son.*

Then she thought of Julie, and she cried out to her mother, "Mama, *now* I understand!"

Lori stood upright as the figure of her mother looked up as the vision faded. At the sound of Lori's outburst, the ENT doctor and Herr Schmidt rushed into the room.

The doctor quickly moved towards the bed where Joseph lay, with eyes closed and mouth smiling. He examined Joseph, and then turned to Herr Schmidt.

"He is at rest now," the doctor said.

A cold sweat broke out over Lori's body as she left Joseph's room. She had to sit down. Right in front of Lori, as she stood alert and awake beside her brother, their mother's form was hovering over Joseph's deathbed. She had seen and felt their mother in the room. Her head was whirling.

The doctor approached her and said, "You look ill. Are you all right?"

With eyes wide, she stated, "My mother was there. In the room. She took Joseph with her. Did you see her?" Lori grabbed a few tissues off the bedside table and blew her nose and wiped at her eyes, catching her breath.

Herr Schmidt brought her a glass of water and led her to a chair. Both he and the doctor shook their heads.

"Maybe you should rest. I can give you something to make you more comfortable," the doctor said.

Lori just smiled, taking the water and sitting down. "I believe Einstein, in his space and time theory, said, it is possible the past, present, and future might all exist at once. I *did* see my mother."

"Was ist das?" the doctor asked Herr Schmidt inquisitively. *"Ist sie zitiert Einstein?"*

"Sie sah ihre tote Mutter." Herr Schmidt shrugged and tried to explain the supernatural to the clinical doctor to no avail.

"Unsinn!" the doctor replied, passing it off as utter nonsense. *"Diese Frau braucht einen starken drink."*

(The lady must have had too much to drink!)

Epilogue

Lori felt like her family history should be preserved for future generations. After recording all she knew up to the present time, she continued to write in her journal. Maybe someday she will make it into a book.

"This last year has been a journey through laughter and tears. The trip to Germany gave me an understanding of my family's history. The child in me will never forgive my mother, while the adult Lori cries in pain for what my mother went through. If only she could have talked to me about her life, our relationship would have been so different. I feel blessed to have met my brother Joseph before he died. So many wasted years not knowing that he was alive. He left me financially fit for the rest of my life, which will help, especially after I've had to pay several bills Jerry accumulated.

"Last month I buried Adele, my dearest friend, my soul mate. She put up a courageous battle against breast cancer. It hurt so much to watch her slide away from us. When my Julie was on her death bed, I was so young and naive that I never really believed it would happen. Now older and wiser it was somehow easier to accept, maybe because death is no longer a stranger to me.

"I am lucky to have Rain in my life. She won't let me spend time complaining or acting old. We don't have a history like Adele and I had, but slowly we are building one, and for now we have both agreed that we need a rest from men.

"The highlight of my life is my granddaughter, Cate. I am on my way to celebrate her first birthday. She is an adorable blue-eyed bundle of love. I know we will be the best of friends. I've thought about moving back to Chicago to be near her, but I've fallen in love with Arizona, and my blood has thinned out. Just landed at O'Hare Airport and I am shivering already."

Lori Braun Weinberg Brill
Feb. 08, 2003

About the Author

Native Chicagoan Charlene Wexler is a graduate of the University of Illinois. She has worked as a teacher and dental office manager and as a wife, mom, and grandmother.

In retirement, her lifelong passion for writing has led to her creation of several essays, short stories, and novels. Among her books are: *Lori*, *Murder on Skid Row*, *Elephants in the Room*, *Murder Across The Ocean*, and *Milk and Oranges*.

Coming Soon!

CHARLENE WEXLER'S

MURDER ACROSS THE OCEAN

American widow Lori Brill thought she'd have an uneventful vacation in London visiting her granddaughter, Cate. At the airport she ran into Josh, her high-school boyfriend. This resulted in an unexpected night of passion in a London hotel. Lori was all smiles as she stepped out of the shower the next morning, until she saw Josh's bloody corpse lying in the bed. Who killed Josh?

Made in the USA
Monee, IL
06 September 2023

42214545R10219